JENNIFER BRODY

THE UNITED CONTINUUMS

The Continuum Trilogy
BOOK 3

TURNER
PUBLISHING COMPANY

Turner Publishing Company
Nashville, Tennessee
New York, New York

www.turnerpublishing.com

The United Continuums

Cover design: Maddie Cothren
Book design: Glen Edelstein

Library of Congress Cataloging-in-Publication Data

Names: Brody, Jennifer, author.
Title: The united continuums / Jennifer Brody.
Description: Nashville, Tennessee : Turner Publishing Company, [2017] |
  Series: The continuum trilogy ; Book 3 | Summary: "Aero leads a group
  insurgents from the Second Continuum to overthrow his rival Supreme
  General Vinick and unite his space colony's military forces, while Seeker
  takes on a secret mission back to her home colony to reinforce Earth's
  defenses and protect the First Continuum against an even greater threat.
  Meanwhile, Myra's nightmares have become a reality as the Dark Thing
  hurtles toward Earth with designs on eradicating the planet's fledgling
  populace. The only thing standing in the way are the three Carriers and
  those who would join them to fight against a second coming of the Doom"--
  Provided by publisher.
Identifiers: LCCN 2017009010 | ISBN 9781681622620 (pbk. : alk. paper)
Subjects: | CYAC: Science fiction.
Classification: LCC PZ7.1.B758 Un 2017 | DDC [Fic]--dc23
LC record available at https://lccn.loc.gov/2017009010

9781681622620

Printed in the United States of America

To all those who dream of building a better world from these ashes.

Don't lose hope.

You are not alone.

CONTENTS

I know not with what weapons World War III will be fought,
but World War IV will be fought with sticks and stones.

—Albert Einstein

We are only as strong as we are united, as weak as we are divided.

—J.K. Rowling, *Harry Potter and the Goblet of Fire*

Chapter 0
NOBEL LAUREATE

Before the Doom

Professor Theodore Divinus heard his name echo through the Stockholm Concert Hall as the symphonic music swelled to a crescendo, accompanied by vigorous applause.

"Professor Theodore Divinus, on behalf of the Royal Academy of Sciences, I wish to convey our warmest congratulations, and I now ask you to step forward and receive your prize from the hands of His Majesty the King."

When Divinus struggled to his feet, a dizzy feeling swept through him. It could have been from euphoria—or simply the stiff collar of his designer tuxedo slowly choking off his air supply. Tugging at his collar, he proceeded to the stage and padded across the blue carpet emblazoned with an "N" inside a white circle. He accepted the award from the king and then turned to bow to the crowd. More applause rippled through the hall like a rumble of thunder. He bowed two more times, bobbing his head.

I'm now a Nobel Laureate in Physics, he thought in disbelief as he made his way back to his front row seat on wobbly legs. Though he'd spent almost his whole life with that aspiration lodged in his heart, he had never believed that it would happen. Only two short days ago, in the midst of a raging nor'easter, he'd boarded a plane at Logan Airport and flown to Sweden to give his lecture on nuclear fission—and now here he was shaking hands with the king of Sweden. How strange it was that so many countries kept up the ruse of supporting an antiquated monarchy when it was only for show.

He sat through the rest of the ceremony in a state of bliss— yes, that was the word for it, wasn't it? He clapped when it was called for, sat quietly through the musical portions, all the while wishing that it would never end. His prize was clasped in his lap. He could feel the weight of it radiating through his thighs like it was radioactive. The Nobel Banquet was set to follow immediately after at Stockholm City Hall.

Divinus gathered his prize and was flowing along with the crowd making for the exits when he felt his handheld buzz in his jacket. He fished it out and saw a text message.

From: Rhae Lynn Bishop

Congrats, you sly dog. Helluva accomplishment. You got there first . . . but I'm next. You owe me a proper date when you're back in Cambridge. xxRL

The message was accompanied by a few emoticons. This made Divinus's lips kink into a smile. They were colleagues, having met in graduate school and both ascended to professorships, hers in History and Literature with an emphasis on Digital History, and his in Physics. More recently, their friendship had morphed . . . well . . . into something else. But it was still in the early stages—that delicate, flittering, heart-thumping, gut-wrenching phase—and he didn't want to jinx it by giving it a label.

He fired off a witty response (or at least, he hoped it was witty) and was making for the exit when he felt a firm hand grip his elbow. Then he heard a stern voice by his ear.

"Professor Divinus, will you please come with me?"

Divinus turned to see a man dressed in a tuxedo. He was middle-aged with close-cropped hair and broad shoulders. At first glance, nothing about him stood out, but then Divinus glimpsed something peeking from underneath his crisply starched jacket.

It was a gun.

The man gripped his elbow harder. "Professor, come with me."

His gray eyes were steely—and it wasn't a question this time.

"But where are you taking me?" Divinus managed, feeling the crush of the crowd pressing in on them, struggling toward the exits. The man lowered his voice.

"Professor, I'm not at liberty to divulge that information. All I'm authorized to say is that it concerns a matter of national security."

"And if I refuse?" Divinus asked as the crowd streamed around them, oblivious to the espionage taking place in their midst. He wondered how many other agents were strategically placed in the crowd, watching them. "What about the banquet?"

"I have permission to take you by force," the man said without hesitation. His hand slipped inside his jacket. Divinus saw the flash of a hypodermic needle. "Though I hope that does not become necessary. The choice is yours, Professor."

Divinus elected to go with the man, his award still tucked under his arm but mostly forgotten. They moved swiftly through the dispersing crowd, the hum and thrum of upbeat chatter chasing them out of the hall and into the dark Stockholm streets.

Rain splattered down from the sky in thick droplets. Divinus exhaled, and his breath came out in smoky tendrils. He could taste snow in the air—the rain would change over soon. Though it was only early evening it felt like midnight, the sun having set well before two o'clock. December in Stockholm was a special kind of winter that put even his home of Cambridge, Massachusetts, to shame. Why they chose to hold the ceremony in the dead of winter seemed counterintuitive, but he knew that it was held on the anniversary of Alfred Nobel's death, the founder of the prize that he now gripped under his arm.

A black Mercedes sped up to the curb and screeched to a halt, kicking up a puddle. "This way, Professor," the man said, jerking open the door to the backseat. It was only as Divinus climbed inside that he realized his shiny black shoes—Ferragamos newly purchased for this occasion—had been soaked through with the frigid water.

Thwump!

The man climbed in after him and slammed the door, and the car raced off into the bitter December night. On closer inspection, he saw that the car was armored with reinforced glass. "Now can you tell me where we're going?" Divinus asked.

The man didn't reply. He just stared back with those gray eyes.

"How about your name? You seem to know mine."

Still nothing. Divinus gave up and slumped in his seat. The man pulled out a handheld and scanned the screen, keyed in a message, and returned it to his inside coat pocket. Divinus sighed in annoyance, but the man didn't appear to care. He wished he could slip off his shoes, or at the very least strip off his sodden socks, but his unease kept him locked in place as his feet gradually went numb.

A thousand scenarios flashed through his head. What could they possibly want with him? Had he unknowingly committed some crime? Smuggled something through the airport that wasn't allowed? Did they suspect him of being a terrorist? Or a political agitator of some sort?

But that seemed farfetched. He was only a scientist—hell, he didn't even follow politics. Maybe it was a case of mistaken identity? He'd seen that happen once in an action movie when he was a kid. The main character was an ordinary man forced to go on the run after the government confused him with a terrorist. Regardless, Divinus was certain this situation would be cleared up quickly and he'd soon be at the banquet, sipping champagne and feasting with his fellow Nobel Laureates. That thought reassured him. He sank down into the plush leather seat, hugging his prize like a security blanket.

About fifteen minutes later, they skidded to a halt in front of an abandoned building on the outskirts of the city. Divinus peered through the window, flexing his feet to return some blood flow. It was fully snowing now, dusting the ground and frosting the rooftops of the derelict buildings that lined the pot-holed street.

What are we doing here?

Divinus took one look at the man and knew it would be an exercise in futility to ask him. The man ushered him from the vehicle and through the front door, passing more men in suits as they went. The man led him up a rickety staircase that coiled to the third floor. A dilapidated door hung crookedly from its hinges. The man pushed it open.

Another Nobel Laureate stared back at him.

"Madam President?" Divinus sputtered. He'd contemplated a hundred different scenarios on the way here—but not this one. "What . . . are you doing here?"

Last year, President Olivia Barrera won the Nobel Peace Prize for her work on immigration reform—a choice that provoked controversy with the rival political parties back home—but that didn't explain her presence here today. Maybe it was to congratulate him for winning? But that thought evaporated as soon as Barrera opened her mouth.

"Professor Divinus, thank you for coming on such short notice," Barrera said. Her amber complexion looked flawless in the dim light. Her hair was smoothed back into a tight bun. "I apologize for pulling you away from the festivities. The Academy knows how to throw a classy party. But the matter is of utmost importance."

Barrera led him over to a pair of plush, velvety chairs set in the center of the room. They looked out of place in this rundown apartment—peeling wallpaper, water leaks staining the ceiling panels, warped floorboards, plywood nailed to the windows.

"Professor, may I offer you a drink?" Barrera asked. She held up a crystal decanter filled with Scotch.

Divinus acceded to the offer and soon found himself sipping the amber liquid from a heavy tumbler. It burned his throat and he coughed, but it did calm his rattled nerves. Absently, he felt the weight of the box with his medal resting in his lap. Barrera sat in the chair across from him and loosened the silk scarf around her neck. Divinus wished he could do that same with his bowtie but didn't dare. Barrera sipped her drink.

"Madam President," Divinus ventured. "Why am I here?"

Barrera took another sip. "I'll cut right to it. The arms race is heating up. North Korea and Pakistan are involved, of course. But also rogue groups with unpredictable leaders. The energy markets are drying up, and that's driving a new wave of fanaticism across multiple regions—the Middle East, Russia, South America."

Divinus felt his head spinning as he tried to keep up. "But, Madam President, if I may . . . how does this concern me?"

Barrera took another sip and met his eyes. "Professor, you are aware of the weapons applications of your research? I can only surmise that someone as brilliant as yourself—now a Nobel Laureate, no less—would understand the consequences."

Divinus felt as if the air in the room had constricted. He tugged at his collar, trying to suck more air. It took a him a moment to find his voice. It emerged strangled. "Of course . . . though you must understand, that was never my intent."

Barrera nodded. "Our intent is often subverted, is it not?"

Divinus felt the truth of that like a blow to the gut. He could only nod in response.

"Professor, level with me," Barrera said. "How worried should we be if these rogue groups obtain your technology? Our military intel came back. It looks bad."

"Can't you stop them?" Divinus said.

"We've tried, but one group kidnapped a scientist from Russia—a physicist named Sergei Nabokov. My briefing indicated he was your research assistant. Then last week, they hijacked a load of radioactive material bound for a reactor in Iran. They call themselves the Salvation of Humanity. Their leaders are preaching about the end of the world, the corruption of humanity, the decadence of society, and the sins of the modern age. They're threatening to build a doomsday machine—and detonate it. We tracked them across the border but lost them in the mountain region of Afghanistan."

"They're building the Doom?" Divinus said. The tumbler of Scotch almost dropped from his hand. The possibilities flashed through his head. The fire and ash and the millennium of obliteration that would inevitably follow. "Madam President, it would mean the end of the world as we know it. No one would survive such an event."

Barrera set her lips. "Then it is as I feared."

"Why didn't I hear about this? They have Sergei?" Divinus remembered his assistant fondly—a diminutive man with a thick accent and unbridled enthusiasm in the lab. He'd graduated and accepted a teaching position in Moscow a few years back.

"We kept the kidnapping out of the press for security reasons," Barrera said. She sipped her drink calmly. "We don't want to induce panic. But even if we stop the Salvation of Humanity, others extremist actors are trying to build their own doomsday machines. We may succeed in delaying their weapons programs for a time, but our risk calculations show that it's inevitable someone will eventually succeed."

"And you believe they will detonate it? I thought deterrence theory would prevent that from happening. The United States, China, Russia, India . . . supposedly they've all had the Doom for years, yet nothing bad has happened. They know mutually assured destruction would wipe everyone out, including them. That keeps us all safe."

Barrera shook her head. "Deterrence theory applies only to rational actors. I'm sorry to say, but these rogue groups don't fall into that category. Their leaders have been very clear on this point. Make no mistake—if given the chance, they will use it."

Divinus felt the blood drain from his cheeks. "Wait . . . you're saying the Doom could actually happen?"

"Yes, our predictions point to that probability. They worship the end of the world. They want it to happen. They believe that the Doom will wipe out all the sinners, and then the Chosen people will ascend to heaven and reap the rewards of the afterlife."

"That's completely insane."

Barrera cracked a wry smile. "Since when has that ever stopped humankind from believing in all sorts of harebrained religions?"

Divinus knew Barrera was right. The great history of their species flashed through his mind—and all the insane tales once heralded as the absolute truth.

"They have the raw materials? And they have Sergei?"

"Correct."

"You're right, it's only a matter of time. The Doom is inevitable."

"Yes, Professor. Now you understand why I'm here."

A long moment passed before Barrera spoke again. "What if we could save some people? In a bunker somewhere? Or maybe on the International Space Station? I don't know if China and Russia would go along with the plan, but Japan would back us."

Divinus shook his head. "This isn't about merely surviving the initial event. We're talking about a thousand years of toxicity and radioactivity and devastation—a planetary surface bereft of all organic matter and life. Not only would they have to survive at least a millennium in exile, but they'd return to a barren wasteland."

The president exhaled and took a sip from her glass. The wear and tear of the job showed plainly on her face; under a year in office, and already her hair was sprouting out mostly white. When she ran for the highest office in the land as a young senator from Oregon, she planned to focus on health care expansion, immigration reform, and a domestic poverty agenda. Not on this; never on this.

"Professor, are you saying there's no hope?" Barrera said. Her eyes had taken on a bleary quality, dulled by the alcohol and the undesirable news. "We're doomed?"

Guilt ripped through Divinus. Without him, this conversation wouldn't be happening. They wouldn't be in this room talking about the end of the world. He steepled his hands under the long strands of his beard. He'd grown it out for the ceremony, thinking it would lend him an air of distinction. Now he regretted his vanity. He could see it for what it was—a shallow disguise for the monster he had become. He clenched the box with the medal resting in his lap; now he resented it.

"That is why they call the weapon the Doom, isn't it?" Divinus said. "Make no mistake, this event will be catastrophic beyond any imagining."

Barrera grimaced. "So there's nothing we can do? That's what you're telling me. I came here out of desperation, despite the wishes of my closest advisors."

Divinus thought for a moment. "Madam President, it will require immense preparation and secrecy. We would have to devote the remainder of our lives to this project. My university possesses resources and funds greater than any other institution on Earth. Our landholdings alone are formidable. We just launched a new research vessel—a mining rig designed to look for rare space minerals. That's in addition to our Mars colony and our ship headed for deep space to search for extraterrestrial life. We also have several deep-sea facilities studying the trenches and a handful of underground labs."

Barrera swirled the amber liquid in her glass and took a measured sip. "Your university does have more resources than the federal government. That last mortgage crisis hit us hard— we're still recovering. Our credit rating was downgraded. We don't even have a space program anymore. NASA was shuttered in the last round of budget cutbacks. An international cooperative runs the space station. We've got three astronauts up there, but they had to hitch a ride on China's shuttle. The headlines aren't exaggerating. We're virtually bankrupt."

Divinus thought fast. Of course, he knew about the financial strains and the loss of the shuttle program. "Madam President, I'll meet with the Harvard Board of Overseers. With their backing and the assistance of my fellow professors, we may have a chance."

Barrera raised her eyebrows. "A chance? That sounds promising."

"It's slimmer than I'd like," Divinus admitted. "And we must act immediately. And you can't tell anyone, not even your cabinet. Only your most trusted advisors."

The president downed the rest of her Scotch and summoned her chief of staff. They whispered to each other. The paunchy man frowned and shook his head.

"Madam President, that violates protocol—"

"I don't care about your damned protocol," Barrera cut him off. "These are extraordinary circumstances, and they call for extraordinary measures."

That settled it—Barrera turned back to Divinus.

"Professor, Marine One is at your disposal. Make haste back to Cambridge, and keep me informed. I'll do everything I can to assist you in this undertaking."

Divinus stood, abandoning the box with his medal on the chair. It would find its way back to him a few days later, ferreted to his office by a Secret Service agent. By then it will have lost its luster, and he will shove it deep into a drawer in his desk, shamed by the mere fact of its existence cementing him as the progenitor of the Doom. He followed the chief of staff—a smarmy man named Reed Porter Quaid III—from the room.

They hastened down the creaky staircase and out into the chill of the night. Snow drifted down, sticking to the black wool of his tuxedo. Divinus's mind was operating at breakneck speed, assembling the elements they would need. He would reach out to Professor Singh right away about his supercomputer project. He also needed to contact the Astrobiology and Astrogeology Departments about their research vessels, the study abroad program about the Mars colony, the Geology Department about their underground labs, and the Marine Biology Department about their deep-sea research stations.

He pulled out his handheld to dash off a quick text to Professor Bishop. He would need her expertise not only in deciding what to archive, but also in determining how to organize the immense swath of human history and cultural knowledge.

What to preserve? What to jettison?

And lastly—and perhaps most importantly—he would need her to help him *choose*. Whom would they save in these colonies? Whom would they forsake to the Doom? The study of history had never seemed so pressing, so urgent, so relevant to their very survival as it did in this moment. His fingers flew over the handheld.

To: Professor Rhae Lynn Bishop

Flying back to Cambridge tonight. Emergency . . . can't go into it here . . . but I need your help if I'm going to pull this off. Meet me at my office in 6 hours. I'll text u when I land.

It sent with a pleasing chime. A few seconds later, the handheld beeped with a response.

From: Professor Rhae Lynn Bishop

Theo, I'm intrigued. Emergency? Flying back 2nite? What about the banquet??? Pull what off?? Damn you, not gonna get any work done now. CU later.

A short time later, Divinus boarded Marine One in a blur of thoughts. He barely registered it when they lifted off over Stockholm. He pressed his face to the window, feeling the cold bite of the clear pane. The lights of civilization twinkled like a million artificial stars below them. *We created all of this*, he thought, *and it takes only one bad actor to wipe everything out. Creation and destruction—opposing impulses contained within the beating heart of humankind.* He thought about the rise and fall of ancient kingdoms, the catastrophe of the World Wars—all three of them—the way they always rebuilt after each upheaval, each scarring of the Earth, each demolition of empires.

"Aeternus eternus," he whispered like a prayer, an old phrase he'd picked up in his undergraduate Latin classes. *Eternal, everlasting, world without end.*

But humanity had never faced a challenge as daunting as the Doom.

Will we survive this time?

The only answer was the whirring of the transport's engines as they beat back against the blustery, snow-studded skies, whisking him over the expansive blackness of an ocean and back to Cambridge.

PART I
COLLISION COURSE

The future's uncertain, and the end is always near.

—Jim Morrison, *Roadhouse Blues*

If you try and lose then it isn't your fault. But if you don't try and we lose, then it's all your fault.

—Orson Scott Card, *Ender's Game*

Excerpts from
THE LOGBOOK OF SUPREME
GENERAL BRYANT STERN
(The Twelfth Carrier of the
Second Continuum, Outer Space)

*All entries pertaining to the disappearance
of the Fourth Continuum*

[295 P.D.] . . . I sense a disruption through the Beacon. The sensation is impossible to describe. It's subtle yet powerful, like a nightmare when you can't remember what it was about. I'm being *haunted*. That's the only word for it. I visited the Foundry and had them conduct a full examination of my Beacon, but it's functioning flawlessly. Nothing appears amiss. I must be experiencing emotional hazards. Perhaps the stress of command is affecting me? The prior Carriers assure me through the Beacon that my anxieties will pass in time. They all felt the same pressure when they became the Supreme General. I made an appointment with the Medical Clinic anyway. Hopefully, they can help me repress my emotional state . . .

[295 P.D.] . . . I had my first communication with the Fourth Continuum's new Carrier today—Commander Shira Ramses. She appears to be adjusting to her role, having taken over after their prior Carrier passed away last week. I respected Commander Thaddeus and regretted his passing, but I must confess . . . Commander Ramses has grabbed my attention in a way that I didn't realize was possible. Our first bonding was quite memorable, though it makes me blush to recount it here. The Beacons connected our minds in a way that felt . . . well . . . *pleasurable*. Of course, I realize that's an emotion and forbidden by our society because it makes you weak and clouds your decision-making. Still, our communications have become the highlight of my week . . .

[296 P.D.] . . . I sensed another disruption through the Beacon today. It feels like something bad is about to happen. It's been troubling me all day. Of course, I know this is a sign of emotional weakness. Thankfully, my regular communication with Commander Ramses cleared my head. She talked about breakthroughs they're experiencing in their scientific research. Her enthusiasm is contagious, though I must confess that I can't follow the complex formulas and equations that so excite her. Alas, science was never my strongest subject at the Agoge. I excelled in Falchion-to-Falchion combat and the History of Earth Before Doom. I was especially fascinated by the Greek and Roman civilizations, both how they were built and how they were destroyed and the dark age that emerged . . .

[296 P.D.] . . . The disruption is growing stronger, and now I can remember the nightmares. A dark, faceless figure haunts me as soon as I close my eyes. Every night, this monster attacks me with shadowy knives, and I fight it off with my Falchion. But last night the blades nicked my shoulder. I woke up with blood staining my pillow. Another visit to the Foundry showed nothing abnormal with the functioning of my Beacon. They sent me straight to the Medical Clinic. The doctor suspects night terrors. He says I injured my shoulder thrashing around in my sleep. He prescribed medication to suppress my dreams. Starry hell, I pray it helps. When I look in the mirror, I see the dark circles imprinted under my eyes from poor sleep. It's impairing my ability to command my army . . .

[296 P.D.] . . . Finally got some rest last night. No dreams, just a black curtain that descended as soon as I shut my eyes and didn't lift until the automatic lights illuminated my private barracks. I still feel groggy but more rested than I have in many weeks. However, when I tried to connect with Commander Ramses for our weekly communication, my Beacon failed to respond. The medicine the doctors prescribed seems to be interfering with my ability to communicate through the Beacon. I sat down with one of the oldest Forgers, who first bestowed my Falchion upon me at the Agoge. I trust him above all others. He explained that the Beacons function using complex biological interfaces that connect directly to my neural network. The drugs must be impairing that connection somehow. So I have two choices—I can suffer from night terrors and maintain my connection to Shira, or I can take the drugs but lose all my abilities with the Beacon. A great sorrow has settled in my chest. Never before have I doubted my ability to serve my colony, but now I wonder if I shouldn't report to the Euthanasia Clinic, declare myself an emotional hazard, and have them end my life so the Beacon can pass to a more worthy Carrier . . . I am in a state of total despair . . .

[296 P.D.] . . . The disappearance of the Fourth Continuum was reported today. One minute, they were on our sensors, a tiny blip blinking on the dark side of Uranus, and the next, they had vanished. We calculated their last known coordinates and have embarked on an emergency rescue mission. It will take us several weeks to reach their position. Meanwhile, the only thing keeping me sane is the hope that they're still out there somewhere and we'll locate them soon . . .

[296 P.D.] . . . After three months of orbiting Uranus and searching for the Fourth Continuum, I'm forced to conclude that they crashed into the planet, sinking through the upper gaseous layers and into the icy liquid center. But how their ship failed, or even why they journeyed to this location, remains a mystery. I deeply regret the weeks spent out of contact with Commander Ramses. Nobody except the Order of the Foundry knows the true extent of my struggles. The guilt haunts my every step. I have managed to wean off the medication, and the night terrors haven't returned. My doctor thinks that the dreams were a fluke and the medication cleared them up, but the old Forger worries that they were caused by something more complex. He has me under strict orders to report to the Foundry immediately if I sense any more disruptions through the Beacon . . .

[296 P.D.] . . . My despair has deepened. Only regular visits to the Foundry are keeping me stable. The old Forger suspects that it's caused by losing contact with Commander Ramses. The bondings we experienced through the Beacons were extremely powerful, akin to the feelings produced by romantic love, which is deeply forbidden in our society and something that I had never experienced before. Of course, I have my betrothed and engage in connubial visits when the Clinic for Procreation and Population Maintenance summons me. We have produced three healthy offspring, but I feel no emotional attachment to my betrothed. However, Shira was different. Maybe the old Forger is right. The sorrow of losing her is driving me crazy. It's insufferable, this heartbreak. How can humans stand to be in love if it means feeling like this when their loved one vanishes? . . .

[296 P.D] . . . To combat my despair and survive the next seven hundred years in exile, I have ordered the Second Continuum to undertake a new mission to find another planet to call home. The Majors have taken to calling it Stern's Quest. Today marks the first day of this new mission. Will we survive—or meet the same fate as the Third and Fourth Continuums? Will we find a new home planet? I don't know, and it's both terrifying and thrilling. The one thing I haven't confessed to anyone, not even the old Forger, is my secret motivation for embarking on Stern's Quest. It sparks and flames in my heart like a comet. Maybe the Fourth Continuum is still out there somewhere. Maybe they didn't perish on Uranus after all. Maybe journeying to the outer reaches of the stars is the only way I can reconnect with Shira . . . this hope is the one thing that keeps me going . . .

[318 P.D.] . . . I've reached the end of my life. My body

is beginning to fail. Today, I have my appointment with the Euthanasia Clinic. After I'm put under, my Beacon will pass to the next Carrier, a young girl named Captain Arrow Jordan who graduated at the top of her class from the Agoge and commands a combat unit. She is being summoned to the bridge as I dictate this final logbook entry. Under my command, the Second Continuum has journeyed into the deepest reaches of galaxies yet unnamed except by letter and number codes. Despite our valiant efforts, we haven't located a new home planet. Each one we identify as being potentially inhabitable turns out to possess some fatal flaw—toxic levels of chemicals in the atmosphere, violent atmospheric storms, extreme temperature variations. Earth remains one of a kind—an anomaly in the vast and desolate universe. Despite how far we've traveled, we haven't encountered any signs of the Fourth Continuum. Shira is truly gone. Over twenty years have passed since they vanished, but the ache of her loss still tugs at my heart. My night terrors—the ones that separated us—also never returned. I curse them to this day for driving us apart, even if we would have had only a few more weeks together. That would have felt like an eternity in my mind. I officially recuse myself from duty. This is the final logbook entry of Supreme General Bryant Stern.

—THE NATIONAL OPERATION TO ARCHIVE HUMANITY

THE FOURTH CONTINUUM

. . . One of three interstellar colonies of the Continuum Project, built into a space vessel originally designed by Harvard University astrogeology professors as a mining rig to scour the galaxy for rare minerals . . .

. . . The demographics of the colony were heavily tilted toward scientists and mathematicians. Based on a mandate set forth by their first Carrier, Professor Helen Ramses, for the first three hundred years of their existence they devoted their resources to furthering scientific research into the nature of human consciousness. During this period, there are no records of uprisings or civil unrest within the colony. Their society appeared peaceable and unremarkable. They maintained regular communication with the Second and Third Continuums . . .

. . . That changed in 296 Post Doom. While orbiting Uranus, the colony vanished. Why they traveled to that location remains a mystery. Under the command of Supreme General Bryant Stern, the Second Continuum embarked on a rescue mission. But when they arrived at the last known coordinates, they found no trace of the ship or her crew . . .

. . . Stern sent out emergency signals and deployed several units to search the moons, but a surface mission to Uranus remained out of the question. Had the Fourth Continuum crashed into the planet, it would have sunk through the upper layers of hydrogen and helium and into the planet's liquid, icy core. There would be nothing left of the ship to find. Eventually, after months of orbiting Uranus and sending out emergency signals, Stern was forced to conclude that the Fourth Continuum had perished . . .

. . . That conclusion would prove false. In 1000 Post Doom, when the time finally arrived for the surviving colonies to return to the First Continuum and restart life on Earth, the Fourth Continuum reappeared just as suddenly as it had vanished seven hundred years before. Their ship was now equipped with a massive artillery, even more powerful than the Second Continuum's army. Led by their Carrier, Commander Drakken, they contacted the First Continuum and issued a threat. The other Carriers had to surrender immediately and Professor Divinus was to turn over the secret of the Doom, or Drakken would destroy them and everything that they held dear . . .

—THE NATIONAL OPERATION TO ARCHIVE HUMANITY

Chapter 1
THE UNVEILING

Commander Drakken

He went by many names.

The Dark Thing. The Fourth Carrier. Descendant of the Chosen. Commander Drakken. His birth name was Ramses, but he had discarded it when he ascended, having endured the great testing. His skin was marked with scars—ropy, twisted veins of raised tissue that crisscrossed his torso and extremities, hidden beneath his crimson robes and contained by a tight girdle that kept his flesh in one piece. His physical form remained his weakness—the repulsive frailty of the human body.

Curse this flesh, he thought with disgust.

His Beacon flared with fresh intensity now that they had returned to their home galaxy. He revered the device. It allowed him to transcend his flesh and select his preferred form—a dark shadow. He had worked hard to control his mind and cloak his identity. But that plan had been foiled. He felt fresh anger ripple through him.

Those Carriers will pay. They will all suffer.

Besides, it made no difference. It only moved up his

timetable. He knew his place in the world. He knew why his people had endured and suffered and ascended. They were returning for one reason, and one reason only: *the Doom.*

It had forsaken them. It destroyed their home world. It laid ruin to all manner of flora and fauna. But it had also created them. It spawned a new world order. It forced the next evolution of the human race. It weaned out those who were unworthy—the frail, the weak, the damaged, those who weren't Chosen—and even then, those who could not survive the exile. The Third Continuum was corrupt and gluttonous. Artists and poets and painters and philosophers. What kind of existence could they possibly hope to create? They deserved what they got. The air leak was a mercy.

His people were scientists. They knew what it took to survive.

The Fourth Continuum had gone further than any other civilization. They'd probed the outer reaches of the universe. They'd faked their own disappearance to free themselves from the tyranny of Professor Divinus's project. It was the only way to continue their evolution into the Superior Beings—a collective consciousness.

Drakken pushed through the wires jacked into his brain that boosted the Beacon's power. He felt his consciousness flow through the ship's many levels, through the immaculate laboratories manned by the Superior Ones in their lab coats, and into the black netherworld of outer space. He reached for the First Continuum. He reached for Professor Divinus. He felt a connection lock into place. He issued his demands:

The Doom. The Doom. The Doom. The Doom.

Once they possessed the secret that had eluded them, they would truly be the most powerful beings in the universe. Soon it would belong to them.

Chapter 2
SEVENTEEN

Myra Jackson

The automatic lights flooded her chambers, ratcheting up their intensity to mimic daybreak. Myra stopped pacing around her room, glancing at her bed. Sheer curtains unspooled around the tucked-in sheets and unrumpled pillows.

Yet another night of not sleeping, she thought with a sigh.

She padded into the bathroom, peering at her face in the mirror. The stark light caught her cheekbones. The dark circles under her eyes had deepened into bruises. Her caramel skin took on a sickly pallor. Red filaments shot through her eyes. Her wiry curls jutted out like she'd shoved her fingers into an electrical socket.

But she didn't want to waste energy on showering, just like she didn't want to sleep. Not when the fate of their entire world rested on her slim shoulders. She didn't feel up to the task. *Who am I but a sixteen-year-old girl from a remote colony buried in a trench under the sea?*

Wait, how many days had passed since she escaped from her home? She did a quick calculation, coming up with a number that rattled her—eight weeks and three days. That meant her birthday had come and gone without her noticing.

I'm seventeen now, she thought.

Seventeen. She let the word roll around in her empty head, so much emptier now with the Beacons deactivated. If she were back home in the Thirteenth Continuum, Maude would have thrown her a festive party in her overstuffed compartment, complete with freshly baked buttercake, ginger beer, and all the sweetfish Myra could eat. She would have made a wish and blown out seventeen candles to the cheers of her best friends in the whole world. They never would have let her forget her birthday like this.

But two of them—Paige and Rickard—were dead, and Kaleb had been captured by the Second Continuum's space colony, along with her brother, Tinker. The chances of any of them surviving long enough to celebrate another birthday were slim.

Slim to none, she thought with a shudder.

A solid week had passed since they received the communication from Commander Drakken. His threat ran through her head for the millionth time, ushering a wave of dread as potent as the first time she heard it:

Surrender now and turn over the secret of the Doom, or we'll destroy everything that you hold dear . . . I know who you love—and exactly how to destroy them.

The Fourth Continuum was returning to Earth. According to Noah's latest estimate, they were traveling fast and were about four short weeks away. Meanwhile, Supreme General Vinick was holding her friends hostage aboard the Second Continuum. Even worse, in the darkest depths of the ocean, her colony was running out of oxygen, yet a rescue mission remained impossible without a submersible or the raw materials to build one, both of which they lacked.

Every time Myra thought through their situation, it seemed just as hopeless as the last time. Her mind stretched beyond their atmosphere to the vacuum of space and then dove back under the ocean, plunging through the miles of saltwater and rock and impenetrable darkness, pinging back and forth and leaving her head spinning.

Yet still no solution came to her.

She flung herself on her bed, fluttering the curtains and crumpling the covers. Hopelessness descended on her hard and fast, but she couldn't give up now. She returned to pacing around her room. She was fast wearing down the soles of her flimsy canvas shoes. It was a bad habit that she'd picked up from her father. Last she saw him, he was chained up in the Pen back in the Thirteenth Continuum. She had no way of knowing if he was still alive. Most likely, she knew with a sinking of her heart, Padre Flavius and the Synod had already put him out to sea.

She pushed that thought from her mind but quickly found herself dwelling on her brother instead. She missed Tinker like a pipe to the head, but at least she knew he was alive. Noah had hacked into the security feeds from the Second Continuum. Tinker was locked up in the Disciplinary Barracks, along with Kaleb, Wren, and the Forger.

Myra skidded to a halt, glancing at her Beacon. It remained dark and lifeless. She longed to discuss everything with Aero and Seeker, but since the Beacons had been deactivated, it felt like a wall had gone up between her and the other Carriers. Despite the intimate moments they'd shared, Aero seemed like a distant stranger now.

Aero, oh Aero, she thought sadly.

But he could no longer hear her thoughts, so her call went unanswered. As she paced her room in the dawn light—or rather, the approximation of it by the automatic lights—she found herself thinking of the world from Before Doom. In these imaginings, she was Elianna Wade. She remembered Tulsa, Oklahoma, with its amber waves of wheat, sweet as the songs they sang in her elementary school, the blazing heat of the unfiltered sun, the cicadas humming in the sweaty crush of evening, the skies stained purple with the last rays of sunlight, her family waiting for her in their sagging farmhouse while she raced through the fields, catching fireflies and shuttling them into an old tomato jar, the tin lid pierced with a knife's tip.

Even though her Beacon was switched off, these memories were still seared into her brain. She'd downloaded them when she bonded with the strange device—

The door to her chamber beeped, announcing the arrival of the service bots and snapping her out of her ruminating. The funny little machines zipped into her room and started straightening her pristine bed, cleaning her untouched bathroom, whisking away her uneaten rations, shooing her out of their way with their clawed appendages and insistent beeping. They were her only source of company these days.

When they left and the door beeped shut behind them, silence settled over her chamber, thick and stifling. She returned to her pacing. A few days into her seventeenth year on this planet, and still she couldn't see a way out of this mess.

It's hopeless.

Myra snatched her tablet off the trunk and approached the door. She was headed for the chamber that housed amphibians to check the cryocapsule levels. She signaled for the door to open. It obeyed automatically with a sharp beep. Just as she stepped into the corridor, a disembodied voice cut through the recycled air.

It belonged to Noah.

"Carriers, report to the control room."

Chapter 3
SURVIVAL ISN'T COWARDLY

Aero Wright

O ne hundred," Aero counted out as he finished yet another set of push-ups.

His muscles quaked under the thin fabric of his tunic. Thanks to the protein-laden rations and daily bouts of calisthenics, he had put on a thick layer of muscle that padded his tall frame. He bounced back to his feet. Sweat dripped down his face, pooling in his collarbone.

Despite his weariness, his fingers twitched, longing to unsheathe his Falchion and morph it into a broadsword. It took everything in his power to still his hands. The golden blade dangled uselessly in its scabbard. He needed to conserve what little power remained in his weapon. It was fast draining without the Forger around to charge it. Noah was trying to come up with a work-around but so far hadn't succeeded.

He dropped into another round of push-ups, counting them out like the Drillmasters back at the Agoge, the military school aboard his former home in the Second Continuum. "One . . . two . . . three . . . four . . . five . . . six . . ."

He reached one hundred.

But still his mind reeled from everything that had happened in the last week. He missed Wren. He pictured her locked up in the Disciplinary Barracks, guarded around the clock by soldiers. She hated sitting still; she was probably going mad from it. A smile twisted his lips when he remembered some of her more challenging yet endearing qualities. But it vanished a split second later.

Starry hell, the Fourth Continuum's coming for us.

He envisioned his home colony preparing for war—combat units running drills in the simulators, the Order of the Foundry charging Falchions, Supreme General Vinick and the Majors ensconced on the bridge, hashing out their battle strategy. They'd pulled back into a defensive position. Undoubtedly, they'd picked up Commander Drakken and the Fourth Continuum on their sensor arrays. A quick analysis of the scans would reveal the power of Drakken's arsenal.

Aero reached for his Falchion again and had to stop his hand. He wanted nothing more than to be back home with his combat unit, prepping for battle. Action was his strength—not all this waiting around underground, trying to come up with a plan. He was a soldier above all else; he wasn't much of a strategist. He had always left the more complicated aspects of commanding an army to his father, the last Supreme General. Aero liked following orders and issuing them down the chain of command.

The rushing tide of emotions threatened to overwhelm him. One thought screamed louder than the rest: *Myra . . . I want to talk to Myra.*

Since their Beacons were deactivated, she'd been avoiding him. He saw her only briefly when she appeared for their strategy meetings with Professor Divinus and Noah in the control room before retreating to her chambers and shutting her door. He tried to talk to her after yesterday's meeting, but she didn't want to listen.

"Myra, is everything okay?" he asked, pulling her aside

before she could wriggle through the door and vanish back to her chambers. "You look tired—"

"What does it matter how I look?" she cut him off.

"I'm just worried about you," he managed weakly. "That's all."

Seeker watched their exchange with her sharp eyes, though she kept her mouth shut. Myra sidled toward the door, trying to slip past him. "Look, if we don't find a way out of this mess, we're all dead anyway. You heard that message from Drakken, didn't you? He wants the Doom. He intends to destroy everything—and everyone we love."

He felt a rush of helplessness and struggled for words. Before he could say anything else, she slipped past him and headed back to her chambers, leaving him in the control room with Seeker.

Professor Divinus—or rather, his projection—leveled Aero with a sympathetic gaze. "Don't take it personally, my son. She's under a lot of pressure. You all are. This situation with the Fourth Continuum's return is troubling and unprecedented, to say the least," he added, flickering with worry.

"Of course, Professor," Aero said and then hurried back to his chambers. His face felt hot, and he felt embarrassed for letting his emotions get the better of him.

Why do I care so much what Myra thinks? he chided himself, though he knew the answer plain as the automatic lights blasting down on his room—*I love her.* He had never been good at handling his emotions. His society despised emotions; they valued detachment and logic above all else. Why was he such an emotional hazard?

The door to his chambers beeped, snapping him out of his thoughts. Was it Myra? Hope got the better of him, but then he saw a stooped figure lope into his room on all fours. A dead rat dangled from her jaws. Seeker spat it out on the floor and grinned a toothy smile that came off more like a scowl. The rust tinge of blood coated the hair around her mouth and her hands, which elongated into razor-sharp claws.

"A successful day hunting in the corridors?" Aero said, raising his eyebrows.

"Ratters try to escape, but Seeker finds them in the Darkness of the Below," she growled, nudging the tiny carcass. "Seeker snaps their filthy little necks."

With that proclamation, she stalked around the rat, then sat back on her haunches and ripped into the tiny creature's torso. Blood spurted out, staining the floor black. Without the Beacons connecting them, she seemed to be reverting to her feral ways. Her home colony, the Seventh Continuum, had lost their electricity and technology, living in the total darkness of the underground, devolving into a barbaric culture, where only the Strong Ones thrived and Weaklings hunted and served them.

"What should we do about Drakken and the Fourth Continuum?" Aero asked, hoping to engage Seeker in a strategy discussion. He perched on the edge of his bed.

"Drakken is the Strongest of the Strong Ones now," she said, taking another bite of her prize. "We are the Weaklings . . . there's nothing we can do."

"But surely there must be something?" He snatched a tube of rations from the tray left by the service bots. He peeled it open, swallowing the gluey paste.

Seeker lowered her voice. "Flee . . . we can flee now."

He flinched at the idea. "Isn't that cowardly?"

"Survival isn't cowardly," she growled. "Why wait around to die?"

"But we can't leave yet. Noah controls the elevator. Even if we could get up to the surface, a combat unit from the Second Continuum is guarding the door. They'd take us prisoner and throw us in the Disciplinary Barracks with our friends."

Seeker narrowed her eyes, taking on a sly appearance. "Seeker found another way back to the Brightside . . . secret back way . . . Noah doesn't even remember it."

Aero wasn't surprised that she had stumbled upon another door. Since they had arrived here, she'd been prowling the dark passages of the First Continuum nonstop.

"Where will you go?" he asked. "You can't go back home. Drakken knows the location of the Seventh Continuum from your Beacon. It's not safe there."

"Doesn't matter. Seeker will find a safer place. Seeker hunts and explores . . . Seeker is very good at finding things." She slunk over, rubbing her back against his leg. "Strong One, will you come with Seeker?" she purred affectionately.

Aero shook his head. "I can't leave them."

"Them?" Seeker growled, shooting him a confused look. "They aren't alive—the one with no smell and the one who is only a voice. You don't want to leave Myra."

Despite her animalistic qualities, Seeker was clever and intuitive. That was how she had survived this long, despite being a Weakling.

He wanted to argue that it was his duty to stay in the First Continuum and serve out his time as a Carrier. That fleeing was a cowardly act that went against his most fundamental instincts and training. But those weren't his real motives, and they both knew it. "Fine," he admitted, feeling heat in his cheeks. "I don't want to leave Myra."

Seeker snorted. "Myra doesn't like you anymore. She stays in her room . . . keeps the door closed. You should leave her. Why do you care about that Weakling?"

He felt his heart quake and threaten to rend in half. Seeker had a point—why did he care so much about the girl? He thought back to their nightly bondings, when their Beacons melded their consciousnesses together while they slept. But those shared dreams were long gone, lost with the dimming of the Beacons. And now Myra seemed like nothing more than a stranger—and a hostile one at that.

He wanted to stuff his emotions back down into a deep, dark place from which they would never emerge, like he'd been trained to do at the Agoge after his mother abandoned him on their doorstep on his fifth birthday, as was her duty. But once these emotions had been let loose—once they had run rampant through his mind and his heart—he found that he could not force them back down. They refused to go quietly. Instead, they popped up in his daily life and then assaulted him in his dreams.

In short, they were driving him completely mad.

"Seeker, I'm sorry," Aero said, fidgeting with the empty tube of rations. He felt embarrassed by his emotional weakness. "I wish I could, but I can't go with you."

Seeker shrugged. "It's your choice, Strong One."

She didn't say anything else. She stalked to the door and vanished into the corridor. It contracted behind her with a beep. Aero pictured her galloping through the First Continuum, weaving through the golden cryocapsules that filled the immense subterranean chambers with their promise of one day revitalizing the surface, populating it with animal and plant life, rebuilding some of what had been lost in the Doom. The images that he'd studied at the Agoge from Before Doom flooded his brain.

But if Drakken had his way, none of this would come to pass. The Continuum Project would be nothing more than a failed experiment—the final proof that humanity's prime impulse was destruction above all else. That they weren't worth saving after all. "Starry hell," Aero muttered and returned to his push-ups.

Some time later, while Aero was in the midst of an especially challenging drill that involved squats and arm movements, Noah's voice cut through the staid air.

"Carriers, report to the control room."

Chapter 4
STAY OR GO

Seeker

The Darkness of the Below called to her.

Seeker bolted from Aero's room and into the next chamber, zigzagging through the cryocapsules. She glanced inside one that was labeled *Buteo jamaicensis,* though she had no idea what it meant. Embryos floated behind the clear panel, lit up from below with murky emerald light. This chamber housed *birds.* Myra had told her about them when they first got here, before the Fourth Continuum returned and changed everything.

Filthy, stinking Drakken. He's the Strongest of the Strong Ones.

She tore away, propelling herself forward with both her arms and legs. She galloped through another few chambers and past their cryocapsules (*amphibians* and *insects*) and then into a narrow tunnel that branched away, curving through the underground. The light panels on the ceiling faded out behind her. Construction equipment lay abandoned in this tunnel. She emerged into another chamber. Half-built cryocapsules filled part of the enormous space. They never finished it.

The Doom interrupted their plans.

Seeker inhaled and smelled dirt, rock, and squirmy, scratchy creatures that lived in the Darkness of the Below. Her eyes could see nothing now. The Light was long gone from these tunnels—that was just how she liked it. Noah's sensors didn't extend to this part. Usually, Noah was monitoring her every move; only here was she alone at last.

Navigating by smell and touch alone, she pounced on an unsuspecting nest of buggers and devoured them, avoiding their poisonous pinchers and crunching their exoskeletons in her sharp teeth. Satisfied, she licked her lips. Her belly stretched out, full and bloated. She lumbered over to a cozy corner, napping until the pressure in her abdomen lessened. Then she retraced her steps, veering down a different tunnel.

Her hands and feet kicked up grit as she ran at full speed. She skidded to a halt when she reached her secret destination. *The Door in the Wall.*

She'd stumbled upon it while hunting. This was a special door—a secret, long-forgotten back door. Golden and marked with the seal. She traced the outline of the snake swallowing its own tail, entwined around the ancient words:

Aeternus Eternus

Sensing her presence, the door receded into the bedrock with a deep rumble that rattled the passage. She cowered down, pressing her hands to her ears until it stopped, and then peered into the blackness. She knew what lay beyond— the Moving Room. It was waiting to carry her upward, hurtling through miles of solid rock.

It would transport her back to the Brightside.

She sat back on her haunches and thought about it. She was tempted. Very tempted. She could leave now. She was only a Weakling; she wasn't a Strong One.

This wasn't her fight.

Her heart beat faster, thumping like a primal drum and repeating a mantra—*survival at all costs.* She felt for her wrist. Her Beacon was dark and cool to the touch. It had released its grip on her mind. She was free to choose her own destiny now. Noah wasn't influencing her thoughts anymore. She'd even started to forget about Jared, the first Carrier from her colony. His voice seemed like a distant memory now.

Her best chance was to flee in the Moving Room and run away as fast as she could—and to forget about Aero and Myra and Tinker and Noah and Professor Divinus and the Continuum Project. She shouldn't care about them. *Caring* made you weak. *Caring* made you die. Seeker needed to look out for herself now. That's how she'd survived for this long. Most Weaklings didn't make it past their birthing season.

She wasn't sure where she would go exactly.

Really, did it matter? This world was full of dark caves and pits in the ground and bugger nests and ratters. That was all she needed, wasn't it? Some shelter, some darkness, and something to fill her belly? What else was there?

Tinker, she thought. *Poor Tinker.*

Seeker sat in front of the Moving Room and thought about her options for a long time. Long enough for her legs to go cold and numb, despite their thick shrouding of hair. She'd almost made up her mind to leave, when something stopped her.

Her ears pricked up. She cocked her head.

A voice cut through the stagnant air of the tunnel. It wasn't very loud, but her ears were sharp. "Carriers, report to the control room," Noah announced.

Stay.

Or go.

Stay.

Or go.

Stay.

o   o   o

Seeker passed by Divinus's cryocapsule. The old man's face stared back at her with milky, blue eyes. "No smell," she muttered as she bolted past. "Not alive."

She continued to the control room, where she found Myra and Aero already seated at the long table with Professor Divinus at the head. His projection radiated with emerald light. Though Seeker hated sitting, she crawled into a chair and forced herself into an unnatural upright position. A projection of the Fourth Continuum blazed to life overhead, rotating in three-dimensional resolution. Drills jutted out of the sides of the ship like bugger stingers. It was hurtling through space toward them.

Seeker glanced at Myra. Her face looked sallow and pinched; dark circles shadowed her eyes. Next to her, Aero fidgeted with the hilt of his Falchion. Seeker could sense the divisions that had sprung up between them, as solid and impenetrable as rock. Dejected, Seeker shrank down in her chair, snaking her arms around her rib cage.

"There's been a new development," Professor Divinus said, quivering with concern. "Noah updated his calculations on the Fourth Continuum. They'll be on our doorstop in six weeks. If we're going to implement a plan, we'd better do it fast."

Chapter 5
ANY MEANS NECESSARY

Major Danika Rothman

Danika marched down the corridor. Outside a window in the side of the mothership, she glimpsed their preparations for war. Their solar sails remained furled, tucked under the smooth, curved wings of the ship, but blasters poked through the hull. Further out, a combat unit was running flight drills. Their transports zipped through space, trailing twin tails of gas and fire. A flash of light erupted as one fired a blaster.

Danika had just left a security briefing on the bridge, where Major Doyle confirmed their worst fears. "Supreme General Vinick, we finally broke through their cloaking shield. It appears the ship bears the markings of the Fourth Continuum."

Starry hell, that's impossible, Danika remembered thinking as she gazed at the long-lost colony projected on the monitors in three-dimensional clarity. The ship looked exactly like the images she'd studied in her history classes at the Agoge. It was nothing like their sleek, polished vessel. It was dark and clunky, fitted with drilling rigs.

"Weapon capabilities?" Vinick asked, pursing his thin lips. Absently, he stroked the hilt of his Falchion belted to his waist. His eyes stayed locked on the monitors.

"We're still running scans," Doyle said, his fingers flying over his console. "But the preliminary data indicates they're heavily armed with nuclear warheads."

A hush fell over the bridge.

The Supreme General turned to Danika. "Major Rothman, interrogate the prisoners. Find out what they know about the Fourth Continuum. Is this a separate threat? Or some kind of trap? Their reappearance can't be a coincidence."

"Yes, sir," she said with a salute.

"Major, I grant you permission to use any means necessary," Vinick added as his hand closed around his Falchion, morphing it into a dagger. "Do not fail me."

Snapping out of her memory, Danika tore her eyes from the window. She followed the corridor to the right, her boots clacking on the polished floor. A soldier from the Medical Clinic trailed behind her, carrying a tray laden with hypodermic needles. Another soldier from a combat unit, Captain Leroy Malik, marched to her left. A thin, half-moon scar marked his upper lip, a souvenir from his Krypteia, their grueling test to graduate from the Agoge. He was emotionless and built like a tank, the kind she'd seen pictures of in the archives from World War II. They'd trained at the Agoge together. He would obey her orders without hesitation; he would do whatever was necessary.

A combat unit rounded the corner, marching in tight formation with their Falchions belted to their waists. Captain Tabor snapped off a crisp salute.

"Major Rothman," she said formally.

Danika saluted back. "State your business, Captain Tabor."

"We're going to run a simulator drill," Tabor said. "A surface deployment."

Danika felt her lips twist in satisfaction. The Fourth Continuum posed a serious threat, but her colony had their own army with skilled soldiers. They would not be easily defeated. "Proceed, Captain," Danika said. "May your soldiers fight well."

Tabor's unit traipsed past. Their footfalls died out, swallowed up by the ship's many corridors on their way to the simulators. Danika watched them, taking pleasure in the sight of soldiers who followed their orders and performed their duties without hesitation. *Unlike the deserters*, she thought with a surge of hatred. She'd always despised rule breakers, even back at the Agoge. A memory surfaced, the edges soft and blurry—the way they often were, especially with things you'd rather forget.

Lillian.

Unbidden, the name shot through her head. Lillian was her biological sibling, though they shared no relationship apart from their attendance at the same school. Lillian was only a year behind her. In Lillian's Fourth Year, she got caught in a cheating scandal. As Danika would later learn, the girl struggled in math and had been placed on academic probation. Desperate to pass her class, Lillian hacked the tests from the Drillmasters' secure archives. They discovered the breach and traced it back to her sister.

As punishment, Lillian was banished, packed into an escape pod and forsaken to the vacuum of space. Her life-support systems and rations would hold out for a few weeks at the most. Then she'd either starve or suffocate—Danika wasn't sure which fate would befall her first—but either way, she'd be dead. No habitable planets existed in their immediate vicinity. Space wasn't even a place; it was a void, an absence.

Lillian Rothman.

"Danika, save me! Don't let them banish me!"

The pitiful girl cried out for help as the soldiers dragged her down the corridor toward the Docking Bay. She used Danika's first name, not her surname, as was protocol. That small slip hardened Danika's resolve. The girl was flawed; she was weak. Soldiers like her threatened their society, their way of life, their ability to survive.

The girl had to die.

Keeping her face a mask devoid of emotion, Danika watched with her fellow classmates as the soldiers shoved Lillian's small body into the escape pod, locking her inside. Her sister pounded on the door with her fists. Danika could see her struggling on the monitors, but the sound was muffled by the thick insulation.

"Proceed, Major Doyle," Supreme General Brillstein ordered.

Did he look pained when he gave the order? Danika studied his face, but it snapped back to neutral before she could get a solid read on it.

Doyle hit a series of buttons on his handheld to launch the escape pod. Danika watched it grow smaller and smaller on the monitors—a tiny speck cast against the blackness of space—and felt relief. Her biological sibling was an emotional hazard. Worse yet, the girl reflected poorly on Danika's genetic records. They shared a surname, and the girl had polluted it. *Good riddance*, Danika thought.

These deserters deserved no better than her biological sibling. Vinick's orders ran through her head. *I grant you permission to use any means necessary.* She would do her duty. She would prove that Lillian was an anomaly in her family line.

"Major Rothman?" Captain Malik said. "Isn't this the wrong way?"

Danika snapped back to reality. She was standing in the Docking Bay in front of the escape pods. The long row spanned the corridor. She must have taken a wrong turn, a left instead of a right? *Starry hell, what is wrong with me?*

Malik and the soldier from the Medical Clinic stared at her. She could read the doubt on their faces. "Of course, Captain Malik," she backpedaled. "I just had to check on something. Soldiers, it's this way to the Disciplinary Barracks."

She pivoted and reversed course down the corridor, trying to stuff the memory of Lillian back down and pretend the emotions clawing at her insides didn't exist.

o   o   o

A few tense minutes later, Danika came to a halt in front of the Disciplinary Barracks. Five armed guards stood outside with their Falchions already morphed.

"Major Rothman," they saluted and waved her through. One soldier hit a button to unlock the door.

Danika marched through it and came face-to-face with Wren Jordan. The deserter's face contorted with hatred. Wren shoved a little boy behind her back and motioned to the Forger, who stepped in front of the injured boy. *Kaleb Sebold from the Thirteenth Continuum*, Danika knew. Thick bandages girdled his torso. His serious wounds were only now scabbing over and starting to heal, though they would leave scars. Apparently, they'd been inflicted by the cannibalistic inhabitants of the Seventh Continuum.

The Forger glared at her. "Major Rothman, I was traveling under direct orders from my sworn brothers and sisters. We don't fall under your jurisdiction—"

"Silence, brother," Danika said, gripping the hilt of her Falchion. "You're a deserter, just like the others. Your precious Order can't protect you anymore. You're at the mercy of Supreme General Vinick and the Majors now."

The little boy peered up at her from between Wren's legs. His eyes fixed on her Falchion. He didn't look afraid, more curious. Kaleb took a step toward her.

"Major Rothman, I demand you release us at once," he said in a haughty voice. "My father sits on the Synod of the Thirteenth Continuum. You have no right to hold us captive like this. My home colony is dying. We have to rescue them right away."

Wren rolled her eyes. "Save your breath, Sebold. Major Rothman doesn't have a heart, just a block of ice in her chest. Doesn't have much of a brain either. She can't think for herself. She only follows Vinick's orders."

Danika wasn't supposed to feel any emotions, but fury exploded in her chest. She *was* only following orders, like she'd been trained. Wren would suffer for her insolence. Danika had every bit of authority she needed. She reached for a hypodermic needle from the steel tray. It glinted under the light of the overhead panels.

Fear passed over Wren's face. She knew what the needle contained; it was a serum derived from a long-extinct species named *Paraponera clavata*, also known as the bullet ant. It was famous for delivering the most painful sting on Earth. The venom acted instantaneously, creating excruciating waves of pain that crashed over your body and then receded, only to crash over it again. It didn't affect the heart or lungs, so it wasn't lethal. But that was the point. Of course, their doctors had amplified its effects. And they'd added a healthy dose of a truth serum. Nobody could resist it.

Wren's upper lip trembled, but she bit down on it. "Major Rothman, you're going to have to go through me first," she said, motioning for the little boy to hide under the bunk. He scrambled away, gazing out through the legs.

"No problem, deserter," Danika said, gesturing for Malik to hold Wren down on the cot. "Let's have a chat about the Fourth Continuum, shall we?" She hit a button and turned toward Wren. The thick door to the barracks contracted behind them and locked.

But it did not contain Wren's screams.

Chapter 6
STALEMATE

Myra Jackson

Six short weeks?" Myra said. "Professor, are you sure?"
Her mouth tasted bitter with fear. Images from Draken's communication materialized overhead—armed soldiers in matching uniforms and nuclear warheads ready to be launched. Around the control room, computers whirred and beeped.

"I've analyzed their speed and trajectory," Divinus replied as the images shifted to the ship. "They'll decelerate as they near Earth. But unless the Fourth Continuum alters their path, Noah's calculation is correct. The margin of error is small."

They all took this in.

"Have we learned anything new about the Fourth Continuum?" Aero asked. His eyes were locked on the projection. It faded in and out of focus. "Maybe a weakness we can exploit? Or a flaw in their defense systems?"

"Very little, I'm afraid," Divinus said with a shake of his head. "Noah's still having a hard time locking onto their signal."

On the monitors, the ship vanished again only to snap back into existence a second later. "Noah finished compiling his report on the Fourth Continuum using the downloads from Captain Wright's Beacon and the historical records from our archives," Divinus continued. "And well, it's pretty thin. Not much is known."

"Professor, projecting the data now," Noah said as it materialized overhead.

Myra skimmed over it, picking out key phrases: *Originally designed as a mining rig to scour the galaxy for rare minerals . . . the makeup of the colony was heavily tilted toward scientists and mathematicians . . . orbiting the dark side of Uranus . . . the colony suddenly vanished . . .*

Divinus manipulated the report, flipping through it. "Noah's scans haven't been productive. The Fourth Continuum has sophisticated cloaking devices. We've never encountered anything like them before. Even tracking their location has proven challenging. Basically, the last seven hundred years of their existence remains a mystery. We don't know why they vanished or where they've been all this time."

"But we do know why they've returned," Myra said darkly. Her eyes locked on the image of their ship. "Drakken made that perfectly clear in his message."

Seeker raised her hackles. "They want . . . the Doom."

Silence descended over the table.

"Remember how Noah used the Beacons to make us run into the elevator?" Aero ventured. "Could we hijack Drakken through his Beacon the same way?"

"Alas, I wish it were that simple," Divinus said. "Proximity matters. You were standing right on our doorstep. We couldn't have done it when you were hundreds of miles away. Also, your minds are still untrained at controlling the Beacons. You haven't erected security protections, so to speak, while Drakken is extremely skilled with his device. He's created layers of security. Not even Noah can hack through them."

"That's correct, Professor," Noah said. "And it's not from lack of effort."

Myra felt frustration building under her skin like an itch that wouldn't go away. More than anything, they needed to find a way out of this stalemate. She had hoped that Noah's report would reveal a clear path forward. But if anything, it only added to their confusion. What had happened to this mysterious space colony? Why did they disappear all those years ago? Where were they all this time? What were they doing?

Divinus flickered with regret. "Carriers, I'm saddened to report that my sworn brothers and sisters prepared for many contingencies and possibilities, but we didn't plan for a situation like this one. Of course, we have some minor defenses in place to protect our underground haven, but nothing that can avert such a severe attack."

His words echoed through the control room.

"Starry hell, you're right," Aero said, frustration making his voice quiver. He gestured around the table. "What good are the five of us against Drakken's forces? Professor, no offense, but only three of us are able-bodied. I'm a trained soldier, but even I can't defeat a whole army alone. Plus, my Falchion is draining. It's got a few good swings left in it, but it needs a fresh charge. I'm lucky it hasn't melted down yet."

"Let's not forget, Vinick is still holding our friends captive," Myra added. A knot lodged in her throat, but she pressed on. "He needed them to bargain with us. But with the reappearance of the Fourth Continuum, we don't know what Vinick wants anymore."

"My dear, you're correct," Divinus said. "Noah's analysis no longer applies in the face of this larger threat. They're still in orbit, and their solar sails remain dormant."

Noah projected an image of their sleek vessel. Their sails were furled under the wings. Something swarmed around outside the ship, emitting quick flashes of light.

"What are those lights?" Myra asked, pointing at the projection.

"They appear to be smaller transports," Divinus replied. "They're swarming around the mothership in complex patterns."

Myra squinted at them. "Why are they doing that?"

"They're preparing for war," Aero said, his eyes fixed on the projection. "They're running combat flight drills. I'll bet the simulators are in operation around the clock. The Foundry must be working overtime to charge Falchions."

"So Vinick thinks they can fight back against the Fourth Continuum?" Myra said, feeling a hopeful fluttering in her chest. "That sounds promising. Maybe they can defeat Drakken for us? Vinick has a whole army at his disposal, doesn't he?"

"He does have an army, but they were always intended to be a peacekeeping force by design," Aero explained. "Our Falchions are deadly weapons, but they're not capable of inflicting destruction on a mass scale like Drakken's arsenal."

"Then why even bother to prepare for war?" Myra asked with a frown.

Aero thought for a moment. "The Majors must have detected the Fourth Continuum in their vicinity. That would explain why Vinick pulled back into a defensive position and withdrew his troops from our doorstep. I'm guessing these drills are a show of strength—a bluff to frighten Drakken and keep him from attacking them first."

Myra took that in. "Vinick is hoping they'll target us instead?"

"Yes, that's my best guess," Aero agreed. "Vinick is hoping that Drakken will blast open our front door, so then he can sweep in and scavenge whatever is left."

"If there's anything left," Myra added darkly.

Holographs of the two space vessels appeared overhead, both hostile forces. Seeker shifted uncomfortably in her seat. Her eyes had a glazed look, the kind she got when she was tired of following their conversation. Myra could sense the discord between them. She glanced down at the golden cuff encircling her right wrist.

All these Continuums, all divided in their intentions, in their loyalties, in their priorities. Even their Carriers were divided. She could tell that Seeker had reverted to her old ways—that she wanted to escape from the First Continuum, abandoning them to their fate. Aero also seemed at a loss without orders, routine, and the structure of his old existence. The Beacon had given him something bigger to follow. It issued orders that he was more than happy to obey. But without its connection, he seemed lost and adrift.

Myra gazed down the table, her eyes flicking from Aero to Seeker to Professor Divinus. She could sense Noah hovering around them, not human exactly, but still a being with intelligence and ability. And in that moment, she came to a decision. All the confusion of the past week, all the indecision and failure to find a way forward evaporated. Without any shred of doubt, she knew exactly what they had to do.

"Our only hope lies in uniting your Continuums."

Her voice came out loud and clear and utterly certain. Even Seeker looked up and paid closer attention. Aero glanced over. "Unite our colonies? What do you mean?"

"Exactly what I said," Myra replied. "We have to bring your colonies together, so we can fight back against Drakken and the Fourth Continuum. My people are unreachable in their trench without any submersibles." Her voice caught in her throat, but she forced it out. "Otherwise, I know the Thirteenth Continuum would help us."

"You're talking about the Second and Seventh Continuums?" Aero said. "You do realize my colony is ruled by a hostile leader. And Seeker's world is . . . well . . ."

"Weak and feeble," Seeker growled. She blinked in the harsh light of the control room. "Weaklings afraid . . . and Strong Ones mostly crushed to death."

"Look, I know it's a long shot," Myra said, but she felt hope stir in her heart. "But it's our only choice. We have to unite them into one force."

Divinus looked hesitant. "My dear, you're talking about building an army."

"An army to defend the First Continuum," Myra said with a quick nod. "Aero, your people are trained soldiers, right? They already have an army. And Seeker, yours are survivors. I've seen them fight." She flinched at the memory of losing Paige.

"But what about Vinick?" Aero asked. "My people are soldiers above all else. That means they'll follow his orders without question. And there's another tiny hitch. I've been banished from my colony and labeled a deserter. Sorry to mess with your grand plan, but turning my colony to our side would prove difficult—if not impossible."

"The Strong Ones . . ." Seeker said. "Some dead, but not all. Weaklings not united . . . out for themselves . . . don't trust others . . . only care about survival."

"I never claimed it would be easy," Myra said stubbornly. "But there must be a way to unite your people together. Otherwise, we may as well surrender to Drakken now and turn over the secret of the Doom. We're dead anyway."

Divinus steepled his hands under his beard. "It's risky, there's no question about it. But my dear, you're right. Uniting the Continuums may be our only hope."

"I concur, Professor," echoed Noah. "Based on my limited data on the Fourth Continuum, Commander Drakken and his army are too powerful. If we are divided, then we will fall. We need reinforcements. Even then the odds are still unfavorable."

"But it would give us a chance, right?" Myra said. She leapt to her feet and started pacing around the control room. Her mind was flying at high speed. "Aero, you'd have to go back to the Second Continuum. Find a way to overthrow Vinick and enlist their army. Seeker, you'd have to return to the Seventh Continuum. Recruit as many Weaklings as you can and bring them back here. Maybe some Strong Ones survived and will join our cause. By the Oracle, we need as many soldiers as we can get."

"Right, how am I supposed to do that?" Aero said in disbelief.

"Well, I don't know," Myra admitted. "We'll have to come up with a plan. What other choice do we have? Wait down here until Drakken blasts down our door?"

"What about you?" Aero asked, watching Myra pace in a loop. "What are you going to do while Seeker and I are back in our colonies trying to recruit this army?"

A smile crept over Divinus's face. "Myra is going to stay here with me and Noah. We'll have many preparations to make if this plan is going to succeed."

"What about your colony?" Aero asked. "The Thirteenth Continuum is running out of oxygen. If we don't launch a rescue mission soon, won't they suffocate?"

Myra felt a deep shiver start in the base of her spine. She thought of her father and Maude and the Bishop twins and everyone else back home in her deep-sea colony. "They're unreachable without a submersible, and we can't build one without the raw materials. Plus, it won't matter if we save them only to have Drakken kill us."

She skidded to a halt and locked eyes with Aero. "Just promise me that you'll rescue Tinker and Kaleb from your colony," she said. "Promise that you'll try."

Aero nodded solemnly, gripping the hilt of his Falchion.

"I swear it, even if it's the last thing I do."

"There's one more thing," Myra said, raising her right arm. The Beacon clung to her wrist, still dark and lifeless. "We have to reactivate the Beacons. Ever since they were turned off, it's like we've dissolved into our own separate factions."

"My dear, we deactivated them because they had fulfilled their purpose," Divinus said. "Reactivating them could prove dangerous. Let's not forget that Commander Drakken is a Carrier too. He can spy on you and manipulate your thoughts with the Beacons. We don't know the extent of his powers yet."

"Can't you deactivate his Beacon?" Aero suggested. "And turn ours back on?"

Divinus shook his head. "He anticipated we might try that, or attempt to control him through his Beacon. For starters, he's still too far away for us to exert any real influence over him. He's also trained his mind to shut us out. Plus, it appears that special modifications have been made to his device that shield it from Noah's control."

Myra let out a frustrated sigh. "They've thought of everything."

"Well, they've had seven hundred years to prepare," intoned Divinus.

Myra took up her pacing again. Her canvas shoes slapped against the concrete floor. "I don't care if it's risky, we need the Beacons. Not only to keep us bonded together, but also to communicate once we go our separate ways." She glanced over at Aero. "Isn't that how the space colonies used them back in the day?"

"Yes, the space Carriers used the Beacons to communicate that way," Aero confirmed. "The Order of the Foundry also had a way of communicating with the Carriers directly, though I don't know how it worked exactly."

Noah projected the blueprints for the Beacons overhead. The images materialized, showing the combination of nanotechnology and biological interfaces.

Divinus pursed his lips. "The Beacons are bonded to your nervous systems, your brains, your cellular structures—in short, to the very essence of your beings. You understand the risks of reactivating them?"

"Drakken?" Seeker growled. "Spy on us . . . try to hurt us."

Divinus nodded. "Yes, he will use the Beacons to spy on you. You'll have to learn how to shut him out. The less he learns about our plans, the better."

Aero glanced around the table. "I don't know about you, but I was struggling with that before my Beacon went dark. It's not like my Falchion. I can't control it very well."

"Me too," Myra admitted. "Drakken was in my dreams as the Dark Thing. He did horrible things to me. I don't ever wish to go through that again."

"Commander Drakken is focused on Myra," Noah chimed in. His voice seemed to emanate from everywhere and nowhere all at once. "It appears that she has the strongest neural connection to the Beacon, so he was feeding off her energy somehow."

"It was terrible . . ." Myra shuddered, remembering how he attacked each night, enveloping her in his shadowy form and sucking away her life force.

"My dear, I fear the risks are too great," Divinus said, flipping through the data on the Beacons. "If Drakken succeeds in infiltrating your thoughts and learns about our plans to unite the Continuums, he will work to counter us. It would be much better if we could operate in secret. Reactivating the Beacons will render us vulnerable."

"The professor is right," Aero said. "He'll figure out our plans for sure."

"Drakken . . . nasty and dangerous," Seeker growled.

Myra stopped her pacing. "Wait, I've got an idea. Drakken will spy on us, right? Mostly in our dreams? So instead of shutting him out, what if we let him in?"

Aero looked shocked. "Are you crazy? I've seen what he does to you."

"Just hear me out," Myra continued and lowered her voice. She explained her plan in detail, speaking quickly. When she finished, they all looked resolved.

"So then it's decided?" she asked. "We'll reactivate the Beacons and unite your Continuums?"

"Or die trying," Aero said, seizing the hilt of his Falchion. "Starry hell, this is one crazy plan." He broke into a grin. "I'm just sorry I didn't think of it myself."

"Strong Ones and Weaklings," Seeker growled. "One people."

Divinus rose from the table. His robes rustled as he manipulated the screens over their heads, keying in codes. He stood back. "Noah, reactivate the Beacons."

With a great flash of emerald light that engulfed the control room, their armlets blazed back to life. Myra felt a rush of adrenaline surge through her body, through her nerves, through every single cell in her body, and zap her brain. In that moment, she was Aero and she was Seeker—they were united for the first time in many long days.

Her consciousness spanned beyond the confines of her

material body, to the outer reaches of space, to the darkest depths of the underground, to the trenches of the deep seas, and beyond, through space and time. She fell through the breadth of human history, through world wars, ancient empires, cities leveled to dust and then rebuilt, through creation and destruction galore. And then she heard a familiar voice echo through her head.

It was Elianna—the first Carrier of her Beacon.

"Myra . . . I'm here . . . I'll always be here . . . I never left you."

Chapter 7
THE SPARE PARTS ROOM

Jonah Jackson

Stella and Ginger led the way through the darkness. Only the bluish beam of their flashlight lit their path. Jonah shuffled after them, feeling the pipe scraping against his back. Maude, Greeley, and the rest of the Goon Squad, her security detail, crawled behind them single file. The passage was too narrow to allow for anything else.

"This way—to the right," Stella hissed behind her. The flashlight flashed over her freckled face and wiry orange hair, lending her a ghostly appearance.

"Right," Ginger whispered to Jonah, who passed the message down the line. He followed the two girls, but his thoughts were fixed on his daughter. Myra had learned how to navigate through the colony undetected, using the pipe and duct system. When she rescued the Bishop twins from the Pen, she taught them about her secret ways.

"Myra," he said under his breath. *I know you're up there on the Surface. By the Oracle, I'm coming for you*, he promised himself. *Even if it's the last thing I do.*

Following the twins, their raiding party snaked right. The next pipe spit them out into a larger passage, which had once carried water but was now abandoned. Their hands splashed down into puddles. The steady *drip-drip-drip* of water followed them. Jonah felt relief at the pipe's wider girth. When had he developed claustrophobia?

In his younger days, when he'd first pledged to Engineering, his job involved frequent excursions into the pipe and duct system to repair burst water mains, sewage leaks, and any other problems that sprang up due to the advanced age of the colony's infrastructure. But that had been a long time ago. When he became the Head Engineer, his duties morphed into more of a desk job. Clearly, he'd gone soft.

Stella and Ginger hurried ahead. They could walk stooped over; the adults still had to crawl. After a few more twists and turns, the twins came to a halt over a square grate set into the pipe. Chilled air hissed over them and drew goose bumps to Jonah's skin. He shivered slightly and peered through the grate.

"This is it," Stella whispered and clicked off her flashlight. "Sector 10."

"The Spare Parts Room," Ginger added and pointed through the grate.

"You lassies sure 'bout that?" Greeley asked, joining them by the grate. His large frame crammed into the small space. "Feels like we're all the way over by Sector 2. Though my head could be mixed up from those turns. These pipes are a bloody maze."

"We know the secret ways by heart," Stella replied.

Ginger exchanged a look with her sister. "Myra taught us."

"How many Dissemination workers down there?" Greeley asked. The big Hocker was the head of Maude's security detail. Hockers were the ones who had been kicked out of their trades and lost half their Victus, or Synod-issues rations. Before the uprising and the shuttering of the Souk, they survived by trading homemade goods at the market.

Jonah squinted through the grate. The vast sector was coated in a thick layer of dust and mostly cast in shadow despite the blazing of the automatic lights. Junk filled the room and spanned up to the ceiling—hunks of metal and all manner of spare parts. He guessed Dissemination had a filing system for how the sector was organized, but Jonah couldn't decipher it. It looked completely disorganized.

"Looks like only two workers inside," Maude said. Though she was approaching seventy, her eyesight was still sharp. "One woman behind the checkout desk, plus a pledge to retrieve the spare parts and make deliveries to other sectors."

"Penelope Reed," Jonah said, recognizing her plump figure. The woman let out a raspy cough as she flipped through the dusty receipts. "Dissemination must have transferred her from the Com Store after the Synod put Stan Decker out to sea. That pledge is her son, Bailey. He used to make deliveries to the Engineering Room."

"Stan Decker," Greeley said. It took him a minute to place the name. "Isn't he the Factum who helped you?" Unlike the Hockers, who had been expelled from their trades, the Factum made up the working class and received their full Victus from the Synod. Both the Factum and the Hockers served under the Plenus, made up of the chancellors who sat on the Synod and the priests from the Church of the Oracle of the Sea.

"Stan was a brave man," Jonah confirmed. "He helped me smuggle out parts so I could build the submersible in secret—and he paid for it with his life." Myra, Tinker, and their friends had taken that vessel when they fled to the Surface.

Maude swirled her hand over her heart. "The Holy Sea rest his soul," she muttered in prayer. The other Hockers followed suit and repeated the phrase. Their superstitions still ran deep.

"How many 'Trollers guarding the sector door?" Jonah asked.

"Only five," Greeley said. "My squad scoped out the corridor yesterday. The Synod don't care about no Spare Parts Room, else they'd have a larger detail."

"Baron Donovan and Horace Grint?" Maude said, glancing back at him. "Aren't they in charge of this sector? I read your report this morning."

"Yes, Cheif," Greeley said, but then he frowned. He exchanged a look with his security detail, which everyone called the Goon Squad. "Chief, this mission is too dangerous for you. You ought to hightail it back to the Engineering Room. Or at least hang back in the pipes until we clear the 'Trollers from the sector."

"Greeley's right," said Pratt, a Hocker with a long, stringy beard. "Chief, you're too important to the Surfacers. The Synod would love to get their perfumed hands on you. You know what Padre Flavius will do if he catches you."

Jonah shuddered. He flashed back to his time locked up in the Pen. Padre Flavius had visited him regularly to dole out his favorite punishment.

"He'll torture you in the unbroken darkness," Jonah said. His hand felt for the scars that lined his back, thick raised veins of pink flesh. "Until you beg for Padre Flavius to put you out to sea. Because it will seem like a mercy. But he'll refuse, and the beatings will continue. It's not just physical— the psychological torture is the worst part."

Maude shot them all a stubborn look. "Greeley, I know it's your job to protect me, but I'm sick and tired of sitting on my arse while you do the dirty work. By the Oracle, I started this rebellion—and I mean to see it through."

Her hand snaked to the insulated handle of the pipe belted to her waist. The weapon was Jonah's own design. They all carried one, even the Bishop twins.

"Yes, Chief," Greeley replied. Pratt also backed down, though he didn't look happy about it. They knew better than to argue with her. Once again, Jonah was reminded why his widowed neighbor had become a formidable rebel leader.

The Hockers passed around a tin of axle grease, which they smoothed over their arms and bare shoulders. The grease blackened their skin. That was followed by a flask of firewater. All the Hockers, including Maude, took strong pulls of the acrid liquid, though Jonah declined the alcoholic brew. He wanted to keep his wits about him.

"Ready?" Maude said. She unsheathed her pipe and felt for the button set into the handle. Her thumb settled into the groove. "Surfacers, on my count."

Greeley and the others drew their pipes in response. Stella and Ginger clutched smaller versions that Jonah had specially made for them. Their green eyes glinted in the light leaking through the grate. Jonah felt his heart flutter wildly in anticipation. His fingers cramped, but he kept them wrapped tightly around his pipe's handle.

"One, two, . . . three," Maude counted softly. "To the Surface!"

Jonah quickly unlatched the grate and swung it inward. Greeley leapt through the vent with surprising speed for his large size. His greased shoulders slid through the narrow opening. He landed on the floor in a crouch with his pipe raised. The other Hockers landed around him, one right after the other. Jonah followed suit, though his landing was far less elegant. He stumbled and almost toppled forward.

"What's . . . happening?" the Dissemination woman yelped. She leapt up from her desk. Bailey ran over, his bare feet dusty from racing through the stacks. Likewise, his cheeks were smudged with dust, grime, and the Oracle knew what else.

"Ma, they're Surfacers," he hissed. "Look at their uniforms."

"Surfacers," she stammered. Her eyes fixed onto their blue garb with the golden symbol stitched into the lapel—a clenched fist with the index finger pointing up. Her mouth formed into a scream. Before she could get it out, Greeley seized her and clamped his large hand over her mouth. The woman struggled in his arms.

"Keep your mouth shut," Greeley growled in her ear. "Unless you want to feel the bite of my pipe."

Seizing on the distraction, Bailey took off for the back of the sector. But Stella and Ginger chased him down. They nimbly weaved through the towering heaps of parts that threatened to topple over and crush them. They cornered him at a dead end.

"Please . . . just don't hurt me," Bailey begged, thrusting his hands in the air. The twins stood over him with their pipes raised. Dust motes danced around their silhouettes.

"We won't hurt you," Stella said. "Swear it on the Oracle."

"Unless you give us a reason," Ginger added with a menacing grin.

Bailey nodded mutely. The twins herded him back to the front of the sector. After soliciting a promise not to scream, Greeley released Penelope from his grip. She clung to her son tightly. Her frightened eyes combed over the rebels' faces.

"What do you want with us?" she said. Her voice warbled, thick with fear. "We're only Factum, following the rules and staying out of trouble. Please . . . I'll do anything. Just don't hurt my boy. I lost my girl to the Pox when she was only a babe in swaddling clothes. The Synod denied my appeal for another child. Bailey's all I've got left."

Maude lowered her pipe and fixed the woman with a tender gaze. "My dear husband and two children succumbed to the last great Pox outbreak. I've lived as a widow ever since, scraping by as a Hocker. Your trade sided with the Synod, but the Surfacers wish your family no harm. We want to help you."

"But we've heard . . . terrible stories . . ." Penelope said.

Greeley snorted. "That we torture and kill babes?"

"And eat them for breakfast?" Pratt added, patting his belly.

The woman nodded fearfully. Her eyes darted to their clothing. "And that you skin them and use their leather hides to line your uniforms."

"Lies spread by Padre Flavius and the Synod," Maude said. Her eyes flashed with anger. "They're the ones who imprison and torture children in the Pen—not us."

"Yeah, they're the true heathens," Stella said darkly. "They killed our parents. Put them both out to sea." Doubt sparked across Penelope's face.

"They locked us up in the Pen," Ginger added. "And we're only kids. Not much younger than Bailey here. Myra Jackson rescued us."

Penelope swirled her hand over her chest. "She's a sinner and a heathen!" she hissed and spat on the floor. "Don't you dare speak her unholy name. Padre Flavius should have put her out to sea when he had the chance."

"More lies," Maude shot back. "Myra Jackson is a hero. Padre Flavius, the Synod, the Patrollers—they're the sinners. They've forgotten our true purpose. We were never meant to stay under the sea. We're supposed to return to the Surface—"

"Blasphemy!" the woman cut her off. She let out a raspy cough. Her son shot her a worried look. "You'll bring about another Doom by uttering the banned words."

"Bullocks," Maude said. "The only *doom* that will befall us is if we stay down here. The Animus Machine is failing. It's breaking down. This man—Jonah Jackson—is the Head Engineer. Even he can't fix it. Do you know what that means?"

It was Bailey who replied. "We're running out of oxygen, aren't we? That's what's been making everyone sick, isn't it? The shortness of breath. The dizziness. The fatigue. The longer lines at the Infirmary. I knew something wasn't right."

Maude nodded. "And fast."

"No . . . it can't be," Penelope stammered. "I saw the orange flag. The Synod said it was just an allergen release from Farming. Nothing to worry about."

"Lies, lies, and more bloody lies," Greeley sniffed. "Padre Flavius is the one who should be put out to sea. Jonah told the Synod about the Animus Machine."

"And they decided to do nothing," Pratt added with a disgusted expression. "Except Padre Flavius demanded more sacrifices. He's the true heathen."

"Exactly," Jonah said, approaching the Dissemenation workers. "Our only hope is to return to the Surface. My daughter led the way, but it's our task to follow her. We need your help to save our colony. Will you join us?"

Bailey exchanged a look with his mother. "Ma, listen to them. I think they're telling the truth. I've noticed the shortness of breath too. When I run through the stacks or make deliveries. And your wheezing and cough—it's getting worse, isn't it?"

She thumped her chest. "It pains me terribly. The doctors think it's my allergies kicking up with the pollen release. But the medicinal tonics aren't helping."

"What if it's not allergens?" Bailey said. "What if it's hypoxia?"

"Then the Oracle help us," she replied. "We're doomed."

Bailey turned back to the rebels. "If we agree to help you, you must promise that no harm will come to us. My mother . . . she was only following the rules."

"Of course," Maude said. "I swear it on my life."

"And the Oracle?" Bailey asked.

Maude winked. "And the Oracle and the Holy Sea."

Bailey nodded and clasped his mother's hand. They peered at the rebels expectantly. "What do you need us to do?"

Chapter 8

ABANDONED IN THE NIGHT

Commander Drakken

Drakken felt a surge that sucked him into the dreamscape. His Beacon lit up with a green charge and propelled him from his ship, through the insulated walls, out into the black void of space. He hurtled like a meteor and exploded into another world, crashing down on the desolate surface. He flowed up from the crater like smoke, shielding himself with his mind. His Beacon continued to throb.

Where am I?

Untold miles of scorched land spanned around him. The sun sparkled like a black pearl in the apex of the sky. The edges of the world were frayed and blurry, still incomplete. But always this world was expanding, coming into sharper focus, filling out with new topography. A jagged mountain range poked at the obsidian sky. That was something new. The Carriers fashioned this landscape with their minds, networked together by the Beacons. This place marked the ghostly crossroads of their consciousnesses. The physical manifestation of where their neural synapses connected.

After a long moment, Drakken realized why he'd been summoned here. He could feel it with each electric pulse from the device encircling his wrist. *They've reactivated the Beacons.* When the other Carriers disappeared into the First Continuum, his connection to their minds had been severed, much to his annoyance. Then Noah had broken through his cloaking shield, forcing him to alter his carefully laid plans.

But no longer.

Drakken could feel the power of the reforged connection rippling through his being. Using his Beacon, he probed for the girl. He knew she was in the dreamscape. She was the only one who could summon him to the crossroads. Her connection to the Beacon was stronger than the other two Carriers—Aero and Seeker—combined.

Myra . . . Myra . . . Myra . . .

Drakken sent out his signal and searched for her—and something pinged him back. Spreading out over the blackened terrain, he flowed like a foul mist after the signal. He crested the newly raised mountain range, and there—set into the cliffside—he came upon a massive door. It was golden and marked by the Ouroboros seal. His amorphous form slammed into the barrier and ricocheted off it, as if repelled by an ancient spell.

Is this some protection the girl has erected to defy me?

Fury shot through him, hot and fiery. He would break the door down; he would find the way in. His mouth watered at the prospect of feeding off the girl's energy. It had been many days since their last bonding. He summoned every bit of his power, drawing raw energy from his Beacon, from his people, from their beating hearts, from their ship, from the nuclear core of their reactor. He gathered it and released it at the door.

An emerald blaze exploded out of his Beacon.

The golden metal began to soften in the inferno. It melted, dripping down the mountainside and revealing an elevator. Inside, he saw a crumpled form.

"They left me alone . . ." Myra let out a strangled sob.

Her whole body shook from the force of it. The Beacon on her wrist throbbed erratically. "We had a plan . . . but Aero and Seeker backed out. They fled from the First Continuum through a secret door. Seeker only cares about herself . . . and Aero loves Wren more than me . . ."

"What did you expect, Carrier?" Drakken said with a jeering laugh. "Your friends abandoned you, just like they did after the Trial. They always abandon you."

Using the Beacon, he could rove freely through her mind, extracting her worst memories. He forced her to relive the moment the Patrollers arrested her, pulling her out of her class and tossing her into the Pen. He also made her re-experience the pain of her expulsion from school and her closest friends avoiding her in the corridors, even after she was released. He enjoyed using her memories against her. Her pain was his pleasure.

"But I thought . . . Aero loved me . . ." she sobbed.

"Nobody loves you, Carrier," Drakken snarled and descended on her, enveloping her in his shadowy tendrils. She screamed and flailed, but it did no good. She was frail and alone. She hadn't mastered control of her Beacon yet. He could taste her terror and her sorrow on his tongue; he fed on them, suckling her life force. He rifled through her mind, plucking out her deepest thoughts. Her memories played out as if in real time:

The girl waking from a deep slumber, traipsing down a darkened corridor. Finding Aero's room empty, then Seeker's also empty. Running frantically through the passages, searching for the other Carriers, stumbling upon a secret door hidden in an abandoned chamber—and an empty elevator. Discovering a note left inside:

Myra,
Seeker is gone. She left in the middle of the night through a secret back door. I'm so sorry . . . but I have to leave too. I can't stop thinking about Wren. It's driving me mad. I hope you'll find a way to forgive me one day.
—Aero

Drakken let out another laugh. The girl was the last Carrier left in the First Continuum. Noah was only a computer, and Professor Divinus a projection. It will be easy to invade their haven and extract the secret of the Doom.

Now it's all mine for the taking.

PART II
STRATAGEM

Let your plans be dark and impenetrable as night, and when you move, fall like a thunderbolt.

—Sun Tzu, *The Art of War*

Chapter 9
THE LAST CARRIER

Myra Jackson

Myra woke with a scream on her breath and knew they were gone.

Seeker and Aero.

Both gone.

She didn't have to look in their chambers to confirm that depressing truth; she could feel their absence like a missing limb. She pushed herself up from her bed, the silken covers sloughing off her thin frame.

She was pale and shaking. She dragged her wrist from under the covers. Her Beacon throbbed weakly. It was drained of energy, like her body. With another bout of trembling, she remembered what she'd endured during the night. While she slept, the Dark Thing had preyed upon her, feeding on her life force and delving through her mind, through her deepest, darkest secrets, savoring the terrible loss of her friends.

The other Carriers.

I'm the only one left in the First Continuum.

This sanctuary—constructed to preserve life and

knowledge and culture and technology—now felt like a tomb. And all the while, the Fourth Continuum was hurling through space with a massive arsenal intending to blast right through their door.

It felt hopeless.

Chapter 10
RAMPING UP FOR WAR

The Order of the Foundry

The dull creaking came from his joints.

The old Forger swished across the Foundry, his crimson robes rustling around his ankles. As he went, he switched off the golden machines and flicked off the overhead light panels. He glanced at the newly forged Falchions suspended in the middle of the Foundry, as if floating on air. They shimmered with their fresh charge. He counted seven of them. Those were only the blades forged in the last twenty-four hours.

He had always taken great pride in their work, but now he couldn't suppress his disdain for their accelerated production schedule, their blindly ramping up for war without thought of consequences or strategies that might avert a conflict. This went against their most fundamental teachings, the ones that had sustained the Second Continuum through their millennium-long exile in the cold vacuum of space.

Nothing I can do about it, he reminded himself. *Supreme General Vinick won't change his mind. He's stubborn, prideful, and foolhardy, just like he was as a student at the Agoge. He doesn't see the error of his ways—he never will.*

Men like Vinick had started all the great wars in history, the Forger knew from his studies. They always believed they were right, even in the face of all evidence to the contrary, even when the future would condemn their actions harshly.

That realization made the Forger feel older than his one hundred and two years. He was the eldest of his sworn brothers and sisters, having outlived even the most generous life expectations of his people. He attributed his longevity to a combination of fate, carefully selected genetics, moderate eating, low-impact calisthenics, and a sizable dose of luck. Though he feared his luck might finally be running out.

Their current situation was tenuous at best. He could feel this truth in every brittle bone and stiff joint in his body. Vinick was bent on eroding the Order of the Foundry's autonomy, granted to them by the First Ones in their founding charter. Any misstep, any action that appeared to undermine Vinick's authority, could cause it to collapse altogether. Worse yet, Vinick was holding one of their sworn brothers captive in the Disciplinary Barracks, in defiance of their laws. So far, Vinick had resisted the Order's call for their brother's release. They'd already dispatched two emissaries to the bridge.

"He's a security threat and a deserter," Vinick scoffed at them. "Thus, he doesn't receive the protections outlined in our charter. You're fortunate I don't detain the rest of your Order for harboring a traitor in your midst—or banish you from our colony."

The old Forger continued across the Foundry. He frowned at the readout on the next machine. The power supply was dwindling faster than usual; it was in danger of being over-worked. He patted it, feeling blistering heat emanating from the smooth metal.

"Rest now, old friend," he whispered to the machine. "I fear I can grant you only a few precious hours to recharge. Tomorrow will be another long day."

He felt a shudder ripple through the golden metal in

response. He harbored a special fondness for this particular machine, the first he had trained on after the Order selected him, pulling him out of the Agoge when he was only a child. It was a machine—yes, of course—but it was also a living, breathing organism. It didn't have moving parts like conventional mechanical devices. Instead, it functioned using a flawless blend of nanotechnology and biology that seemed less like science and more like magic.

The old Forger flipped the second-to-last light panel. It flared and shut off. Tucked away on the lowermost level of the Second Continuum, the Foundry fell into shadow. The rest of his Order had already taken to their bunks. They needed their rest. The old Forger was always the last to retire, such was his burden. Lately, his Order been working around the clock for one reason and one reason alone.

They were ramping up for war.

"These are troubling times," he had informed his Order after Vinick and the Majors briefed him on the sudden reappearance of the Fourth Continuum. The response from his usually staid brothers and sisters had been immediate.

Questions rang out like blaster fire, rapid and staccato: "Brother, where has the Fourth Continuum been all this time?"

"Brother, do they have a Carrier? Who commands their ship?"

"Brother, what does the Fourth want? Why have they returned?"

The old Forger did his best to respond, though most answers still remained a mystery. "My sworn brothers and sisters, precious little is known about the Fourth Continuum," he said, gesturing to the circular windows that dotted the Foundry, revealing the black void of space. "Their cloaking devices are stronger than anything we've encountered before. The Majors are trying to break them, but so far they haven't succeeded. Nor has the Fourth opened up communication lines with us. However, we do know three things—they have a Carrier, and they're bound for the First Continuum."

"Brother, what's the third?" said one of his young sisters. Her clean-shaven head gleamed under her crimson hood. The old Forger tugged at his beard agitatedly.

"They're armed with nuclear weapons."

Frightened whispers crackled through the Order. The old Forger raised his hands for quiet. His robes slipped back, pooling behind his calloused elbows. It took them a long moment to calm down. Then another question shot out at him.

"Brother . . . the Doom? Do they possess it?"

It was the young sister again, recruited two years ago out of the Agoge. Her lips trembled as she spoke. When the old Forger was her age, he had never tasted war. *And this is only its precursor*, he reminded himself. The worst was yet to come.

He shook his head. "Nothing from Major Doyle's initial scans indicates they possess that terrible secret, thank the stars. Though we can't be sure."

Before they could ask more questions, he plowed forward. "Our colony is ramping up for war. Supreme General Vinick has ordered us to forge new Falchions. He plans to arm the youngest students at the Agoge."

His Order rumbled their disapproval. "Brother, that's blasphemy!"

"Brother, it takes time to master the art of the Falchion!"

"Brother, the bonding could prove perilous to those untrained to handle it. Incidents are documented in our Archives. Many young souls have perished."

The old Forger raised his hands again. He felt gratitude for their sovereign realm, where they could speak freely without concern for the Supreme General or the Majors over-hearing their deliberations.

"My sworn brothers and sisters, I'm aware of the risks. But it would be dangerous for our Order to refuse the Supreme General's demands. He's looking for any excuse to usurp our autonomy. I fear this would give him exactly what he wants. He could brand us as traitors, like our young brother being detained in the Disciplinary Barracks."

This was met with cold, hard silence—the Order knew that antagonizing Vinick could prove hazardous to their very existence.

"Regarding Supreme General Vinick's request for new Falchions, are there any further objections?" the old Forger asked. "Speak now or forever hold your peace."

The silence endured; it lengthened and deepened, enveloping the Foundry in its icy embrace. Even the machines seemed to sense it. Their whooshing and whirring softened, as if they too were holding their breath.

The old Forger nodded in acknowledgment of their sacrifice. Their principles were the foundation of their Order, and to compromise them in this way—to put the youngest students at the Agoge at risk by forging weapons that they weren't prepared to wield—was a weighty concession to make. And they did not make it lightly.

"As you know, each Falchion requires a high level of skill and precision to forge, so we will be instituting a new schedule. Commencing immediately, we will sleep for only four hours a night in order to meet Vinick's demands. When we sleep, the machines will also need to rest and recuperate. I pray that we all survive this test."

With that edict, the Foundry's preparations for war had commenced.

The old Forger knew he should sleep, but tonight he had a mission. *A secret mission*, he reminded himself. With a creak of his knees—was it audible only to him or to the wider world?—he reached the furthest end of the Foundry, where the ceiling sloped down and tapered into a snug alcove. A single light panel remained illuminated; it shone down in a narrow pool and spotlighted their Archives—shelves stacked to the ceiling and laden with ancient tomes so heavy that they made them sag in places.

His eyes grazed over the books, feeling a prickle of pride. This was the summation of his Order's knowledge, culled over the years, scrawled out with ink and pen on thick parchment, festooned with illustrations made of curling letters and golden paint smeared into black outlines, like the handwritten books made by monks during the Middle Ages in the time Before Doom.

The old Forger approached the first shelf and ran his finger over it, coming up with a thick layer of dust. He felt a burst of sadness at the neglect. The library seemed to get visited less and less as the years crept along. His younger brothers and sisters simply didn't have as much appreciation for the sacred work of their ancestors.

His Order's rationale in creating the Archive was simple— if the First Continuum failed and their computer systems were destroyed, either by a power surge or other ill-fated happenstance, then these handwritten books alone would endure. They would outlast computer chips and wires and hardware and machine intelligences. The simple act of putting pen to paper grasped at a type of immortality; it defied time itself.

Of course, a book could age beyond recognition, the ink fading to nothing, the pages curling up and crumbling to dust. But before that happened, his brothers and sisters removed the tomes from the shelves and copied them onto parchment anew. His Order had an intricate system of rotating through the shelves and duplicating the texts. Each manuscript bore the distinctive handwriting and embellishments of the individual author. The old Forger could identify them simply by scanning a random page.

The old Forger paced down the second row, stopped at the correct spot, and pulled down a weighty tome. His arms shook as he lifted it. He approached a table and set it down with a thunk. The light pooled over the cover, battered and faded—*The Teachings of the First Ones*. Below that was scrawled *Preserved by the Order of the Foundry*.

He flipped through the crumbling pages, his eyes skimming over the ornate cursive, decorated with gold lettering and illustrations. He ran his fingers over a miniature Ouroboros, tracing the outline of the snake swallowing its own tail. He found the passage that held one of their most sacred teachings:

When all hope is lost and night seems longer than day

And those with evil in their hearts and death on their lips

Come to destroy everything we have endeavored to save

Only then will he emerge to lead us back to our true home

The Chosen One who carries the Beacon and lights the way

The old Forger bent over the text, his brow knitted together. He thought of the Supreme General—*Jaden Vinick*. He pictured the man's narrow face, beady eyes, and sharp nose. He could still remember when Vinick was a skinny boy with high combat scores at the Agoge. The old Forger never would have selected him for their Order. Even back then, Vinick possessed the same character flaws—envy, vanity, a quick-flaring temper, little patience for studying. This man was not the true Supreme General.

He has evil in his heart and death on his lips, the old Forger thought with a frown. Vinick did not carry the Beacon; he would never carry the Beacon. That honor—or was it a burden?—had passed to Captain Aero Wright.

He was their rightful Supreme General.

The old Forger bent over the table and combed through the dusty tome, searching for any references to the Fourth Continuum. He pulled more books down and cracked open their battered spines, the pages flying under his fingertips, his eyes firing across the pages. Worrying phrases jumped out at him, scrawled in ornate script:

Human experimentation. Weapons development. Networking synapses to amplify cognition. Using the Beacon to power it all. To connect and bind them together.

He flipped faster. The dust made him sneeze. His vision blurred. His eyes weren't what they used to be. He'd need to visit the Clinic for a tune-up soon. Only there never seemed to be enough time with these dastardly war preparations.

As a bone-shattering weariness overtook him, the old Forger pushed back from his desk and rubbed his eyes. His brothers and sisters would stir in their bunks soon, needing to return to their work. He had to replace the books in the Archives before they rose. Out of the corner of his eye, he caught a flash of emerald light.

An old machine lodged in the back of the Foundry blazed to life.

The old Forger looked over with a start. "By the stars, how can this be?" he whispered when he saw which machine had caused the disturbance.

The Colloquium Machine had been defunct for nearly seven centuries, a relic preserved mostly for archival purposes, something interesting to show the students from the Agoge when they toured the Foundry on their field trips with the Drillmasters. The last time it had been in active use was when the three space colonies still used their Carriers to communicate with one another.

The old Forger rushed over, feeling deeply unsettled. Despite its lack of use, the Colloquium Machine was spotless and bereft of any decay. It gleamed even in the dim light of the Foundry. Dials, knobs, and levers marked the control panel. They bleated with light. He tinkered with the knobs and toggled the levers, trying to lock onto the signal and amplify it. He hit the right sequence, making the screen blaze to life.

INCOMING SIGNAL FROM CARRIER

Fear shot through the old Forger's body. *Is it Commander Drakken?*

His heart thudded in his chest as he manipulated the levers. But then another Carrier appeared on the screen, projected in perfect three-dimensional clarity.

It was Captain Wright.

The projection quivered and threatened to vanish. "Don't lose the signal," the old Forger muttered. He flipped levers, his arthritic joints in agony from the effort. But he ignored it, sighing with relief when the projection stabilized.

Captain Wright appeared to be piloting a transport— one belonging to the Second Continuum, from the looks of it. Through the cockpit window, the old Forger glimpsed the blue sky mottled with vaporous clouds. They looked unthreatening. With a blinding flash, the sun peeked through them—*oh, the sun*—and lit up the world. In the distance, he could just make out the ocean, sloshing and churning with white-capped waves.

Captain Wright lives—and he made it to Earth.

The old Forger felt a youthful longing stir deep within his heart. When he still was a boy at the Agoge, before the Forgers chose him for their Order, he dreamed of being a soldier deployed to Earth. He snapped out of his memories as Captain Wright spoke, his voice coming through loud and clear, despite the countless miles separating them. As he spoke, his Beacon flared bright as the sunlight peeking over his shoulder.

"Brother, I need your help."

Chapter 11
THE COLLOQUIUM MACHINE

Aero Wright

Their escape from the First Continuum went according to plan.

Or mostly according to plan, Aero thought as he piloted the transport through the clear skies. Absently, his fingers slipped through the gash in his tunic, feeling the shallow wound sliced into his left shoulder. Fresh blood wet his fingertips. *The opponent who left that mark is no longer breathing*, he thought, taking no pleasure in that knowledge. He dispensed with his adversaries only if there was no other way to win the battle.

In the middle of the night, he and Seeker had fled from their chambers and down the corridors of the First Continuum. They traveled light. Aero carried a rucksack stuffed with ration tubes. His Falchion was belted to his waist. He sported his old combat boots, paired with a loose-fitting tunic and trousers. Seeker didn't need clothes. Her thick hair kept her warm in the brisk chill of the underground. But she had a rucksack filled with her most recent kill strapped to her back.

"Secret door, this way," Seeker growled over her shoulder, her eyes sharp in the dim glow cast by their Beacons. She ran on all fours, her hands and feet finding the way. She was so sure-footed and nimble that Aero could barely keep up.

"Right . . . just slow down," Aero grunted as she hooked right, leaving him skidding on the loose gravel and scrambling to reverse direction. "I'm not from the Seventh Continuum. My people can't see in dark corridors."

"Strong One, follow my Beacon," Seeker said. "I can see for both of us. Hurry up, it's this way." She didn't slow her pace; if anything, she ran faster.

Aero gritted his teeth and tried to trust his feet to find the path. This part of the First Continuum was unfinished. Derelict construction and mining equipment peppered their path, as if abandoned in the middle of a shift. Loose wires hung down from the ceiling but posed no risk; no electricity reached this far.

Seeker skidded to a halt before a golden door. Aero almost ran blindly into it, righting his course only at the last minute. He stopped when his nose was an inch away. Seeker snickered at his clumsiness, though it sounded more like a growl.

"Careful, Strong One," she chided. "Secret back door."

Using their Beacons, they activated the door, boarded the elevator, and braced themselves against the railing as it accelerated with a rusty squeal. About twenty minutes later, it spit them out in the middle of a courtyard framed by crumbling redbrick buildings. A sliver of moon hung in the sky, allowing the stars to steal the show and blaze like a million pinpricks. Snow blanketed the ground, remnants of the recent blizzard. It had melted and refrozen into black ice in places, which made the terrain treacherous.

"This way," Aero said once he got his bearings.

The old maps flashed through his head, fed into his brain by Noah through the Beacon. They were standing in the old Radcliffe Quadrangle. This used to be a separate university where only women matriculated, before they were permitted to integrate into Harvard University. Aero found it hard to believe that women had been kept separate, their abilities judged inferior. In his home colony, women attended the Agoge with men, fought alongside them, and ascended to command posts. He knew from experience that their abilities were equal to their male counterparts, if not superior.

Thank the stars for progress, he thought with a rueful shake of his head. *Wren won't believe this when I tell her about it.*

"Very quiet now," Aero whispered to Seeker.

They crept down the ancient streets, picking their way over the rubble and around the dilapidated buildings that once marked the great city of Cambridge. They had to be careful not to slip on the black ice. When they reached Harvard Square, Aero led them through Johnston Gate, framed by two lopsided posts, and into the Yard.

He signaled for Seeker to hold back, his hand slipping to his Falchion. He spotted their target—a sleek transport from the Second Continuum hovering a few feet off the ground. Its engines rumbled with power meant to blast the ship into space.

"Filthy ship . . . filthy flying," Seeker muttered, raising her hackles. She had developed a healthy distaste for flying, having lived her whole life in an underground colony. "Not natural. We should stay on the ground . . . safer that way."

"Flying is the fastest way to get back to the Seventh Continuum," Aero whispered. "And the only way to get to the Second. I can't exactly run to outer space." He gestured to the sky with its smattering of moon and stars.

"Fine, Strong One. Have it your way," Seeker shrugged, though she didn't look happy about it. Her scowl was visible even in the pale moonlight.

The ship appeared unguarded. It shimmered like spun silver under the cascade of moonlight. In the distance, one courtyard over, Aero could just make out the roofless ruin that was Widener Library, the ancient repository which housed the First Continuum.

"Seeker, can you sense anyone?" he asked, scanning the Yard.

Seeker combed over the crumbling buildings with her big eyes. She rose up on her hind legs and scented the air. Aero took a cautious step toward the ship.

Suddenly, Seeker cocked her head in alarm.

"Strong One, wait . . . not safe! It's a trap!"

But it was too late. A shrill whistle pierced the still night. Aero hadn't spotted the sentry posted on the top of University Hall across the Yard.

"Halt, intruder!" yelled the sentry. "Soldiers, we're under attack!"

A blaze of golden sparks exploded and lit up the Yard as the combat unit attacked, rushing out from their encampment in the next courtyard. Aero counted about twenty soldiers. In one smooth motion, he unsheathed his Falchion and shifted it into a broadsword. It morphed slowly. He could feel the weakness of the charge.

Just one more battle, he promised his blade. *Then I'll get you recharged, I swear it. Starry hell, don't melt down on me.* Next to him, Seeker arched her back and bared her razor-sharp teeth. The first soldier had almost reached them with his Falchion raised.

"Private, you don't have to attack us," Aero yelled to the soldier. He tried to explain to the soldier that he wanted only to hijack their transport, not to kill them. But of course, the soldier wasn't interested in talking about it. He wanted to fight.

"Fine, have it your way," Aero said with a shrug.

He twisted away from his opponent's katana. The sharp blade whizzed past his ear, searing off a few locks of curly brown hair. But the soldier had overreached. He lunged past Aero, slipping on the black ice and falling down hard. Aero kicked his Falchion away. It skidded to land by an overturned bronze statue of a man dressed in flowing robes and seated in a chair. Aero hadn't used his Falchion . . . yet.

Seeker swiped at the next soldier, dodging his pike with a spin move. The soldier's leg spurted blood from a deep gash. She whipped her head up.

"Strong One, watch out!" she growled. "More soldiers coming!"

Aero had only a moment to regroup before the soldiers fell on them. Their Falchions blazed from their scabbards, shifting into various weapon forms and oozing sparks—swords, pikes, battle-axes, maces.

Seeker lunged at the next soldier, deftly avoiding his mace and slashing at his legs with her claws. Blood burst from his thigh as he went down screaming. He didn't get back up. Aero wielded his broadsword with great force, parrying off three soldiers with one swing. Then he shifted it into a shield to block another series of blows. He could feel his Falchion fading with each action; he had to be precise in how he used it.

"Die, deserter," yelled one soldier with a pike.

Whoosh!

The long spear clipped Aero's shoulder, slicing into his flesh. Blood bloomed from the wound, dripping down his arm. Aero didn't think twice; he ducked and shoved his sword deep into his opponent's rib cage.

The boy went down with a gurgle, blood erupting from his throat.

Aero dislodged his sword from the boy's chest. It came out with a sickening crack. He hated that he had killed the young soldier, but the boy had left him with no other options, not if he wanted to survive this night.

"To the stars," Aero murmured under his breath. "My fellow soldier, you fought bravely and died a clean death in battle. That is our greatest achievement."

The other soldiers pulled back to regroup. They'd lost three men, two felled by Seeker and one by Aero. The soldiers all shifted their Falchions into pikes and then attacked again with the long spears.

"Die, deserter!" they screamed as they stormed across the Yard.

Aero could feel his blade draining of power. It was sparking less brightly. It had only one precious swing left in it. Though it went against his every instinct not to stand his ground and fight back, he whispered to Seeker, "Run!"

They broke for the transport.

Aero heard the other soldiers running behind them—pounding feet, angry shouts, the metallic clattering of their Falchions. He slid over the ice, slamming into the side of the transport and feeling the cold bite of metal. He hit the button to open the door.

But nothing happened—it was locked.

Seeker growled and pivoted to face the soldiers bearing down on them. She arched her back and extended her claws. "Noah, if you can hear me, do it now!" Aero hissed, feeling his Beacon flare in response. "Come on—*now*!"

The soldiers had almost reached them.

"Noah, override the lock!" Aero yelled.

Nothing happened again.

"Damn it," he cursed and gripped his blade tighter, feeling the weight of the broadsword and simultaneously the weakness of its charge. It had one good swing left in it, and then it was done for. They were both done for. His Falchion would melt down, leaving him a psychological wreck as the bond was violently severed.

But then he heard a voice in his head. *Lock override successful*, Noah communicated. His Beacon flashed, and so did Seeker's. They could both hear it.

With a sharp hiss, the transport's door yawned open, and a stairway unfolded. Aero vaulted up the stairs before they touched the ground, with Seeker on his heels.

"Noah, seal the door!" he yelled. "Hurry up!"

The door retracted and locked behind them.

The soldiers pounded on the hull, but they were too late. Aero had seized control of their ship. He scrambled into the cockpit, sliding behind the controls. The ergonomic chair hugged his back. They didn't have much time. Undoubtedly, the soldiers had raised the alarm and reinforcements would be on their way from the Second Continuum.

Seeker claimed the copilot chair next to him. He glanced

at her, missing Wren like a dagger to the heart. That was her spot.

"Noah, unlock the controls," Aero said, pushing his thoughts into the Beacon. A second later, the controls lit up. He heard Noah's voice in his head again.

The ship is yours, Captain Wright. Have a safe flight.

"Hold on," Aero said to Seeker. "Time to get out of here."

He hit a series of buttons and firmly gripped the controls. They blasted off, sailing into the night sky and leaving the soldiers and the Harvard Yard far below.

o   o   o

The night was clear, and the flight was smooth.

Aero flipped on the cloaking shield and verified that it was working. The readout said max power. He felt relief that they could fly undetected. Only then did he set their course. Using the data from Noah, Aero plugged in the coordinates for the Seventh Continuum and then engaged the automatic pilot. The instruments would alert him if anyone started tailing them, but that was unlikely with the shield at full strength. Outside the cockpit, the sky brightened, signaling day would break soon.

"We did it," Aero said and grinned. In the propulsive rush of flight, he felt his muscles relax finally. This was where he felt most at home—with the ship's controls in his grip and a pair of wings under him. Seeker did not share his feelings and gripped her armrest like her life depended on it.

"Filthy flying," she muttered, peering warily through the cockpit at the miniaturized landscape below. "Not natural . . . should fall out of the sky."

"At least we'll be there soon," Aero said. "ETA two hours and twenty minutes," he read off the instrument panel.

"Two hours . . . too long," Seeker replied unhappily.

Aero chuckled but then settled into his seat for the duration of the flight. Lulled by the soft purr of the engine, his mind drifted back to Myra, as it always did when given half a chance. He missed her already, though he'd been gone for only a few short hours. *Starry hell, get a grip*, he told himself then fretted that she'd heard that.

That fear was confirmed a second later when his Beacon throbbed and a throaty laugh echoed through his head. He'd recognize it anywhere. It was Myra.

I heard that. I can read your mind, remember?

Seeker shot him a sly look. She could hear Myra too. Aero tried to ignore the flaming feeling in his cheeks. Instead, he pushed his thoughts into the Beacon and sent Myra an image of him flying the transport.

Mission accomplished, he communicated. *We hijacked the transport. Three casualties on the other side, I'm sorry to report. Plus, a lot of angry soldiers.*

Nice work, she pinged him back. *But don't get too cocky, Captain Wright. That was only the first part of the plan.*

Don't remind me, he communicated. *So how'd it go with Drakken?*

Myra didn't answer in words—instead a torrent of emotions hit him, knocking the wind from his chest. He felt her pain and fear as Drakken attacked her in the dreamscape. He heard Seeker moan. She could feel it too. Aero's hands trembled and dropped from the controls. He nearly cried out in agony, but then the sensation faded away.

Our strategy worked, Myra communicated. *I lured Drakken into my dream. He bought my story about you and Seeker abandoning me in the middle of the night. He doesn't suspect our true purpose. He thinks we're weak and fragmenting.*

It worked alright, Aero shot back. *Too well.*

What does that mean? Myra asked.

Myra, it's too dangerous, he thought, feeling the sudden dryness of his mouth. His protective instinct flared. *We don't know if it's safe . . . if he could kill you.*

It's only a dream, she reasoned. *It's not even real.*

You know that's not true.

Well, it's the only way, she communicated, stubborn as always. Even her thoughts felt stubborn. *We discussed it already. Don't worry about me. I can handle Drakken.*

Like you did last night? He's feeding on your life force . . . he tortures you!

She didn't argue with that. Instead, her thought hit him like a door contracting in his face: *Trust me to do my part, as I trust you to do yours. Keep me posted.*

With that missive, she cut off the connection.

Seeker caught his eye. She'd heard their whole disagreement. "Myra not happy with you, Strong One," she said and patted his arm sympathetically. "You should leave her alone and stop telling her what to do. That's what she wants."

"And what if Drakken kills her in her sleep?" he muttered.

"Myra knows the risks," Seeker said, picking at the hair on her arm. She plucked out a clump of dirt. "She can look after herself. She's a Strong One too."

"By the stars, I hope you're right."

Despite his misgivings, Aero prayed their ruse had bought them some time. Of course, he would never abandon Myra like that. It went against his every instinct, but Drakken didn't understand that. He understood only manipulation and pain.

Aero pushed that dark thought from his mind and double-checked their cloaking shield. It was still at max power. He felt relief—they could fly undetected. He shut his eyes and sought the guidance of the long-dead Supreme Generals, the former Carriers of his Beacon. *Supreme Generals, I need to get a secret message to the Order of the Foundry*, he thought, pushing his energy into the Beacon. *Is there any way?*

The chattering of the generals intensified, making his head ache from too much information crowding his neural synapses. But then they quieted. One voice rang out loud and clear—it was his father, Supreme General Brillstein.

My son, there might be a way, his father communicated. *The Colloquium Machine hasn't been used for centuries, but listen closely and we'll explain how it works.*

Aero didn't hear him as much as he felt his father's knowledge flood through him—through every cell in his body—and then he opened his eyes. He pushed every ounce of his energy into the Beacon. His consciousness expanded beyond the cockpit, beyond Earth's thick atmosphere, out into the void of space, through the thick walls of the Second Continuum's hull, into the bowels of the mothership. His energy flowed into the long-forgotten machine. He felt the complex circuitry and malleable metal whirring to life—and then he could feel that somebody else was listening.

The old Forger materialized before him, his visage projected by the Colloquium Machine. Aero spoke to him as though they were standing in the Foundry together.

"Brother, I need your help."

The Forger looked surprised but quickly composed himself. Though the Foundry was dark, Aero could make out a new batch of Falchions floating in the background. He then knew with certainty—the Second Continuum was preparing for war.

"Captain Wright, greetings," the Forger said with a bow. "The Order of the Foundry serves the Carrier of the Beacon and the rightful Supreme General. My sworn brothers and sisters are at your command. What do you need us to do?"

Aero took a deep breath and projected his thought.

"Sanctuary."

The old Forger looked shocked. "It's been many ages since we've invoked sanctuary. It's risky—Supreme General Vinick doesn't respect the old ways."

"Brother, I realize the risks, but not acting is more dangerous. It would imperil everything we believe in." As quickly as he could, Aero laid out their plan. The old Forger listened to everything. "So brother, will you help us?" Aero finished.

The question traveled untold miles, reverberating out of the Colloquium Machine and through the Foundry. But still the Forger hesitated. He was thinking of his Order, Aero knew, of the risk to his brothers and sisters should they agree to this plan.

"Brother, time is short," Aero prodded, feeling doubt welling in his gut. "You've never failed me. So tell me, what is your answer? Everything depends on this."

The old Forger didn't speak.

He only bowed his head in acquiescence.

Chapter 12
NOT WELCOME

Seeker

Seeker, welcome home," Aero announced.

With a few deft maneuvers, he piloted the transport down. It plunged vertically, stopping to hover a few feet off the ground. The nozzles blasted out rippling waves of heat. He hit a button, triggering the door. It gaped open and the stairs descended, thunking down on an icy patch of snow. Seeker unfurled herself from a tense ball.

"Welcome . . . what is welcome?" she growled, peering at the snow-covered mountainside. Her visor shielded her sensitive eyes from the midday sun. Her stomach felt twisted into knots, like when she'd eaten something rotten.

Aero's brows knitted together. "Well, let me see . . . I guess it means to be gladly received. Or something along those lines."

She shook her head adamantly. "Seeker not welcome," she said, fear twisting her stomach more. She thought she might retch. "Seeker stole the Gold Circle and the Feast. The Strong Ones furious . . . they want to kill Seeker."

"Right, sorry." Aero grimaced. "It's just a figure of

speech. I wasn't thinking."

Seeker was even more confused by that statement.

"Figure of speech?"

Aero hit buttons on the console. The engine purred into conservation mode. He flicked through his flight checklist. "Right, that means it's a saying. Like *good morning* or *nice to see you*. Just because you say it, doesn't mean it has to be true."

Seeker frowned. "Why say things if not true?"

"Just to make conversation, I guess. You're right, it's stupid."

"Stupid," she agreed with an emphatic nod. "Seeker not welcome . . . but this is home," she added to clarify which part of his statement was true.

Seeker struggled out of her harness—Aero had insisted she wear it despite her growls of protest—and staggered up on all fours. She still felt disoriented and nauseous from the flight. She reached up to make sure her visor was secure before peering outside. They'd landed on a high plateau cradled by the mountains. A bitter wind whipped through the passes, hurling errant bits of snow and ice at the ship.

Winter, she thought. It was still winter.

Seeker inhaled the crisp air, pulling it into her lungs. Despite her many complaints, she would miss this about the Brightside—the way it tasted like clean, fresh spring water on her tongue, and the way it washed through her nostrils with the scents of dirt and rock and snow. Unlike the sunlight—*the stinking, burning light*.

That she wouldn't miss, not one bit.

Seeker didn't wait for Aero to unbuckle his harness. After hours of being cooped up in the transport, she longed to stretch her legs. Her muscles twitched and pleaded with her—*go, go go!* She bounded down the stairs and onto solid ground, instantly feeling better. Her stomach settled and stopped churning. She glanced back at the ship.

"Filthy flying," she growled for good measure.

It didn't make any sense that the ship could fly like that. Why didn't they fall out of the sky? What held them aloft in thin air? Why didn't they crash to Earth and burn into blackened bits of ash? *It makes no stinking sense.*

Aero craned his head through the door. "Sure you don't want me to stick around?" he called, cocking his eyebrow. His hand felt for the hilt of his Falchion.

Seeker shook her head. "No . . . better if go alone."

Aero hesitated. "Are you sure? Things got a little sticky last time we were down in the Seventh. We killed many Strong Ones, but some might have survived that avalanche. And well, I'm guessing they hold a grudge."

Their Beacons flared in tandem, as Myra's ghostly voice interjected itself into their conversation. *Seeker is right—time is short. Aero, you must go to the Second Continuum. You're supposed to follow my orders, remember? I'm in charge now.*

Amusement colored that last part, but she was serious. Aero raised his hands in surrender. *Starry hell, you're both stubborn,* he thought, forgetting it wasn't private.

Myra's voice shot through their heads.

Aero, I heard that. I can hear your thoughts, remember?

Me too, Seeker communicated.

Well, now I do, Aero thought as his cheeks flushed pink.

Through the Beacon, Seeker could feel that Myra was laughing and Aero also let out an amused chuckle, but she didn't understand what was so funny. She often felt like an outsider when the other Carriers were around.

Now get going, Myra communicated. *I'll be monitoring your progress.*

Her presence faded away as the communication ended.

Aero tossed a rucksack to Seeker, who caught it in midair. She felt the weight of her haul nestled inside—ratters and buggers that she'd rooted out of the tunnels of the First Continuum. She was bringing them as an offering for her people, a way to bargain her way back into their good graces. If there was one thing they understood, it was fresh kill. No matter how much they hunted, there was never enough to go around.

Seeker slung the pack across her back. She was about to

bound away when something tugged at her chest. It was a strange sensation, almost like she didn't want to leave . . . almost like she was injured or frightened. What was wrong with her?

She met Aero's gaze through her visor. "Thank you . . . Strong One," she growled, feeling self-conscious about her sudden burst of sentimentality.

"You're welcome, Seeker," Aero replied with a salute.

Seeker smiled a toothy grin. "That another saying?"

"I suppose it is," he said. "See . . . you're learning."

Seeker laughed a deep, rasping sort of laugh that sounded more like a growl. But then she turned serious. She shifted her pack, settling it onto her shoulders. "Be careful, Strong One. Your people very angry. You not welcome in your home either."

He grimaced. "No, I don't suppose I am."

Their Beacons flared, and they heard Myra's voice urging them to *bloody get going already and stop wasting time.* Aero grinned and patted the side of his ship.

"Next stop—outer space," he declared as the wind lashed through his hair. It had grown out over the last few weeks, dipping into his eyes. He waved farewell.

"Seeker, good luck with your people down there."

She thrust one spindly hand in the air. "Fly home, Strong One."

With one final salute, Aero ducked back into his transport. The stairs retracted behind him, and then the door hissed shut. The engines revved, shooting out flames that seared the snow. Water droplets splattered Seeker's fur as the ship vaulted straight up into the air and vanished behind the gathering clouds. Seeker could hear the roar of the engines for a few seconds, but soon even that was swallowed up by the sky.

Seeker was left alone on the plateau. The wind heaved at her, chilling her flesh. She tasted cold water. Snow would fall again soon. Her gaze fell on the Door in the Wall, set into a sheer cliffside a few hundred yards away. Seeker, Myra, Aero, and their companions had used this secret exit to escape from the Seventh Continuum, fleeing from the Strong Ones with the help of the Weaklings, who finally rose up against their oppressors and fought back. But that felt like a lifetime ago. Maybe longer.

Time is relative, Jared communicated. He was the first and only prior Carrier of her Beacon. *That all happened a few weeks ago, at least by my calculation. I was deactivated for some time. But your emotional experience makes it feel longer.*

Did she detect hostility in his voice?

"Not my choice to deactivate . . . missed . . . you," she growled.

The words came out garbled with emotion—that filthy pulling in her chest—but she meant them all the same. It was true. She'd missed Jared. After spending most of her life alone, focused only on survival, it was nice to have a companion— even if he'd died centuries ago and existed solely in her head. Then she felt stupid for thinking that.

You'll never be alone again, Jared replied. *Even after you die, the Beacon will download and preserve your essence. You will live on. We'll always be together.*

Friend, Seeker thought back.

Yes, friend, Jared echoed. *Now go home, Seeker.*

Urged by her Beacon, Seeker adjusted her rucksack and loped toward the door. Since she bonded with the Beacon, so much had changed. The Weaklings had risen up against the Strong Ones. They killed Crusher and some Strong Ones, but as Aero had pointed out, many still survived. It wasn't just her home that had changed; she had changed too. She was returning home as a Carrier now.

Questions tumbled through her brain. What would she find in the Darkness of the Below? Could she unite her people? Inspire them to fight back against the Fourth Continuum? Get them to care about something beyond their own basic survival?

Jared's voice shot through her head.

You can and you must; it's our only hope.

Seeker not welcome, she thought back.

Jared nudged her through the Beacon. *Don't you see? This is our chance to liberate our people, lost to the long years in the depths of the earth, resorting to cannibalism and other vile practices to survive at all costs. If we cannot unite them for this cause, then what was it all for? Survival alone isn't enough—we need redemption.*

Seeker felt that word resonate through her soul:

Redemption.

Yes . . . that was what they needed. Who cared about *welcome?* That was an empty word; it meant nothing. *Redemption.* Now that Seeker understood.

Buoyed by that thought, Seeker steeled herself against the wind and approached the door. It gleamed in the winter light, despite the shrouding of snow dusting its surface and obscuring the golden metal.

"Aeternus eternus," she chanted.

She pushed all her energy into the Beacon. In response, the door began to dilate with a rumbling noise. Clumps of snow and debris tumbled down, stinging her eyes. She pressed herself to the cliffside and waited for it to abate. The metal retracted liquidly into the rock, until it vanished as if it had never been there at all.

Seeker peeled herself away from the cliff. Air gusted out of the Moving Room. She caught a whiff of mold, rotting flesh, sulfur, and dust. She inhaled deeper, savoring the stench. It comforted her; it made her feel almost . . . *welcome.*

It smelled like home.

Seeker clambered into the Moving Room and crouched down, hugging her rucksack to her chest. She felt the lumpy contours of its precious offerings. As if sensing her presence—her willingness to descend—the Door in the Wall contracted with another deep rumble. The Brightside diminished to a tiny pinprick and then disappeared, as thick darkness rushed back into the Moving Room. Seeker tilted her visor back and opened her eyes wide, no longer fearing the burning light.

Abruptly, the floor lurched away. She experienced a horrible somersaulting sensation like she'd lost her balance. Her ears popped painfully. She cried out and crushed her rucksack to her chest. As the Moving Room plunged even faster, carrying her into the Darkness of the Below, one panicked thought rushed through her head:

Will I ever see the Brightside again?

Chapter 13
SIGNAL-TO-NOISE RATIO

Myra Jackson

Seeker made it to the Moving Room.

Myra felt elated as her Beacon flared and delivered this news—in fragments of images, tatters of thoughts, vivid streaks of emotion straight from Seeker's neural synapses. But once the elevator started to descend, carrying Seeker down to the Seventh Continuum buried miles beneath Earth's surface, the connection fizzled out.

Myra's elation evaporated.

"Noah, what's happening?" she called out. Her eyes were still shut tight. She was trying to keep her mind blank and calm . . . trying yet failing. Her heart rate sped up, and her palms felt sweaty. That certainly wasn't helping matters.

"Losing signal from the Seventh Carrier," Noah replied, unnecessarily. Myra already knew that much. "Signal-to-noise ratio is one to one," he added.

Myra fought to reestablish the connection, trying to quiet the noisy rush of her thoughts and emotions and fears, but it faded until it was gone altogether.

"Signal lost," Noah reported.

"Seeker . . . I'm sorry," Myra said in frustration. She opened her eyes, feeling tears prick them. Seeker was alone now and heading into hostile territory.

My dear, have faith, Divinus said, his voice cutting through her frustration. *The Carrier chooses the Beacon— but the Beacon also chooses the Carrier. Seeker's bonding was no mistake. She was destined to lead her people out of the darkness.*

Professor Divinus materialized in the control room. He wore his crimson robes that looked too perfect to be real. *That's because they aren't real*, Myra reminded herself.

Divinus read her thought—the Beacon enabled him to do this.

"Is this better?" he asked as his robes rematerialized with a sizable hole in the left sleeve and a stain of indeterminate origin smeared on the lapel. "Your feedback is most welcome. We're still working out the kinks in the projection."

"Yes, we are," Noah chimed in. "Professor, I'm helping you, aren't I?"

"Of course, old friend. None of this would be possible without you."

"Thank you, Professor," Noah said, sounding pleased.

Myra smiled at their banter—and felt the deep ache in her knees. She was seated in what the professor called lotus position, with her legs crossed and her hands resting lightly on her knees. According to him, it was an ancient pose used for meditation. But after a few hours, it cut off the circulation in her extremities.

She unfurled her legs, wincing. "By the Oracle, why is this so hard?"

Divinus swished over. "My dear, be gentle with yourself. You're attempting to maintain two separate connections with untrained Carriers with thousands of miles separating you," he pointed out. "Did you expect that would be easy?"

"Easier than this," she sighed. "This is worse than studying for my Apprentice Exam, worse than being tortured by the 'Trollers. My mind keeps wandering, my knees and my backside bloody hurt, and I'm so bored of sitting still that it makes me want to scream or tear my hair out." She massaged her sore calves. "Or maybe both."

Divinus laughed. "At least you still have a sense of humor."

"Professor, that's a small consolation when the fate of the free world rests on your shoulders," she quipped. She craned her neck back. It popped audibly.

"My dear, do you need a break?" Divinus asked, concern flashing over his features. "Perhaps some nourishment or a walk through the chambers?"

"I can have the service bots deliver some rations," Noah added.

Going for a stroll and letting her muscles unkink themselves and her mind wander did sound tempting. Plus, she derived comfort just from being around the cryocapsules.

But her stubborn streak rose up.

"No, I want to try again."

She forced her legs back into lotus position, even though her knees complained with another angry pop. Divinus looked like he wanted to object, but then he gave in.

"One more time, my dear. But then I must insist that you rest. Is that a deal?"

"Deal," she said impatiently.

"Close your eyes, my dear," he directed in a soothing voice. "Clear your mind, feel the pulsing of your Beacon, feel the currents running through your body and connecting you to the other Carriers."

Myra did as he instructed, sinking into herself. Once she achieved stillness, once her mind quieted its turbulent whir of thoughts and emotions, she reached for Seeker and tried to pick up her signal again, but she heard only white noise. She abandoned that connection for now and instead concentrated on finding Aero. She experienced a rush of sensation as their minds clicked together. Myra projected her thought:

Aero, can you hear me?

Aero startled but then relaxed. *I'm not used to this mind-reading stuff. I miss seeing you in real life already. Your disembodied voice isn't cutting it.*

Me too, she thought, savoring the connection. She could see through his eyes—the transport's control panel lit up with lights, the stars and planets exploding beyond the cockpit. And she could feel the harness strapping his body into the pilot's chair.

Any updates? she asked.

The question crackled between their Beacons. Aero replied:

I've engaged the transport's cloaking shield. The Second Continuum shouldn't be able to detect my approach until I'm about to land in the Docking Bay. The Order of the Foundry has agreed to help me. But this hasn't been attempted in over seven centuries.

Do you think it'll work? She tried to keep the fear out of her thoughts, but the emotion leaked through anyway. Aero picked up on it.

It doesn't matter what I think, he communicated. The connection started to fade. *The plan is already set into motion. All we can do is hope for the best—*

And then the signal terminated.

One second she was connected to Aero—their thoughts and emotions intermingled like they shared one brain—and the next he was gone. She cracked her eyes open and found herself alone in the control room. Alone with a stiff neck, aching knees, and a worried heart. She knew that Aero was flying right into danger.

If their plan failed, then Vinick wouldn't hesitate to kill him.

o   o   o

Myra wound her way through the First Continuum, trying to soothe the concerns cycling through her mind. She veered down the corridor, yearning to spend some time with the cryocapsules. The machines reminded her of the Engineering Room back home, where she'd always felt like she belonged. They would offer her some comfort.

But a voice chided her—*You promised to rest, my dear.*

"Professor, I'm just going for a quick walk," she hedged.

The more tired and weak you become, the greater the danger. You need to rest and keep up your strength. Commander Drakken is waiting to exploit you.

Myra knew better than to argue.

"Fine," she said—and in truth, her eyelids felt terribly heavy. She reversed course and headed to her chambers. The service bots had tidied up, laying out tubes of rations and freshly laundered clothes and towels, all stacked on the trunk at the foot of her bed. She munched on the sticky paste, which stuck to the roof of her mouth. Then she burrowed under the covers. The gauzy canopy fluttered in the cool hiss of the air vents, but sleep wouldn't come, no matter how hard she tried.

She thrashed around, feeling restless. Her brain needled at her with anxious thoughts. Had Seeker reached the Seventh Continuum? Had she made contact with her people? And what about Aero? Had he docked with the mothership?

Her mind crawled with questions—and there was only one way to answer them. Before she could second-guess herself, she sat up and assumed lotus position. She shut her eyes and pushed her consciousness into the Beacon, feeling for the other Carriers.

Aero . . . she called out. *Seeker . . .*

But somebody else answered her summons.

The dreamscape materialized around her. She had only a second to orient herself—the fuzzy borders at the edge of the world, the sleet coating the ground, the obsidian clouds crowding the sky—before the Dark Thing descended on her with its shadowy tendrils flailing like knives. Her Beacon throbbed weakly. She wasn't strong enough to fight Drakken off, so she did the only thing she could:

She ran.

Her legs pumped hard despite their weariness; her feet skidded over the sleet-slickened ground. But the Dark Thing chased after her like a poisonous fog.

He was gaining on her.

She tried to run faster but slipped on the ice. She jerked her head back—and saw the black fog bearing down on her.

She scrambled up, ignoring the searing pain from her skinned knees. She reached the unformed edge of the dreamscape and skidded to a halt, nearly tumbling into the sheer chasm that lay below, spanning into blackness.

She was trapped.

Myra spun around, her breath lashing out of her lungs in panicked bursts. The shadow gathered in front of her, like clouds building up before a violent storm, and then lunged at her with its dark tendrils deployed like daggers. They stabbed at her, and one pierced clean through her shoulder. She grimaced as blood escaped the puncture wound, staining her tunic dark red. She collapsed to the ground and convulsed—

And then she woke up.

It took a moment for her eyes to adjust to the stark light of her room. The automatic lights blazed down, simulating midday.

"It was a dream . . . only a dream," she whispered, trying to calm herself. Sweat coated her forehead. "Drakken can't hurt me. I'm safe inside the First Continuum . . ."

Her voice died in her throat when she saw blood staining her sheets, dark red and unmistakable. She bolted upright and jerked her hand to her shoulder, wincing from pain. Her tunic was wet with blood. That made her panic even more. She slid it off her shoulder, revealing a deep puncture wound where Drakken had stabbed her.

Her mouth opened, but she was too scared to scream.

Chapter 14
CLEAR TO LAND

Major Danika Rothman

A shrill beep roused Danika from sleep. She swung her legs around quickly—*too quickly*—and bumped them against the sharp edge of the bedside table.

"Starry hell . . ." she cursed, massaging her bruised knee. She wasn't used to the layout of her new room yet. Now that she was a major, she had her own private barracks. Like everything on the ship, the room was austere—a compact space with a bunk, a bedside table, a small desk, and a trunk. But it was an upgrade over her previous accommodations, where she had shared a tiny room with nine other soldiers.

Her communicator continued its shrill cry.

She swiped it off the bedside table. "It's Doyle, damn it," she muttered when she saw his face leering through the screen. She waited for the fog of sleep to be replaced by a heady rush of adrenaline. She cleared her throat and clicked it on.

"Major Rothman, report to the bridge," Doyle said tersely.

"Sir, what's the situation?" she asked, tugging on her boots and belting her Falchion to her waist. She hurried toward the door, communicator in hand. The screen showed

Doyle's pinched, slumberous face. *Guess I'm not the only one who got roused from sleep.* He was already stationed behind his console on the bridge.

"We'll brief you when you arrive."

With that, her communicator went dark.

o   o   o

Danika took the elevator to the top level. Her head still felt jumbled, full of broken dreams. *Was I dreaming about Lillian again?* She peered through the clear paneling at dark void of space, hoping to shake the revulsion that accompanied that question.

She's dead, she reminded herself for the hundredth time. *She was banished from our colony. That cowardly girl is never coming back—*

The elevator doors opened, snapping her out of her rumination. Danika was greeted by a blast of chill air. She marched onto the bridge, halted, and snapped her hand to her brow. Scattered around the control room, the other officers manned their consoles. Vinick stood with his back facing her and his eyes glued to the windows.

"Supreme General, you summoned me?" Danika said, her nerves flaring. "Is this about the interrogation? I tried to get the deserters to talk like you ordered, but they proved resistant. I'll try again later today. Captain Dalton from Medical says that if we don't give Wren Jordan enough recovery time, then the serum could kill her—"

"This concerns another matter," he said, pivoting to face her. He clutched his Falchion, morphed into a dagger. His face looked haggard, and his thin lips more bloodless than usual. "It's about the deserter Aero Wright."

"Aero Wright?" Danika said, taken aback. "What about him? He's trapped in the First Continuum. We left a combat unit behind to guard the door."

"Well, he's not trapped there anymore," Vinick said with a scowl.

"Sir, what do you mean?" Danika said, her mind grappling for an explanation. "Wait, he escaped? How did he get past our combat unit? We should deploy the probes to scan for him right away. Maybe we can catch him before he gets too far."

"Major, there's no need for that," Vinick said and signaled to Doyle.

Doyle hit a few buttons on his console. A transport materialized on the monitors. Danika scanned the insignia. "Aero Wright hijacked one of our ships?"

Doyle nodded. "He dropped his cloaking shield and popped up on our sensors about ten minutes ago," he said, hitting more buttons. "He's headed straight for us."

"Sir, he's coming here?" Danika said. "Why would he do that? That's a suicide mission. It doesn't make any sense."

"Major, you've studied his files," Vinick said. "What's your analysis?"

Danika thought through everything she'd learned. "He's an emotional hazard, that much is clear from his records. So his actions are rash and unpredictable."

"But why come back here?" Vinick demanded. "He's not stupid, even if he is an emotional hazard. He graduated from the Agoge at the top of his class."

She searched her mind. "Sir, it's his companions. He wants to rescue the prisoners. He's attached to Wren Jordan. Captain Dalton from Medical even suspects that he *loves* her." She pronounced that word like a curse.

"The boy cares about his companions," Vinick agreed with a distasteful expression. "But why e drop his cloaking shield? Why give up the element of surprise?"

Danika thought about it. "It's almost like he wants us to know he's coming . . ." she replied. "That's the only explanation."

"But why?" Doyle said, pushing back from his console.

"Sir, I don't know," Danika said in frustration. "I wish I did."

The uncertainty hung in the recirculated air of the bridge. Aero was headed straight for them. He had turned off his cloaking shield. Doyle was right—none of this made any sense. *The element of surprise is a soldier's greatest weapon.* The ancient teaching from the Agoge shot through her head. So why would Aero give it up?

"What's the deserter's ETA?" Vinick asked, fiddling with his Falchion.

"Fifteen minutes," Major Wright reported, looking up from her console. From the deserter's files, Danika knew that Major Wright was Aero's biological mother. But her face remained impassive. If she harbored any attachment, she was skilled at hiding it.

"Supreme General, what do you want to do?" Doyle asked. He flipped to his targeting software, locked onto Aero's ship. "Should we fire on the transport?"

Danika held her breath in anticipation of Vinick's order. She knew she should suppress her emotions but couldn't; they were too powerful. *Is this the moment when I finally get to witness the deserter's death?*

"Major Dolye, let the deserter board us," Vinick said after a long moment. "I want him to reach us alive so we can recover the Beacon. Then we can kill him."

Danika felt the air deflate from her lungs, chased by the bitter aftertaste of disappointment. Doyle also seemed disappointed but closed his targeting software. "Sir . . . are you sure?" he said, his voice hitching. "The deserter is dangerous."

Vinick let out a scathing laugh. "One boy soldier with a fading Falchion against a whole army? Remember, we captured his precious Forger. I doubt his weapon is even functional anymore. I wouldn't be surprised if it's melted down already."

"Yes, sir," Doyle said quickly, knowing better than to press Vinick further. He was thin-skinned and hated having his judgment questioned.

"ETA . . . ten minutes," Major Wright called out from her console.

Vinick's eyes snapped to Danika. "Major Rothman, collect three combat units and go to the Docking Bay.

Allow the deserter to dock his transport and board our ship unhindered. Then kill him and recover the Beacon. Is that understood?"

"Yes, sir," Danika saluted as her heart skipped a beat. She'd felt disappointed that she didn't get to see him get blown apart on the monitors by their torpedoes.

But this was even better.

o   o   o

Danika paid a visit to Captain Tabor first, finding her in the simulator control room. Her unit was running a combat drill on Mars. Swords sparked against battle-axes; maces against shields; pikes against broadswords. The clamor of battle played over the monitors, filling the control room with grunts, clangs, rustling, and screams.

"Major Rothman," Tabor said with a crisp salute. Nervousness played across her features. "What brings you down here? Surely, it's not another observation of my unit. Major Wright conducted one last week."

Danika wasn't used to eliciting such a reaction. Only a few weeks ago, Captain Tabor had been her commanding officer. But that was then, and this was now. Everything could change in a nanosecond.

"Captain, I need you to pull your soldiers out of the simulators and accompany me to the Docking Bay," Danika said, trying to make her voice sound deeper.

"The Docking Bay?" Tabor said, taken aback. "But why?"

That bordered on insubordination. Soldiers were supposed to follow orders from their superiors and not ask questions. But Danika couldn't bring herself to reprimand her former commander. Tabor's short, wiry hair was shot through with white. Her ebony skin cracked with wrinkles and old battle scars. She'd been leading a combat unit for almost four times as long as Danika had been alive.

"The deserter Aero Wright," Danika replied, lowering her voice. "He stole a transport and plans to dock. My orders are to kill him and retrieve the Beacon."

Surprise played over Tabor's features, followed by studied composure. "Yes, Major," Tabor said and started pulling her soldiers out of their simulation.

Danika collected two more combat units—one from the Mess Hall and one from their barracks. Flanked by Captains Tabor, Grimes, Malik, and their soldiers, Danika marched to the Docking Bay. Grimes had deployed to Earth with her to track the deserters, and Malik heralded from the same class at the Agoge. She trusted both of them.

Her communicator beeped in her ear. "ETA . . . five minutes," Major Wright reported over the connection. "Docking Bay 14 engaged."

Feeling a thrill, Danika gripped the hilt of her Falchion and led the soldiers into the Docking Bay. Transports rested in individual bays. The air felt lighter. They were on the outer edge of the ship—far away from the mothership's centralized gravitational drives. She ordered Captains Malik and Grimes to clear the area of the Engineering units.

Docking Bay 14 flashed and an alarm went off, signaling an incoming transport. "Aero Wright, you are clear to land," Major Wright communicated.

Danika heard the directive and signaled to her soldiers to surround the bay. They stood five deep with their Falchions morphed into their preferred weapon forms. Danika commanded her blade to shift into an ahlspiess, a thrusting spear with a razor-sharp point. She heard the transport click into the dock and a sharp hiss as the bay pressurized.

The door dilated, revealing the transport. The engines powered down and shut off, as the cooling vents engaged. "This is Aero Wright. Confirming successful dock."

Danika heard the deserter's voice and felt a shudder of revulsion. The soldiers around her shifted—they could hear it too.

The transport's door opened with another hiss. The stairs descended, clicking down on the floor. She saw his worn boots first. Then the deserter disembarked and marched toward them. He was dressed in strange, loose-fitting clothing. His hair had grown indecently long. His Falchion was sheathed; his hands raised in surrender.

Danika felt a thrill—the deserter wasn't even going to put up a fight. "Captain Tabor, kill him," she ordered. "Grimes and Malik. You're backup."

Chapter 15
SURVIVAL OF THE STRONGEST

Seeker

The Door in the Wall opened with a deep rumble.

A gust of stale air wafted into the Moving Room. Seeker inhaled the familiar smell of the underground—rot, sulfur, rocks, and dust. She even got a whiff of ratter. This made her break into a grin. Beyond the elevator lay thick darkness.

She loped out of the Moving Room, feeling the rucksack bouncing on her shoulders. The throbbing light of her Beacon pierced through the blackness. The Door in the Wall contracted behind her with another rumble that shook the cavern. Rocks and grit skittered down from the ceiling. Seeker shielded her head and hugged the wall, waiting for it to subside. When the dust settled, she peeled her eyes open.

Rubble still blocked the tunnel's entrance, left over from the standoff with Crusher and the Strong Ones. She saw something sticking out from under a massive boulder. She leaned in closer, holding up her Beacon to illuminate it.

It was a severed hand.

Seeker wasn't repulsed; rather, she felt curiosity curling in her gut. She poked at it with her foot. The hand was shriveled and grayish. The stiff fingers looked like they'd been nibbled on, probably by ratters.

"Filthy Crusher . . ." she hissed, kicking dust over his hand. He'd tormented the Weaklings, ruling their world with brute force and resorting to cannibalism when they failed to deliver enough offerings. She didn't feel sorry for him, not one bit.

Seeker backed away and observed the cavern. She definitely couldn't go through the main tunnel with the avalanche blocking it, but there were other ways to get around if you were nimble and sure-footed. Instead, she turned her attention to the wall, spying shallow handholds in the sheer rock. She remembered the Weaklings helped them escape by straddling the top of the cavern and hurling rocks down at the Strong Ones.

"Weaklings smarter than Strong Ones," she said under her breath. She was about to start climbing the wall, when she felt a jolt through her Beacon. It came from Myra. It felt like an alarm. With each pulse, Seeker caught a quick series of images:

Dark tendrils stabbing through the air.

Stabbing at her shoulder.

Blood splatters on white fabric.

Seeker tried to hold on to the signal—*Myra, what's happening?*

But the connection fizzled out, if it had even been a connection at all. Seeker still didn't understand the Beacon or fully trust the strange messages it sent her. But she couldn't shake those frightening images. They felt real, and they felt dangerous.

"Jared," Seeker growled. "Did you see that?"

Her Beacon throbbed and delivered his response:

Drakken.

"What happened? Is Myra . . . hurt?"

I'm not sure, Jared communicated. *The connection was fragmented . . . but whatever happened involved Drakken and Myra . . . and it wasn't something good.*

Seeker felt chilled. "Drakken not good," she agreed.

She considered fleeing back to the Moving Room and taking it to the Brightside . . . but then what? Aero had already left for the Second Continuum. She was hundreds of miles away from the First Continuum. It would take her weeks to reach it on foot.

You must carry out your part of the plan—everything depends on it, Jared communicated. *That's the only way to help Myra now. You know that.*

"Sorry, Myra . . ." Seeker whispered. "Can't help you."

Doing her best to ignore her worries, Seeker nimbly scrambled up the wall and clambered onto a narrow ledge. Smaller tunnels fed into the cavern. Following Jared's directions, she chose one that would carry her toward Agartha and the center of the colony. The tight passage snaked through solid rock. The floor was coated with a thick layer of dust. She heard the scratching of tiny feet. Ratters were fleeing from her intrusion into their domain. She felt the urge to hunt, but now wasn't the time.

Up ahead, she heard the faint echo of voices:

Seeker, Seeker,
Can't get any weaker!
She creeps and she sneaks,
Sticks her nose where it reeks!

The singsong melody was familiar; her reaction to it was immediate. She froze and strained her ears, picking up shuffling sounds coming from around the next bend. It sounded like more than one of them. She listened closer. Actually, it sounded like a whole pack. She jerked her eyes down. In the throbbing glow of her Beacon, she spotted large footprints marring the dust. They were too big to be made by Weaklings.

That was when she knew—*The Strong Ones found me.*

Her heart thudding, Seeker turned to run. Pounding footstep erupted in the tunnel behind her, blocking her escape route. She was trapped. In the flashing of her Beacon, she saw the huge figures stampede into the tunnel—jaws cracked open, razor-sharp teeth and claws. A hand seized her ankle, yanking her backward. Other hands clawed at her neck. They clamped onto her limbs and dragged her into the next cavern.

She fought back with claws and teeth, breaking their grip and scrambling away. She was about to run for it, when she heard their pitiful cries.

"Strong One . . . don't hurt us!"

"Seeker . . . help us . . . please help!"

Seeker turned around, her eyes falling on the pathetic creatures. Five of them huddled in the cavern. Their faces looked sunken, their cheeks hollowed out. Their bellies were swollen. She couldn't believe it—the Strong Ones were *starving*.

"Seeker . . . we're hungry . . ." whined a huge female with black-tinged hair. She rolled over, exposing her belly. Her ribs protruded like knives. "Please help us . . ."

Seeker stared at them in shock. She still couldn't believe the change in their fortunes. "Slayer, what happened?" Seeker growled, recognizing the Strong One.

Slayer's eyes narrowed. "The Weaklings . . . they took over . . . after they killed Crusher. They stopped bringing us offerings and threw us out of the castle. Their pack barricaded the door. We tried to fight back . . . but too many of them . . ."

"Why not hunt for ratters and buggers in the tunnels?" Seeker asked.

Slayer frowned. "We tried . . . but ratters too fast and sneaky. Buggers have sharp pinchers and poison." She held out her mangled hand. It was riddled with punctures that oozed and looked badly infected. Some buggers could inject venom.

"The Strong Ones forgot how to hunt," Seeker said, feeling the disdain rise in her gut. "Your pack sat in the throne room, eating our offerings and growing fat and lazy. You're pathetic . . . and now you know what it's like to go hungry."

Seeker turned to go, but Slayer latched on to her leg.

"Oh, Seeker, the Strongest of the Strong Ones . . . please don't leave us," she pleaded, tightening her grip. Desperation flashed in her eyes. "Seeker brought the Light back to the Darkness of the Below. Seeker the Carrier came back to save us."

Seeker hesitated. She felt her Beacon nudge her.

Seeker, you have to help them, Jared communicated. *The Strong Ones aren't any different than the Weaklings. We are one people. And we need to build an army. The Strong Ones know how to fight. They can help us.*

Seeker knew he was right. She tore open her rucksack and tossed them a few fat ratters. "Strong Ones, feast now . . ." That was all she got out before they descended on the carcasses. A fight broke out between Slayer and Brawler.

"No fighting," Seeker yelled, pulling them apart.

Once the they finished eating, having picked the ratters clean, Seeker spoke to them. Her eyes flicked over the Strong Ones. They had lost muscles mass, but their massive frames could be rebuilt with proper nutrition and training.

"Slayer, are there more Strong Ones?" Seeker asked.

Slayer nodded. "Yes . . . many more . . . starving in the tunnels."

"Do you consider me the Strongest of the Strong Ones?" Seeker asked. She held up her wrist, so the Beacon's emerald glow fell over them.

"Yes . . . yes!" Slayer said and signaled to the others.

They all bowed down and started chanting. "We worship the Light in the Darkness. May the Light never go out, so long as we shall live . . ."

"Slayer, I need your help," Seeker said, gesturing for them to rise. "I've come back to lead our people to the Brightside. I need you to gather the rest of the Strong Ones together and lead them to the Door in the Wall. Do you know where it is?"

"Yes . . . the Door in the Wall . . . Slayer knows it."

"Go now," Seeker said. "Find your people. I'll meet you there."

Seeker turned to leave, but Slayer stopped her again. Her saucerlike eyes refracted the Beacon's glow. "Strong One, where are you going?"

"To Agartha," Seeker replied, cinching the straps on her rucksack and readjusting the weight. "I need to find the Weaklings. We need their help too."

"Be careful," Slayer said. "Weaklings . . . sneaky and dangerous."

o   o   o

With Slayer's warning fresh in her mind, Seeker barreled through the tunnels. The passage curved and forked again and again, but she knew the way by heart. Her hands and feet were sure; she never slipped, never missed a step. She burst into a massive cavern. A rock bridge arced over a deep chasm, and beyond it lay the ancient city of Agartha. Without the Beacon to illuminate it, the city had fallen into darkness.

Seeker bolted across the bridge, smelling the stench of rot and decay wafting up from the chasm. She remembered how Paige jumped to her death, sacrificing herself so she wouldn't slow them down. Though Seeker hadn't been overly fond of Paige—the feeling was mutual—sadness stabbed her gut like hunger pangs.

Poor little Weakling . . . she thought as she passed under the city's gates and into Agartha. Her hands and feet slapped the cobblestone pathways. She darted between the crumbling stone buildings and past the burbling fountain. She stopped to slurp water and then passed into an narrow alleyway. It spit her out a hundred feet from the castle.

The door to the main entrance still gaped open, but the Weaklings had barricaded it with rocks to keep the Strong Ones out. That way was impassable.

Seeker strained her ears; she could hear muffled voices coming from inside the castle. There must be another way in. She circled around to the back. She could see grooves worn into the sheer wall. So that was how the Weaklings got in and out. They were more agile and lighter than the Strong Ones. Climbing came naturally to them.

Very clever, Seeker thought.

She scrambled up the wall, using her sharp claws to seek out handholds. She reached the arched window and squirmed through it, leaping down and landing in the middle of the throne room. Her Beacon's glow washed over the spacious chamber, revealing hundreds of child-sized creatures. Their eyes jerked up in surprise.

They snarled, snapping their teeth at her.

The pack surrounded her, clutching sharpened bones fashioned into spears and knives. The Weakling seated on Crusher's throne rose, shielding his eyes from the Beacon. He wore a tattered robe slung across his shoulders. His eyes narrowed to slits.

"Seeker . . ." Rooter growled. "You came back."

Chapter 16

DOES THIS MEAN I COULD DIE?

Myra Jackson

Myra felt the deep puncture wound in her shoulder.

Drakken, she thought and started shaking. The dream felt fuzzy, hovering on the edges of her consciousness, but she remembered him stabbing her shoulder with his shadowy tendrils. More blood oozed from the wound, leaking through her fingers. In a distant and detached way, she knew that she was probably going into shock.

Professor Divinus materialized in her chambers.

"My dear, is everything okay? Noah sensed your elevated blood pressure—" he started, but then his eyes fell on her shoulder. His projection shuddered "Noah, send the service bots to Myra's room right away. Inform them it's a medical emergency."

"Yes, Professor," Noah said with a chiming sound.

Divinus hurried to her bedside, but stopped short. He was only a projection and couldn't tend to her injuries. "My dear, what happened?"

"Drakken . . ." she managed through gritted teeth. More blood leaked from her wound. "I had a nightmare . . . but it felt real."

"Drakken did this to you?" Divinus said. "In a dream?"

Myra nodded, feeling faint from the blood loss. "I shouldn't have tried to contact Aero again. I wasn't strong enough. It was my fault. Drakken invaded the dreamscape. He was the Dark Thing. He attacked me, and then I woke up and saw the blood."

"He's progressing," Divinus said with another worried flicker.

In a blur of motion, the door to her room beeped and the service bots zipped inside. Metal appendages cut away her tunic, injected her with pain medication and antiseptic solution, and wielded a needle and thread, sterilizing and stitching up her wound. Another bot stood by with sterile bandages clutched in its claws. Yet another started trying to change the dirty sheets and make the bed with her still lying in it.

"Away with you," Divinus said, shooing that bot away. "Leave the bed alone. Noah, no cleaning now. They can do it later. Please change their programming."

The service bot beeped angrily but then reversed and zipped into the bathroom, where it started scrubbing the already pristine shower.

Once the bots finished stitching and bandaging Myra's shoulder, they injected her with more meds. Then they retreated from her room in a blur of whirring wheels and electronic chirping. Divinus lingered by her bedside. He reached out to feel her forehead, but his hand passed through her like vapor.

"Rest now, my dear," he said softly.

Before Myra could protest—or even shake her head—Divinus vanished from her room as if he'd never been there at all. Her head swam woozily. She wasn't sure if it was from the blood loss or pain meds, or maybe both. She sank into her pillow, still stained with fresh blood, and fell into a deep slumber.

o   o   o

When Myra woke, she wasn't sure how much time had passed. The automatic lights glowed brightly, simulating midday. Had it been a whole day? Or only an hour? Time was impossible to follow in the stillness of the underground.

Wincing from pain, she climbed from bed, padded into the bathroom, and stripped off her soiled clothes. Fresh bandages girdled her shoulder. The service bots must have changed them at least once while she was sleeping. She wasn't sure if showering was a good idea, so she wiped herself down with a washcloth, slipped into a fresh set of clothes laid out on her trunk, and headed for the control room.

As soon as she stepped into the corridor, the service bots zipped past her to tidy her room and change the stained sheets. She left them to their fussing. Her shoulder throbbed with each step, but it was dull and manageable thanks to the pain meds. She clenched her teeth against it, passing through several interconnected chambers and into the hallway that led to the control room. She heard voices up ahead.

"I'm not sure she's strong enough yet," said Divinus. "This was a mistake."

They were talking about her. Myra slowed her pace and kept her ears sharp. Her stomach clenched in anticipation.

"Strong enough for what?" Noah asked.

"Drakken."

Myra had the irrational urge to swirl her hand over her chest, but stilled her hands. She couldn't revert to superstitious gestures now. They wouldn't save her.

"I can handle Drakken," she said, stepping into the control room. "I'm strong enough. I was just tired and got sloppy. I should have listened to you, Professor."

"My dear, were you spying on us?" Divinus asked.

The service bots zipped into the control room, depositing water and ration tubes on the table. One started dusting it, but Divinus shooed it away. Myra helped herself to a cup of water and drank it in one gulp. She hadn't realized how thirsty she was.

"Eavesdropping is rude," Noah chimed in.

"Right, I'll keep that in mind the next time you're debating my imminent demise," Myra quipped, but then her shoulder throbbed. "Holy Sea, that stings."

Divinus regarded her seriously. "My dear, this is no joking matter. You're lucky Drakken didn't kill you. The Beacons were designed to connect the Carriers together, but I never imagined they could be used as a weapon. Needless to say, this goes beyond anything we anticipated. We're still trying to figure out how Drakken did it."

She looked down. "It's happened before . . . with Aero."

"He hurt you?" Divinus raised his eyebrows. "Wait, why didn't you tell us?"

She shook her head quickly. "No, the first time we bonded, he was trapped under a thick layer of ice. I had to cut him free and sliced my finger in the dream. When I woke up, there was blood on my pillow. My finger was cut in the exact same spot."

"So that makes two incidents?" Divinus asked.

"Yes, that's right," Myra said.

"Then it's as I feared. This wasn't an anomaly."

"Anomaly?" Myra said. "What do you mean?"

"We've been exploring alternate theories for your injury."

"That's great," Myra said. "You don't believe me."

"My dear, your memory isn't scientific proof," Divinus said, manipulating the screen and summoning blueprints of the Beacon. "We're still running tests to figure out how it would be possible for Drakken to weaponize the Beacon. But the fact that you've experienced two identical incidents makes your version of events more plausible."

"Professor, I know what happened," Myra said defensively. "I'm telling you that the connection can transcend the dreamscape. Just look at my shoulder. Obviously, I'm not making this up. Check the security feeds. I didn't sleepwalk or hurt myself."

Noah spoke up. "Myra is correct. I reviewed the security feeds. She never left her bed. Her shoulder is concealed by the comforter, so I can't be sure exactly when the injury occurred. But you can see she was having a nightmare."

Noah projected the footage of Myra in her bed. She was moaning and writhing in her sleep. Her face contorted with pain, and then blood bloomed on the sheets. "There!" Myra said, jabbing her finger at the feed. "That's when it happened."

Noah froze the feed. It paused on her bolting upright. Her eyes were wild with fear, her hair sweaty, her tunic stained with blood. Nobody else was in the room with her, not even the service bots. The blood seemed to appear out of nowhere.

It took Myra a second to find her voice. A sick feeling swam in her stomach. "Professor, does this mean I could die in my dreams?" she asked.

Divinus quivered with worry. His eyes were fixed on the feed. "Yes, we must assume that all the Carriers are in danger. This doesn't apply only to you."

"Look, it's my fault," Myra backtracked. Her hand darted protectively to her Beacon. "I shouldn't have tried to contact Aero when I was exhausted. I let my defenses down. But I can shut Drakken out. I can keep him from hurting me again."

The professor let out a slow exhale. Myra knew it was only an affectation, but it did make him seem more human. "The closer Drakken gets to Earth, the stronger he becomes." Divinus flicked his wrist, pulling up the Fourth Continuum's ship. "He's still four weeks out, but his power is already growing. Given this development, I have no choice but to recommend that we deactivate the Beacons. It's too dangerous."

"No, our plan depends on us staying connected," Myra protested, remembering how alone she felt without the device. "Plus, we know nothing about Drakken. Maybe I can crack his protections and find a weakness that we can use to defeat him."

"My dear, don't you understand?" Divinus said. His projection shuddered and looked older than usual. "Drakken could use the Beacon to kill all of you without even setting foot on Earth. Is that what you want?"

"I'm willing to risk it," she said stubbornly. "Besides, it was my idea to send Aero and Seeker back to their colonies. I'm not going to cut them off. What if they need our help? What if they need Noah? I won't abandon them like that. I know what it feels like to lose your friends when you need them the most . . ."

Myra trailed off as the fatigue, strain, and meds hit her all at once. She started to feel dizzy. Divinus looked at her in concern. "My dear, you need to rest. Only . . ."

"Only what?" she managed to get out. The world look dimmer; the edges of it were blurry. She gripped the edge of the table to remain upright.

"I pray you wake up tomorrow," he finished. "I'll have Noah send the service bots to give you an injection that will suppress your dreams. But we've never administered it for this purpose. We're not sure it can protect you from Drakken."

o   o   o

Myra returned to her room, trudging along as if through molasses. Everything felt far away, except her shoulder, which was alive and sharp with pain. Hugging her arm to her chest, she crawled into bed. Her nerves sent out alarm bells. Wincing, she stared at the ceiling. She missed her friends like an invisible wound that ached more than her shoulder. She also missed her home colony, cradled by the dark tides of the sea. This underground world felt stagnant and stale; it felt like a dead place.

Her thoughts turned to her father. *Papa, I'm sorry I can't save you. I wish you were here. I feel so lost without you. I don't know what to do.*

It was Elianna who answered.

You're doing the best you can. That's all any of us can ever do.

My best isn't good enough, Myra thought. *They're all going to suffocate.*

Don't underestimate them. I know your people. They're descended from my family. They're more resilient and capable than you think. Don't give up hope yet.

You're right, Myra agreed, but doubt plagued her anyway.

The service bots zipped into the room to change her bandages and give her the injection. She felt the medicine shoot into her bloodstream like lead weights dragging her into unconsciousness. The Dark Thing didn't visit her dreams, but neither did Aero or Seeker. With the medication clogging her neurons, she couldn't sense them at all. Not even Elianna could penetrate her drug-induced stupor. Myra felt cut off from everyone that she knew and loved—and helpless to change anything.

Chapter 17
OLD JUNK

Jonah Jackson

The tower of spare parts crashed down in Sector 10. The Dissemination worker dashed toward the sector door. She swiped her tattoo under the scanner. It beeped its approval, and the door dilated. The Patrollers whipped around with their pipes.

"Patrollers, come quick!" Penelope cried. "Aisle D collapsed. My son, Bailey—he's trapped under the parts. By the Oracle, you have to help him."

Baron Donovan frowned. He stood just outside the door in his black uniform, fidgeting with his pipe. His face flashed with annoyance.

"Padre Flavius said not to abandon our post for any reason—that includes rescuing Dissemination workers. Summon your own trade for help."

"Patroller Donovan, have mercy," Penelope begged. She pointed to the rubble, barely visible through the thick dust clogging the air. "My son's trapped under those parts. He could suffocate by the time Dissemination gets here."

The other Patrollers shifted uncomfortably. One of them caught Baron's eye. "Patroller Donovan, Bailey's a good kid," Horace ventured. "He was a year ahead of us at the Academy, remember? He's loyal to the Synod. Shouldn't we help him?"

Baron looked irritated, but then he saw the faces of the pledges under his command. They looked mutinous. Their eyes kept darting to the rubble trapping the boy.

"Fine, Patroller Grint," Baron grumbled. "But let's make it quick. Padre Flavius won't grant us the same mercy if he catches us away from our assigned post."

The Patrollers marched into Sector 10. The dust made them cough. They reached the back of the sector and started digging through the rubble, shifting mounds aside. Penelope stood back and watched. She wrung her hands together.

"Bailey, hang on!" she called. Her face was tense with anxiety. Dirt smudged her cheeks. "Just a little bit longer, baby. By the Oracle, don't die on me."

As the Patrollers dug through the rubble, a shadowy figure silently moved past Penelope and headed toward them. As he crept closer, his foot landed on a brittle piece of metal. It crunched under his weight. Baron whipped his head around.

"Ambush!" he yelled. "It's a bloody trick—"

Greeley hit the button on his pipe and jabbed it into Baron's chest. *Zap!* Baron writhed and collapsed on the floor. Foam frothed from his lips. Pratt and the other Surfacers dispatched the rest of the Patrollers. Patroller Grint broke Pratt's arm with his pipe, but Maude zapped him in the chest before he could inflict further damage.

"Serves 'em right!" She patted the insulated handle of her pipe. "Let the 'Trollers see what it feels like to be on the other end of a pipe for a change."

The rebels disarmed the Patrollers, stripping away their pipes and binding their wrists with hempen rope. Baron stirred and woke. His eyes narrowed to slits.

"Holy Sea, it's the Chief!" he yelled when he spotted Maude. "Heathen, you'll pay for this!" But then Jonah gagged him too. He struggled anyway.

"Oh sit still, you bloody prig," Pratt muttered and zapped him again.

Baron went limp—and this time he stayed down. Jonah felt for the Patroller's pulse and then straightened up. He wiped the sweat from his brow. It came off in a puddle. "He'll be fine, except for a splitting headache when he wakes up."

Maude plugged her fingers between her lips. She let out a shrill whistle. "Bailey, my boy!" she called. "You can come out now. It's safe."

Bailey crept out from where he'd been hiding in the next aisle. The avalanche was only a diversion. He gaped at the unconscious Patrollers.

"What are you going to do with them?" he asked.

Maude rested her hands on her hips and glared down at Baron. "We should put them all out to sea, don't you think? Give 'em a taste of their own medicine."

Penelope looked horrified. But then Maude patted the woman's arm. "Don't worry, that's not our way. The Surfacers aren't like the Synod."

"To the Surface!" Greeley and the other rebels began to chant.

Jonah joined in, feeling elated that their ruse had worked. Greeley grinned and patted him on the back. Jonah didn't detect even a hint of animosity from the big Hocker. Instead, it felt like they were on the same team finally. Factum, Hocker—it didn't matter anymore. They were in this rebellion together.

Maude turned to the Goon Squad. "Greeley, have your people cart these 'Trollers back to the Engineering Room for debriefing. Let's find out what they know." She shifted her gaze to Pratt, who hugged his broken arm to his chest. "And Pratt, get yourself to Doctor Vanderjagt straight away. She'll patch you up like new."

"Yes, Chief," they both said and saluted.

Greeley signaled to his men. He slung Baron over his shoulder like the heavy Patroller weighed nothing. The rest of the Goon Squad followed suit, carting the Patrollers away and leaving Maude and Jonah alone with the Dissemination workers.

"Now what?" Penelope asked. Her tremulous voice echoed through the cavernous sector. The spare parts towered over them, casting angular shadows across the floor.

"Now we wait," Maude replied. "They'll be back any second."

"Who will be back?" Bailey asked, glancing around nervously.

His question was answered a few seconds later when the grate over his head retracted. Bailey staggered back in alarm, but then two pale faces peered through it.

"Girls, it's safe," Maude called. "You can come down."

Ginger leapt through the grate, landing on all fours. Stella followed her sister. The twins saluted Maude. "Chief, Sector 8 is secure," Stella reported.

"Yup, the Docks are under our control," Ginger added. "We took many 'Trollers captive. Minimal injuries to our people. The new prototypes worked like a charm."

"Thanks to Jonah," Maude said with a nod of her head.

Jonah felt warmth creep into his cheeks. "Well, I'm not the one who wielded them," he said, patting his pipe. "I'm sure the Surfacers fought bravely."

"Oh, don't be so bloody humble," Maude said but then grew more serious. She turned to the Dissemination workers. "Time isn't on our side, I'm afraid. Let's start sorting through this old junk. Jonah, care to do the honors?"

He nodded and fixed his attention on Penelope and Bailey. "You know this sector better than anyone," he said, pulling a scroll from inside his uniform and unfurling it. The end smacked the floor. "I'll need your help to locate these parts."

He handed the list over to Penelope. She squinted at the curling parchment through her thick glasses. They made her eyes look impossibly large. "Highly irregular parts on this order. Nobody's wanted anything to do with them in ages."

Bailey peered over his mother's shoulder. "Yeah, and that's a long list," he said, letting out a low whistle. "What're you gonna do with all those parts?"

"Build a fleet," Jonah replied.

"A fleet of what?" Penelope asked, still scanning the list.

"Submersibles."

Off their frightened looks, Jonah plowed ahead with an explanation. "During the Great Purging, the Synod ordered Engineering to destroy our submersibles, along with any records from Before Doom. The Head Engineer, my predecessor from the early days of our colony, objected to the Synod's decree. He knew it was pure madness. But he couldn't defy the Synod—at least, not directly. He knew what they'd do to him."

Bailey nodded. "They'd have put him out to sea. They probably wouldn't have even bothered with a trial before the Chancellors."

"Exactly," Jonah said. "So the Head Engineer did the next best thing. He ordered his trade to demolish the submersibles, complying with the Synod's demands. But he saved the parts and created the Spare Parts Room. He thought they might be useful in the meantime. Or maybe one day, if we overthrew the Synod . . ."

Bailey's eyes widened. "We could rebuild the subs."

"Wait, you're saying they were hidden back here all this time?" Penelope said, glancing around the sector. "Right under our noses?"

"Ingenious plan, don't you think?" Maude chuckled.

Jonah brushed the dust off a hunk of metal, revealing a silvery shimmer. It looked like the tail to a sub. "After Engineering disassembled the submersibles," he went on. "The parts looked like nothing more than a bunch of old junk. They carted them away from the Docks and hid them back here. The Synod never knew any better."

"Bloody fools," Maude said.

Jonah grinned. "Yup, their ignorance just saved our colony. Without these parts, we wouldn't be able to build one sub, let alone a whole fleet. We lack the ability to manufacture new parts. The science was lost in the Doom or destroyed in the Great Purging. But we don't have to start from scratch— we've got the Spare Parts Room."

o   o   o

The Surfacers marched through the sector door. They clutched all manner of parts hoisted over their shoulders or loaded onto rickety carts, making for the Docks in Sector 8. That's where they would rebuild the submersibles, right next to the portals that opened to the sea. "Greeley, grab that tail," Stella ordered. "The one that Bailey tagged."

"Careful with it now," Ginger chided him. "It's fragile."

"You lassies are bossier than the teachers at the Academy," Greeley muttered. But he did as they said. He knew better than to disobey them with Maude so close by.

Bailey darted down the aisles, tagging parts with red tape, while his mother scoured their files, flipping through the crumbling parchment and checking it against Jonah's list. "Bailey, Section 3 . . . Aisle B," she called out. "Rudder."

"Yes, Ma," Bailey said, scampering off barefoot. He disappeared down a dusty row to flag the part. It took him only a minute to find it, even in the messy piles.

The logic of Dissemination's filing system still eluded Jonah, but Penelope understood how to decipher it, and Bailey knew where to find the parts. Jonah wondered if it was designed to be confusing on purpose—if it was part of his predecessor's ruse to hide the parts from the Synod. *If so, he did a bloody good job of it*, he thought.

A few hours later, the Spare Parts Room had been nearly emptied. The rebels carried out the last of the tagged parts. Maude joined Jonah by the sector door. The automatic lights dimmed, signaling that day would soon transform into night.

Maude produced a flask of firewater from her hip pocket. "To Dissemination and the Spare Parts Room," she said, uncorking it and taking a long pull. She passed the flask to Jonah. "Never thought I'd drink to the likes of that snooty trade."

Jonah hesitated. "Isn't it premature to celebrate? We've got to rebuild an entire fleet of subs. My Engineers are skilled, but we've got so many new workers to train. And what about

Padre Flavius and the Synod? They're going to be furious when they hear about the raids. They're sure to notice the missing 'Trollers eventually."

"Mark my words, Jonah Jackson," Maude said with a wink. "It's never premature to celebrate. Good tidings are few and far between in these dark days. We've got to toast 'em, while we still can."

"But aren't you worried? Even a little bit?"

"Hockers live our whole lives on the brink of starvation," she explained. "Or expecting the 'Trollers to crack our heads open with their pipes. Or the next Pox outbreak to carry us off to the Holy Sea before we can get into the Infirmary." She gestured around the shadowy sector. "So this is no different— just a different set of worries."

Jonah nodded and raised the flask. "Then I propose another toast. To the Hockers and their ingenuity," he said, tipping it to his lips. He felt the fiery burn and braced himself but didn't cough. He was growing used to the fire-water, he realized. It hit his stomach and relaxed the tension in his neck.

He gazed around the Spare Parts Room, nearly stripped bare. Maude was right. They'd pulled off something important today. His mind flashed to the blueprints—the light blue lines etched onto dark paper that he'd used to build his proto-type. They'd use the designs to weld the ancient ships back together, piece by piece, part by part.

Maude took another sip before pocketing her flask. "Now, let's get our Programming recruits in here to change the codes on that sector door."

"Code heads?" Jonah said. "You trust them? Their trade's loyal to the Synod. They've always envied the Plenus and hoped to join their perfumed ranks."

"Lonnie and Ingrid Knox harbor no love for the Synod," Maude said, her eyes flashing darkly. "They were some of the first Factum to defect and join our rebellion. I recruited them after Padre Flavius put their nephew out to sea."

"Carter Knox?" Jonah said. "He was my Engineering

apprentice. He was helping me with my plan to return to the Surface when the Synod caught him."

"The Holy Sea take his soul," Maude said and swirled her hand over her heart. "I can still remember his Sentencing. Lucky for us, his aunt and uncle are genius Programmers. They'll change the codes so that their own trade can't even hack them. That ought to keep the Synod and the 'Trollers out of our sectors."

Jonah nodded, though he felt worry tugging at his gut. Even the firewater couldn't drown it out. Like the rest of his trade, he'd never trusted the Programmers. He supposed it was because they seemed to love their computers more than their fellow humans, unlike the Engineers, who harbored a healthy respect for their machines but recognized that their true purpose was to keep the colony running.

"That's lucky indeed," he said, tamping down his fears.

"Right, we need all the luck we can get," Maude said. "It seems in short supply these days." She swiveled around and lumbered toward the sector door.

Jonah lingered behind. The automatic lights dimmed even more, casting the room into darkness. He thought of his predecessor who had the foresight to preserve the submersible parts down here. His name had been forgotten, swallowed up by the long years, like so many other things in their history, the past wiped clean when the Synod rose to power and started to destroy everything.

Maude nudged his shoulder. He smelled firewater on her breath. "Jonah Jackson, what're you doing dillydallying? Hurry up, we've got work to do."

Chapter 18
THE DOCKING BAY

Aero Wright

A ero Wright, you are clear to land," Major Wright communicated.

Aero heard his mother's voice in his headset. "Roger that, over," he replied, keeping his voice devoid of emotion. *She's only a soldier doing her duty*, he reminded himself. Hating her was a waste of his energy and would only distract him. The mothership's external portal yawned open in expectation of his arrival.

The transport shuddered as it locked onto Docking Bay 14 and glided weightlessly—*almost gracefully*, Aero thought— through the circular opening. He couldn't take all the credit for the smooth landing. The computer did all the hard work, performing the calculations to match the spin and acceleration of the mothership, burning the thrusters and executing the tricky docking maneuvers. He remembered the first time he ever docked a transport, back when he was still a student at the Agoge:

"Welcome back," the Drillmaster said through the communicator. "You locked on your first attempt." His voice was stern. The Drillmasters never expressed any other senti-ment, but Aero could tell he was impressed.

He grinned like a fool. "Thank you, sir."

Wren shot him an annoyed look from where she was buckled into the crash couch next to him. "Don't let it go to your head," she said in a teasing voice. She hit a series of buttons on the console. "You'd be lost without my copiloting skills. Remember that asteroid you almost sideswiped during the obstacle course run?"

"Duly noted," Aero said. "But for the record, it came out of nowhere."

She lifted her eyebrow. "Oh yeah?"

"I swear, it wasn't there when I checked the monitors."

"Excuses," she said. "I stand by my statement—you'd be lost without me."

The memory soured as he snapped back to present. He glanced at the empty copilot's chair next to him. *Wren was right*, he thought. *I am lost without her.*

The transport settled inside the Docking Bay as the external portal contracted. The bay pressurized with a blast of air that engulfed the ship in dense vapor. Aero powered down the engines and engaged the cooling systems. He hit a button to broadcast his message through the entire ship, not just back to Major Wright on the bridge. "This is Aero Wright," he spoke into his communicator. "Confirming successful dock."

He unbuckled his harness, shrugging it off, and clambered to the door, hitting a button on the way. The door hissed open as the stairs unfolded and touched down. He marched down them with his hands raised in surrender. Armed soldiers surrounded his ship with their Falchions morphed and raised. Aero counted three top combat units.

His eyes darted to their leader—it was Danika. "Captain Tabor, kill the deserter," she ordered with a sneer. "Grimes. Malik. You're backup."

The three commanders advanced on Aero. Captain Tabor morphed her Falchion into an executioner's sword. Aero recognized the weapon form right away. He'd learned about it at the Agoge. The two-handed blade was rarely used in combat and had only one historical purpose—decapitating criminals. Captain Grimes shifted his Falchion into a battle-ax, while Captain Malik wielded a lengthy broadsword.

Aero didn't flinch back in fear. He didn't unsheathe his Falchion either, though it went against his every instinct. Instead, he kept his hands thrust over his head.

"I surrender," he said simply.

Grimes and Malik hesitated. Even if he was a deserter, striking down an unarmed opponent who had surrendered went against their teachings. This infuriated Danika.

"Don't listen to him!" she snapped, waving them forward with her ahlspiess. "He's a liar and a traitor. You can't trust anything he says. Your orders are to kill him and retrieve the Beacon."

"Yes, Major Rothman," Tabor said, signaling to Grimes and Malik. She stood well over six feet tall. Her muscles rippled as they hoisted the heavy sword, making it look effortless. Grimes and Malik flanked her. Aero remembered them from the Agoge due to their stellar combat records, though neither of them were in his class. If he allowed himself to feel anything in this moment, it would have been terror. But he kept his emotions tightly corralled. They wouldn't help him against trained soldiers.

"Major Rothman, can't we talk about this?" Aero said, his hands still raised. "I'm very reasonable. I didn't kill you when I had the chance, remember?"

Around them, the Docking Bay had gone still. Usually, it pulsed with frenetic activity—transports docking and taking off, being serviced by Engineering units, supplies being unloaded and dispersed throughout the colony. Danika smirked back at him.

"Trying to appeal to my emotions? You really have lost your mind, haven't you? Supreme General Vinick was right. You're an emotional hazard—and you will die for it."

"Now Vinick has you committing murder?" Aero said.

"*A good soldier will not strike down an opponent who has surrendered.* Surely, you remember our teachings."

"You're a traitor and a deserter," Danika said. She gripped her pike so tight that her knuckles turned rigid and white. "Our teachings stopped applying to you the second you fled from the mothership. The penalty for desertion is death by beheading."

Aero's eyes snapped to Tabor's sword. But still he didn't unsheathe his Falchion. Not that it would have made a difference. His weapon was drained of power. Shifting it now would cause it to melt down. Not to mention the three combat units surrounding him. Instead, he laid down his Falchion, knelt down, and bowed his head.

"So be it," he said. "I surrender—and I ask for sanctuary."

He made sure that when he made his appeal, he engaged his communicator so that it broadcast to the entire colony. The soldiers shifted uncomfortably. Whispers shot through their ranks like a virus. "Sanctuary . . . the deserter asked for sanctuary . . ."

"But nobody's done that in hundreds of years . . ."

"Silence—that's an order!" Danika barked. Her face turned bright red. She paced in front of her soldiers. "Don't listen to the deserter! He's just trying to confuse you."

Her communicator went off with a private line. "Starry hell," she cursed and clicked it on. "Supreme General Vinick—" she started.

"Major Rothman, what's the holdup?" he cut her off. He was screaming; his tinny, nasal voice could be heard by everyone in the Docking Bay. "Why isn't the deserter dead? Why is he talking to my ship? Damn it, where's my Beacon?"

"Sir . . . I'm handling it," Danika stammered.

"No more excuses. Finish him—now!"

The line went dead.

Danika's face turned purple with rage. The soldiers looked even more uncertain now. Doubt was spreading through their ranks. Despite the private line, they'd overheard Vinick screaming at her. Danika marched up to Tabor. "Stand down,

Captain," she barked through gritted teeth. "I'll finish the deserter myself."

Looking relieved, Tabor backed away. "Yes, Major."

Danika shifted her Falchion into an executioner's sword. Aero kept kneeling with his hands pressed to the back of his head. He tilted his neck up.

"Major, are you denying my request for sanctuary?" he asked.

Again, he made sure his communicator was live, broadcasting his voice to the entire ship. He was sure that Major Doyle was working to cut off his line, but he hadn't succeeded yet. Noah had rigged it up with special security protections.

Danika pressed the heavy sword to his neck. It gleamed with a fresh charge.

"I deny you sanctuary, deserter," she said coldly.

Aero nodded in resignation. "I knew you wouldn't show me any mercy."

"*No mercy in the face of weakness,*" she quoted back to him. "I bear the shame of having been betrothed to you. That will end now."

"It wasn't my fault, you know," Aero said, his voice cracking with regret. "The doctors at the Clinic paired us together. They use us for our genetics. They don't care how the match will affect us. I hated the idea of being wed to a stranger, so I looked at my file during an appointment. I knew your name, but not your face. Even so, I should have found you and told you about it. We could have had the match annulled."

"Too late," Danika said. She raised the sword.

The sound of slippered footsteps echoed through the Docking Bay, accompanied by a commanding voice.

"Major Rothman, stay your blow."

Chapter 19
THE WEAKLINGS

Seeker

Rooter stared down at Seeker from the throne.

"Seeker, what brings you back to the Darkness of the Below?" he asked, sweeping his tattered robe from his shoulders. He gestured to two Weaklings stationed by his side. "My scouts warned me you were coming. They caught your scent in the city."

The Weaklings formed a loose circle around Seeker, still clutching their bone spears and knives. Some shielded their eyes from the Beacon's glow, while others gazed at it with rapt attention.

"Rooter . . . old friend," Seeker said, bowing down to seem smaller. She knew Rooter from when they used to hunt ratters in the tunnels for the Strong Ones. They came from the same birthing season. "Are you the Strongest of the Strong Ones now?"

Rooter let out a bitter laugh. "We're the Weaklings," he growled. "We will always be the Weaklings, no matter how many ratters and buggers we stuff in our bellies. We would never betray our pack like you did."

"But you're sitting on Crusher's throne," Seeker said, raising her hackles as the Weaklings tightened the circle and closed in on her. She didn't like feeling trapped. Though the creatures were child-sized, there were hundreds of them.

Rooter's eyes flashed with anger. "Mine . . . now! Banished the Strong Ones from the city. The Weaklings rule Agartha now. We don't need those dirty, filthy creatures."

"I saw Slayer in the tunnels," Seeker said, adjusting the straps of her rucksack. "The Strong Ones are starving to death. We should invite them back into the castle—"

"They deserve to starve!" Rooter cut her off. "They're lazy and forgot how to hunt and feed themselves. That's our only law—survival of the strongest."

The Weaklings snapped at the air with their teeth and raised their weapons in support. Seeker felt a rush of sadness. "Then we're no better than Crusher," she said softly. She raised her wrist in the air, letting the Beacon's glow wash over the throne room. "We are one people, remember?"

"Liar, we are the Weaklings!" Rooter growled. His pack circled closer, pointing their bone spears at her. "Seeker . . . you abandoned your pack. Why should we let you come back now? We should banish you to the tunnels like the Strong Ones."

Seeker's heart thumped in her chest, as her Beacon pulsed brighter and faster. The Weaklings had changed, she realized. They were no longer the docile, subservient creatures she'd left behind when she journeyed to the First Continuum.

The Weaklings circled closer. Their bone spears pricked at Seeker's skin. Their big eyes reflected the light from her Beacon, glowing like a hundred red moons.

"Please don't hurt me," Seeker said, cowering away. Moving slowly, she removed her rucksack and unzipped it. "I come in peace . . . I brought offerings."

Rooter snarled. "This better not be a filthy trick! I know you're sneaky. I remember how you betrayed Crusher and freed the prisoners from the Black Mines. They named you Seeker for a reason."

"No filthy tricks . . . look for yourself," Seeker said,

upending her rucksack and spilling out the dead ratters. She had given a few to the Strong Ones but kept most as an offering for her old pack. The closest Weaklings scented the pile and licked their lips. If there was one thing they understood, it was fresh kill. She just prayed it worked.

She picked out the plumpest ratter and held it out to Rooter. "Here . . . feast on this," she growled, bowing down before him. "And grow big and strong."

Rooter looked like he was going to refuse. His lips curled back, exposing his sharp teeth. But then he grinned and clapped Seeker on the back. "Old friend, join your pack," he said, accepting the ratter. "We always have use for good hunters."

o o o

Hunting parties set out from the castle at all hours, returning with their haul from the tunnels, which they dumped in front of the altar. Seeker was allowed to feast with the pack until her stomach bulged, but she wasn't invited on the hunting trips.

Soon, she started to grow antsy from being cooped up in the castle. She also needed to send an update to Myra through the Beacons. But Rooter never left his throne and rarely took his eyes off her. He didn't trust her.

Seeker had no choice but to rest with the pack. She curled up by the altar with her head on her rucksack. Rooter's main scouts—two Weaklings named Crawler and Greaser—settled down next to her. She recognized them from back when they used to hunt in the tunnels for the Strong Ones. She slept fitfully, missing her chambers back in the First Continuum. She had never slept in a bed before. The softness repelled her at first, but she quickly grew used to the comfort. The stone floor cut into her hip bones, and she woke a few hours later sore and thirsty. Her tongue tasted like grit.

But the water pitchers were empty. They needed to be refilled. Maybe this was her chance. She snatched up two of the pitchers, tucking them into her rucksack. She glanced around the room. Tiny skeletons littered the floor, left over from the recent feasting. The Weaklings were fast asleep, including the scouts. Their soft breathing and occasional snores peppered the quiet room.

Seeker crept by their bodies, careful not to disturb them. She reached the window and was about to scale the wall—

"Going somewhere . . . Seeker?"

Rooter's sleepy voice cut through the room. He was slumped on the throne. His bloated belly protruded from his robes. Blood stained his lips and chin.

"Need water," Seeker said. "Pitchers empty. Going to the fountains."

Rooter narrowed his eyes. "If you're not back soon, I'll send my scouts. Don't betray my trust."

"Yes . . . back soon," Seeker said. She didn't wait for him to change his mind. She scrambled through the window and away from the castle.

A horrible feeling rollicked in her guts, sloshing and burning. When the Weaklings rose up and took over the colony, she expected that everything would change for the better. But nothing had changed. If anything, the Weaklings were worse than the Strong Ones—crueler and more cunning. She could see that now. She had no doubt that the pack would turn on her if she made one wrong move. That thought made her swallow hard, though her mouth was horribly dry.

Once she passed into the city, Seeker ducked into an alley and tried to message Myra, but her attempts were met with silence. They were too far apart, separated by untold miles and shielded by solid rock. She didn't even try to reach Aero—he was bound for a place even farther away. She just hoped they were both safe.

Giving up, she galloped down the cobblestone streets and burst into the central square. The fountains burbled away. Elevated pipes carried water to them, pumping it out of springs and delivering it to the city. One was warm for bathing, and the other cool for drinking. She approached the latter and drank steadily and deeply until her belly hurt.

She backed away, wiping her mouth. The dark castle loomed in the distance, staring down at her. Rooter's scouts could track her movements by following the light of the Beacon. She needed to return to the castle soon or they'd come looking for her. But when she started back after refilling the pitchers, Jared's voice shot through her head.

Go right, Seeker.

She jerked to a halt, feeling confused.

But the castle is the other way. Why do you want me to go right?

She peered down the dark alley to the right. Doors lined it at even intervals, leading to crumbling two-story dwellings. Though it was forbidden for Weaklings to enter the city, Seeker had explored many of them, searching for special objects from Before Doom to add to her collection in her secret cave.

I want to show you something, Jared communicated.

Seeker felt her curiosity prick up; it drowned out her anxieties. She bolted down the alley. *Two doors down,* Jared directed, *on the left side of the alley.* She skidded to a halt in front of a dwelling marked "451." The door hung loosely from its hinges. She had to shove hard to force it open. The frame splintered, shattering and sending up a cloud of dust. Coughing and her eyes stinging, she staggered into the main living space.

Go upstairs, Jared communicated.

Seeker obeyed, taking the steps two at a time, and emerged in a long hallway. Jared directed her to the door at the end. It led to a bedroom. Her eyes fell on a bed, draped in a patchwork quilt. Everything was covered in a thick layer of dust.

My mother's room, Jared communicated. His words were accompanied by quick memory flashes. *A woman covered in bloody pustules. Radiation eating away at her flesh. Jared sitting by her bedside, knowing he will succumb to the same affliction soon. He tries to get her to drink water from a pitcher. He feeds her iodine pills that she vomits up in a pool of blood. Her insides are liquefying, her cellular structure dissolving.*

Another flash:

She inhales and exhales, releasing her last rattling breath.

Jared's emotions rushed at Seeker. She felt his despair and sadness like they were her own. *A long time ago,* he communicated. *I used to live here. I'm sorry, I got distracted. I wanted to see her room one last time. But it's not why I brought you here.*

Jared directed Seeker back to the hallway and into another bedroom. *This was my room,* he explained. *There . . . on the dresser . . . do you see it?*

Seeker approached the dresser, her eyes falling on the object. It was a photograph preserved under glass in a silver frame. The frame was badly tarnished, and the picture was splotchy and fading. Seeker picked it up and studied the image. A woman had her arms wrapped around a child with floppy black hair and wide brown eyes, while a sprinkler sprayed them with water, refracting the light into multicolored shards.

It's you, isn't it? Seeker thought. *With your mother?*

We were playing in the backyard of our old house, Jared replied. *It was summer break from school, and I'd just turned ten, though I was still taking classes at the community college two days a week—Calculus and Applied Physics. It must have been over a hundred degrees and humid. My mother set up the sprinkler so we could run through it and cool off. She made a pitcher of instant iced tea—the kind flavored with sugar and lemon. Not real, of course. It was artificial and tasted like candy—*

Suddenly, two forms crowded the doorway. They clutched bone spears and aimed them at Seeker. "You said you were going to the fountains," Crawler growled. "And now we find you creepin' about the city."

"Rooter won't be happy," Greaser added, his eyes darting to the Beacon on her wrist. "He don't trust you. Neither does the rest of the pack."

"Sorry . . . I got lost," Seeker backpedaled.

Greaser looked suspicious, but Crawler pulled him aside. "Come on, let's get her back to the castle," he whispered.

"Rooter doesn't need to know about this."

"But she lied about the fountains," Greaser hissed. He pointed his spear at Seeker. "You can't believe her filthy story. There's a reason they call her Seeker. She's known for sticking her nose where it don't belong."

"Weaklings were banned from the city. She doesn't know her way around, that's all," Crawler said. His golden eyes glowed in the Beacon's light. "We'll tell Rooter if it happens again. No need to tell him now. She hasn't done anything wrong."

"Fine," Greaser grumbled. "But I still don't trust her."

While the scouts were busy arguing, Seeker tucked the photograph into her rucksack. She could have sworn that Crawler saw her do it. His eyes were sharp; they had darted to her when she moved her wrist. But he didn't say a word.

Instead, he led her back to the castle. His feet padded on the cobblestone streets. She followed the hairy curve of his back, wondering why he'd helped her. Why didn't he cart her back to Rooter and tell him everything? Why didn't he make her turn over the object? But she didn't dare ask the question with Greaser following so close behind.

As she ran, Seeker could feel the weight of the photograph tucked in her rucksack. She knew that it was important, and she knew what Jared wanted her to do with it. But she had no idea if it would work.

It will work, Jared communicated.

How do you know? Seeker thought back.

Because it has to work, Jared replied. *It's our only chance.*

His words haunted her thoughts as she barreled after Crawler, back toward the castle. Her Beacon pulsed faster and brighter, mimicking her racing heart. If their plan failed, then Rooter would kill her. He was already suspicious; that's why he'd sent his scouts. She'd gotten lucky this time. But her luck was bound to run out. She sent one last thought to Jared as they bolted under the gates and galloped into the drafty castle.

We don't have much time.

Chapter 20
SANCTUARY

Aero Wright

Major Rothman, stay your blow."

Aero jerked his head up, his eyes landing on the cloaked figures. The Forgers hurried into the Docking Bay in a rush of crimson. Their slippers muffled their footfalls. Danika was about to decapitate Aero. Her sword's razor-sharp blade stopped only an inch from his neck. The old Forger glared at her from under his hood.

"The Order of the Foundry has voted to grant Aero Wright sanctuary." His voice shot out as if fired from a blaster. "Major, withdraw your Falchion. Or my Order will never charge your blade again, so long as you shall live."

Danika hesitated, her sword still poised over Aero's neck. She licked her lips nervously. "Brother, your Order has no authority here. I'm operating under direct orders from the Supreme General. Aero Wright is a deserter. He abandoned his unit and fled to Earth. The sentence is death by beheading."

The old Forger narrowed his eyes. "He has invoked sanctuary. Did you not hear him? His plea went out to the entire ship." He swept his arms around at the soldiers. "Do you dare strike down an unarmed refugee in front of all these witnesses?"

The rest of his Order swarmed across the Docking Bay toward Aero, their shaved heads concealed under their hoods. Most sported long, scraggly beards. The soldiers backed away, giving them a wide berth. Uneasy whispers shot up and down their ranks.

"The Forgers rarely leave the Foundry . . . and all of them at once . . ."

"Soldiers, don't let them pass!" Danika yelled. "That's an order!"

But the soldiers were too afraid of the Forgers. They lowered their Falchions. The Order surrounded Aero, shielding him from the soldiers with their bodies. Danika withdrew her Falchion and backed away, dragging her heavy sword with her. Her communicator went off, but she ignored it. Fear rippled across her face.

When she didn't answer, Vinick's voice blared through the loudspeakers. "Treason, this is treason!" he shrieked. "The Forgers have no jurisdiction here! This is my ship, and Aero Wright is my prisoner!"

The old Forger frowned. He reached for Aero's communicator and clicked it on, so his voice broadcast to the entire ship. "I speak for the Order of the Foundry. My sworn brothers and sisters hereby grant sanctuary to Aero Wright. This ancient protection dates back to Before Doom. Any soldier who attempts to strike him down violates the sanctity of my Order. We have come to escort him back to the Foundry in peace. We ask only that you allow us to return to our domain unhindered."

Vinick screamed back over the loudspeaker. "Soldiers, strike them down! That's an order! Or you will all be court-martialed! You cowards, attack them!"

The soldiers whispered amongst themselves, but they didn't dare take up arms against the Forgers. They relied on the Order to charge their Falchions, their most precious possessions. Even Captain Tabor appeared humbled by their presence.

"Brothers and sisters, you may pass," she said, stepping aside to let them through. She signaled to Grimes and Malik, who followed her lead. They gestured to their combat units. They also withdrew their Falchions. Satisfied, the older Forger turned to Aero.

"Aero Wright, come with us."

Aero followed the Forgers across the Docking Bay. Once they'd put some distance between them and the soldiers, he whispered to the old Forger. "Brother, what took so long? That was cutting it a little close." He rubbed his neck ruefully.

The old Forger smiled. "Well, it took time to rally these old bones into action. Most of my brothers and sisters aren't accustomed to leaving the Foundry."

Aero cocked his eyebrow. "Keeping me on my toes?"

"That too," the old Forger chuckled.

Vinick's voice blared ship wide again. It had taken on a shrill, desperate quality. "Kill them, you fools! That's an order! I don't care if they're wearing stupid robes! The Forgers are traitors! Kill them now—or you will suffer the consequences!"

Aero hesitated. They'd reached the end of the Docking Bay and were about to pass into the corridors. His eyes flicked back to the soldiers. He felt suddenly guilty.

"What will happen to them for disobeying Vinick's orders?"

The old Forger's eyes darkened. "I wouldn't put bloodshed past Vinick, but even he can't be that stupid. These are his top combat units. He'll need them, especially with the reappearance of the Fourth Continuum. Who else will defend our colony?"

Aero nodded. "Commander Drakken makes Vinick look like a pacifist."

"Indeed, these are trying times," the Forger said, giving his beard a worried tug. "But first things first. Let's get you back to the Foundry and figure out our next move."

"Thank you, brother," Aero said and meant it.

o   o   o

The Forgers escorted Aero back to the Foundry without incident. No soldiers ambushed them in the corridors or waited
to intercept them on the lowermost level of the ship. The first
part of their crazy plan had succeeded. He was still alive. He
had flown a stolen transport right into the mothership, where
three combat units were waiting to kill him, and walked away
without shedding a single drop of blood. *Or losing my head,*
he thought. But it had been awfully close. His neck tingled at
that reminder.

As they neared the door to the Foundry, his Beacon flared.
Aero realized that he needed to update Myra. He shut his
eyes and searched for her through space and time.

The first part of the plan worked. I'm with the Forgers now.

Myra's response didn't come right away, and when it
did, the she sounded weak and uncertain. *Thank the Oracle,*
she communicated. *Keep me posted on the next phase of the
plan . . . I'm dealing with some complications here . . . more
later . . .*

Her voice broke up and fell silent.

Aero crumpled his brow. Why had she been so short with
him? What complications? Worse yet, why did her signal feel
so weak?

Before he had time to decipher her message, they reached
the Foundry. The door morphed, dilating into the walls. Scattered around the vast room were the strange, golden machines
used to forge the Falchions and charge them.

Usually, the Foundry hummed and thrummed with
activity, but now it was deserted. Some of the machines looked
like they'd been abandoned in the middle of performing some
important task. They flared with golden light as if irritated
by their neglect. Aero had been here many times to charge
his blade, but now the space took on a whole new meaning—
this was his sanctuary. He had never come here before with
the intention of staying beyond the short time that it took to
maintain his Falchion's charge.

The old Forger approached the door and did something
Aero had never seen him do before. He whispered some

strange words under his breath, passed his hand over the golden metal, and locked it. The door sealed with a thud.

"Emergency precaution," he explained when he saw Aero's expression. "I don't think the Supreme General will do anything rash, but better safe than sorry."

"That another one of your teachings?" Aero said. The Foundry always had an open-door policy. Soldiers could visit anytime they needed help with their weapons.

"Nope, merely common sense."

The old Forger ushered him to the back of the Foundry, which housed their sparse living quarters. Each nook was outfitted with a simple bunk, a bookshelf, a metal desk and chair, and a desk lamp. "You must rest now," he said. "You've been through combat and space travel. We can pick this up tomorrow. This bunk belonged to my young charge. But it's not being occupied right now."

"Xander..." Aero whispered, remembering his companion who accompanied him to Earth. No personal possessions cluttered the space, aside from a sleeping gown folded neatly on the shelf and a dog-eared copy of the Order of the Foundry's teachings, which lay on the desk.

The Forger smiled at the memory. "Yes, that was his name before we chose him from the Agoge. He's being held with your other companions in the Disciplinary Barracks. It's guarded around the clock. But we'll discuss that after you rest."

Aero wanted to object, but he felt weariness in every millimeter of his body. His muscles ached. His head felt foggy and heavy. He was no good to anyone like this. The old Forger was right. He needed to rest and recharge, much like his Falchion.

As if reading his thought, the old Forger held out his hands. "Well, hand it over. I see you've been neglecting your weapon."

"Not exactly my fault," Aero replied, unsheathing the blade. It flared once, weakly. The metal shuddered and rippled. The old Forger looked alarmed.

"My son, why didn't you say something sooner? Your Falchion is close to melting down. We must recharge it right away, or it may not hold together. Rest now, and tomorrow we'll try to broker a deal with Vinick. I fear it may prove difficult."

"Yes, brother," Aero said. "But we've got one piece of leverage."

He held up his wrist, where the Beacon pulsed with emerald light. The device could be removed only if he were dead. The old Forger met his eyes. "I pray it doesn't come to that," he said and then rushed away in a swirl of crimson.

Aero watched as the Forger weaved through the Foundry, slipping between the machines and heading for a middle-aged Forger that Aero recognized. She looked distressed when she saw the state of his Falchion. She whispered something to the old Forger—something sharp and disapproving. Probably about how Aero had neglected his weapon. Then she took the Falchion and shooed the old Forger away. She approached the largest machine and placed the Falchion inside the incubator, where it levitated in thin air. A green-tinted dome shot out, enveloping the blade. With a liquescent shudder, the Falchion melted into molten gold as it began to charge.

Aero wanted to watch her work on his blade, reforming it into a sword. He wanted to stay awake until she finished and his Falchion was safely back in its scabbard, but his eyelids drooped, one and then the other, and his knees buckled. He slumped on the edge of the bunk, feeling the mattress compress under his weight. *Wren*, he thought as he lay back on the pillow. He pictured her face and wispy blond hair. *Tomorrow, I'll figure out a way to rescue you. I swear it on my Falchion.*

Rescue me? he imagined her saying. *Starry hell, you owe me. It's payback. How many times have I saved your sorry ass?* His lips twitched into a grin, and everything dissolved into a dream-ridden sleep.

PART III
HEARTS AND MINDS

And now here is my secret, a very simple secret: It is only with the
heart that one can see rightly; what is essential is invisible to the eye.

—Antoine de Saint-Exupery, *The Little Prince*

Chapter 21
DEFIANCE

Commander Drakken

The Fourth Continuum cut through space, slicing through the vacuum and barreling toward their ancestral home. Drakken pushed his powers beyond their usual limits. He wanted to test his boundaries. The closer he got to Earth, the stronger he grew.

The dreamscape came alive around him, the edges blurry where it was still unformed. He focused his considerable power on summoning the girl. He had learned her schedule, picked up on her patterns. He knew when she slept and when she woke to the automatic lights. He'd worked to sync their routines. During their last encounter, he wounded her. He could still taste her blood. He savored the memory, yearning for more. It was better than any of the drugs that had helped extend his unnaturally long life.

He probed the dreamscape for her, but it was empty.

Where was the girl?

Why didn't she appear?

He projected his thoughts, flowing beyond the thick walls of his ship, through the nothingness of space and the dense atmosphere, across the volcanic ruin of Earth, down the elevator shaft and toward the First Continuum, through the corridors and into the girl's room, where she slumbered under a thick comforter. He felt a thrill at the immensity of his power. He had never bridged the dreamscape like this before.

He surged toward her like a malevolent shadow. His tendrils shot out and groped for the girl, but then—

He was repelled as if he had slammed into a concrete wall. Pain radiated through his body like an electric shock. His mind returned to his ship with a sickening jolt.

The girl defied me!

Drakken gripped his commander's chair in anger. His body burned as if on fire; he was injured, badly. Sensing his distress, the chair shot him full of medicines. As a blanket of numbness enfolded him, he sank down and shut his eyes. Before he nodded off, he sent an order to his disciples. *Power,* he thought, *I must have more power.*

In their pristine laboratories, scattered across the many levels of their ship, they got to work on the problem like a well-oiled machine. They would find a way to boost his power—or they would pay for failing.

Drakken stopped fighting for consciousness. He let himself drift away in an opioid-induced haze. Dimly, he thought of the girl. The other Carriers were formidable opponents, but they didn't wield nearly as much power she did. They weren't who he needed to defeat. One soothing thought cycled through his drug-addled brain:

Hearts and minds, I will destroy you.

Chapter 22
BRAIN DAMAGE

Myra Jackson

Myra woke from the deepest, darkest slumber of her life. Her mouth tasted like cotton; her tongue felt furry. Her head weighed a thousand pounds. She pushed herself up, emerging from under the comforter that had been her tomb. Slowly, the room came back into focus. *I'm alive,* she thought. *The drugs worked—I didn't dream.*

She glanced at her wrist. The Beacon throbbed slowly, almost lethargically. *Drakken couldn't reach me.* But the flip side tore at her heart—*Seeker and Aero.*

They couldn't reach her either. She wanted to try contacting them, but she felt too numb from the sedatives. Aero was with the Forgers; his plea for sanctuary worked. But could he broker a deal with Vinick? And had Seeker reached the Seventh Continuum?

She hated herself for being so cowardly when her friends needed her. Hiding behind a chemical veil in her comfortable bed. Sleeping the day away. Worrying about a little flesh wound. She felt for her shoulder, wincing from a sharp stab of pain.

Okay, maybe a big flesh wound. But still . . .

The automatic lights faded up, blasting her. She shielded her eyes and staggered into the bathroom. Her face looked sallow in the mirror. She splashed water on it and slurped from the faucet, wiping her mouth. She squirted some toothpaste in her mouth, swished it around, and spit in the sink. She was in the middle of changing into a fresh tunic when the door beeped and the service bots rushed in. They started cleaning.

"What happened to privacy?" she muttered, turning to grab her shoes before they could sweep them aside. The bots beeped at her in annoyance. She straightened up, startling at the crimson figure who had materialized in her room.

"My dear, you're alive," Professor Divinus said with obvious relief.

"Wasn't Noah monitoring my vitals?" she said, letting the irritation seep into her voice. She wasn't sure if it was a side effect of the drugs or merely her natural personality. "I'm betting you invade my privacy in all sorts of ways."

"Indeed," Divinus replied. A sheepish look flashed over his features. "Please understand, it's a necessary precaution. However, Drakken can harm you in ways that aren't purely physical. We can't monitor those properly with our instruments."

"Oh, you mean brain damage?" she said, tapping her forehead.

Divinus managed a weak smile. "Did Drakken attempt to contact you?"

Myra sat down on the bed, feeling overwhelming exhaustion. She wanted to crawl back under the comforter and never get up again. Let the drugs do their job. "He stayed away. I didn't have any dreams that I can remember. But Seeker and Aero . . ."

"You couldn't communicate with them either," Divinus finished. He clasped his hands at his waist. "Well, I'm afraid you can't have it both ways."

"So either Drakken attacks me when I'm sleeping and maybe even kills me, or I take drugs to keep him away, but I can't contact Seeker or Aero?"

The service bots started changing the bandages on her shoulder. When they peeled the gauze away, pain shot down her arm even though her blood was still thick with sedatives. She jerked her arm, making them beep in alarm.

"Right, that seems to be the situation," Divinus replied.

Myra took that in while the service bots finished bandaging her shoulder and left with a squeal of their mechanized wheels. The door to her chambers contracted.

"Look, I want to try again," Myra said. "Once the meds wear off."

Divinus flickered with fear. "My dear, I can't recommend that. It's too dangerous."

"I concur, Professor," Noah chimed in. "I've run various simulations and weighed the risk factors. The probability of her surviving another dream encounter with Commander Drakken is statistically low. Most likely outcome—Drakken will kill her."

Myra felt frustration pricking at her scalp. She hated the way they were calculating the odds of her demise almost as much as she hated being told what to do. Besides, she had never believed in probabilities. If she had, then she never would have come to the Surface. She tugged on her canvas slippers and started for the door.

Before she exited her room, she glanced back at Divinus. "You can't stop me."

o   o   o

Myra weaved through the cryocapsules, feeling the deep chill emanating from inside them. She pressed her face to a clear panel and watched the embryos drifting in their frozen slumber. She glanced at the placard—*Buteo Jamaicensis*. She was in the chamber housing birds. Coming here made her feel closer to Tinker. He loved hearing about the fanciful, winged creatures. *Will you ever get to fly again?* she wondered.

She kept expecting Divinus to materialize or Noah to answer her question, but they were keeping their distance. They could probably sense her irritation. She also couldn't sense Elianna, another side effect of the drugs. They were still making her drowsy, so trying to contact Aero and Seeker wouldn't work right now. She had to wait, which made her regret taking them even more, despite the risks.

She meandered through the interconnected chambers, passing between the cryocapsules, wondering what it would be like to be locked inside them like Divinus. When she grew tired of wandering, she sat on the floor. The concrete bit into her thighs through the thin cotton tunic. She hated feeling helpless. She needed to do something.

Anything.

Or she might go crazy.

"Noah, are you there?" she asked. Her voice echoed through the chamber. She felt silly for talking out loud when she was clearly alone. But then Noah answered her.

"Yes, Ms. Jackson," he replied. "I'm always here."

"Please, call me Myra."

"Yes, Myra."

"That's better," she said, hopping to her feet and dusting off her pants, though there was no need. The service bots kept the place spotless. "Do you have a Spare Parts Room around here? Somewhere you keep extra junk? Stuff you don't use anymore?"

"Let me see," Noah said and fell quiet for a second. "There's a storage closet located off Chamber 12. I'll have the service bots show you the way."

Myra heard mechanical whirring. When the bots burst into the chamber and spotted her, they emitted excited beeps. With their metal appendages, they hooked her pants and dragged her across the room. She followed them through several more chambers connected by corridors before they reached their destination.

Chamber 12 was located deeper in the colony. She hadn't been this way before. The service bots tugged her over to a nondescript door. One of them beeped at it impatiently. It responded by dilating.

The storage closet turned out to be the size of a compartment back home, with shelves spanning the length of it and stacked to the ceiling. Myra spotted electrical wiring curled around thick spools, pipes, computer circuits, hunks of metal, and other raw materials. Her heart beat faster. She approached the nearest shelf and picked out a motherboard. She blew on it, making a cloud of dust take flight. The bots crowded around her legs, beeping for attention. She looked down at the funny little machines.

"Tools?" she asked. "Do you have any tools around here?" One of the bots beeped out an affirmative response. "Great, can you bring them to me?"

That provoked another round of beeping as they communicated with each other. After arriving at a consensus, the bots zipped off from the storage room, returning a few minutes later lugging a heavy box behind them.

Myra tried to flip it open, but the hinges were rusty and resisted moving. One of the bots zipped over and spritzed the hinges with oil. "Thank you," Myra said, giving the bot a pat on the head. It beeped with elation and whirred in circles.

Myra turned her attention back to the toolbox. The lid swung open easily. Inside lay all manner of tools, organized into sectioned trays. She selected a wrench, feeling the heft and quality of the workmanship. "Now we're talking," she said to the bots. All this time alone was making her grow attached to the pint-sized machines.

They let out a chorus of happy beeps.

Myra had just started pulling out tools when Noah's voice reached her ears. "If you don't mind my asking, what are you going to do with all those tools?"

"I do mind actually," Myra said, feeling annoyed. Nothing she did around here was every private. It made the 'Trollers' surveillance back home seem laid back. But then she softened her tone. He was only a computer—he didn't know any better.

"Right, I can't build a submersible to reach my home colony. Like the professor said, we lack the necessary parts and can't manufacture new ones. But maybe I can jerry-rig some kind of probe to deliver a message to them. It probably won't be able to withstand the pressures of the trench, but maybe it can get deep enough."

"Intriguing idea," Noah said. "An unmanned probe would be far simpler to design and construct. It wouldn't need to carry oxygen or life-support systems."

"Or worry that the pressure will crush it and kill somebody," Myra added. "But it's a long shot. Even if it reaches the Thirteenth Continuum, they'd have to be looking for the signal. Also, if the Synod intercepts the probe, that wouldn't help us."

"I concur," Noah said. "The probability of your project succeeding is low. Especially with the Animus Machine breaking down. I reran your father's calculation. His projection was optimistic. It could shut down at any moment. They're fortunate if it's still working at all. They could have suffocated to death already."

"Well, that's great news," Myra muttered. She felt panic tug at her gut. She started riffling through the shelves, selecting parts. Keeping busy seemed to be the only way to keep her sanity right now. "Why didn't you tell me?"

"My calculation could be wrong," Noah said. "I don't have enough information. Plus, there's nothing we can do about it, given our current situation."

"Then I'd better work fast." She pulled down a spool of wiring.

"I hope you don't consider my question insensitive," Noah ventured, "but why bother building the probe if the odds of success are so low?"

"Because it feels good to do something with my hands again," she said. Ignoring her throbbing shoulder, she dragged a heavy sheet of metal off the shelf. It brought a cloud of dust with it. The bots beeped in alarm and started suctioning it out of the air. "Besides, it's better than sitting in my room, waiting for everyone I love to die."

"That's an emotional response," Noah said.

She released the metal with a loud clatter that sent the bots scurrying away. She wiped sweat from her brow, feeling better than she had in weeks. "Then I'm an emotional person, I guess," she said with a shrug. "Always have been."

"How perplexing," Noah said in a thoughtful tone. "I enjoy my work and find it stimulating. But I do not experience love. In fact, I don't even understand the concept. It makes you act illogically and against your own self-interest."

Myra couldn't help it—she burst out laughing. It made her shoulder ache.

"That it does."

o   o   o

A few hours later, Myra finished working on the preliminary design. The probe didn't look like much yet—just wires, circuits, and metal loosely cobbled together. She hadn't even started the welding yet. But it was starting to take shape. Every engineering project had to start somewhere, like her father always said. She replaced the tools. She didn't believe in keeping a messy tool rig. Her father had taught her that too.

Papa, I hope you're still breathing down there, she thought. *I'm trying to reach you.* She pushed back against the sadness that threatened to flood her chest.

"Noah, I'm going to need welding tools tomorrow," she said before she left the supply closet and headed for the control room. She found Divinus at the head of the long table, where he always sat. Surveillance footage swirled above his head. She saw the Fourth Continuum's clunky vessel—still winking in and out of existence, bound for Earth—and the Second Continuum's sleeker ship, still hovering in orbit.

"Still locked out of the surveillance feeds?" Myra asked. She took a seat next to Divinus. His face looked haggard, almost skeletal. She regretted snapping at him. "I'm sorry about earlier. I just feel so helpless when I'm cut off from everyone."

"My dear, no need to apologize. These are trying circumstances that would wear on even the toughest souls." Divinus returned his gaze to the feeds. "The Second Continuum's strengthened their security measures, but we're working to crack them. However, the Fourth Continuum's network remains impenetrable."

Myra frowned. "Noah can't break in?"

"Not likely," he replied. "Their security protections go beyond anything that we've ever encountered before. It appears that their ship is controlled by a network, but it's not only computerized. Some biological component seems to power it."

"Drakken," Myra said. "He's the reason we can't get into their systems. He's the biological component. We don't need to hack their ship—we need to hack him."

Divinus raised his eyebrows. "What do you mean?"

"Look, I don't know how he does it exactly," she said, holding up her wrist with the Beacon. It flared with emerald light. "But I can use the Beacon to find out."

"My dear, it's too risky. He could kill you."

Her eyes flashed with defiance. "Everything is dangerous now. I want to try again. And no more drugs. I'm done with that. I need to stay sharp."

"My dear, please be reasonable—"

"It won't work," Myra cut him off. "My whole family is stubborn, and once we've made up our minds, there's no changing them. You're wasting your time."

All the fight drained out of the professor. He shrugged his shoulders, making his robes flutter weakly. "As you wish, my dear," he said in resignation.

Divinus couldn't disguise his worry as he guided her through the meditation. She assumed lotus position, with her legs crossed and her hands resting lightly on her knees. She closed her eyes, blocking out the external world and sinking deep into her unconscious mind. She felt herself surging into the dreamscape. Her Beacon's pulsing slowed, matching the rhythm of her heart. Her eyes locked onto a shadowy figure. *The Dark Thing*, she thought and flinched away. Fear streamed through her blood. The professor was right. She should have listened to him. She wasn't ready for this yet.

Her shoulder started to burn like it was on fire. The Dark Thing flowed toward her, extending his tendrils like knives. But then she heard a voice echo through the dreamscape. *Welcome back, Myra,* Aero said as his Falchion exploded with sparks and chased the Dark Thing away. *Damn it, where have you been? I've missed you.*

Chapter 23
REPLACEABLE

Major Danika Rothman

Danika felt fear gurgle in her gut. The whoosh of the elevator carrying her to the bridge only made it worse. Her eyes were fixed on the window, but she didn't see the view. All she could see was Aero kneeling in front of her with his head bowed, her sword stopped an inch from his neck. But what happened? Why wasn't the deserter dead? She'd been asking herself that question over and over since the standoff in the Docking Bay.

The answer never changed.

Because I froze, that's why. Like a foolish coward.

She was a trained soldier. That shouldn't have happened. *The Forgers, this is their fault,* a little voice in her head spoke up. It was an excuse, even if it was a good one. She doubted that Vinick would buy it. *I'm no better than Lillian,* she thought. *I'm weak and feeble-willed like my sister, and so I'll suffer the same fate.*

The elevator doors deposited her onto the bridge. She was greeted by a blast of circulated air and a sharp voice. "So, you finally decided to respond to my summons?" Vinick said. She couldn't see his face—his back was turned to her, his eyes fixed on the windows—but she could hear his trademark sneer in his voice.

"Sir, I don't know what came over me," she started, feeling heat blazing in her cheeks. "The Forgers . . . they actually left the Foundry! All of them! My soldiers refused my orders and allowed them to enter the Docking Bay—"

"Why didn't you set an example and strike the Forgers down yourself?" Vinick said. He drew his Falchion and shifted it into a dagger. "They are only men and women, are they not? They can bleed, can't they? And they're unarmed. They refuse to carry the very weapons they forge. They say it goes against their teachings, the fools."

"But they're the Forgers," she said, realizing how lame it sounded. "To strike them down . . . well . . . that goes against all of our teachings."

"You sentimental fool," Vinick said. His face twisted with fury. "You let your emotions govern your actions. I should declare you an emotional hazard and banish you. You wouldn't be the first from your genetic line to show weakness."

Danika felt like she'd just been stabbed. "Sir, my sister . . . was an anomaly. I'm nothing like her. I can assure you—"

"I'm not so sure," Vinick said in an icy voice.

Danika felt panic setting in. She knew the eyes of the Majors were boring into her, but she refused to look at them. "Sir, I'm sorry. I can make it up to you."

"Appealing to my emotions won't work, Major. You're replaceable. Just like your sister. We can't afford to have emotional hazards polluting our ranks."

"Of course, sir," Danika said, feeling ashamed of her outburst. She hated herself right then the same way that she had hated Lillian for her weakness.

"Sir, do you want to banish Major Rothman?" Major Doyle asked from behind his console. His manner was rote and casual, as if he were discussing mundane administrative affairs, not considering whether they should end her life.

"She disobeyed your direct order and ignored your summons. We've banished soldiers for less."

"I agree with Major Doyle," said Major Wright coldly. "She's an emotional hazard, like Aero Wright. We can't have soldiers like them infecting our ranks."

"Supreme General Vinick, should we take a vote?" Doyle asked, gesturing to the other Majors stationed around the bridge.

Danika considered begging for her life. But that wouldn't work—it would only make it worse. Besides, if she was going to die, she didn't want to die like a sniveling coward. *If they banish me, I won't go like Lillian*, she promised herself. *Crying and begging like a child. I'll march into the escape pod with my head held high.*

The bridge was silent. The soft whisper of the ventilators, the occasional beep from the sensor arrays—these were the only sounds. Danika's heart thumped so hard, she marveled that nobody else could hear it. If they chose banishment, her prospects were bleak. She shifted her gaze to the grayish planet hovering outside their windows.

Even if she made it to Earth in one piece in the escape pod, the planet was scorched and bereft of life. She would have nothing to eat and nowhere to go. Certainly, the First Continuum wouldn't take her in.

Not after what I've done, she thought.

"Not yet," Vinick said finally. "The Foundry is on lockdown. Until we agree to meet with them, they're refusing to charge any Falchions. For obvious reasons, this puts us in a difficult situation. Major Rothman may still be of some use to us."

Danika exhaled. It felt like more than oxygen left her body. "Thank you, sir," she said. "You won't regret it, sir! I swear it on my Falchion. I'll make you proud."

"Don't thank me until you know what I've got in mind," Vinick said, exchanging a look with Doyle. Before she could reply, he added, "Major Rothman, return to your barracks and await further orders. Is that understood?"

"Yes, sir," Danika said and saluted crisply. Then she retreated from the bridge and boarded the elevator before Vinick could change his mind.

The doors contracted behind her. Only then did she let her shoulders sag in relief. She gripped the railing for support, feeling her knees go wobbly. A cold sheen of sweat graced her upper lip. She knew how close she'd come to death.

As she stood clinging to the railing in the elevator, she made a vow: *I won't disappoint the Supreme General again.* Her hand slipped down and gripped her Falchion's hilt. *Next chance I get, I will kill the deserter. That's a promise.*

The sight of her barracks had never been so welcome. She stumbled through the door and collapsed onto the bunk. She screamed her rage and fear into the foamy softness until her voice went hoarse and her throat felt raw. Only then did she finally lapse into a dream-riddled sleep. Over and over again, in her dream, Aero bowed his head and she raised her sword to strike him down. And over and over again, she froze, every muscle in her body locking up like concrete. He laughed at her weakness. And then all of her soldiers pointed at her and laughed too.

Shut up! All of you! Shut up!

But her lips wouldn't move. They were frozen. The scene played and replayed. Aero bowed his head. She raised her sword. She froze. Then the laughter. Again and again—until she burst awake. She thrashed off the blanket and screamed:

"Shut up! All of you! Shut up!"

All that emerged from her raw throat was a croak. She sat on the edge of her bunk, shaking and gasping for breath. She caressed the engraved hilt of her Falchion, feeling a soothing calm wash over her.

"Aero Wright. Deserter. Traitor. I will kill you." Her voice came out in a rasp.

Her communicator buzzed. It was Doyle. She clicked it on.

"Major Rothman, report to the bridge immediately," he said. "The Supreme General has an important task for you."

She forced her voice out. "Yes, sir."

Chapter 24
PULL YOUR WEIGHT WITH THE PACK

Seeker

Seeker spent the next two days holed up in the castle with the Weaklings. Hunting parties set out each day, but she still wasn't invited. She watched Crawler scramble through the arched window, feeling her legs ache with the desire to hunt. Crawler and his party returned later with plenty of fresh kill, more than the Weaklings could eat. Despite Seeker's continued appeals to have mercy on the Strong Ones, Rooter refused.

"The filthy, stinkin' beasts deserve to starve," he growled from the throne when Seeker dared to broach the subject again. He glared down at her. "It's revenge for every Weakling they feasted on and tossed into the chasm."

Seeker felt the Weaklings watching her every move, listening to her every word. One scooped up a fistful of buggers and delivered them to Rooter on his throne.

"But haven't the Strong Ones suffered enough?" Seeker said, feeling the steady pulsing of her Beacon. It lit up the throne room with emerald light.

"Never," Rooter said. He snapped his jaws shut over the word like it was a morsel of food. "Not until every last one of them dies from hunger."

The Weaklings stomped their feet on the floor, expressing their support for Rooter. They had crept over and stood in a loose circle around Seeker.

"No more talk of Strong Ones," Rooter said with a magnanimous sweep of his arms. He tattered robes fluttered in the filtered air. "The Weaklings are the only ones who matter now. Our people survived and rose up to claim our rightful place."

The Weaklings stomped their feet again.

"Of course, Rooter," Seeker said, bowing down to appear submissive. She knew when to push her case—and when no amount of pleading would work.

Instead, Seeker crept back toward the altar. She'd assumed that the Weaklings would be on her side and easy to convince to join their cause. That it was the Strong Ones who would stand in her way. But it was the other way around. She had already wasted too much time vying for the pack's acceptance—and she hadn't even broached the idea of returning to the Brightside and the First Continuum. It was still too risky.

Patience, Jared cautioned. His voice echoed through her head, making her Beacon throb faster and brighter. *Wait for the right time . . . they'll come around.*

Rooter hates me, Seeker thought back. *The Weaklings have always been weak and afraid. They can't think for themselves. They will do whatever Rooter says.*

He doesn't hate you—he fears you. There's a difference.

But why? I'm small and weak.

Because you carry the Beacon. Jared's voice pierced through her skull. Feeling protective of the ancient device, Seeker cupped her wrist to her chest.

Rooter wants the Beacon, doesn't he?

Yes, he will try to take it. That's why we need a plan.

Seeker retreated to the altar, where she'd staked out a spot. She found her rucksack and rustled through it for the photograph that Jared had shown her. Her fingers alighted on the hard edge of the frame. She stroked the grooved metal. Jared was right; she needed to be patient. She would do her best to fit in. She would stick close to Rooter and the throne room. She wouldn't mention the Strong Ones again.

She would wait . . . for her chance to hunt.

o o o

The next day, Rooter summoned Seeker and four other Weaklings over to his throne. Seeker recognized his scouts—Crawler and Greaser. Rooter's eyes darted to the Beacon on her wrist. They lingered there for a long moment, before he dispatched the group to the tunnels to hunt. "Seeker, pull your weight with the pack," he growled from his perch. His hands rested on his distended belly. "Don't come back empty-handed."

"Yes . . . Rooter," Seeker said, bowing low. "Seeker is very good at finding things. Seeker will find ratters and snap their filthy, stinkin' necks."

Rooter licked his lips in anticipation. "May you hunt well and return with fresh offerings for your pack." The pack thumped their feet in support.

Seeker trailed after her hunting party, following them through the window and into the city's cobblestone streets. The air smelled sulfurous and rotten, but it was better than being cooped up in the castle. As she galloped forward, she felt the glorious exhilaration that came only from running full speed. She hated being confined anywhere. Having enough to eat wasn't worth losing your freedom, she decided. She would rather starve. They vaulted across the bridge and into the black tunnels.

Seeker had to be careful. Her hand jerked to her wrist, fingering the golden cuff. She didn't like the way Rooter had been ogling it. *He will try to take it*—Jared's warning shot through her head again. She wouldn't put it past Rooter to have her killed on this hunting trip and make it look like an accident. Then he could claim the Beacon for himself. She couldn't let that happen. She caught the faint scent of ratters.

"Ratters," she growled. "That way." She pointed down the narrow passage to their right. The others skidded to a halt and smelled the air.

"More than one," Crawler added. His eyes glowed like red coals in the Beacon's glow. "Hopefully, fat ones. Rooter's been hungrier lately." He frowned, and Seeker sensed an opportunity. *They're not all happy with Rooter,* she thought.

"But I smell a bugger nest two tunnels over," Greaser said, scratching his face with his foot. His voice had a nasal, whiny quality. "Fat, juicy ones . . ."

"Rooter prefers ratters," Crawler said. "You know that, Greaser. If we return with only buggers, he will be angry. He might even banish us from the castle."

"Why don't we split up?" Seeker interjected, keeping her voice casual. She shrugged. "Twice as many offerings that way. Won't that make Rooter happy?"

"Rooter said to stay together," Greaser said, sounding uncertain. "Though more fresh kill to go around . . . that does sound good. Rooter would like that."

Crawler caught Seeker's eye and held her gaze. Regular feasting had done wonders for him, she could tell. His cheeks were no longer sunken; his eyes looked bright and clear. "Yes . . . he would be happy. Seeker can come with me to hunt ratters. Greaser and Trencher, go after that bugger nest. Meet back at the bridge?"

"Fine, under the gates," Greaser agreed. He signaled to Trencher. They split off, vanishing into the tunnel ahead. Their footsteps faded out, consumed by the gloom.

Seeker and Crawler went the other way. As they ran, they matched their footfalls, keeping them as silent as possible. Seeker produced a shred of cloth from her rucksack, binding it around the Beacon to conceal the glow. Thick darkness washed into the tunnel. Her eyes took a moment to adjust; she had grown used to carrying light with her everywhere that she went.

In the crush of darkness, her other senses grew stronger. She could hear Crawler's breathing, the rustling of his hair, and the soft padding of his hands and feet against rock. She could smell him too. But it wasn't unpleasant—a bit of spice and sweat and also blood, rusty and tangy. They fell into an easy rhythm together, pausing to smell the air and then adjusting their course based on the tiniest sensory clues.

They came to a fork, where the scents diverged down two different tunnels. "One ratter that way," Seeker whispered. "And one down the other tunnel."

Crawler's voice reached her ears. "You want to split up?"

Seeker couldn't be sure—was there suspicion underlying his tone? "Split up and meet back at the gates?" Seeker suggested. She fought to keep her voice neutral. "More ratters for Rooter that way."

There was a pause, and it seemed to elongate in the darkness.

"Fine, see you back at the gates," Crawler said at last, and then he bolted down the tunnel to the right. "May you hunt well," he called back over his shoulder. His footfalls dropped off as he rounded the next bend.

Seeker lingered in the tunnel. *Does Crawler suspect something?* she wondered. *Is he under orders from Rooter to keep an eye on me?* But then he wouldn't leave her alone in the tunnel . . . unless it was a trick. She strained her ears, listening for sounds of him doubling back to follow her. But the tunnel remained silent, aside from the soft hiss of the air vents and the faint scratching of ratters in the tunnel ahead. Even if she didn't hear him coming, she would smell him if he followed her. She knew his scent now.

Reassured by that thought, Seeker bolted down the tunnel. The smell of ratter grew stronger. The scratching grew louder. She envisioned the creature's circuitous route through the colony. Two more turns, and she pounced on the poor creature. She shook it once in her jaws, snapping its neck cleanly. She tucked the limp ratter into her rucksack. Then she caught another scent.

The instinct to hunt took over completely. In short order, she bagged six more ratters—big ones—and stuffed them into her rucksack. Sweat dribbled down her brow, but it felt good to be hunting again. She lapped at a trickle of water spilling out of the ground. Her tongue brushed the cold granite and tasted dirt. But the water was cool and clean, fresh as the deep mountain springs from which it emanated.

Still panting hard, Seeker sat back on her haunches and unwrapped the Beacon. Emerald light spilled out like mist and lit up the tunnel. Stalactites spiked down from the ceiling, casting unruly shadows. Suddenly, something stirred in the tunnel. Seeker sensed a slight shifting of light and shadow. She snapped her head around and raised her hackles. The shrill rush of adrenaline charged through her bloodstream.

She heard faint rustling noises.

And then a hunched figure crept into the light.

Chapter 25
THE ARCHIVES

Aero Wright

Aero woke with a smile affixed to his lips. "Myra . . ." he whispered.

For a blissful second, he imagined that he was back in the First Continuum with Myra only one door away. But then his vision resolved, and he remembered where he was—in the young Forger's bunk at the back of the Foundry. Myra was thousands of miles away from their ship, tucked beneath the scarred surface of the Earth.

It was only a dream.

His eyes flicked to the circular portal set into the wall, where a cluster of transports ran combat drills a few clicks away from the mothership. They balked and dove, cutting sharp turns through the void of space. The ships fired simulator torpedoes, which emitted a flare of orange light when they hit their target but caused no damage.

How long before the Fourth Continuum is within range, he wondered with a stab of fear, *and those combat drills become real?*

A simulator torpedo slammed into the nearest transport, obliterating his view in an explosion of orange sparks. He couldn't worry about the Fourth Continuum yet. There were too many other problems to confront first. He needed to win his colony over somehow. And he had to free their friends, still being held captive in the Disciplinary Barracks. *One thing at a time*, his father reminded him. *That's the best strategy.*

Easier said than done, Aero said with a grimace.

Worries paraded through his head nonstop these days. He missed being a soldier, only a cog in a much bigger machine, where all he had to do was follow orders and command his unit, and his father was the Supreme General with the weight of their survival on his shoulders and the Beacon on his wrist.

My son, those days are over, his father said. *You must learn to compartmentalize your fears—or they will overwhelm you. Then you'll be no good to anyone. Trust me, I know. The burden of command is not something to take lightly.*

He heard a soft rapping on the door.

"Come in," Aero called out. He glanced around the sparse living quarters. The compact room was smaller than the barracks that the soldiers shared, yet it had more character. The bedposts had been engraved with snakes. Their tubular bodies wrapped around them, spiraling down to the floor where they ended in clawed feet.

"Thought you might be awake," the old Forger said as he opened the door and stepped in. He looked like he hadn't slept a wink. But he managed a weary smile for Aero. He carried something in his arms, wrapped in crimson cloth.

"My Falchion?" Aero said, his hand twitching with desire.

The old Forger smiled. "Freshly charged."

Aero accepted the blade, feeling the fresh charge surge up his arm. "Thank you, brother," he said, returning it to its scabbard. He felt the reassuring weight of the sword hanging from his waist. "How close did it come to melting down?"

"Too close," the Forger said with a frown. "Another day, and it would have been beyond our abilities to salvage it. I'm just thankful you got it to us when you did."

Aero smiled weakly. "Wasn't my choice, that's for sure."

He tugged on his loose tunic and slid into his boots. He

fastened them, the buckles clicking into place. It felt strange to be wearing civilian clothes from the First Continuum, instead of his usual silver uniform. "How long was I asleep?"

"A solid six hours," the Forger said. "Not that I was counting."

Aero scratched his head. Instead of short stubble, his fingers pawed through long, curly tendrils. His hair had never been this long before. The Forger noticed his expression. "A lot has changed since you've been gone, hasn't it?"

"I feel like a stranger in my own colony."

The Forger's eyes darted to the Beacon. "Well, you're not the same person anymore. It's only natural to experience a certain degree of disorientation."

"Because I'm a Carrier?" Aero said. "Banished from my colony? Hiding out in the Foundry like a refugee? While my friends are locked up like common prisoners?"

The words tumbled out before he could stop them. He could hear the fear and anxiety buried in his voice. He hated himself for showing emotion. He ran his hand through his hair again in frustration, feeling the curls tug at his scalp and produce a burst of pain. He had the urge to lop it all off with his Falchion.

The Forger shot him a sad smile. "All of those things, I'm afraid. And many more that you haven't discovered yet. But let's deal with one situation at a time."

"Vinick," Aero said darkly. "Has he responded to our demands?"

"Our hope is that we may broker a settlement agreement," the Forger replied. "I dispatched two emissaries from the Foundry to request a meeting with the Supreme General and the Majors. Major Doyle turned them away from the bridge, so my Order has taken the extraordinary measure of putting the Foundry on lockdown."

"Lockdown?" Aero said in surprise. "You mean . . ."

"We're not charging any Falchions," he replied in a pained voice. "We've locked our door. It's not controlled by the central computer, so only my sworn brothers and sisters can access the Foundry. Of course, I hope it's a temporary measure and that Vinick agrees to our demands soon. I've got a feeling this will force his hand. As their weapons begin to fade, his soldiers will grow restless."

Aero fidgeted with his blade. All his life, the Foundry had had an open-door policy. Any soldier could visit it at any time, either for a fresh charge, or to discuss a problem with how their weapon was morphing, or even just to seek a little solitude from the daily grind, as Aero often did over the years. "Think Vinick will give in?"

"News of the lockdown should have reached him," the old Forger said. "We've already turned away several soldiers who came by seeking a fresh charge."

"You'll let me know when you hear from him?" Aero said.

"Of course," the Forger replied with a bob of his head. "You'll be the first to know. Now come with me. I've got something to show you."

Aero hesitated, his curiosity piqued. "Brother, what is it?"

A twinkle lit up the Forger's eyes. "Just follow me."

o   o   o

The old Forger swished across the Foundry. Aero followed him, though less gracefully. They weaved throw the golden machines, coming to a halt in an alcove tucked all the way in the back. Aero hadn't even known it existed. The nook had shelves stacked all the way to the ceiling. Dusty, old manuscripts were heaped onto them. The whole place smelled of must and decay. Aero felt his nose twitch, and he sneezed twice.

"Brother, what is this place?" he asked once he recovered.

"The Archives," the old Forger replied. He moved over to a teetering stack of books piled on a desk. He cracked the top one open, releasing a sizable puff of dust. "Since our inception, the Order of the Foundry has kept our own secret records. They're recorded by hand, indexed, and filed on these shelves."

"But why?" Aero asked, feeling the dust tickle his nose and urge him to sneeze again. He repressed it. "The central computer keeps records and logbooks."

"The Foundry exists as a separate entity. We thought it the best way to keep our records separate as well. Anything that's digitized is vulnerable to prying eyes. It can be hacked, or even destroyed with the flick of a button. We wanted to create something more permanent. Also, it serves as a backup should the ship's computer fail."

"I guess that makes sense," Aero said, running his finger over the cover of the manuscript. The binding felt like rough canvas. He flipped it open, revealing ornate, sloping handwriting adorned with gold leaf. "These are books, right?" he said, remembering his history classes at the Agoge. "This is a . . . library, isn't it?"

The Forger let out a hearty laugh. "Indeed, my young friend," he managed after a moment. "You were taught that libraries went extinct, weren't you?"

"After the worldwide conversion to digital in the age Before Doom," Aero confirmed. "That's what the Drillmasters taught us. Everything went digital."

"Not everything," the Forger said, patting the book. "We like the old ways. Sometimes they're better, safer even. Some books are straight records of our history. Some contain our philosophy, while others pertain to our ancient science and how we forge and maintain the Falchions. Others are merely fanciful stories."

"Stories?" Aero said, scrunching his brow. "But what purpose do they serve?"

"Not everything has to serve a purpose," the old man replied. "But if you ask me, stories teach us things about our very nature. They show us what is possible, what could happen if we take certain paths. They're lessons disguised as entertainment."

"If you say so," Aero said uncertainly. He had a hard time understanding how a made-up tale could have any value. "Brother, why show me the Archives? Aren't we wasting time? Shouldn't we be focused on Vinick and trying to broker a deal for the release of the prisoners?"

The old Forger pursed his lips. "All things in due time,"

he replied in a calm voice that annoyed Aero. "Rushing won't improve the odds of a favorable outcome."

Aero sighed. "You sound like Professor Divinus."

The Forger smiled. "Maybe there's a reason for that."

He motioned for Aero to join him by the desk. A young Forger, whom Aero recognized from the Agoge, hurried over with a tray. Aero smelled the pungent, spicy aroma of the Forger's tea. His mouth started watering.

"Thank you, brother," the old Forger said, accepting the tray. "You always prepare the best brew." The younger man flushed with pride and bobbed his head. Then he retreated across the Foundry. The old Forger poured them each a cup of tea. Aero eyed the fresh pastries laid out on a platter.

"Please, help yourself," the old Forger said. "You must be famished."

Aero didn't have to be told twice. He tore into a pastry, feeling a jolt of pleasure when the spongy, sweet bread hit his tongue. It sure beat the bland food served in the Mess Hall or the rations doled out by the service bots in the First Continuum. He gulped tea to wash it down and then tore into two more pastries.

The Forger took a measured sip of his tea. "You asked why I brought you here," he said. He patted the stack of books piled high on the desk. "These volumes contain everything that we recorded about the Fourth Continuum before they disappeared. As you can see, my brothers and sisters kept meticulous records."

Aero's eyes tracked over the tomes. Their spines were labeled with dates, all occurring in the first three centuries Post Doom. "Nobody else has seen these?"

The Forger shook his head. "Only my Order has access to the Archives. Based on the condition of these manuscripts . . ." He flipped open the top volume to reveal its yellowing, curled pages. The ink was badly faded. "I'm guessing that I'm the only one who has read these pages in a long time."

"Brother, we need to transmit this information to the First Continuum right away. Maybe it could help Professor Divinus and Myra." Aero set his tea down and frowned. "Only, I'm guessing Vinick is monitoring your communications."

"Indeed," the Forger replied. "Major Doyle is jamming them. We can't transmit any data, not without going through Vinick first. I doubt he'll agree to help us."

Aero picked up another pastry and finished it in two bites. "Right, harboring a known deserter probably hasn't gotten you on Vinick's good side."

"Vinick has a good side?"

They both laughed but then turned serious again. Aero's eyes flicked to the books. "So I'm guessing you haven't told Vinick about the Archives yet."

The Forger sipped his tea. "These manuscripts don't pertain only to the Fourth Continuum. They also contain sensitive information about my Order. As I'm sure you can understand, my sworn brothers and sisters don't want them falling into the wrong hands. I'm breaking our rules just by showing you the Archive."

"So where does that leave us?" Aero asked.

A moment passed while they both sipped their tea. It had cooled to room temperature and no longer tasted very good. A thick film had collected on the top. Aero pushed his mug away. His eyes flicked over to the Colloquium Machine. The old Forger followed his gaze and broke into an approving smile. "My thoughts exactly."

"Do you think it'll work?" Aero asked.

"Well, it's never been used for this purpose before," he replied, furrowing his brow. "But we should be able to scan the relevant documents and transmit them to Ms. Jackson through her Beacon. Then Noah should be able to download the data."

Aero cocked his eyebrow. "Brother, that means digitizing the Archives."

"Well, I must admit hard books do have their limitations," he allowed, grudgingly. "I've already put it to a vote. My Order has approved taking this measure."

Aero peered at the dusty volumes piled on the shelves. Drakken and the Fourth Continuum still seemed like a distant and mysterious threat. They knew so little about them, except that they were flying toward Earth at high speed with the power to destroy everything that they cared about.

"Let's do it then," he said, sounding more confident than he felt.

Chapter 26
ONLY A PROJECTION

Myra Jackson

Myra lowered the welding mask and bent over the deep-water probe. A shower of sparks fell in a curtain around her. She smelled the tang of burning metal and tasted it in her mouth. The service bots scurried away in fright. Circuit boards, spools of wire, metal scraps, and clunky tools were scattered across the drafting table that she had rigged up in the supply closet by stacking boxes and laying metal sheets across them.

The weld pool built up on the seam. She finished the seal, let the torch cool for a few seconds, and flicked off the machine. She flipped back her mask, wiping away the sweat that had collected under it. She felt a rush of satisfaction.

"Check it out," she said, pointing to the probe.

The service bots zipped over, racing around the probe. It resembled a miniature submarine, like the one her father had built, except that her design didn't have a pressurized cabin or carry oxygen tanks or any supplies.

"Careful, it's still hot," she cautioned when one bot stuck out its appendage and got too close. It beeped in irritation, zipping away to sulk. She'd grown fond of the little machines, since they were her only real companions down here.

Suddenly, she felt a tug at her Beacon, accompanied by a flash of emerald light. The service bots beeped and scurried around her ankles. *Incoming communication,* Elianna's voice rang through her head. *I'm receiving some kind of signal.*

Myra felt a burst of fear. *Drakken.*

No, it's not Drakken.

Myra felt a surge of relief. *Is it Seeker? Or Aero?*

It's unclear . . . this signal feels different . . .

Different how?

It's not coming from a Beacon.

But how is that possible? Myra wondered.

Elianna didn't reply right away, but then her voice came through. *I have no idea, but it's locked onto your Beacon with great strength. Beginning transmission now.*

Myra felt the world around her turn blurry and dim—the supply closet, the drafting table freighted with tools, the service bots racing around her ankles and emitting worried beeps—and then they vanished from her view. She felt a strange wrenching sensation, like her body was being separated from her mind. The feeling intensified, making her ears ring, and then it ceased and she was somewhere else altogether.

But where was she?

She glanced around, taking in the vast room filled with rows upon rows of golden machines. But they weren't cryo-capsules; this wasn't the First Continuum. Red-cloaked men and women bent over the machines, adjusting levers and buttons. Their shaved heads gleamed under the automatic lights as they rushed around in their slippered feet.

One woman bent over a translucent dome of emerald light and extracted something from it. The elongated object shimmered with golden light. It was a Falchion, Myra realized. They were Forgers. Was this the Second Continuum?

The woman with the Falchion headed straight for her. Myra expected that she would be surprised to see a stranger standing here—or at least, step around her and offer an apology. But the woman walked straight through Myra as if she wasn't there.

She can't see me, Myra realized. *It's like I'm here . . . but I'm not really here.*

"Welcome to the Foundry, Ms. Jackson."

The voice came from behind Myra. She wheeled around to see an old man dressed in crimson robes. He looked straight at her like he could actually see her. "I'm glad to see you've arrived safely. Well, technically, your body is still back in the First Continuum. But your consciousness is here in the form of a projection."

"Right . . . where is here exactly?" she asked, feeling disoriented.

"The Foundry," the old man replied.

She gazed around in astonishment. "So I'm in the Second Continuum?"

"The one and only," he replied. "Currently, we're orbiting Earth." He gestured to a circular window set into the thick wall. "Look, you can see for yourself."

Myra followed him over. It felt strange to be here . . . yet not really here. Her feet glided over the floor like she was walking on air. Everything around her appeared soft and unfocused. She gazed through the window.

A soft gasp escaped her lips. "It's . . . so beautiful."

What she glimpsed defied all imagination. Earth hovered below their ship, illuminated by the flaming light of the sun. Swirls of cottony clouds obscured the grayish land formations and patches of deep blue. *The oceans,* she realized. She pushed her gaze right, where she could see the polished, silver exterior of the Second Continuum, tapering to a propulsion engine of some kind, she guessed, though it did not resemble any engine she'd ever encountered in her engineering studies.

The old Forger smiled. "If you think that's beautiful, I should show you the images from Before Doom."

It wasn't easy, but Myra pulled her gaze from the window and fixed it on the old man. "How am I standing inside the

Second Continuum?" she asked. "And why can you see me and talk to me, but the other Forgers can't?"

She held up her hand, watching as it faded in and out of being. Her brain was having a hard time wrapping itself around the concept that her consciousness had been suddenly projected into outer space.

"Here's the simplest answer I can give," the old Forger said. "I summoned you here using ancient science developed by my sworn brothers and sisters. They developed a way to communicate directly with the Carriers through their Beacons."

"But I thought only the Carriers could communicate with each other that way?" Myra said, trying to make sense of this new puzzle.

"My Order specializes in the same science that the First Ones used to make the Beacons. We modified it and used it to create the Falchions. They function using the same nanotechnology and biological interfaces." He smiled when he saw the puzzled look on her face. "If you follow me, I can show you how it's done."

He led her over to a machine tucked unobtrusively in the back corner of the Foundry. "This is the Colloquium Machine," he explained, taking a seat in front of it. "You perceive me as walking around and talking to you. But really I'm seated in front of this screen, communicating with you."

Myra squinted at the machine. "How does that work?"

The old Forger patted the top, coming away with his hand streaked with dust. "I'm still getting the hang of it myself. The Colloquium Machine is so ancient that even I'm not sure how it works. This is the first time I've tried the projection setting. Anyway, the machine has certainly come in handy since Aero decided to come back."

In the rush of disorientation that came along with being projected into space, she'd forgotten about Aero. "Where is he?" she asked. "Can I talk to him?"

The old Forger tilted his head toward an alcove set in the back corner, lined with shelves heaped with old manuscripts.

A figure stirred in the shadows. He made his way over, stepping into the light. He scratched his nose and sneezed.

"Sorry," Aero said. "I think I'm allergic to books."

Myra couldn't help it. She rushed over and tried to hug him, but her arms passed through his body. "Sorry," she said, matching his grin. "I'm only a projection."

His smile didn't waver. "I'll take what I can get."

"So, you're responsible for kidnapping my mind?"

He nodded. "Yeah, well, we need your help." Then as quickly as he could, Aero told her about the Archives and how nobody else had a copy of these records. She followed him down the nearest row. Her eyes passed over the shelves. "A real library . . ." she said. "I thought they all went extinct after the digital conversion."

"Not all of them. The Forgers like the old ways. They also have some benefits. If the computer records ever get destroyed, then they still have these as a backup."

"Like in the Great Purging," she said. "That's genius."

"Well, the Forgers are pretty sharp."

He came to a halt in front of a desk with a stack of books piled precariously on it. Her eyes swept over the spines, reading the hand-scrawled dates.

"Here's everything we have on the Fourth Continuum," Aero said. "The old Forger has been working on scanning these books. Using the Colloquium Machine, we'll transmit the data to you. That way, Vinick can't block our communication."

She eyed the books. "I hope it helps us defeat Drakken."

Her face darkened, and her hand darted to her wounded shoulder, though her projection didn't have bandages encircling it. "Myra, what is it?" Aero asked, noticing her expression. "What happened?"

"Drakken," she said. Her projection vanished and then snapped back into existence. "Sorry, I think my emotions overwhelmed the signal. Drakken attacked me in the dreamscape. He stabbed my shoulder. And, well, when I woke up . . ."

Aero's eyes flashed with worry. "It had happened in real life too."

She nodded. "When I woke up, there was blood everywhere. The service bots patched me up and gave me medicine. It's only a flesh wound, thank the Oracle."

"But Drakken could have killed you," Aero said. His voice sounded ragged, fearful even. Myra met his gaze. "The dreamscape isn't safe anymore."

"Well, it's only a theory at this point," she said. "But Drakken is growing stronger. The professor thinks it's related to him getting closer to Earth. He wants to deactivate the Beacons. But I refuse to be cut off from you and Seeker—"

"Myra, the professor is right. It's too dangerous."

She shook her head, feeling that stubborn streak flare in her blood. "No, I can keep Drakken out. I've been practicing my exercises. I'm getting stronger."

"When you're awake. But what happens the next time you're asleep? Listen, I won't risk Drakken killing you. We should turn them off."

She searched his face. "And go back to complete silence? Remember how it fragmented us? How it tore us apart? How we couldn't sense each other anymore? How we felt like strangers? We need the Beacons—they're the key to everything."

Aero set his lips. "They're also the dagger that Drakken will use to stab you in your sleep." His words hung in the air. The tense moment enveloped them. Her stubbornness smashed up against his worry. It felt like a stalemate.

Myra drifted over to him. "The Beacons make us stronger, don't you see? They bind us together and keep us united. Besides, how else can you contact me without Vinick intercepting it? Or transmit all this data from the Archives?" She paused, feeling a rush of fear. "Also, how am I supposed to know if you're still alive up here?"

"Fine, but we have to be careful. Promise me."

"I promise—"

She started but then flickered. The old Forger worked the

levers and hit buttons on the Colloquium Machine. "Signal interference," he called out. "I don't know how much longer we can hold on to her connection."

Myra glanced around the Foundry, sensing that she could be ripped away from this place at any moment. The Forgers were working on their machines as if she wasn't there. They couldn't see her. A large golden door stood at the other end of the room.

"Tinker, Kaleb . . . they're being held on this ship, aren't they?"

Aero followed her gaze to the door. "They're on another level in the Disciplinary Barracks. It's guarded around the clock by armed soldiers. I haven't been able to visit them, though I've been assured they're mostly unharmed."

"Mostly unharmed?" Myra said, flickering again. "That's not exactly reassuring."

"Solid intel, though secondhand. Many soldiers remain loyal to the Forgers. I can't leave the Foundry. Vinick has posted a combat unit outside that door. The Forgers have granted me sanctuary, but it protects me only if I stay in here. As soon as I leave, Vinick has the right to do with me as he pleases. And well, I don't like my chances."

"What about me?" she asked. "I'm a projection. The soldiers can't see me. If you tell me where Kaleb and Tinker are being held, I bet I could find the barracks."

"I guess it's worth a shot," Aero said. "Brother, do you think it'll work?"

The old Forger nodded. "My dear, once you leave the Foundry, I don't know if your projection will be strong enough. I'll hold on to your signal for as long as I can. But if I lose it, then you'll simply vanish from our ship."

After receiving directions from the Forger and bidding farewell to Aero, she floated over to the door. She steeled herself, pushing her energy into strengthening her projection, and passed through the barrier. It felt strange not having to comply with the physical limitations of the world. She floated past the combat unit of soldiers guarding the Foundry. They had their Falchions clutched in their hands. They didn't even notice when she passed right through them, gliding down the smooth corridor.

Myra came upon two soldiers, marching away from the Foundry. "Deserter's camped out in there with the Red Cloaks," the first one muttered, scratching her temples with the hilt of her Falchion. It was morphed into a short, curved sword.

Myra's ears pricked up. That was what they called the priests back home.

"More like *Turn Cloaks*," the other soldier replied. He had a battle-ax laid over his shoulder. Myra caught sight of the name stitched into his uniform:

Captain Lucius P. Zakkay

His comment produced a smirk from his companion. "All I'm saying is the Supreme General can't be happy with the Forgers," she went on, oblivious that Myra was following them down the corridor like a ghost. "They're harboring a traitor."

Zakkay turned more serious. He lowered his voice. "You don't think Vinick would actually try anything, do you? I mean, the Foundry . . . it's protected." He tightened his grip on his Falchion nervously. "We need them to charge our Falchions."

"No, of course not," she said quickly. "I'm just saying, it doesn't look good."

Myra followed them into an elevator. In theory—she realized only later—she probably could have floated up through the floor to the next level, but her mind hadn't yet shaken those preconceived limitations. It complied with rules of the physical world even if they didn't apply to her projection. The Foundry was located on the lowermost level of the ship. She waited with the soldiers while the elevator jettisoned them to the top level. She let the soldiers exit first and then continued down the corridor.

She could feel her projection growing weaker the farther she traveled from the Foundry. She glanced at her hand.

Before it had appeared solid, but now it looked translucent. She could see through it. *I really am a ghost now,* she thought.

Not exactly, Elianna responded. Humor tinted her voice. *And I should know, since I'm the real ghost around here. I've been dead nearly a thousand years.*

Myra reached the end of the corridor and turned right, following the old Forger's directions. Doors lined either side, leading to difference barracks, but she knew her destination; she could tell by the six guards posted outside the door. They didn't notice her. She floated through the door and into the Disciplinary Barracks.

Her form grew even more transparent. She fought to hold onto the signal and felt it stabilize. Her eyes landed on Tinker. He was curled up in the bunk, wrapped in a crinkly silver blanket. The young Forger was meditating on the floor in a cross-legged position, his lips moving but producing no words. Kaleb and Wren sat across the room with their backs propped up against the wall. Wren had strange marks on the inside of her elbow. The whites of her eyes were bloodshot, like she'd burst all the capillaries.

From screaming, Myra realized with a shock. They'd been tortured. Myra glanced at Kaleb. His arm bore the same markings; his eyes were also bloodshot.

Tinker, she thought. Her lips moved but no sound emerged.

Nobody looked over—they couldn't hear her. Her eyes roved over Tinker's face, taking in every feature. He looked older. He had lost a lot of baby fat. His cheeks were more defined. He also looked like he'd grown an inch. Could that happen? She drifted over, feeling an ache in her heart like a physical force. *Tinker,* she thought again. *I'm here. We're going to get you out of here. Aero is working on it. We have a plan.*

She was only centimeters from his face, but he stared right through her. But then he shifted his gaze slightly—it could have been a coincidence—but his eyes locked onto her face. His eyes widened. He sat up straighter, the blanket sloughing from his shoulders. Her heart beat faster. Could he see her?

Could he sense her presence? She reached out for him, her transparent fingers extending, but then she flickered—

This time, her projection didn't snap back.

She felt a wrenching in her being. Her consciousness was hurled back toward the Earth, through the vacuum of space, down through the atmosphere, and plunged deeper and deeper through layers of rock.

Then everything went dark.

When Myra woke up, she found herself splayed on the floor of the supply closet. The service bots beeped around her anxiously. The welding mask lay a few inches away from her outstretched hand. She could feel gravity pressing her into the cold floor.

She sat up, her head pounding fiercely. The service bots beeped in concern, but she shooed them away. Memories of the Second Continuum rushed through her head. Was that dream real? Or did she faint while working and simply imagine it all? The confusion overwhelmed her, but then she heard Elianna's voice in her head.

Data being transmitted from the Second Continuum, she said in her pleasant voice. *Should we inform Noah so he can begin the download?*

Chapter 27
SUBSTITUTE SOLDIER

Major Danika Rothman

anika marched toward the Foundry with Supreme General Vinick and Majors Doyle and Wright. Their boots smacked the ground in a rhythmic pattern. They trailed two emissaries from the Foundry, whose slippers muffled their footsteps.

They came to a halt in front of the Foundry. The doors were locked and guarded by soldiers from one of their combat units.

"Captain Zakkay, stand down," Vinick barked.

He'd ordered the soldiers to guard this post after the Foundry locked their doors. He didn't trust the order. *And with good reason*, Danika thought bitterly.

"Yes, sir," the soldier replied, snapping off a salute. Danika recognized him right away. Zakkay came from Aero's old unit, but he harbored no positive feelings for the deserter. He signaled to his soldiers to back away and let the Forgers through.

They approached the door and began the complex process to unlock it. Once they'd decoded the door, the metal rippled and retracted into the wall. A rush of warm air greeted them. Danika inhaled the unique fragrance of the Foundry—a mix of singed metal and the strange tea that the Forgers brewed and drank all through the day.

"Majors, stay close to me," Vinick whispered. "Is that understood?"

"Yes, sir," Danika whispered back. The other Majors nodded their agreement.

They proceeded into the Foundry. One of the oldest Forgers came to greet them, but Danika's gaze immediately snapped to the man behind him—Aero Wright. She felt her nerves jangle, but she worked to control them. This was the first time she'd seen him since the Docking Bay.

"Supreme General Vinick," the old Forger said and bowed deeply. "May I offer you a refreshment?" Danika watched him closely. She knew he couldn't be trusted.

"Brother, I accept your offer of hospitality," Vinick said stiffly.

Aero's eyes brushed past Danika, coming to rest on the soldier standing to her left. It was Major Wright, Aero's biological mother. When he saw her, his whole countenance seemed to harden. He quickly looked away.

"Shall we sit?" the old Forger asked, already lowering himself onto a pillow.

One of the younger Forgers raced over with a tray laden with a steaming pot of tea and some food. Her mouth started watering at the sight of it. The young Forger set the tray on a table, which was surrounded by overstuffed pillows.

"Yes, brother," Vinick replied, though he appeared uncomfortable with the arrangement. But he signaled to the Majors to follow suit. They took seats on the pillows, while the old Forger poured tea into mugs and passed them around.

Danika had a hard time arranging herself on the pillow. Her uniform was pliable and her joints were nimble, but her Falchion clanged against the floor. Even worse, Aero claimed the pillow next to her. Why couldn't he sit somewhere else?

She didn't want to look at him, so kept her eyes aimed at the mug of steaming tea clutched in her hand. It was singeing the hell out of her palm. *All this technological advancement,* she thought, *yet no handles on their cups.*

"Welcome to the Foundry," the old Forger said. He raised his cup in salute and sipped his tea. "Supreme General Vinick, thank you for accepting our emissaries and agreeing to this meeting. I trust they delivered our demands?"

"Of course, brother," Vinick replied. He took one sip of tea, grimaced at the bitter taste, and set it aside. "I hope we can settle this diplomatically. I'm sure we can all agree that putting the Foundry on lockdown was an extreme and unnecessary measure."

Danika could feel tension crackling in the air. She shifted uncomfortably on her pillow, trying to avoid looking at Aero. She could hear him breathing next to her.

"So do I," the old Forger said. "We do not wish to keep the Foundry on lockdown. It goes against our teachings. Are our terms acceptable?"

"As I'm sure you'll understand, we cannot grant the deserter a pardon outright," Vinick said in a reasonable voice. "We have rules to follow. I can promise he'll receive a fair trial by the Majors. In exchange for turning him over to us, we will release the prisoners to your Order, but only after the Majors have rendered a verdict."

"That wasn't the deal," the old Forger said. His voice remained calm, but anger flared in his eyes. "A trial by the Majors is unacceptable. Their neutrality in this matter is impaired. We've requested that Aero Wright receive a trial by combat."

A hush fell over the room. *A trial by combat?* Danika thought. She couldn't believe they'd made that request. It was highly unusual.

"A vulgarity, don't you think?" Vinick said. "I wish you'd reconsider. We haven't conducted a trial by combat in many centuries. A trial by the Majors would be much more civilized and less likely to stir up unrest in the ranks."

Vinick smiled warmly, but the old Forger shook his head. "Our terms are clear and very fair. We could harbor Aero Wright indefinitely and keep the Foundry on lockdown. It's well within our rights to offer him sanctuary and the protection of the Foundry. It's also our decision whether we reopen our doors to your soldiers."

The smile faded from Vinick's face, replaced with a look of fury. "Refresh my memory. What would this trial by combat entail?"

The Forger pulled out an old parchment scroll. He began reading from the colony's charter. "The accused may request a trial by combat against his main accuser to prove his innocence on the field of battle in Falchion-to-Falchion combat."

The Forger looked up and exchanged a glance with Aero, who quickly nodded his head. *So this was all the deserter's idea*, Danika thought. *Very clever.* He knew that a trial by the Majors would result in a death sentence. Fighting bought him a chance.

Vinick raised his eyebrows. "His main accuser?"

"That would be you, Supreme General," Aero said, speaking up for the first time. His eyes bored into Vinick. "You're my main accuser. Does anybody doubt that?" He let his words hang in the air. "You're not afraid to face me again, are you?"

"Of course not, boy," Vinick snapped. "I fear no soldier."

The Forger nodded. "Then we are agreed? A trial by combat?"

Vinick whispered with Doyle. A few heated seconds passed. He straightened up. "Brother, your terms are acceptable," Vinick said. "But on one condition."

"Condition?" the Forger said. "What's that?"

"My increased responsibilities in light of the reemergence of the Fourth Continuum have kept me from my customary Falchion training," Vinick said.

Aero narrowed his eyes, but the old Forger shot him a pointed look and held up his hand. "Supreme General, I don't see how that's relevant—"

"I want to choose a soldier to fight in my place," Vinick interrupted.

"A substitution?" the Forger said. "That seems highly unorthodox."

"There's precedent," Vinick replied and gestured to Doyle.

Doyle pulled out his tablet and started reading. "During wartime, if challenged to trial by combat, the Supreme General may select a substitute to duel in his place. The choice of the substitute soldier shall lie solely at the Supreme General's discretion."

Danika felt a shiver run up her spine. *Vinick was expecting this*, she realized. *He and Doyle came prepared. Acting surprised was only a ruse to get his way.*

"Thank you, Major Doyle," Vinick said with a curt nod.

He turned his attention back to the Forger. "Brother, surely you must agree that we are at war." He gestured to the fresh Falchions floating across the room. "It's the reason your Order has been laboring around the clock to produce new blades."

The Forger nodded. "Indeed, these are troubling times, to say the least. Nobody doubts that. Will you excuse me for a moment? I must consult with my Order."

"Of course," Vinick said. "Take all the time you need."

The old Forger and Aero rose from their pillows and crossed the room, where they huddled with the other Forgers. Danika could hear their muffled voices. She caught parts of what they were saying. ". . . think it's a dirty trick . . . can't be trusted . . ."

That was Aero.

". . . no leverage . . . they've agreed to all the other terms . . ."

". . . must get our young brother back . . . wrongfully imprisoned . . ."

Danika glanced at Vinick, who sat calmly sipping his tea. He appeared untroubled by this turn of events. Meanwhile, Doyle stood up with a grimace.

"These cushions aren't good for my joints," he grumbled. Then he made a show of stretching his legs and parading around the room to loosen them up.

After another minute of heated discussion, the old Forger

and Aero returned to their cushions. Doyle followed suit, claiming his place next to Vinick. He was clutching his tablet. He quickly darkened the screen. Vinick glanced around the circle.

"Brother, has your Order reached a decision?"

"We agree to your terms," the Forger said. "But you must name your substitute now. We won't accept any last-minute changes. So whom do you choose?"

Vinick smiled and fixed his gaze on Aero. "Major Rothman is my choice. I believe you're already acquainted, aren't you? Her combat marks at the Agoge were impressive. Almost as good as yours."

Danika looked up in surprise. The Supreme General had chosen her. That was a great honor. Aero leaned in and whispered in the Forger's ear. Danika caught a snippet.

". . . messing with my emotions again . . . it won't work this time . . ."

The Forger nodded and straightened up. "Supreme General, you may amend the agreement naming Major Rothman as your substitute."

"Thank you, brother," Vinick said, and they shook hands on it.

Doyle scrawled on his tablet. He passed it to both men to sign and then to Aero lastly. Once they had all signed the agreement, Doyle read aloud from it.

"The trial by combat between Aero Wright and Major Danika Rothman will take place at 0900 hours tomorrow," he said in his throaty voice. "Falchion-to-Falchion combat in the simulator. The controls will be set to kill. It will be a fight to the death. The Forgers will select the venue in consultation with the Majors, but it shall remain a secret from the participants until the trial by combat commences. The trial shall be made public, so that any soldiers who wish to view it may tune in to the feed . . . "

While Doyle continued reading, Danika poured a fresh cup of tea. She took a sip, but it scorched her tongue. With a grimace, she set the mug aside, slopping tea onto the table.

The young Forger rushed over to mop it up. Her eyes roved over his shaved head and crimson robes. He was only a year or two behind her at the Agoge.

How different their paths, she thought. He lived with this ancient Order, while tomorrow she would be fighting for her life with the powerful weapons they forged.

Her thoughts were interrupted by the old Forger. "Major Rothman?" he said with a questioning look. He held out his hands, but she stared back in confusion.

"Major Rothman, hand over your blade," Vinick said.

"My blade, sir?" she stammered. "Is that wise?"

Vinick rolled his eyes. "Would you rather fight without a fresh charge? We've come to a mutually beneficial agreement. The Order bears us no animosity."

"My dear, I promise to take good care of your blade," the old Forger said. He peered at her with a kindly smile. "We are sworn to serve the Falchions. We would never tamper with one of our creations or seek to destroy it. You can trust us."

"It's Major Rothman," she snapped before handing her blade over.

The old Forger accepted it with a bow and passed it to the younger Forger, who shepherded it over to the other Forgers. They got to work charging the weapon.

Danika felt naked without it, but Vinick was right. She needed a fresh charge for the duel tomorrow. They all stood up. Vinick and the old Forger shook hands while Doyle transmitted a copy of the agreement from his tablet. Aero turned to Danika. "Good luck, Major Rothman. May the strongest soldier win tomorrow."

"Good luck," Danika repeated, but inside she was seething. *This is my chance*, she thought. *Tomorrow, you will feel the sting of my blade piercing your heart.*

"Majors, let's reconvene on the bridge," Vinick said. Doyle caught his eye and passed his tablet to Vinick. "Did you get everything, Major?" Vinick whispered.

It was soft, but Danika heard it. Her ears pricked up.

She glanced at the tablet as Vinick thumbed at the device.

Images of the Foundry flashed over the screen. Doyle must have snapped them during the meeting, when he made a show of stretching his legs. But what did he want with them? Before Danika could ask about it, Vinick leaned in close. She could feel his breath on her neck.

"Hope you're ready to fight, girl. This is your chance to redeem yourself after that unfortunate incident in the Docking Bay. You don't want to fail twice, do you?"

"No, sir!" she said with a salute. "I am the stronger soldier. I will vanquish the deserter. He has grown weak and idle during his time in exile, while I've been training and practicing my drills. I'll be ready for him."

"Very good, Major," Vinick said. "I hope it's true for your sake."

Chapter 28
THE HUNTING TRIP

Seeker

Seeker felt her body clench with fear as the figure crept into the tunnel.

Did Rooter tell his scouts to kill her and make it look like a hunting accident? He'd been eyeing the Beacon, coveting it. Well, they could try to take it from her wrist, but she wouldn't give up without a fight. She crouched down low, raising her claws.

The figure crept closer.

Seeker scented the air—and relaxed.

"Don't hurt me, Strong One," Slayer purred, throwing herself at Seeker's feet. "Saw the Light in the Darkness. Followed it into the tunnel . . . and found Seeker."

Seeker lowered her claws. She sniffed the air to make sure Slayer wasn't being followed. "Slayer, stop groveling," she said, feeling pity for her former tormentor. "Also, I'm not a Strong One—I'm a Weakling. Always have been, always will be."

"Yes, Weakling," Slayer said eagerly. "Always Weakling."

Her stomach looked bloated from hunger. Licking her

lips, she eyed Seeker's rucksack. Seeker gripped the straps tighter, feeling protective of her haul. It was an old habit. "Slayer, did you find the other Strong Ones? Hiding in the tunnels?"

"Yes . . . found them," Slayer replied, dancing from foot to foot. "Told them nice Seeker returned with the Light in the Darkness. Brought offerings for Strong Ones, and wants to lead us back to the Brightside. The Strong Ones want to come with you."

Seeker felt a burst of hope. "How many?"

"About a hundred," Slayer said, counting them out on her fingers. Noticing Seeker's disappointment, she grew nervous. "That's all that's left from our pack. The rest starved or threw themselves into the chasm after the Weaklings banished us."

"Could there be more?" Seeker asked. "Maybe hiding in the tunnels?"

"A few stragglers maybe."

Slayer tugged at Seeker's arm, trying to lead her down another tunnel. "Seeker, this way. Strong Ones waiting for you at the Door in the Wall. Ready to go now."

Seeker shrugged her off and shook her head. "Not yet, I need more time. I have to get the Weaklings to come with us. Their leader watching me and making it hard."

"Rooter?" Slayer said and spat on the floor. "He's a filthy, sneaky, stinkin' creature. Crusher should have feasted on him when he had the chance."

"No more feasting," Seeker growled. "That is done."

"Of course, no feasting," Slayer nodded, appearing chastised. "Just be careful. Rooter can't be trusted. He's worse than Crusher. You'll see—"

Suddenly, rustling noises erupted in the dark tunnel. Slayer jerked her head around and sniffed the air. When she caught the scent, her eyes flashed with fear.

"Weaklings coming back . . ."

Her eyes snapped back to the rucksack, so Seeker tossed her two ratters. Slayer snagged them out of the air with her teeth, dragging them down the tunnel.

"Slayer, find the stragglers," Seeker whispered as she crept away. "Bring them to the Door in the Wall, and wait for me there. Do you understand?"

"Yes, Weakling." Slayer hissed and vanished into the Darkness.

The rustling grew louder. Crawler reappeared in the tunnel. His eyes darted to her Beacon. Seeker fought the urge to conceal it. He carried ratters in his mouth. He spat them out on the floor. "Saw the light in the tunnel. Seeker, catch any ratters?"

She pulled out her offerings. "Only five . . . but they're fat and juicy."

"Six for me," Crawler said, adding his ratters to her pile.

She stuffed their haul into her rucksack. Their bodies felt warm and malleable. They hadn't been dead long enough to turn stiff and cold. She glanced around. It was just her and Crawler in the tunnel. She might not get a chance to talk to him alone again.

"Rooter will be pleased with our offerings," she ventured, invoking the proper platitude while watching Crawler closely to gauge his reaction.

He eyed her carefully. "Rooter keeps us safe and our bellies full."

"But you hunt and do all the work," she pointed out. She was treading on dangerous territory now. "While Rooter sits on his throne and grows fat and lazy."

Seeker could feel her heart fluttering like a wild creature. Her cheeks felt warmer than usual; sweat broke out over her entire body. Crawler sensed her physical reaction to him. His nostrils flared, and a smile twisted his lips.

"Better than it was under the Strong Ones," he growled in a low voice. "When we were starving in the tunnels. He tells us what to do and keeps our pack together."

"Food and shelter. That's all?"

"That's all Weaklings care about. Can't think for ourselves."

"Some of us are different," Seeker said as her Beacon flared brighter and faster, giving away her racing heart. She winced—she should have covered it up. "*Seeker, Seeker, she creeps and she sneaks . . .*" Crawler sang softly under his breath. "*Sticks her nose where it reeks . . .*"

Seeker grimaced. "Nasty song—Strong Ones made it up."

His eyes locked onto her. "Beautiful song . . . Seeker is different. Seeker found the Door in the Wall and went to the Brightside. Seeker claimed the Gold Circle."

"Well, it's not as great as it sounds," Seeker grumbled. Her cheeks felt even hotter. He reached for her hand—the one with the armlet encircling her wrist.

"You're not the only one who can think for herself."

He shot her that knowing look again. Before she could reply, he tugged her down the tunnel. "Let's get back to the bridge, or the others will be suspicious."

o   o   o

They galloped through the tunnels and back toward Agartha. Seeker was faster and bolted ahead. She knew the way by heart. Thoughts stampeded through her brain, flying faster than her hands and feet skittering over the rock path.

Why did Crawler hold her hand? Why did he say all those nice things about her? She didn't know, but her heart raced faster—and it wasn't from physical exertion. Clearly, he wasn't happy with Rooter. Maybe more Weaklings felt like he did.

That gave her hope.

She started across the bridge, but Crawler grabbed her hand and pulled her back. His lips brushed against her ear. She could smell him—sweat and spice and dust. "Heard voices in the cavern," he hissed. "You were talking to *them*, weren't you?"

Seeker squirmed in his grip. He *knew* about the Strong Ones. "It's nothing . . ." she stammered. "I just feel sorry for them. Gave them ratters . . . that's all."

His grip tightened. "It's more than that—and we both know it."

"Listen, I came back for a reason—"

"No, I don't need to know," Crawler cut her off. His eyes bored into her. "Safer that way. I'll keep your secret from Rooter . . . if you promise me one thing."

She swallowed hard. "What's that?"

"When you go back to the Brightside, take me with you." His voice was barely audible, but she could hear it. "The Darkness of the Below isn't my home anymore."

Crawler held her gaze for another long second.

Then he pivoted and charged across the narrow bridge. Seeker felt her heart thumping in her chest. *He knows*—she thought—*and he wants to come with me.* They rejoined their hunting party by the city's collapsing gates. Though her heart was still racing, Seeker tugged open her rucksack, showing off the size of their haul.

"Eleven fat ones," she bragged.

Greaser grinned. "Rooter will be pleased."

o   o   o

Indeed, Rooter was pleased with their offerings when they piled the ratters and buggers in front of the altar. He stood up from his throne, his knees popping. *He sits too much*, Seeker observed. *He grows lazy and weak.* "Fresh offerings," Rooter proclaimed to the pack. His voice reverberated through the room. "Weaklings, tonight we feast."

The Weaklings stomped on the floor.

"Feast!" they chanted. "Feast!"

Seeker felt sickened that they were using that filthy word, but she did her best to hide it. Rooter turned to her. His eyes fixed onto her Beacon. He licked his lips. "Seeker, you hunted well," he said. "So you will be my special guest at the Feast."

"Thank you, Rooter." She bowed down low. She could feel jealous looks digging into her back from Bruiser and Trencher, though she would have gladly traded places with either of them. She didn't want to be Rooter's *special* anything.

"Seeker, now rest up," Rooter said. "You must be tired from hunting."

Crawler shot her another knowing look before he slunk away, casting himself down by the altar for a nap. *Take me with you*, she remembered him saying and felt a secret thrill. She tried to shake it off, but the feeling lingered anyway. She rooted around on the stone floor for a comfortable position. Her mouth watered at the prospect of the Feast, but then it turned sour with fear. She probed for Jared with the Beacon.

It's time, isn't it? she thought as her eyelids grew heavy. *At the Feast.*

Her Beacon flashed, letting her know that Jared approved.

At least, after days of waiting around, everything would finally come to a head. Comforted by that thought, she curled into a tight ball and felt truly drowsy for the first time since she'd arrived back here. Crawler would follow her to the Brightside, and so would the remaining Strong Ones. But would any other Weaklings come with them?

She knew only one thing for sure.

Whatever happens, Rooter isn't going to like it.

o   o   o

Seeker didn't wake up gently—she was jerked from sleep by rough hands.

"Let me . . . go!" she snarled, trying to wriggle free.

More hands clamped down, yanking her up. Fear shot through her blood. The Weaklings dragged her to the altar and threw her down. She leapt to her feet, her eyes landing on Rooter. He sat on his throne with a treacherous grin pulling at his lips.

"Rooter . . . what's happening?" Seeker asked.

His smile deepened into a leer. "You're my special guest at the Feast."

"Special guest?" she repeated, trying to make sense of what was happening. But her head felt heavy and clogged with sleep.

The Weaklings surrounded her, clutching knives and spears carved from sharpened bone that glinted in the light from her Beacon. Seeker staggered back, tripping into the pile of offerings—ratters, buggers, and tubers recently dug up with clumps of dirt still clinging to their roots. The Weaklings licked their lips and looked . . . *hungry*.

The Feast, Seeker thought dimly.

She felt a deep shudder of revulsion. When the Strong Ones ruled their colony, that word had carried a different connotation—it meant cannibalism. That was when a horrific thought dawned on her.

They're going to eat me.

Chapter 29
IN ONE PIECE

Aero Wright

A ero, you'd better come back in one piece," Myra said. Worry creased her face, making her look older than her seventeen years. "Do you bloody hear me?"

She faded and threatened to vanish.

"I'm losing her signal," the old Forger called from behind the Colloquium Machine. He toggled a few levers and twisted a knob, making her projection snap back.

"One piece, roger that," Aero said with a grin.

She didn't look any less worried. "Are you sure this is the only way?"

Aero reached for her, but his hand passed right through her projection. "We discussed it, remember?" He spoke quickly. Their time was limited, not only because they might lose her signal, but also because 0900 hours was fast approaching.

"Yeah, I know. So why do I feel so anxious?"

"Nerves before combat are a common affliction. So is vomiting."

She laughed in spite of herself. "Thank the Oracle, I don't

feel like puking. How can you seem so relaxed? You're the one putting your life on the line."

"Right, I've done this before," he said with a wry smile. "Remember, it's the only way to get Vinick to release our friends. If I can win the trial by combat, he's agreed to restore my standing in the army. That will grant me access to the ship and soldiers. Maybe I can convince them to throw their support behind us.."

"Vinick can't be trusted," she warned with a nervous shake of her head. Her curls tussled around, looking so life-like. "How do you know he'll keep up his side of the deal?"

"The Forgers transmitted the agreement to the entire ship. By now, every soldier has seen it. His signature is right there, authorizing my release if I prove myself in a trial by combat. If he reneges on the deal, then the whole ship will know of his treachery."

"Fine, but what if you lose? Don't underestimate your opponent."

Across the Foundry, the Forgers were busy charging his Falchion. He had already donned his lightweight deployment suit. His empty scabbard pulled at his waist like an amputated limb. "Now you sound like Wren. She's always worrying about me."

"Is that such a bad thing?"

"No, it's good. It means you care."

"Well, that's one way to put it."

"Fine, what word would you use?" he said, shifting uncomfortably. His neck started to feel hot. He tugged at his collar. "This emotion stuff still feels weird."

"Right . . . I love you," she mumbled quickly, her cheeks flashing crimson. "Now don't go messing it up by dying on me. Is that understood, soldier?"

He cocked his eyebrow. "Now you're mocking me."

She glowered at him, but somehow it made her appear even more alluring. Her projection looked so real—so life-like—that it was painful not to be able to reach out and touch her. His Beacon flashed and betrayed his thoughts.

"Alluring, huh?" she said with a quirk of her lips.

"Right . . . sorry." He fidgeted with his empty scabbard. Combat didn't make him feel sick, but talking to Myra about his feelings made him want to puke out his guts.

"And?" she prodded with a cock of her eyebrow.

"If it makes you feel better, I promise not to die yet," he muttered, feeling heat scorching his cheeks. "I've faced Danika in combat. She's a strong soldier. Her combat marks at the Agoge were high, but I defeated her once already." He paused, still fidgeting with the scabbard. "Only, something about her selection has been bothering me."

Myra floated toward him. "What is it?"

He frowned. "Why choose her over a more experienced soldier?"

"Because Vinick trusts her?" Myra suggested. "Also, he's used her to stir up your emotional state before. He could be resorting to the same dirty trick again."

"Yeah, I thought the same thing at first. So did the Forgers. But Vinick isn't dumb. He knows I'd be expecting that, so I'd be less likely to fall for it this time. Plus, I'm better at controlling my Beacon. It's not likely to undermine me like that again."

"You're right," she agreed. "It's suspicious."

"Thought so," he said. "Glad it's not just my imagination. Wren wouldn't have agreed with me so easily."

"I'm not Wren."

The way she stared at him sent shivers up his spine. It was true—Myra wasn't like Wren at all. She was strange, unpredictable, and impulsive, but also deeply intelligent. Wren harbored an emotional streak too, but she controlled it. Her mind always ran to the practical. That made her a great soldier, one who could keep a combat unit on their toes and running on a tight schedule. But Myra was something else altogether.

A tentative voice snapped him out of his thoughts.

"Your Falchion is charged," the young Forger said, the one who had served them tea. He passed the blade to Aero, who accepted it gladly. He took a few test swings, feeling it cut through the air. It surged with the fresh charge. Satisfied, he sheathed the blade in his scabbard, feeling the comforting weight of it pulling at his waist.

He noticed Myra watching him with a strange expression. The Forgers couldn't see her. It probably looked like he was talking to himself, but he didn't care.

"Don't look so damn pessimistic," he said. "It's not like I'm walking into my funeral. Where I come from, combat is a reason for celebration. You should be happy for me. I'm about to prove my innocence through my prowess as a soldier."

"And end someone else's life in the process," she said with a disapproving frown. "That's no cause for celebration—at least, not where I come from."

"Better than ending my own," he shot back.

"Right, I know," she said, sounding frustrated. She wrenched her hand through her hair. "I just wish there was another way. One that didn't involve certain death for you or for a young girl ordered into battle by her commander. She's just following orders."

"True, but I've got a feeling it's personal."

"Because you were betrothed?"

"Yup, that," he said, blushing again. But then he turned more serious. "Myra, we're fighting a war now. There are going to be casualties on both sides. Lots of them. You've got to make peace with that somehow. It's the only way we're going to survive this. If you think Vinick is bad, wait until the Fourth Continuum shows up."

"You're right, but that doesn't mean I have to like it." She floated over and locked her eyes on him. "Promise me—you won't kill Danika unless it's the only way."

He saluted. "Yes, I swear it."

The old Forger called over. "I'm afraid 0900 hours is approaching."

Myra's projection started to dissolve in front of his eyes.

"Remember, I'm coming back," he said quickly. "The

next time we speak, you'll be with Tinker and Kaleb. I'm going to send them home. That's another promise."

And then she was gone.

He wasn't sure if she'd heard the last thing he said. The old Forger slid back from the Colloquium Machine and hobbled over. He looked older, Aero noticed. This struggle was wearing on him. "Come on, let's go," the old Forger said. "My sworn brothers and sisters are going to escort you down to the simulator to make sure you arrive safely."

"You mean, to make sure Vinick doesn't try anything?" Aero said.

The Forger winked. "That too."

o   o   o

The journey through the corridors was uneventful. The rustling of the Forgers' robes, the soft thuds of their slippered feet did little to calm Aero's nerves, which had finally flared up. He felt a strange sensation—it was fear, he realized. The old Forger glanced back.

"*Fear is only a state of mind,*" he quoted from their teachings. "It's a primitive survival instinct hardwired into our brains to help us survive. But through mindfulness, we can transcend our most primal, intransigent impulses."

"Hardwired," Aero said. "That sounds about right."

The Forger gave him a sympathetic look. "Your opponent will feel it too. Probably more than you. You've fought a duel to the death before. She's never faced such a challenge. Also, she's afraid of failing. I noticed it at our meeting."

"I noticed that too," Aero said. "It's a lot of pressure."

The Forger nodded. "Yes, but I suspect there's more to it. Did you know that Major Rothman had a younger sister?" Aero shook his head. "Well, personal records are private and sealed, of course. But every soldier visits the Foundry to charge their Falchions. We keep diligent records. I pulled Major Rothman's file last night, looking for any useful information. Her younger sister was a shy, sweet girl named Lillian."

"Wait, that sounds familiar," Aero said. "She was banished, wasn't she? I vaguely remember something about that happening when I was a student."

"For cheating at the Agoge," the Forger confirmed. "The girl's sensitive temperament was not valued by the Drillmasters. They tried to train it out of her by treating her harshly. But that only served to break her spirit and amplify her insecurities. She struggled in her classes, resorting to cheating in order to pass. They caught her hacking into the exams. Usually, my Order tries to choose such students from the Agoge before permanent damage can be done, but Lillian slipped under our radar."

The old Forger looked pained. Aero took all this in. "And you think the girl's shortcomings might have impacted her sister?"

"Major Rothman is afraid it could happen to her," he replied. "That she will prove weak, like her sister. Imagine the psychological pressure that could exert on a person. How it might cloud their judgment. Make them do questionable things."

They lapsed into silence, while Aero considered what the Forger had said. He wasn't sure how it helped him, but he tucked the knowledge away.

A few minutes later, they reached the simulators. Major Rothman was already suited up with her helmet fastened. She glanced his way, frowned in acknowledgment, and then unsheathed her Falchion and stepped into the first chamber. The door hissed shut behind her. Looking up from his tablet, Major Doyle marched over to Aero.

"You're late," he said in a curt voice.

His eyes flicked to the parade of Forgers and narrowed in annoyance. "I see you brought your escorts. Well, no need for them now. They can return to the Foundry. Fasten your helmet and report to Chamber 2 right away—or risk forfeiture."

Aero glanced down the corridor. It was empty, aside from Doyle's testy presence. "Where's Supreme General Vinick?" he asked. "And the other Majors?"

"None of your concern," Doyle snapped. He tapped his tablet agitatedly. "I'm running this simulation. The Supreme General has honored the terms of your agreement. His substitute is here to fight in his stead. That's all you need to know." Aero considered pressing his case, but Doyle added, "Two minutes until you forfeit."

Before Aero could say anything else, a helmet slipped over his head and snapped into place. Everything went quiet, muffled by the padding. The sensors wouldn't boot up until he stepped into the chamber. The young Forger who had fetched it smiled at him through the visor and then backed away, rejoining his Order with a swishing of his robes. The old Forger bowed one last time. His face creased with affection.

"I regret that we must return to the Foundry," he said in parting. "We've already been away too long. Our machines require constant tending. Two of my brothers will monitor the trial from the control room. Remember what I told you."

"Thank you, brother," Aero said, his voice muffled by the helmet.

The Forgers retreated down the corridor. Doyle rushed Aero into the simulation chamber. The door hissed shut behind him. Aero felt a sucking of cold air as the room pressurized and dropped in temperature. He settled into the grooves in the floor where he was supposed to stand and unsheathed his Falchion. He would wait to morph it until he knew more about the venue. It was supposed to be a surprise to both of them. A green light flashed on in his helmet. He heard Doyle's voice through the headphones.

"Aero Wright is hereby accused by the Supreme General of being a deserter and a traitor," Doyle said. His message was broadcast to the entire ship along with the feed of the trial. "He murdered Supreme General Brillstein and stole the Beacon."

Aero felt a fresh wave of anger at the false accusations. Vinick was the one who had killed their last Supreme General and framed Aero for it. Aero would never have taken up arms against a commander, especially when it was his own father.

"This is a trial by combat between Aero Wright and Major Danika Rothman," Doyle went on in his droll voice. "The simulator controls have been set to kill. This is a fight to the death. May the strongest soldier emerge victorious."

Aero felt his suit booting up. He was standing in the simulator chamber—and then a second later—the venue materialized in a rush of blinding, midday sunlight.

Where am I? he thought as his breathing sped up.

Once his vision adjusted, the first thing he noticed was that he was standing in a large pit filled with yellow sand. His boots shifted on the unstable turf. He jerked his head around to get his bearings. A towering, cylindrical building rose up around him. It enclosed the pit, effectively caging him inside it. Hundreds of archways dotted the building, spanning several stories high and opening up to bench seating. The venue didn't have a ceiling, allowing the sunlight to beam down with ferocious intensity.

His Beacon pulsed; Aero heard his father's voice. *My son, are there any clues that tell you something important about this venue? Hurry, look around.*

Aero spun in a circle. The pit contained no obstacles. There was no environmental interference. At least, none that he could detect.

It was almost like . . . the venue was designed for fighting.

That sparked a memory. On second glance, something about the structure did seem familiar. Then it clicked—this was the Colosseum, the ancient Roman edifice where the gladiators once fought. He'd learned about it in his history classes.

Suddenly, a hostile voice penetrated the stadium.

"Die, deserter!"

Danika materialized right in front of him. Her Falchion was morphed into an ahlspiess. She jabbed the razor-sharp point at his vulnerable middle. Aero morphed his Falchion into a shield and raised it. Danika's pike deflected off it with a clang, releasing a shower of golden sparks. The Colosseum's benches started to fill up with avatars as soldiers logged into their terminals to watch the trial.

Danika recovered quickly. Cheers erupted from the stands.

"Die, deserter!" the soldiers yelled. The spectators had taken up Danika's battle cry. Buoyed by that and her own adrenaline, she pivoted with a few agile steps, repositioned her body, and stabbed at Aero again with her long spear.

That blow almost skewered his head.

He staggered back, losing his balance, and felt a cold rush of fear. Clearly, Danika had been training hard since they last faced off, while he'd been on the run and unable to practice his drills. For the first time in his life, he doubted his ability to win a fight.

Starry hell, I'm already losing.

That was his last thought before Danika charged again.

PART IV
TRANSGRESSION

War must be, while we defend our lives against a destroyer who would devour all; but I do not love the bright sword for its sharpness, nor the arrow for its swiftness, nor the warrior for his glory. I love only that which they defend.

—J.R.R. Tolkien, *The Two Towers*

Chapter 30
THE SYNOD'S CHAMBERS

The Prisoner

The Surfacers raided Sector 10!"

The prisoner heard pounding footsteps and shouts coming from inside the Synod's chambers. Straining against his shackles, he pressed his ear to the door. He heard muffled voices through the thick barrier, and then more shouting: "What do they want with the Spare Parts Room? Just piles of old junk in there—"

"How many times do I have to tell you? The heathens *want* to spread unrest and blasphemy through our colony. We can't allow news of this raid to leak out. It could cause loyal Factum to panic. Head Patroller, can we contain the damage?"

That was Padre Flavius.

The prisoner cowered away from the door. It took him a long time to gather his courage. Cautiously, he pressed his ear back to the thick barrier. His wrists ached from pulling against the chains. He caught snippets of the Synod's secret deliberations.

". . . changed the codes on the sector doors . . ."

". . . holding our Patrollers hostage in the Engineering Room . . ."

". . . the Docks raided too . . ."

". . . rebellion is getting out of hand . . ."

During his many weeks—or was it months?—of captivity, the prisoner had never heard such alarm in the Chancellors' voices. Such uncertainty. They sounded *afraid* of the Surfacers. Was that possible?

"Fear not, my fellow Chancellors," Padre Flavius thundered in the deep voice that he usually reserved for sermons. "I've poured over the latest reports on the rebels. I've discovered a weakness in their plans. On my orders, Head Patroller Waters arrested some Factum children, pulling them from their compartments in the middle of the night—"

"Factum children? Padre Flavius, are you sure that's wise?"

The prisoner recognized that voice. It belonged to Chancellor Sebold. He felt a memory tug at his muddled brain. It was of the Chancellor's eldest son. *Kaleb* . . . the name shot through his head. But then the memory faded away.

"Chancellor, are you questioning my tactics?" Padre Flavius said. He sounded peevish. "Since when do you care about the lowly spawn of Programmers?"

"Of course not," sniffed Chancellor Sebold. "I don't care about Programmers or their spawn, but their trade remains loyal to us. Won't this push them over the edge? All Factum grow uneasy in these dark times. We must tread carefully."

"I agree wholeheartedly," Padre Flavius said. "And that's why we must resort to these extraordinary measures. Chancellors, I've consulted the Oracle of the Sea. Heathens now threaten us from all sides. This is the only way to defeat them."

"What are you going to do with the Factum spawn?" Sebold asked.

"I've ordered the Head Patroller to torture them—but keep them alive," Padre Flavius said. His voice took on a menacing quality. "Their suffering is the key to our plans. Then let's give their parents a nice little tour of the Pen, shall we?"

The prisoner listened for more objections, but the Chancellors remained silent. No one dared oppose Padre Flavius. "It's settled then," the priest said. "I'll inform the Head Patroller to proceed as planned. As the Oracle commands, so it shall be done."

"Amen," said the Chancellors.

Suddenly, the door dilated in front of the prisoner's nose. He scrambled back, his chains clinking loudly and giving him away. The stench of perfume hit his nose full force, making him sneeze violently. The priest strode into his private chamber. His slippered feet padded over the carpet.

"Heathen, were you eavesdropping on us?" Padre Flavius sneered. "You know that's strictly forbidden. The deliberations of this Synod are secret."

"No, never!" the prisoner stammered. "Mercy, Padre, have mercy!"

"You filthy heathen." Padre Flavius seized the prisoner by the throat and squeezed. "You defile the Oracle with your sins." He squeezed tighter.

Finally, when the prisoner was about to pass out, the priest released his grip. The prisoner collapsed on the floor, gasping for air. The plush carpet felt cool and silken against his cheeks. "Thank you . . . Padre . . . for showing mercy . . ." he croaked out. He crawled over and kissed the priest's feet. "Praise the Oracle . . ."

"Prisoner, what's your name?" Padre Flavius said. When the prisoner didn't respond, the priest kicked him in the chin. Stars danced in front of his vision.

"Heathen . . . heathen," he mumbled. His damaged windpipe burned like he'd gargled firewater. "By the Oracle, sinners don't deserve proper names ..."

"Heathen, tell me you want it."

"No . . . please . . . not again . . ."

Another blow landed on his ribs, forcing the wind from his chest. Then another crashed into his back, making him cry out in pain. He writhed on the carpet.

"Say it," the priest commanded.

"Please beat me . . . purge me of sin . . ."

"As the Oracle commands, so it shall be done."

"Amen . . ." said the prisoner.

In the midst of the brutal beating, when the pain became unbearable, the prisoner's mind left his body behind on the carpet and drifted away. *Kaleb.* The name shot through his head again. It kept him from tumbling over the brink of madness. Another blow landed on his head. White light exploded in his vision, and then the world threatened to go dark, like the permanent dimming of the automatic lights.

But still, the prisoner held on.

He had a secret.

The fetters on his wrists had grown loose as his flesh had shrunk and contracted around his bones. With some wriggling, he could slip them off. He had been too afraid of the Red Cloak to attempt an escape, but now he'd learned something important. The Surfacers had seized control of the Spare Parts Room and the Docks. And there was more—the Synod didn't understand the Surfacers' true motivation. They couldn't fathom why the rebels would covet the Spare Parts Room with its heaps of old junk.

But the prisoner guessed their plans.

Hope stirred in his heart where only despair had settled. It told him to slip his wrists free from the shackles. It told him that he could escape from Padre Flavius. It told him that his chance would come soon. He just had to watch and wait.

And hold on a little longer.

Chapter 31
A MATTER OF PERSPECTIVE

The Order of the Foundry

The old Forger led his sworn brothers and sisters back to the Foundry. They moved at a rapid clip. They rarely ventured outside their domain; partially, it was superstition, but mostly, it was practical. Their machines needed constant monitoring. Also, their protections did not extend beyond the walls of the Foundry. But these were extraordinary times, and they called for extraordinary measures. They reached the Foundry's door.

"Thank you for your brave service," the old Forger said to the soldiers guarding it. He smiled warmly. "It is most appreciated. Captain Zakkay, may we pass?"

"Of course, brother," Zakkay replied. He signaled to the other soldiers. They lowered their Falchions and stepped aside to let the Forgers through.

The old Forger approached the door and began the complex unlocking process. As his fingers danced over the golden metal, manipulating and kneading it, his thoughts drifted back to Aero. By now, he was probably locked in fierce combat. They'd carefully chosen the venue—the Roman Colosseum. They selected it because it was designed for fighting and offered no environmental interference. Aero was the stronger soldier; he could beat Danika in a fair fight. Thus, the venue favored him.

He'd been surprised when Vinick agreed to their choice. But it was a reasonable suggestion, one of the most famed combat arenas in history. More than four hundred thousand gladiators, many slaves, and one million animals lost their lives there. It also made for unobstructed viewing for the soldiers who wanted to tune in. From the emptiness in the corridors, the he could tell that most of the ship had logged in.

The old Forger finished the unlocking process and stepped back from the door. It rippled, dilating into the wall. Warm air rushed out to greet him. He inhaled, feeling his muscles unclench. Being away had made him more tense than he realized. He could sense that their machines needed tending. He started through the doorway, but something stabbed into his back. With a cry of pain, he spun around to see Major Wright.

"How does that feel, brother?"

Her lips twisted into a cruel smile. Her Falchion was morphed into a *nandoa*, a curved sword with a knuckle guard. The tip was coated in blood. *His blood*, he realized, as he slipped to his knees. More blood gushed from the deep wound in his back.

"But we have protections . . ." he sputtered in shock.

"Protections that ended when you stepped out of your precious Foundry," Vinick sneered. He towered over the Forger, casting a long shadow. "You betrayed me when you offered sanctuary to the deserter. Your Order will pay for their deception."

"But . . . who will charge your Falchions?" the old Forger gasped wetly. His hands grasped at his back, as if trying to keep more blood from spilling out.

Around him, he could hear the grunting and screaming noises of a battle. No, that wasn't right. A battle included clanging and explosions of sparks. This wasn't a battle—it was a slaughter. His Order was unarmed. They didn't even know how to fight. The Majors were slaughtering them with the very weapons they had so diligently forged.

"Oh, don't worry," Vinick said. "I'll keep a few of you alive as my slaves—the younger ones that you haven't brainwashed against me. If they refuse to charge our Falchions, there's always torture. That usually proves quite effective."

"But this is . . . wrong . . ." the Forger trailed off.

He could feel his life slipping away. He slumped onto his side, feeling the cold floor pressing into his cheek. His vision went blurry. The blood leaking from his chest had slowed from a gush to a trickle, but that wasn't a sign of improvement.

"That's a matter of perspective," Vinick said with a lazy flick of his Falchion. "The winners write the history texts." He bent down by the Forger, his face contorting into a terrifying smile. "You didn't think I'd actually let you get away with that, did you? Agree to let the deserter win back his freedom and wander my ship?"

"The trial . . . it was a ruse . . ." the Forger said.

He realized the brilliance of Vinick's plan. The trial was a distraction. That's why Vinick had agreed to it so easily. Most soldiers were logged in, watching the feed, so Vinick could conduct his vile mission without interference from soldiers who might retain some loyalty to the Foundry. It was also an easy way for him to dispose of Major Rothman, who failed to kill Aero when she'd had the chance.

"Clever, don't you think?" Vinick said. "By the time the trial is over, I'll feed my soldiers the story that I want them to hear. Just like I fed them the story that Aero Wright murdered Supreme General Brillstein and stole the Beacon."

"Aero . . . will defeat her . . ." the old Forger sputtered weakly.

Vinick laughed. "Brother, sorry to deliver the bad news. But they won't survive the trial, not with what I have planned. They'll both die fighting like the ancient gladiators, putting on a spectacular show guaranteed to keep the viewers rapt until *this* is all over." He wrinkled his nose in distaste at the carnage now littering the corridor.

The old Forger wanted to tell Vinick that he'd pay for his actions. That his soldiers would see through his lies. That history did not reward traitors and murderers. That criminals always paid for their crimes. But that wasn't true, and he knew it.

"By the stars . . . go to hell . . ." he whispered instead.

"Foolish old man," Vinick snorted and left the old Forger's ruined body in the middle of the corridor. His breaths came in ragged gasps now. His brothers and sisters lay around him in unnatural poses, their faces contorted into screams, their blood mingling with the crimson fabric of their robes. A few of the younger ones had been fitted with restraints and were being led away from the Foundry.

Major Doyle arrived in the corridor, carefully stepping over the bodies so as not to sully his boots. He approached Vinick and offered a crisp salute.

"Sir, the trial is proceeding as planned," he reported. "A record number of soldiers logged in to watch. It's almost the whole ship. Luckily, it's a good fight. They're well matched. Major Rothman is faring better than expected. We didn't think she'd last ten minutes. But if she keeps it up, she might even kill the boy."

Vinick shrugged. "Either way, I want them both eliminated. That girl has failed me too many times. Program the environmental interference. Once it's all over, retrieve the Beacon from the boy's simulation chamber."

"Yes, sir," Doyle said. "How do you want to dispose of their bodies?"

"Bypass the Euthanasia Clinic. The whole ship will know they died in the simulation. No need for an official autopsy. Toss them down the incinerator."

"Yes, sir," Doyle said. He pulled out his tablet and hit a few buttons and then looked up. "The environmental interference is engaged. That should take care of them."

Vinick nodded. "Major, you'll issue the official report?"

"The Order of the Foundry attacked the bridge in a surprise ambush, using the trial as a distraction," Doyle said drolly, the lie easily slipping from his lips. "They were armed with the new Falchions they were supposed to have been forging to fight the Fourth Continuum. We had no choice but to defend ourselves against their betrayal."

"Very good, Major," Vinick said. "Soldier dismissed."

The old Forger heard the exchange as he lay slumped on the floor by their feet. Vinick and Doyle marched away, leaving him there to die. He wasn't sure if it was his imagination—the hallucinations of a dying man—but a dark figure stooped down next to him. He laid a cool hand on the old Forger's forehead, stroking it gently.

"Brother, I'm so sorry," Captain Zakkay whispered to disguise his compassionate words. His face crumpled with regret. "I didn't know what Vinick had planned."

He was one of the soldiers who had been left behind to guard the Foundry, so he wasn't watching the trial. He glanced around nervously, but the Majors were too busy rounding up the surviving Forgers and carting away the dead ones to notice him.

"Fetch help . . . hurry . . ." the Forger gasped. "Aero . . . save him . . ."

Zakkay nodded. "Go gently, brother. Don't fight it."

His hand slid from the old man's forehead. Then he slipped away quietly and vanished down the corridor in a full sprint. The Forger took a shuddering breath. He kept his eyes open for as long as he could. Zakkay's boots slapping the blood-slickened floor was the last thing he saw before his heart thumped for the last time.

Chapter 32
SPECIAL GUEST

Seeker

This is filthy and wrong," Seeker begged, backing up and hitting the wall. She was trapped. Fear coursed through her veins. Her Beacon flared faster and brighter. The Weaklings' eyes refracted the light, glowing blood red. They advanced on her with their bone knives and spears, while Rooter watched everything unfold from his throne.

How long had he been planning this treachery?

Seeker glanced around the room, looking for something . . . anything . . . she could use as a weapon. But she came up empty. Even the floor had been swept clean of skeletons. They continued to advance on her.

"Don't listen to Rooter," Seeker tried again. "Weaklings are better than Strong Ones. We don't need to Feast in order to survive. We have plenty of offerings. We know how to hunt. And once we go to the Brightside, there will be even more—"

"Silence," Rooter growled. His lips pulled back from his teeth. "You're a traitor to your pack. You joined the Strong Ones. You stole the Gold Circle and left us behind in the Darkness to die. But we rose up and found a way to survive."

The vitriol in his voice hit Seeker. She felt a tingle of guilt. "No, that's not true," she stammered. Cold rock dug into her back. "I promised to come back and lead us away from the Darkness of the Below, so we could return to our true home."

"Liar! Don't listen to her," Rooter shrieked. "The Darkness of the Below is our home." He gestured to the Weaklings grasping the knives. "Gut her—now."

Bruiser slashed at Seeker with his blade, but she ducked out of the way and kicked. The knife missed her neck, skittering against the wall with a clink.

The circle of Weaklings tightened around her. Seeker could see hunger and bloodlust in their eyes. She thought quickly, trying to find any way out of the situation. "But I carry the Gold Circle," she said as it pulsed with light.

A hush fell over the room. The device held sway over the Weaklings—they'd worshipped it for centuries.

"Not for much longer," Rooter growled. "Seeker is a thief—she stole the Gold Circle from the altar. Weaklings, we must kill her and return it to its rightful place."

The pack chanted in unison, their voices echoing through the room: "We worship the Light in the Darkness. May the Light never go out, so long as we shall live."

Rooter climbed down from his throne. "The Darkness of the Below is our true home. Seeker's stories about the Brightside are nasty, filthy lies! We come from the Darkness. We live in the Darkness. And we shall die in the Darkness."

"Amen," the Weaklings chanted.

The circle tightened again. Bruiser signaled to the other Weaklings, and this time they came at her together with their bone spears. Their eyes looked glassy and blank. It was hopeless, Seeker realized. They would do whatever Rooter said. They couldn't think for themselves. They were weak and feeble-willed. Except for one of them . . .

Her eyes scanned the pack, landing on his face.

"Crawler!" she yelled. "Get my rucksack!"

The Weaklings looked confused, but Crawler understood. He bolted to the corner and snagged it. He pushed through the pack, joining Seeker by the altar. "Sorry," he hissed, thrusting the bag into her arms. "Didn't know what Rooter had planned."

Rooter looked even more furious at the betrayal.

"Weaklings, kill them both," he snarled.

Seeker pawed through her rucksack, her fingers tripping over the sharp edges of the object. She fished it out and held it over her head. The light from her Beacon glinted off the tarnished metal frame that encased the photograph. *They will listen to you*, Jared communicated. *Tell them my story . . . tell them where I came from.*

"Weaklings, listen to me," Seeker said, feeling the reassuring pulsing of the Beacon with Jared supporting her. "I didn't believe the stories about the Brightside either, until I bonded with the Gold Circle and saw the world from Before Doom—the world before our people fled into the Darkness of the Below. We came from the Brightside."

Seeker passed the picture to Crawler, who studied the image and passed it to the closest Weakling in the circle. She looked afraid and glanced nervously at Rooter, who was still yelling for their demise from his throne. But curiosity got the better of her. She seized the frame and stared at the image of Jared and his mother for a long moment.

"Stop her," Rooter shrieked. His jowls wobbled as his voice grew shriller with each utterance. "Seeker tells filthy lies! It's a trick! A nasty, filthy, dirty trick!"

But the Weaklings weren't listening anymore. They continued passing the picture around. The pack crowded in closer to get a better look. They stroked the dusty glass with their fingers, caressing it. They whispered excitedly, all thoughts of feasting forgotten.

"The Brightside . . . the Brightside . . ."

It was as if a spell had been broken.

Crawler glanced at Seeker. "Weaklings, we must listen to Seeker," he said in a loud, clear voice. "Seeker comes from our pack—she's a Weakling! She defied the Strong Ones and journeyed to the Brightside. Seeker can lead us back there."

Bruiser locked eyes with Seeker—and dropped his knife. The rest of the pack followed his lead, disarming themselves. Their weapons clattered to the ground.

"Stop her . . . Seeker's a filthy, nasty liar," Rooter cried weakly from where he was cowering behind his throne. But his pack wasn't listening anymore.

Seeker seized on the opportunity. She climbed onto the throne, thrusting her wrist in the air. The Beacon pulsed brighter with emerald light. "We're not a people born of the Darkness. We are a people born of the Light! And we can be so again . . . only . . ."

"Seeker, what is it?" Crawler asked. "What's wrong?"

"We aren't the only ones," Seeker said. "There are others . . . bad ones, like the Strong Ones . . . only worse. They have evil in their hearts. If we don't return to the Brightside and fight back, then Commander Drakken will destroy everything."

Her Beacon flashed, and for a moment she could feel the pounding of Drakken's black heart like it was lodged in her chest. The connection rattled her, but then it evaporated just as quickly.

He's coming, Jared communicated. *Every second, he gets closer.*

Rooter crawled out from behind the throne. "Weaklings, we should stay in the Darkness of the Below. Safer down here . . . the Brightside is dangerous. The Light burns. You heard Seeker . . . worse than the Strong Ones coming to destroy us."

Nervous murmurs rippled through the pack.

"If we stay down here, we may be safe for a time," Seeker agreed. "But Drakken will hunt down the other Continuums and destroy us. He's coming for us right now."

Silence fell over the room. Seeker could feel she was losing the Weaklings. Their fear was outweighing their curiosity.

"But . . . how do you know this Strong One is coming

for us?" whispered the female, the first one to study Jared's photograph. "How can you be sure?"

"Because I can *feel* him," Seeker said, "through the Gold Circle. He has one too. He stole my memories. He knows where I came from. He promised to destroy our home. My fellow Weaklings, the Darkness of the Below can't protect us anymore."

The pack still looked afraid. But Crawler joined her on the throne, clambering onto the wide seat and adding his voice. "Weaklings, we rose up against the Strong Ones. They were bigger than us, but we defeated them. Together, we are stronger than those who want to destroy us. We must follow Seeker and return to the Brightside."

His voice echoed and died out. Silence rushed back into the throne room.

But then—*Thump!*

The female stomped her foot. Then, one at the time, more Weaklings stomped their feet. The thumps rang out, growing louder and stronger. Even Bruiser joined them, pounding his foot on the floor. Seeker felt the reverberations like a second heartbeat that gave her strength. Her eyes grazed over the Weaklings' faces.

"We must be one pack if we're going to survive," Seeker said. "So will you follow me to the Brightside? Will you fight back against Drakken?"

The stomping drowned out all other noises. And that was when Seeker knew with certainty—her people would escape from the Darkness of the Below at last.

Chapter 33
ENVIRONMENTAL INTERFERENCE

Major Danika Rothman

anika drove Aero back against the barrier. While her opponent was in exile with a fading Falchion, she had used the time to train hard in the simulators and sharpen her skills. Her Falchion felt like it weighed nothing in her grip. She stabbed at Aero, but he ducked away just in time. Her pike ricocheted off the wall, releasing a shower of golden sparks. The avatars roared their approval.

"Danika! Danika!"

The thunderous chant reverberated through the Colosseum. She glanced over the avatars filling the stands. *The whole ship must be logged in*, she thought with a rush of exhilaration. Her momentary distraction gave Aero a chance to recover and reset his feet.

"Listen, you don't have to do this," he pleaded. Sweat dripped down his neck, staining his deployment suit. The midday sun beat down relentlessly. The venue offered no shade at this hour. His Falchion rippled uncertainly in his grasp.

"Do what?" she sneered, stabbing at him. He barely

shifted his sword into a shield in time to deflect her blow. His Falchion's response time was lagging, she noticed.

"Fight me," he managed to get out. "I know you're only following the Supreme General's orders, but he framed me. I didn't kill my father. Vinick did—"

"Liar!" Danika shrieked and stabbed again.

Aero continued to deflect her blows with his shield, soliciting boos and hisses from the avatars. They wanted to see a real fight, not some boring defensive struggle.

"I'm not lying," Aero said, staggering backward. "The Fourth Continuum is dangerous. We have to join together to stop them—or they'll destroy everything."

Danika hesitated. "That has nothing to do with your trial."

"But it does," he said, continuing to back away. "I'm not the real enemy—Commander Drakken is! They have a huge arsenal. Weapons that our people banned over a millennium ago. We don't stand a chance, unless we can unite our Continuums."

"We'll deal with them after I finish you."

She swung at him, barely missing his right shoulder. He deflected her blow, continuing to back away and avoid engaging her.

"Now stop running away like a coward and fight back, damn it," she hissed, losing more respect for him by the second. The crowd booed louder.

"Fight! Fight! Fight!"

"You're making a big mistake," Aero said. He backed up a few more steps.

She laughed coldly. "You've neglected your Falchion drills in your exile. I can't believe I was betrothed to a coward and a deserter like you."

Pain flashed across his face. "I hated being betrothed just as much as you did. They control us. They tell us not to love anyone or express our emotions. They decide who we can be with . . . and where and when it occurs. Is that what you want?"

"Emotions are hazardous—it's for our own protection."

He shook his head. "No, they're not. Listen, there's

another way. I've journeyed to Earth. I've seen it . . . I've *felt* it. I met someone else. She's not from our world. Where she comes from, it's different. People can choose who they want to marry—"

"Shut up!" Danika screamed and stabbed at him. This time her spear clipped his thigh, drawing a spurt of blood. He flinched but didn't drop his shield.

Too bad, she thought as her spear ricocheted off it. She fought harder, her elongated weapon stabbing down and driving him back even more.

"Major, I won't fight you," Aero said. "It's wrong how they pit us against each other like this. You're not my enemy— you're only a soldier following orders."

"You're just saying that because you're losing," she hissed and clipped his other leg this time. His suit was now stained with a mix of sweat and blood.

"I'm tired of fighting my own people. You don't have to follow Vinick's orders. I know you're afraid if you don't kill me, you'll prove that you're unfit to serve, like your sister. I'm sorry about what happened to Lillian, but you're not her—"

"How dare you speak her name?" Danika shrieked. She felt blood rushing to her face in shame. "And how dare you peruse my personal files? That's forbidden."

"They weren't your personal files," Aero said. "The Foundry keeps their own separate records. And I remember . . . when they caught her and banished her . . ."

Tears pricked Danika's eyes. She felt furious at her body for betraying her. "You don't know anything! What it was like to have a biological sibling who betrayed your family's genetic line! To have a black mark on your file that you can't erase!"

Aero shook his head. "No, I don't know. You're right. I wasn't there. But you were . . . weren't you? You can still remember Lillian, can't you? What she did was wrong, but she was young and afraid. She didn't deserve to die. I know that now. Because I left our colony and saw other ways. We can live a different life—a better life."

"Liar," Danika yelled. "Vinick said you'd try to trick me."

Aero shook his head sadly. "It's not a trick. It's the truth."

Danika tried to stuff down the feelings, but her head started to spin. Her boot slipped on the loose sand, making her stumble. It was only for a second, but it was a moment of weakness. Aero could have taken advantage of it, but he didn't move. His eyes stayed locked on her face; his Falchion stayed morphed into a shield.

The crowd voiced their disapproval. "Coward! Deserter!"

"Why didn't you kill me?" Danika demanded when she recovered. She clutched her pike so hard that her knuckles turned white. "You saw me slip. You could've shifted your shield into a sword and ended the trial with one clean stroke."

"I told you," he said stubbornly. "I don't want to kill you. I promised someone." Emotions rushed across his face when he said that last part. Danika felt enraged.

"It's that other girl, isn't it?" she hissed. "The one you left here for."

"I left because Vinick banished me. But yes . . . it's her."

The crowd booed louder. Danika heard shouts of "coward" and "finish him off!" Then they took up chanting her name again. "Danika! Danika! Danika!"

"You're an emotional hazard," Danika said, raising her Falchion. "And so you will die for it. *No mercy in the face of weakness,*" she quoted from their teachings.

She leapt into the air, bringing her pike down hard. It collided with his shield in a blast of sparks. The blow knocked the shield from his arm, leaving him completely exposed. His Falchion landed a few feet away, rippling and threatening to melt down. Their eyes met—and he looked afraid. She relished the moment. It fed her.

"Die, deserter," she said in a cold voice, raising her spear.

Without warning, the venue shuddered under their feet. That was accompanied by an inhuman screeching that made her ears ring. A hush fell over the crowd.

"What was *that*?" Danika said, glancing around franticly.

"Damn, Vinick," Aero said. "It's environmental interference—"

Suddenly, the sand shifted violently under their feet. Danika tucked into a roll and recovered quickly. Aero did the same, scooping up his Falchion and popping back to his feet. He morphed it into a broadsword. The weapon responded instantly with no lag time. He wasn't even breathing heavy anymore. He looked completely recovered.

Was losing all an act?

Before Danika could figure it out, the sand shifted more and threw her aside. A trapdoor popped open. Something large and rectangular rose up from underneath the venue. Dust poured from it, clouding the air. That horrible screeching pierced the arena again. She grabbed her ears in pain. When the dust cleared, her eyes fixed on the golden cage. Through the bars, she saw the flick of a spiked tail, the gnashing of powerful jaws, and a flash of razor-sharp claws. Then a blast of fire ripped through the bars.

Aero ducked out of the way, but it singed his uniform. He dropped and rolled on the ground to put it out. The door to the cage retracted slowly. The beast clambered forth, releasing another burst of fire from its mouth. No, strike that—from its *mouths*.

The creature had three heads.

One was a snake, one a lion, and one a goat.

They all shot out fire.

The crowd roared their approval. They were on their feet now, craning for a better view. Danika stared at the creature in shock. A wave of heat hit her, scalding her skin and making her eyes water. She shifted her Falchion into a shield to protect her face.

"Starry hell . . . what is that thing?" she stammered, backing away.

Her words were drowned out as the creature whipped around with its spiked lizard tail, nearly taking her head off. She ducked just in time. Then the beast lurched at Aero, emitting another unholy screech and unleashing a torrent of fire.

Chapter 34
THE DOCKS

Jonah Jackson

The Docks came alive with frenetic activity. Rebels darted between the partially assembled submersibles, lugging around tools and pushing rickety carts loaded down with spare parts. The Master Engineers used torches to weld them together into seamless machines, handling the more sophisticated aspects of Operation Surface.

"Eight tons per square inch," Jonah said under his breath. He clutched his blueprints to his chest like a talisman to ward off evil. Their subs would have to swim swiftly through the deep, resisting the deadly pressure, and rise quickly to the surface.

That terrible metric plagued him throughout the day, while he paced back and forth supervising the operation, and haunted his dreams at night, twisting them into violent nightmares. There were so many colorful ways to die in the deep, but the extreme pressure terrified him most of all. Some minor flaw in the steel casing, some minuscule mistake in his design, and the pressure would instantly crush them. They wouldn't even make it one short league away from the colony.

A familiar voice cut through the sector, drawing his attention.

"Jonah Jackson, how goes Operation Surface?" Maude called as she pushed aside the thick tarp, ducking under it. She was trailed by Greeley and the Goon Squad, who were armed with electrified pipes. The old signs still dangled over the tarp, a ruse to keep out the Synod and the Patrollers while Jonah built his prototype in secret.

DANGER:
Structurally Unsound

NO TRESPASSING:
By Order of Engineering

"It's going, Chief," Jonah said. "Though not as fast as I'd like."

Maude observed the half-constructed outer shell nearest the opening. The nose and tail had been welded together and the cabin built out with a control panel and bench seating. Sparks flew off a seam, fizzing up the air. Jonah smelled the sharp sulfurous tang of burning metal. He didn't care that it made his nose itch; he loved that scent.

"Is that wee Charlotte with that blowtorch?" Maude asked.

Charlotte flipped back her mask. The torch's tip still glowed deep red.

"Yes, Chief," she chirped. Her long hair was pulled back in a messy ponytail. Sweat dripped off her forehead, but a huge grin lit up her face. "To the Surface!"

"Carry on, lassie," Maude said with a salute. Charlotte flipped down her hood and bent over her work, releasing sparks that danced around her diminutive figure.

"That girl's a natural Engineer," Jonah said, feeling a twinge of pride. It was chased by a rush of sadness. Charlotte reminded him so much of Myra, who had also showed a natural aptitude for their trade. Jonah and Maude proceeded down the sector, surveying the progress. More half-constructed ships lined their path.

"Nice work," Maude said approvingly. "The subs are really coming together, aren't they? I must admit, when I saw all those spare parts, I had my doubts."

"You wouldn't be the first," Jonah replied. "Decker thought I'd lost my mind when I first approached him. Except, he had a more colorful way of putting it."

Maude chuckled. "I'll bet he did! He may have been Factum, but he cursed like a Hocker. I knew him from the market. He loved my sweetfish—and my firewater."

"Equally, I'll wager," Jonah said.

Greeley and the Goon Squad trailed behind them, keeping a healthy distance between them and the subs. He eyed them and swirled his hand over his heart.

"Any word on the Synod?" Jonah asked.

"My brother got a message through to us yesterday," Maude said, lowering her voice. "The Synod was furious when they learned about our raids on the sectors."

"Wish I could have seen the look on Padre Flavius's face," Jonah chuckled. But then he turned serious. "Did Padre Teronius say anything else ?"

"Fortunately, the Chancellors haven't guessed our true purpose yet," Maude said. "They don't understand the value of these sectors. They just think we're trying to spread unrest through the colony. The idea that we'd try to reach the Surface hasn't crossed their minds yet. That protects us for now."

"Their ignorance is a blessing," Jonah agreed, unable to believe he would utter such words. "The longer the Synod stays in the dark, the better. It'll buy us more time. And your brother? Is he safe?"

"For now," Maude said, but strain showed on her face. Jonah noticed it. "Thankfully, Padre Flavius hasn't put our connection together. It's risky, but my brother is too valuable to our cause. I need him to keep spying for us."

They reached the end of the sector and turned back, taking it all in. All around them, Surfacers darted around the construction site. The clanging of hammers, shouting of orders, and hissing of sparks filled the air. Beyond their operation lay ten portals that opened to the sea. Each would soon be filled with a vessel, their cabins crammed with frightened refugees bound for the Surface.

"Never thought I'd live to see such a sight," Maude said softly. Her eyes swept over the Docks. "Or if I did, I imagined it would be the end of the world."

"Our world is ending," Jonah said. "In a way."

"And so we will build a new one above the sea," Maude said. "Upon the bones of our ancestors, the Oracle rest their souls. Your fleet is going to carry us up there."

o   o   o

So weary that his legs could barely support him, Jonah crawled through the pipes and vents, following the circuitous route back to the Engineering Room. A rat scampered ahead, fleeing his flashlight. He remembered once, when Myra was little, he'd pulled out a sack of boric acid. She caught him lugging it toward their compartment's door.

"No, Papa," she pleaded. "Please don't kill the rats."

"And why not?" he said, thrusting his wrist under the scanner.

She darted in front of him, blocking his exit. "They're special."

"Special?" he snorted. "More like, hazardous. They're filthy vermin that spread pestilence and disease through the colony. Plus, they're gnawing on the electrical wiring and driving my workers crazy."

"They're cleaner than the Engineers," she said, still blocking his path. "Royston hasn't had a shower in months. I can smell him coming before I can see him."

That made Jonah laugh in spite of himself. "No argument there."

"And the rats *are* special," she went on, pressing her case. "They're survivors, like us. They deserve to live down here just as much as we do."

Their argument went on for a few more minutes, with him losing ground. Finally, late to work after the Final Warning, he tossed the boric acid down the refuse chute and tramped off to the Engineering Room. He ordered Royston to rig up humane traps around the electrical wiring, and soon the rats learned to avoid that area. They were smart little critters, he had to admit. Maybe Myra was right about them; maybe they did deserve to live down here. He reached the vent that marked his egress.

He wriggled through it, dropping into the Engineering Room. The sector was dark. The automatic lights had dimmed hours ago. He heard snoring coming from the cots in the back of the sector, stacked three levels high. He knew he should sleep too. He had a long day ahead of him. The automatic lights would brighten early and call him back to the Docks. But his mind still jittered with anxiety. He couldn't sleep yet.

A sliver of light was coming from his old office. He pushed the door open, his eyes falling on Maude. She sat behind his desk, pouring over plans for an upcoming raid on Farming, which was heavily guarded by the Patrollers.

"Jonah, what're you doing up at this sinful hour?" Her cheeks glowed rosy from firewater. She slid an empty mug toward him. He raised his hands to object. "Don't dare refuse the wishes of an old lady. Besides, it'll ease your worries and help you sleep."

He cocked his eyebrow. "Old lady? You don't look a day over forty."

"Forty?" she snorted. "You're as bad a liar as the Synod. Plus, my age has its advantages." She uncorked the bottle and dumped ruby liquid into the mug. "Folks tend to under-estimate you. Or better yet, they ignore you altogether. It's like being invisible. And they feel bad for you too, so they do what you want."

"To old age, then," he said and took a sip. He broke into a coughing spasm. Tears leaked from his eyes. "Holy Sea, are you trying to poison me?"

"My special sleep tonic brew," she said, calmly sipping from her mug. "Triple strength. I keep it tucked back here, else Greeley would guzzle it all."

"Good thing," Jonah said hoarsely. "'Cuz that might kill him."

Maude chuckled. "It would take more than firewater to kill 'em.".

"Cheers to Greeley," Jonah said, raising his mug.

They toasted and then sat in silence. It unspooled around them, comfortable and familiar. Jonah could hear the soft hissing of the Animus Machine as it pumped out oxygen and heat. He felt lulled by the firewater and soothing sounds and started to doze in his chair. But then he noticed that the sector had fallen eerily quiet.

The hissing had stopped.

He leapt from his chair, toppling his mug. Firewater stained the maps on the desk. "Jonah, what's wrong?" Maude said, sensing his distress.

"The Animus Machine—"

That was all he got out before the alarm sounded. The oxygen levels were already dropping. He dashed into the Engineering Room and over to the Animus Machine. Usually, it expanded and contracted with a hissing sound, pumping out oxygen and heat to sustain their colony. But the machine was utterly still—it wasn't working.

"Come on, old friend," Jonah muttered. "Don't quit on me now."

He ran his hands over it, feeling for any buttons or seams in the metal, but it was smooth and unbroken. He had no idea how the ancient machine functioned and, therefore, no clue how to fix it. Maude rushed up to his side.

"Jonah, what happened?" she whispered. Her voice wavered with fear.

"I don't know," he said in frustration. "But it's not working."

Drawn by the alarm, the rebels gathered around them. Their eyes locked onto the Animus Machine. They knew what the stillness and the alarm meant.

"Hypoxia . . ." came the frightened whispers.

"We're running out of oxygen . . ."

"Surely, the Head Engineer can fix it . . ."

Mothers and fathers drew their children closer. Jonah could feel their fear like a chill in the air. He continued running his hands over the machine, talking to it in a gentle voice. "By the Oracle, you can't give up yet. We just need a little more time."

But it remained frozen. The alarm kept blaring.

Frustrated, he kicked the machine. He hadn't planned to do it. His foot throbbed and felt broken. But then the Animus Machine let out a rusty clank—and started breathing again. A second later, the alarm stopped. The oxygen levels were rising.

"Holy Sea, that was close," Jonah muttered under his breath, hobbling on his busted foot. Cheers erupted from the crowd.

"To the Head Engineer! Jonah Jackson!"

Maude clapped him on the back. "Jonah, you fixed it!"

Greeley shot him a guilty look and sidled over. "Sorry I ever doubted Maude's plan to break you out of the Pen. Thanks to your trade, we're still breathing."

"Thanks," Jonah said weakly. His abilities had nothing to do with it. It was dumb luck and nothing more. Worse yet, he didn't know how to prevent it from happening again. But he didn't want Greeley or the rebels to panic, so he kept his mouth shut.

He couldn't fool Maude though. She spotted the look on his face. "We need to speed up our timeline, don't we?" she whispered, keeping the smile planted on her face..

"I fear so," he whispered back. "Or it could happen again—"

Pounding on the sector door interrupted them.

"New refugees seeking asylum," Pratt called out from his guard post. He squinted into a special monitor that displayed the corridor outside, set up by their Programmers. "They're alone and unarmed. No 'Trollers or Red Cloaks in the vicinity."

"Pratt, let 'em in," Maude ordered, hurrying over.

Pratt swiped his wrist under the scanner, which beeped

its approval. The refugees rushed through the sector door. Jonah recognized them right away—it was Chancellor Sebold and his wife. They had two of their children with them, a young boy and an infant girl. Their eldest son, Kaleb, had fled to the Surface with Myra.

"By the Oracle, they're Plenus," came shocked whispers from the rebels.

Another figure limped after them. He had broad shoulders, but his frame was emaciated. His face was disfigured by scars and bruises and covered in a scraggly beard. Jonah couldn't make out his features. Was he another family member?

"Chancellor, what brings you to our sector?" Maude asked, placing her hands on her hips. Her eyes bored into him. Her voice did not carry any hint of welcome.

"Please, we seek asylum," Sebold pleaded. "Ever since my son Kaleb left, I've felt my doubt growing like a water leak. I can't ignore it anymore. Padre Flavius has succumbed to madness. He ordered the Patrollers to torture Factum children."

"More children?" the rebels whispered in shock.

"Drown the true heathen!" Greeley shouted.

Sebold's arm snaked around his wife protectively. She stared at the big Hocker while clutching her daughter closer to her bosom. The baby let out a startled cry. They all looked weary and afraid. "Please have mercy," Sebold begged.

Maude met his gaze. "Chancellor Sebold, asylum shall be granted to your family." Her eyes shifted to his wife. "Mrs. Sebold, please don't worry 'bout Greeley. He looks intimidating, but that man's sweeter than my candy."

The little boy's ears pricked up at the mention. She passed him some sweetfish from her pocket. "Little one, don't be afraid," she cooed, tussling his hair. "You're safe here with us. We'll take good care of you, I swear it."

"Thank the Oracle," Sebold said. "Listen, Padre Flavius is planning a secret operation. He's discovered a weakness in your plans, though I don't know what exactly. Torturing the children has something to do with it—"

"Not now," Maude cut him off. She lowered her voice. "All here are sworn to uphold our rebellion, but we still have to be careful. Let's get you Victus and rest first. Then we'll convene the Free Council so you can brief them on everything."

Maude shifted her gaze to the figure behind them. He'd been so quiet that Jonah had almost forgotten he was there.

"And pray tell, who is this fellow?" she asked.

"Padre Flavius was keeping him locked up in his private chamber," Sebold said. "Even I didn't know he was back there. He broke free and caught me sneaking away with my family. He insisted I bring him along."

Jonah shuddered at the sight of the prisoner's mangled wrists. He must have wrenched them out of his shackles through sheer force. It was a miracle that he hadn't passed out from the excruciating pain. Maude squinted at the prisoner's face.

"State your name," she demanded. "Do you also seek asylum?"

"Heathen . . . heathen . . ." the prisoner mumbled, half-mad. He pushed the greasy, matted hair from his face. His eyes darted around wildly. "Heathen . . ."

"Flavius did this to him," Chancellor Sebold said in disgust. Guilt flashed over his face. "I aided and abetted his tyranny for too long. I'll never forgive myself."

The prisoner swiped at his brow, smearing away some of the grime. Jonah felt a spark of recognition. Could it be? He took a few steps toward the prisoner and laid his hand on his broad shoulders. The prisoner cringed away from his touch.

"Please . . . don't beat me . . . have mercy," he whimpered.

Jonah couldn't believe his eyes.

"Rickard?" he said. "Rickard Lynch . . . is it you?"

The prisoner stopped whimpering. He straightened up and met Jonah's eyes.

"That . . . was my name . . . before I defied the Oracle and became a heathen."

Then he collapsed on the floor.

Chapter 35
THE CHIMERA

Aero Wright

The flames shot at Aero, blazing through the Colosseum. His instincts took over—he ducked and scrambled away. The flames licked his back, igniting his deployment suit. He felt a searing burst of heat. He dropped and rolled to put it out and then regained his footing. He spotted Danika on the other side of the venue, trying to get as far away from those fire-breathing heads as possible. Her Falchion was morphed into a shield.

"Starry hell . . . what is that thing?" she gasped

The creature swung around, letting out another high-pitched shriek from its three heads. Aero wasn't sure which one was more terrifying. The goat bore curved horns and resembled a demented devil creature, the lion had huge jaws studded with razor-sharp teeth, while the snake sported a forked tongue and fangs that dripped poison.

"I think it's a *chimera*," Aero yelled across the arena. His back still screamed with searing pain, but he didn't dare lower his Falchion to inspect the damage.

"Chimera?" Danika said, edging toward him. "What the hell is that?"

"Mystical beast from ancient Greece," he replied. Off her surprised look, he added. "Weren't you paying attention in our history classes at the Agoge? It's a hybrid creature that first appeared in the *Iliad*. Damn it, they're not even real."

"What's it doing in our simulation?" Danika said, her eyes glassy with shock. "Vinick promised there wouldn't be any environmental interference—that it would be a straightforward Falchion-to-Falchion fight. He swore it on his blade."

"Yeah, I guess he lied," Aero said. He clutched his sword tighter and crouched down, circling the chimera warily. "Vinick does that. A lot, in my experience."

"Bastard—"

That was all Danika got out before the creature shot out another wave of fire. They both reacted immediately, dodging the flames while keeping their Falchions raised. They were getting better at it. Aero knew the reach of the flames now. He also knew how long they had between attacks. "Thirty seconds," he said.

"For what?" Danika said.

"For it to recharge—or whatever the hell you call it."

"But why would the Supreme General do this?" Danika stammered. "It doesn't make any sense. I've always been loyal. I've sacrificed everything for him."

"Guess he decided we're both expendable."

The crowd let out disappointed hisses. *The fickle appetites of mass humanity*, Aero thought. One second, they were rooting for Danika to kill him, and the next they were cheering for a mythical beast that wanted to roast her.

Roast us both, he corrected himself.

"Get ready," he yelled as the chimera screeched and shot fire at them.

They both dodged it, but this time Danika got hit. Her deployment suit burst into flames. She screamed and dropped her Falchion. Aero tackled her, forcing her to the ground and patting the flames. Once they were out, she shoved him off.

"Why are you helping me?" she asked furiously, even

though he had just saved her life. Her deployment suit was charred and still smoking.

"Don't worry," he said with a grimace. "My reasons are logical, not emotional. We have to fight this thing together—or we're both dead."

Aero kept his Falchion raised in case the chimera lunged at them. But the creature was smarter than that. It reared back and circled them cautiously. That last blast almost killed Danika. It could afford to be patient and wait for its fire-breathing capabilities to recharge. The triad of heads swiveled around, emitting that horrible shrieking noise. Aero realized that it was actually a combination of noises—the snake hissed, the goat screeched, and the lion roared.

"Fine, what's your plan?" Danika said. The fire had incinerated parts of her uniform. He could see her blistered skin through the holes.

"Quick, look for a weakness," he said. "The beasts programmed into the simulators always have one. They were designed to challenge us and improve our training. In order to do that, they have to be fallible."

"By the stars, you're right," Danika said. "I've trained with my unit against some of them. Not as lethal as this creature, but they do always have a weakness."

Aero nodded, keeping his eye on the beast. He studied it closely. Danika did the same. They dodged another round of fire. "Wait, I think the three heads are connected," Danika said, panting hard. "But one has to be in charge."

"You're right," Aero said, picking up on the weakness. "It's the snake's head. It moves first, shoots fire first. I'll bet that's the one we have to take out."

Her eyes roved over the beast. "The snake?"

"The one with the fangs and forked tongue."

"Got it."

Danika morphed her Falchion. Aero glanced at the ahlspiess clutched in her hand. She was skilled with the lengthy spear; it had the longest reach.

"I'll distract it," Aero said. "While you take out the snake's head with your ahlspiess. That's our best shot at killing it."

She glanced at him. "Distract it? How're you gonna do that?"

Aero gritted his teeth. "I don't know, but I'll find a way."

Their eyes met. "Ready?" he asked. "The next fire blast comes in five seconds." The look on her face told him everything—she was ready.

Aero signaled to Danika to split up. She circled around the back of the creature, while he did something stupid. He screamed and waved his arms at the creature.

"Come and get me, foul beast!"

That got its attention. It shot triple blasts of fire at him.

Aero dodged the flames and attacked the creature head on. He darted under it, morphed his Falchion from a shield into a broadsword, and pricked its foot. The chimera shrieked in pain. The snake's head lunged at him. The fangs stabbed down, barely missing his head and sinking into the sand. He slashed at the creature's other foot with his Falchion. It roared again. The lion's head lurched at him. He heard a snap as the jaws clamped down a millimeter from his ear.

The arena erupted with cheering.

The snake's head reared back. It heard Danika circling behind it. Before the creature could change course, Aero waved his arms in the air.

"Is that the best you can do?" he screamed. Blood glinted on the tip of his Falchion. He used the shiny surface of the blade to reflect sunlight into the creature's eyes, further antagonizing it. "Come on, I'm right here! Come and get me!"

The snake's head locked onto Aero. He felt relief, but it was short-lived as the creature emitted another blast of fire. It singed his left arm and shoulder. He dropped and rolled to put the flames out. The smoke cleared just in time to see the creature lunge at him. The snake's head bared its fangs, lethal poison dripping from them.

"Die, beast!" Danika screamed, launching her attack from behind. She leapt into the air. Her arm retracted and released her Falchion at the snake's head.

The golden spear sailed through the air—her aim was dead-on. It pierced the snake's head with so much momentum that it pinned it to the ground with a loud *thunk*. The chimera shrieked, though the tenor of the sound had changed. The snake's head could no longer hiss. Blood gushed from between its jaws. The other two heads flopped around helplessly as life drained out of the creature.

It shuddered again. After another few seconds, the creature dematerialized from the simulation, though its blood still stained the sand. Danika marched over and retrieved her Falchion from where it was skewered in the sand.

The avatars burst to their feet and cheered.

"Danika! Danika! Danika!"

"Well, that wasn't so hard," she said, though her breathing suggested otherwise, as did the blistered skin on her back. She adjusted her grip on her Falchion.

Aero inspected his singed arm, wincing at the charred skin. "Speak for yourself."

"Well, that's over," she said with a shrug.

"Yeah, isn't it better when we work together?"

Danika shook her head. "No, I mean our truce. It's over."

With that, she lunged at him with her pike. It impaled his left shoulder—the burned one. He screamed in pain and clutched at it. She retracted the spear and stabbed again, but he rolled away. Dimly, he could hear the crowd chanting her name. They wanted him dead. Something hard hit his back, pinning him down and forcing the air from his lungs. It was Danika's knee. His Falchion skittered away in the sand.

She raised her spear to deliver the death blow.

"Danika! Danika!" roared the crowd.

Suddenly, another voice echoed through the arena. This one was amplified and came over the speakers. Aero recognized it as belonging to Zakkay, one of the soldiers from his old combat unit.

"Captain Wright, the Supreme General and the Majors attacked the Foundry! It's a bloodbath! They slaughtered the Forgers!"

Chapter 36
BLOODBATH

Major Danika Rothman

Zakkay's message broadcast through the Colosseum.

Danika hesitated, her spear pointed at Aero's heart. The avatars in the stands stopped cheering. "Lies," she cried. "Your dirty tricks won't work this time."

"I swear, it's not a lie," Aero pleaded. He stared back at Danika. He was helpless without his Falchion. "I know that soldier. His name is Lucius Zakkay. He served in my combat unit. Zakkay is many things, but he's not a liar—"

"More dirty tricks," Danika snapped. "You planned this treachery. I'm not listening." She was thrusting her spear at Aero when Zakkay's voice echoed out again.

"Captain, hold on. I'm pulling you out."

Aero's projection started to dissolve. Danika's spear shot out, but it skewered only sand. Aero had vanished. Hisses and boos erupted from the stands.

"Coward," she seethed, but then she felt herself dissolving too.

The Colosseum faded in her vision, and then she was alone in her simulation chamber. She ripped off her helmet, catching sight of her reflection in the smooth door. No blood splattered her cheeks or hands. No sand dusted the laces of her boots. Her suit wasn't charred or burned either. None of that was real. But under the lightweight fabric, she could feel the sting of her blistered skin.

Aero cheated and bested me again, she thought furiously.

Storming to the door, she jammed the button hard. It hissed open, emitting her into the corridor. She expected to find Supreme General Vinick and the Majors waiting outside, but the corridor was empty. Why weren't they monitoring the trial? By now, they should have arrested Aero for exiting the simulation and forfeiting the trial.

Their absence unnerved her.

But she tamped it down and focused on her mission—*kill the deserter*. Her anger took over and propelled her forward. Morphing her Falchion into a dagger, she marched into Aero's simulation chamber. The door was open—highly unusual—and the chamber inside was empty. Aero had already fled.

He thinks he can escape.

She wasn't about to let that happen. A trail of his blood splattered the floor. She followed it back into the corridor and down to the control room. The door was left open too. Also highly unusual. She hurried inside and spotted two mounds on the floor. It took her a moment to register what they were—two dead Forgers. The ones left behind to monitor the trial. It looked like they'd been knifed in the back.

Her eyes snapped to Zakkay and Aero. They stood by the console, speaking in heated whispers. Aero clutched his Falchion in its default form, but he'd let his guard down. Danika charged into the room, slammed him against the console, and knocked his Falchion away. She pressed her dagger to his throat, glaring at him.

"Deserter, what's happening? Tell me now, damn it."

"They killed the Forgers," Aero gasped in a strangled voice. His eyes jerked to the bodies on the floor. He didn't dare move. "Zakkay witnessed it—"

"Who killed them?" Danika demanded. She pressed the

dagger deeper into his neck, drawing a spurt of blood. "The truth or you'll pay!"

"Vinick and the Majors," Aero managed to choke out. "They attacked the Foundry while we were in the simulation. It was a bloodbath. The Forgers were unarmed and couldn't even fight back. They slaughtered them."

"Major, he's telling the truth," Zakkay spoke up. "I saw the whole thing. I was assigned to guard the door to the Foundry. That's why I wasn't logged into the trial like the rest of the ship." His hand drifted to the hilt of his Falchion.

"Stay back," Danika warned. She kept her blade pressed to Aero's throat. "Don't even think about it—or he dies."

"Listen, it's not a trick," Aero said. "Vinick used the trial as a distraction. The Forgers didn't stand a chance."

"But why would he do that?" Danika said. Her brain felt sluggish. She was having a hard time making sense of it. "He's the Supreme General."

"Vinick holds a grudge. In his mind, the Forgers betrayed him when they granted me sanctuary. Of course, I knew it would infuriate him. But I never imagined he'd actually attack the Foundry. They have special protections."

"Sir, he waited until they left the Foundry to escort you to the trial," Zakkay said. Disgust rippled over his face. "So that the protections no longer applied."

"That's even worse," Aero said. "It means he plotted this. He wasn't just acting on emotional impulse. I never should have involved the Forgers. And I shouldn't have underestimated Vinick. I knew he was dangerous and unpredictable. It's my fault."

"No, it's not," Zakkay said. "It's Vinick's fault."

"But I got the Forgers into this mess."

"Captain, I apologize if I'm speaking out of turn," Zakkay said. "But the Forgers wanted to be involved. They made their choice freely. This would have happened anyway. Tension has been simmering for months. I heard rumors in the Mess Hall. Vinick was looking for any excuse to get rid of them."

"That's true," Danika said. Her grip on her dagger slackened. Aero sucked in a grateful breath. "Vinick didn't trust them. He questioned their loyalty."

Aero took this in. "Well, do you believe me now? About my father? About what really happened that day on the bridge, when I bonded with the Beacon?"

For the first time, Danika felt her allegiance wavering. Maybe it was seeing the dead Forgers splayed out on the floor. Maybe it was the chimera that invaded their trial when Vinick had promised no environmental interference. Maybe it was smaller things she'd observed on the bridge. The way Vinick spoke to his underlings. His vindictive streaks. His coldness. His emotional instability. Maybe it was everything combined.

"Maybe," she allowed. She released her hold on Aero, though she kept her dagger pointed at him. He rubbed his neck, coming away with blood. But the wound was superficial. He shot her a self-deprecating smile.

"Does that mean you're not going to try to kill me?"

"Yeah, sorry about that." She glanced down at her dagger, feeling guilty. She shifted it back to its default form and sheathed it. Every movement brought a fresh wave of pain to her singed skin.

"You know, it's not your fault either," Aero said, softening his expression. "Vinick is responsible for all of this. He lied to you too." He turned to Zakkay. "You said they're plundering the Foundry and cleaning up the evidence?"

"Yes, sir," Zakkay said. "They're disposing of the bodies in the incinerators to destroy the evidence. Vinick's going to claim the Foundry attacked the bridge during the trial and attempted to hijack his ship and he had no choice but to retaliate."

Aero looked furious. Danika couldn't believe the intricacy of Vinick's duplicity. *He's been planning this for some time,* she realized.

"That leaves us with only one option," Aero said. "We have to get the truth out to the ship. And we have to hurry.

Every second, they destroy more evidence. They're also bound to notice the environmental interference didn't finish us off."

Zakkay nodded. "Good thing I pulled you out when I did."

"Why . . . what was coming next?" Danika asked. Her shock was fast turning into anger. The more she learned, the angrier she got.

"A massive deluge that would have flooded the arena," Zakkay said, hitting a few buttons and pulling up the simulation program. "Courtesy of Major Doyle. He programmed it. Looks like he did it remotely from his tablet."

Aero grimaced. "Right, and if that didn't work?"

"Volcano eruption," Zakkay said. "They imported the Pompeii program."

Danika frowned. "But why bother with any of that? Why not slit our throats in our simulation chambers? We would have been helpless to fight back."

"Two reasons," Aero said, gesturing to the monitors, which still displayed the empty arena. "Vinick needed to put on a spectacle to keep the soldiers logged into their terminals. That way, they wouldn't realize he was attacking the Foundry until it was too late. It also gave him time to destroy the evidence and spin the story."

"That makes sense. What's the second reason?"

"He needed to make our deaths look natural. Slitting our throats in the simulator would indicate homicide. The Medical Clinic would have to conduct autopsies. That would trigger an investigation. He wanted to avoid all that."

Danika's hand darted to her Falchion. "That cowardly traitor."

"My thoughts exactly," Aero said. "Wait, I've got an idea. Captain Zakkay, are the soldiers still logged into the simulation?"

Zakkay keyed in a few commands. "Yes, it looks like most of them are still logged in. Based on the message boards, they're waiting to see if that was a glitch in the program. They're hoping the trial will start up again." He looked up with a dry smile. "Guess they were enjoying the entertainment."

"Great, can you broadcast a video message into the venue?" Aero asked. "So we can reach the soldiers directly without Vinick interfering?"

"Yes, sir," Zakkay said. He punched in a few commands and then picked up a handheld attachment used to broadcast video into the simulation. He aimed it at Aero. Behind him, on the large screens, Danika glimpsed the arena and the stands populated by avatars representing the soldiers watching from their terminals.

"Sir, it's ready," Zakkay said. "Just tell me when to start broadcasting."

Danika glanced at Aero. He looked disheveled, and that was putting it mildly. Blood stained his face and uniform; nasty blisters covered his neck.

"Pardon me for saying this, but you look like hell," Danika said, frowning at him. "Also, what're you going to say? Shouldn't we discuss it first?"

"There's no time," Aero said. "If we don't act now, Vinick will beat us to it."

"Right, we've got to get our message out first," Zakkay agreed, fiddling with the attachment and adjusting the shot. "It'll help with credibility."

She sighed. "So you're just going to wing it?"

"Pretty much," Aero said. He took a deep breath, squared his shoulders, and stared straight into the lens. "Let's do this."

Zakkay hit a button. On the monitors, Aero's image materialized in the arena. The avatars leapt to their feet and cheered. They thought the trial was starting again.

"Fight! Fight! Fight!" they chanted.

Aero wheeled around to face them, signaling for silence. "Soldiers of the Interstellar Army of the Second Continuum, I'm the Carrier for your colony and the rightful Supreme General."

A hush fell over the arena. Even the message boards ticking over the monitors stopped. Every soldier was paying close attention to Aero now.

His voice boomed out, amplified by the speakers. "That wasn't a glitch in the program. The announcement you heard came from Captain Zakkay. Vinick and the Majors attacked the Foundry and slaughtered the Forgers. They knew you'd be distracted by this diversion, so you wouldn't find out until it was too late."

Nervous whispers cut through the crowd.

". . . attacked the Foundry . . ."

". . . slaughtered the Forgers . . ."

". . . goes against all our teachings . . ."

Aero signaled to Zakkay, who aimed the lens at the dead Forgers. The image broadcast into the arena in three-dimensional clarity.

"That's not all," Aero said. "Vinick murdered my father in cold blood and framed me for his death. That's why he banished me. He's a liar and a traitor. He wants me dead, and he wants the Beacon." He thrust his wrist in the air. "As your Carrier, I returned to Earth, located two other Carriers who survived the exile, and made it to the First Continuum. I met with the First One—Professor Theodore Divinus."

Danika was hearing the story in Aero's own words for the first time. She listened with rapt attention. The soldiers watching the feed seemed to be doing the same.

"I've come back to tell you that Earth is habitable again," Aero continued. His projection shuddered and then stabilized. "I've seen it with my own eyes. Professor Divinus and the First Ones preserved everything we need to recolonize the surface in the First Continuum, as promised. But we face one more grave challenge—the Fourth Continuum. They have a massive arsenal, including weapons our people banned centuries ago, and they want the secret to the Doom."

At the mention of the Doom, shocked whispers roiled through the stands. Aero waited for them to die down before continuing.

"Our only chance lies in uniting our people to fight back against this threat. As soldiers, we've trained for centuries to prepare for this possibility—the emergence of a hostile colony. So, will you join me in fulfilling our destiny?"

At first, nothing happened. The soldiers were too stunned.

But then, one by one, the avatars stood and saluted Aero. *They're supporting him*, Danika thought. *He won them over.* Aero stiffened his posture and returned their salute.

"Commanders, gather your units and then head to the Mess Hall," Aero said. "I'm sending Captain Zakkay to meet you with orders. Be prepared for combat, if necessary. Is that understood?"

"Yes, sir." Their response reverberated through the arena.

"Very good," Aero said. "Soldiers, dismissed."

The avatars started to dematerialize from the stands as they logged out. Zakkay terminated the broadcast. "Nice job, sir."

"Think it'll work?" Danika asked with a cock of her head.

"Guess we're about to find out," Aero said. "Captain Zakkay, you heard my orders? Go to the Mess Hall and gather a few combat units. Pick commanders you trust. Meet us at the elevator to the bridge. Soldier, dismissed."

Zakkay snapped a salute. "Yes, sir," he said and raced off. He vanished down the corridor, his boots leaving bloody footprints on the floor.

On the monitors, Danika saw that the Colosseum now stood empty. Abruptly, portals in the walls opened. A torrent of water gushed into the arena, flooding the fighting pit. If they had still been in the simulation, that would have been their fate.

"Major Rothman, come with me," Aero said, hurrying to the door.

"Sir, where are we going?" she asked, picking up her pace to keep up with him. It was hard to believe that she was actually following his orders.

"The prisoners," Aero said. "I need Wren."

Chapter 37
THE DISCIPLINARY BARRACKS

Aero Wright

Aero marched down the corridor. This was the first time he'd had free rein of the ship since Vinick killed his father. He hadn't realize how much he'd missed his home—the curvilinear passages, the artificial gravity, the astringent scent of recirculated air, the thick windows dotting the corridor, displaying the expanse of outer space.

He glanced back at Danika. "Major, which way?"

"This way, sir," she said, leading him toward the Disciplinary Barracks. Their ship didn't have a prison. They seldom had infractions of their rule-based society. Soldiers followed orders and rarely disobeyed. Also, if they did break the rules, their sentences were usually dispensed quickly—banishment or worse. Either way, long-term imprisonment didn't exist as a concept in their world.

"The prisoners . . . they're unharmed?" Aero asked. This was the first time he'd had anything approaching a normal conversation with Danika. It felt . . . *weird*.

"Mostly," she said in a guilty voice.

"You tortured them, didn't you?"

"I was only following orders. Vinick wanted to know if they had any intel on the Fourth Continuum. He was worried that maybe you were working together."

"Don't tell me you used *Paraponera clavata* venom."

"We did," Danika said, casting her eyes down. "You've seen the data. It's the most effective method of persuasion when interrogating a hostile subject."

Aero felt a rush of anger. "Effective because it hurts like hell. Remember how they made us try it at the Agoge? That's one species I'm going to make sure Professor Divinus doesn't reintroduce. Good riddance to bullet ants and their venom."

They reached a fork in the corridor. She led him right. "If it makes you feel any better, the deserter . . . I mean . . . Lieutenant Jordan didn't give anything up. She screamed until she lost her voice. But she didn't betray you."

"Of course she didn't. She's loyal to the end and tougher than either of us."

"Yes, sir," Danika said. "That she is."

They rounded the corner and came upon four armed guards posted in front of the Disciplinary Barracks. The guards morphed their Falchions into various weapons. Danika grabbed Aero's arms, wrenching them behind his back. He winced with pain.

"Don't worry, I've got this," she whispered. "Just play along."

She marched him up to them. "Captain Grimes, what are waiting for? Open the door at once! I've apprehended the deserter. The Supreme General ordered me to throw him in the Disciplinary Barracks with the other traitors."

Instead of complying, Grimes signaled to the other soldiers. They ambushed Danika, knocking her Falchion away and restraining her. "Starry hell, what're you doing?" she yelled, struggling in their grip. "I'm your superior officer."

"You're the traitor, Major." Grimes turned to Aero and saluted him. "Supreme General Wright, we heard about the Foundry. Gossip spreads fast on this ship."

He pulled out his handheld and flashed it at Aero. The message boards lit up the screen. A few choice words leapt out: *Vinick attacked the Foundry . . . bloodbath . . . slaughtered the Forgers . . . violates all our teachings . . .*

Aero nodded. "That about sums it up."

"Sir, what are your orders?" Grimes asked. "We serve at your pleasure."

The three other guards saluted. "Us too, sir."

"Thank you, Captain," Aero said, feeling uncomfortable at being treated like the Supreme General. He wasn't used to it yet. "I'm grateful for your support."

Danika glared at him. "A little help here, Supreme General?"

"Oh, right," Aero said, enjoying her discomfort just a little bit. "Captain Grimes, release Major Rothman. She's on our side. She didn't know what Vinick was planning either. Also, I need you to release the prisoners."

"Yes, sir," Grimes said and gestured to his soldiers.

They released Danika, who rubbed her sore shoulders and scooped up her Falchion. Grimes keyed a code into the door. It opened with a sharp hiss.

A familiar voice shot through it.

"Starry hell, what took you so long?" Wren said when she saw Aero, sounding more grateful than irritated. She caught sight of Danika. "And what's *she* doing here."

Wren's brash manner told Aero something important—captivity hadn't broken her spirit. Relief swept through him. He hurried into the barracks. The austere room had one cot for the four prisoners and not much else. Tinker popped up from the cot with one of his lopsided smiles. He shoved aside the rough blanket.

"I told you he'd rescue us," he said in his raspy voice. He looked a little taller and thinner, but otherwise the same. Kaleb joined Tinker and grinned at Aero.

"Holy Sea, am I glad to see you." He seemed to have healed from his ordeal in the Seventh Continuum, though scar tissue peeked out from his tunic.

The Forger stood up from where he'd been meditating on the floor. Without access to shears, his hair had grown in. His robes were grubby and stained, but he also looked healthy enough. "Supreme General Wright, I never had any doubts."

"Sorry, I came as fast as I could," Aero said, meeting Wren's gaze. He had the urge to hug her fiercely, but he knew better than to display emotions in front of other soldiers. The guards stood outside the door. "We ran into some interference. As for Major Rothman, she's experienced a change of heart. She's on our side now."

"Right, since when?" Wren muttered. Her eyes looked haunted. Dark circles rimmed them. Clearly, she had suffered from the torture.

Danika strode into the room. "Since Vinick tried to murder me in the simulator." Shame flashed over her face. "Look, I didn't realize Vinick was lying. I was just following his orders."

Wren's countenance softened. "But really, did you have to use *Paraponera clavata* venom?" she said with a dramatic shudder. "An old-fashioned beating would have been preferable."

"I'm truly sorry about that," Danika said. "I wanted to prove myself to Vinick. Maybe I went a little overboard."

Wren shrugged. "Apology accepted, I guess."

"Look, I hate to interrupt this lovefest," Aero broke in, "but we don't have much time. Vinick has probably figured out we're not dead in our simulators. We've got to get to the bridge before he does something crazy."

As quickly as he could, Aero explained the plan they'd hatched—how the Forgers had offered him sanctuary and protected him in the Foundry, how they'd requested a trial by combat. "So it actually worked?" Wren said. "Vinick went for it?"

Aero winced. "It worked until Vinick double-crossed us and decided to slaughter the Forgers while we were in the simulation. He used the trial as a distraction, since most of the soldiers were logged in and watching the feed."

The Forger looked shocked. "Vinick attacked the Foundry?"

Aero met his gaze. "Sorry, brother. He waited until they

left the Foundry to escort me to the trial, and he ambushed them on their way back. They kept the younger ones alive so they can charge the Falchions. I'm sorry to have to tell you like this."

"That lying bastard," Wren hissed, her hand darting to her Falchion. "He lacks the temperament to lead. He's an emotional hazard, if I've ever seen one."

"My words exactly," Danika said. "He also programmed environmental interference into the simulation to kill us. We're just lucky that a soldier who witnessed the attack on the Foundry remained loyal to Aero and pulled us out in time."

"A soldier?" Wren said. "From our old combat unit?"

Aero nodded. "Zakkay, thank the stars."

"He's a good soldier," Wren said without hesitation.

A look passed between them as they remembered how they hadn't always held Zakkay in such high regard. They once considered him an emotional hazard. But he had saved their lives three times now.

"Zakkay helped me broadcast a message to the ship, explaining Vinick's betrayal and asking for support. I dispatched him to the Mess Hall to rally the troops who are loyal to me. They're going to meet us at the elevator to the bridge."

"Right, that's where Vinick will go when he realizes that the ship is revolting," Wren agreed. "Whoever controls the bridge controls the ship."

"Exactly," Aero said, savoring how they always seemed to be on the same page. He'd really missed her.

Before they could head to the bridge, Aero had to do one more thing. He summoned all of his concentration abilities and shut his eyes, pushing his energy into the Beacon.

Come on, Myra . . . answer me.

He was rewarded a second later when her voice cut through his head. *Tell me you're okay . . . that the plan worked . . . that you've got them . . . Tinker and Kaleb.*

Some glitches, but I've got them, Aero communicated back.

In a blur of images and emotions, he downloaded his memories of what had transpired to her, hundreds of miles away in the First Continuum. She experienced his pain and sorrow when he learned about the Forgers and understood his plan for Vinick.

Good luck, Supreme General, she communicated when it was over. *I'll see you back home. Don't forget you promised to come back in one piece.*

The signal terminated.

Aero opened his eyes and blinked hard in the stark light. Slowly, the disorientation passed. He turned to the young Forger.

"Brother, I need you to escort Kaleb and Tinker to the Docking Bay. Put them in an escape pod, and send them back to the First Continuum."

"But I want to help," the Forger protested. "Vinick killed my Order."

"Me too," Kaleb chimed in. "I can fight."

"No, brother," Aero said to the Forger. "I can't risk you getting yourself killed. I'll need you to salvage the Foundry. You're too valuable. You will serve me in other ways." He turned to Kaleb. "This isn't your fight—and you're not a trained soldier. I need to you to look out for Tinker. Myra will kill me if I don't get him back safely."

Kaleb shrugged. "Yeah, she can be stubborn like that."

"Starry hell, you're telling me," Aero said with a grimace.

The young Forger looked like he wanted to object, but he calmed his emotions. "Yes, Supreme General," he said instead. "As long as you promise me one thing."

"What's that, brother?"

"Don't let that traitor lead our colony for one more day. He will bring ruin to our people and destroy everything that we've endeavored to salvage."

Aero gave his assurance to the Forger, who gestured to Kaleb and Tinker to follow him. "Friends," he said, "let's get you home."

"Come on, Tink," Kaleb said. "Ready for another flight?"

Tinker's grin was answer enough. Aero ordered two

guards to accompany them to the Docking Bay and make sure they got there safely. They marched down the corridor and disappeared around the bend. Aero turned to Wren and Danika.

"Let's go," he said. "To the bridge."

o   o   o

When they arrived at the elevator, Aero couldn't believe his eyes.

Hundreds of soldiers packed the corridor, dressed in their silver combat suits and clutching their Falchions. They parted to let him through. As he passed, they saluted him.

"Supreme General Wright, we serve at your pleasure."

Aero felt gratitude tug at his heart. These soldiers had trained with him at the Agoge and taken meals with him at the Mess Hall, and now they'd turned up to support his cause. Wren whispered in his ear, "Just don't let it go to your head, sir."

He caught her eye, and she suppressed a grin. Danika marched behind them with Captain Grimes. They passed through the ranks of soldiers.

Aero whispered back, "Did I mention how much I missed you?"

Wren smirked. "Never doubted it for a second, sir."

"Well, you don't have to be so damn smug about it," he replied. They reached the elevator, where Zakkay was waiting. He saluted them formally.

"Sir, I've gathered the soldiers," Zakkay said. "Aside from a few stragglers, the whole ship has sided with you. They're outraged about the attack on the Foundry. Majors Cole and Kieran fled in an escape pod bound for Earth, but Vinick is holed up on the bridge with Majors Doyle and Wright . . . your biological mother . . ."

Aero brushed over it. He'd let go of any attachment to her. She'd betrayed him too many times; this was just another instance.

"Did Vinick shut off the elevator?" Aero asked.

"Yes, sir," Zakkay said. "But I anticipated that likelihood

and had the Engineering units get to work on bypassing the lock." He stepped aside and hit the call button. The elevator popped open right away. "As you can see, they succeeded."

"Nice work," Aero said. "You've done well."

He clapped Zakkay on the shoulder.

Aero signaled to Wren, Danika, and the other higher-ranking officers to join him in the elevator. They unsheathed their Falchions, morphing them into their preferred weapon forms. Wren clutched a talwer, the curved sword she favored. Aero brandished his broadsword, though he didn't relish it. *I hope Vinick will go quietly so there won't be any more carnage today.*

As do I, my son, his father communicated through the Beacon. *But I know Vinick. We were in the same class at the Agoge, and he served under me. Don't underestimate him like I did. Learn from my mistakes.*

Aero knew that his father was right. He needed to be prepared for anything. He felt a whooshing sensation as the elevator carried them to the highest level of the ship. Next to him, he heard Wren's breathing speed up. She gripped her sword tighter. Her knuckles strained and turned white. The atmosphere in the elevator was tense, like right before a battle simulation. Only this was real.

"Soldiers, once we get onto the bridge, follow my lead," Aero commanded. His eyes swept over their faces, ten of them in all. "Vinick is an emotional hazard. He's dangerous and unpredictable. Is that understood?"

"Yes, sir," they replied. Their voices didn't waver or sound afraid.

By now, Vinick should have realized that they'd hijacked the elevator controls. They wouldn't have the element of surprise. However, the revolt had happened quickly. With any luck, Vinick hadn't grasped the full extent of it yet. The elevator spit them out on the bridge. Aero was greeted by a rush of stale air and a sneering voice.

"Boy, did you come up here to surrender?"

Vinick stood by the window with his gaze fixed on the

view of Earth. Majors Doyle and Wright flanked him with their Falchions morphed and raised. Vinick cocked his head when Aero and his soldiers marched onto the bridge, but he didn't turn around. This was his attempt at a show of strength, but a transparent one.

"You've got it backward," Aero said. "Surrender the ship to me. You've lost your army. Even Majors Cole and Kieran fled in an escape pod."

"What are you going to do if I step down?" Vinick scoffed. "Boy, you can't expect to command a ship of this caliber. You're weak, just like your father."

Wren and his soldiers tensed, but Aero signaled for them to stand down. Diplomacy was the best way to unite the ship and avoid unnecessary bloodshed.

"I'm the Carrier of the Beacon and the rightful Supreme General," Aero said, keeping his voice strong and steady. "Surrender now—and I'll let you live."

Danika's face contorted with rage. "You're going to let him live?" she hissed. "After what he did to us?" But Aero signaled for her to keep her mouth shut.

"Control your emotions, Major."

Vinick pivoted around. He clutched his Falchion, morphed into a dagger—the same form that he'd used to kill Aero's father. "Why should I trust you, boy?"

"Because I'm not like you. I keep my word. Besides, hasn't there been enough bloodshed already? Attacking the Foundry and killing the Forgers . . . that was—"

"Evil," Danika interrupted. "It violated all our laws."

Before Aero could stop her—or do anything but watch helplessly—she launched her ahlspiess at Vinick. The spear sailed through the air and sank into his chest, right over his heart. Vinick screamed, but it turned into more of a gurgle.

Danika glared at him. Hatred lit up her eyes like black fire. "You violated our charter. The punishment for your treachery is death."

Vinick's lips twitched, but all that emerged was a strangled cry. He sank to his knees and collapsed. Within seconds, the life had drained out of him. Danika turned around slowly, as if in a trance. Her eyes were glassy and blank.

"You were going to let him live," she whispered. Her voice sounded choked. "He's dangerous. I couldn't let you do that. It goes against all our teachings."

Chapter 38
OPERATION SURFACE

Jonah Jackson

Rickard thrashed in his sleep. "Padre Flavius . . . please . . . don't beat me!"

Jonah restrained his arms as best he could. Doctor Vanderjagt rushed over and tipped poppy water tonic into Rickard's mouth. Gradually, the thrashing lessened, but he continued to moan. The only word that Jonah could make out was—*Padre Flavius*. It peppered Rickard's mumblings with alarming regularity.

"Rickard's pulse is strong," Doctor Vanderjagt said. She slung her stethoscope over her neck, leaning over to inspect his bandages. "His injuries are healing well."

Jonah caught a whiff of the garlicky pomace packed into his wounds.

"He's lucky he didn't develop blood poisoning," she said, straightening up. "Our medicines work for local infections, but that would have carried him off to the Holy Sea. His vitals all check out. I don't understand why he isn't coming around yet."

"Doctor Vanderjagt—" Jonah started.

"Please, call me Karen." She perched on the stool next

to him. Her face looked pinched with worry. "Myra was my daughter's best friend. I pulled long shifts at the Infirmary and wasn't home much, but I would've had to be blind to miss the bond those girls shared." Her eyes flicked to Rickard. "And they both adored this boy."

"And his friend Kaleb too."

Karen smiled. "The four of them were inseparable, weren't they?"

"That they were," Jonah agreed.

Memories shot through his head of Myra, Paige, Kaleb, and Rickard parading home with Tinker after school, their laughter echoing through the corridors. The colony wasn't the same without them. Karen spied the look on his face.

"I'm guessing that's why you've barely left his bedside for the past week. Aren't you supposed to be supervising our operation at the Docks?"

Jonah felt a stab of guilt. It was true—he'd been shirking his duties. "My Engineering workers are capable," he hedged. "I trained them well, thank the Oracle. They can supervise the operation. I want to stay where I'm most needed."

Karen studied his face. "It's more than that, I'll wager. There's something about the way you look at him. Like you've got something in common . . . like you understand what he's going through."

"Padre Flavius," Jonah said darkly. "When I was locked up in the Pen, he tortured me too. Some wounds never heal. That's why Rickard isn't coming around yet. That's why he's having all these night terrors. It's not a physical problem."

Jonah tapped his forehead. Karen met his eyes.

"We don't have medicines for that kind of sickness," she sighed. She gazed at Rickard with a helpless expression. "I don't know what to do for him."

"Time," Jonah said. "He needs time. And one more thing."

"What's that?" Karen asked.

"Tender loving care."

"Well, that I can provide. I owe him that much for being

such a good friend to Paige. Now, don't you need to get back to your Engine Rats?"

Before Jonah could object, she took his place by Rickard's bedside and shooed him off. "Away with you, Jonah. It's my Infirmary—I'm in charge here."

o   o   o

Jonah slithered out of the vent and dropped into the Docks. He may have been neglecting his duties, but Operation Surface was running smoothly. His workers darted around, putting the finishing touches on the submersibles. His eyes flicked over their fleet—ten vessels preserved from Before Doom. He ran his hand over the cockpit of the nearest sub. A face popped up behind the thick acrylic plastic of the window.

"Aye, aye!" Charlotte said with a grin, hitting the intercom button. "Captain Nemo, at your service. Krakens beware! Don't mess with the *Nautilus*."

She wiggled her arms, imitating the mythical beasts. *Nautilus* was painted across the hull in Charlotte's looping script.

"You've been listening to the Hockers' stories, haven't you?" he said in a mock serious tone. "Lassie, those tales will get you into nothing but trouble."

"Like your daughter?"

"Yup, just like Myra and Tinker. They always loved Maude's stories."

He felt a stab of sadness but forced it back down. Charlotte ran her hands over the controls. She could pilot that sub as well as anyone twice her age.

"The Chief tells the best ones," she said into the intercom. But then her expression turned more serious. "The Surfacers aren't like the Synod, you know. They don't tell us what stories we can tell . . . or what words we're allowed to say."

"Aye, aye, Captain Nemo," he added with a salute.

He left Charlotte to her imaginings. She bounded out of the top hatch and started loading crates of provisions and supplies into the cabin of the *Nautilus*. All around him, the

Docks were bustling with activity. Greeley steered a large crane down the sector, nearly plowing him over.

"Greeley, slow down," Jonah cried, leaping back from the motorized wheels. "You big lug, you could kill somebody. Safety first, remember?"

He was even more peeved when he noticed that Greeley wasn't wearing his work boots or hard hat. Instead, the big Hocker sported flimsy sandals and a hempen cap. He could easily lose a foot—or his head—if he wasn't more careful. Jonah wasn't sure which appendage Greeley considered more important. "Sorry, Engine Rat! Chief's orders, we gotta move up our time frame for Operation Surface."

Greeley attached the grappling claw to the nearest sub. The vessel also sported a name; *Argo* was painted across its hull in blocky letters.

"All set," Jonah said, clapping his hand on the *Argo*. He felt the firmness of her reinforced steel casing under his palm. Using the crane, Greeley hoisted the sub off its pilings and steered it toward the Docks.

"Load her up into Portal 1," Jonah directed.

Greeley nearly clipped the side of the portal, making Jonah cringe. But somehow he avoided disaster and got the vessel inside. Jonah breathed a sigh of relief when the crane released the sub. It landed with a loud thud that rattled the sector.

"Ain't that a lovely sight?" Greeley said, his eyes uncharacteristically welling up.

The Surfacers looked over, breaking into elated cheers. Through the portal window, the exterior lights lit up the trench. An anglerfish darted into the lights. It dangled a lure in front of its monstrous, gaping jaws that shimmered with greenish light. *Bioluminescence,* it was called. Jonah remembered teaching his kids about it.

"That's good luck," Maude said, lumbering over to Portal 1. The monstrous-looking fish stared back at them with milky eyes. A glowing tendril dangled in front of its gaping jaws, meant to lure in unsuspecting prey. "They usually flee from the light."

"Good luck," Jonah repeated. "I'll take it."

o   o   o

That night, they returned to the Engineering Room before the dimming of the automatic lights. Firewater and jovial conversation both flowed freely. They'd finished reconstructing the fleet and loading all the subs into the portals.

But Jonah didn't feel like celebrating. Operation Surface wasn't complete. So much could still go wrong. Instead, he poured over maps in his old office. They contained precious little information about what lay beyond the trench that housed their colony. Where was the First Continuum? How could they locate Myra?

"Curse the Synod and their Great Purging," he cursed, shoving the maps aside. They were of little use. Without proper coordinates, they'd be swimming blind.

"I'll drink to that," Maude said, poking her head through the door. She carried two mugs of firewater. She placed one in front of him, but he shoved it away. She frowned. "You finished building your fleet. Isn't that worth a toast?"

"It's not that," Jonah said, running one hand through his hair. Since this whole mess started, it had grown considerably thinner. "The fleet is more marvelous than I ever imagined. It's the greatest achievement of my Engineering life."

Maude studied him. "What then?"

"Myra had the Beacon to guide her back to the Surface," he explained, gesturing to the maps. "But these are all we've got—and they're useless. So much was destroyed in the Great Purging. Once we ship out from the colony, where do we go? How do we locate the Surface? How do we find Myra and Tinker and their friends?"

She took a measured sip. "That isn't your main worry, is it?"

"What if . . ." he trailed off. He couldn't say it out loud.

"They didn't make it?" Maude finished his thought.

He didn't even try to deny it. "Yes . . . exactly."

She placed her hands on her hips and stared him down. "Jonah Jackson, snap out of it! So long as I've known you—and it's been a bloody long time—you've never given up hope. Not even after you lost Tessa. Not even after the 'Trollers tossed you in the Pen. Not even after Padre Flavius tortured you and told you the truth about killing your wife. We're so close to everything that you've dreamed about. How can you lose hope now?"

"I know, you're right," he said but still wasn't convinced. His doubt lingered like a stubborn oil stain on coveralls. Maude could read it on his face.

"Myra and Tinker and their friends are stronger and more resourceful than even the shrewdest Hockers. Mark my words, they survived and reached the Surface. And they'll find a way to get in touch with us. Now can you drink to that?"

Jonah still felt worry gnawing at his heart, but he forced himself to take a sip from the proffered cup. He could drink to that. It was the least he could do.

"To Myra Jackson," Maude said, clinking their mugs.

o   o   o

His head swimming with firewater, Jonah struggled into his middle bunk. Between visiting Rickard in the Infirmary and supervising the Docks, it had been a long time since he'd slept there. Despite the seldom-experienced comfort of a mattress and pillow under his head, he didn't drift off right away. All around him, he could hear the deep snores of the Surfacers, passed out after a long night of celebrating.

He wasn't sure how much time had passed with him lying there sleeplessly, staring at the coils of the upper bunk, when heard something alarming:

Beep!

Jonah bolted up in his bunk. The sector was dark, but he was sure the noise came from the sector door. The rebels didn't use the corridors to get around anymore. That meant nothing good. That was followed by a slurp. And then shouting:

"It's a raid!" Pratt screamed. "Patrollers . . . Red Cloaks!"

The Patrollers charged into the Engineering Room with their pipes raised. Their flashlights cut through the sector.

Jonah scrambled from his bunk, falling to his knees as chaos broke out around him. His first thought was—*Rickard*.

Ignoring his throbbing knees, he dashed over to the Infirmary, weaving through the panicked rebels. He found Rickard curled in a fetal position on his hospital bed. "Padre Flavius," he whimpered, his eyes darting around. "He's coming for me."

"Right—but we're not going to let him take you."

Jonah slipped his arms under Rickard's shoulders, dragging him out of the bed. Rickard was deadweight in his arms, frozen with terror. "Listen, you have to help me here," Jonah grunted. "I can't carry you all by myself. You're too heavy."

Rickard hung there for another second, but then he found his footing. Doctor Vanderjagt raced over to help her patients, trailed by Maude. "What happened?" Jonah hissed. "How'd they get in? I thought our Programmers changed the codes."

"I can't find hide nor hair of Ingrid and Lonnie," Maude said. "They must have slipped away while we were celebrating last night. I'll wager they betrayed us."

"I warned you those data heads couldn't be trusted," Jonah said.

Rickard moaned in his arms: "Padre Flavius . . . Factum children . . . arrested and tortured . . . Programmers . . ."

"Under duress then," Maude said in an acid voice. "That must be why Padre Flavius arrested the kids. He tortured them to get to Ingrid and Lonnie. They couldn't ignore the suffering of their old trade. Factum bonds run deep—you know that."

Jonah felt his anger soften. He thought of his own trade and loyal workers. What if the Synod was torturing their children? What would he do?

The clanging of pipes echoed through the sector, drawing their attention. Greeley and the Goon Squad fell on the Patrollers with their electrified pipes. The flashlight beams grazed crimson robes. Padre Flavius and his Red Cloaks paraded into the Engineering Room. Over their shoulders, they carried what looked like a stretcher, the kind they used in funeral marches. When Padre Flavius spotted Maude, he gestured to his priests. They tipped the stretcher over. A priest's body tumbled out, landing in a bloody heap on the floor. His face was beaten almost beyond recognition.

"Behold what happens to heathens like Padre Teronius who defy the Oracle of the Sea!" Padre Flavius said in a booming voice. "Patrollers, leave no sinners alive!"

Maude's face crumpled, but she composed her features.

"Surfacers, we've got to evacuate!" Maude yelled to the rebels. "Travel light, leave all your belongings behind! Help the children and elderly! Follow me!"

Maude whispered to Jonah. "Hurry, we have to get to the Docks. Greeley and his squad can hold them off, but not for long. The 'Trollers outnumber us."

They dashed to the back of the sector, where they found Stella and Ginger already prying the grates off the vents. "Head to the Docks," Ginger whispered to the rebels as they climbed into the pipes. The youngest children looked frightened. "Don't be afraid, little ones. Just remember the emergency evacuation drills we practiced."

"Myra Jackson's secret ways will save us," Stella added, helping a little boy who Jonah recognized as Chancellor Sebold's son. "Hurry, make for the Docks."

Maude checked on their progress, then unsheathed her pipe. The rebels were locked in furious battle with the Patrollers, but they were losing ground. Greeley took a pipe to the head and went down hard. He didn't get back up.

"Chief, what are you doing?" Jonah said, catching her arm. "It's too dangerous! You should evacuate now. You heard Padre Flavius—they're going to kill us."

"Not a chance," Maude said. Her voice did not waver. "I can't leave my people to fight these prigs, while I flee like a coward to safer harbors."

Jonah gritted his teeth and drew his pipe. "Then I'm staying to fight too."

"No, you have to go to the Docks! You're the only one

who knows every detail of Operation Surface. You've got to make sure they get out safely."

"But I want to fight," Jonah protested. "Those prigs killed my wife—"

"That was an order," Maude cut him off. "You're too important."

"Yes, Chief," he replied, though he hated it.

He watched as Maude charged across the sector with her pipe raised. "To the Surface!" she yelled as she fell on the Patrollers. She took two down with an electrified swing. Their bodies convulsed. "Drown the true heathens!"

She reached Greeley and helped him up. The big Hocker staggered to his knees. Blood streamed from a deep gash in his forehead. Jonah wanted to stay and watch the fight. But Maude's order rang through his head again.

Go to the Docks . . . make sure they get out safely . . .

Jonah helped Rickard limp over to the nearest vent. He shifted Rickard's weight and helped him angle his body into the narrow opening. "Crawl—you've got to crawl," he whispered in Rickard's ear. "Hurry, we don't have much time."

Jonah heard Greeley scream. "Chief, watch out!"

He glanced back in time to see a pipe bash into Maude's back with a terrible crack. Greeley was there a second later and took the Patroller down, but Maude wasn't moving. She looked unconscious—or maybe dead. Jonah couldn't tell. It took every ounce of his willpower to tear his eyes away. He nudged Rickard, who had started wriggling into the vent when a flashlight hit Jonah square in the face and blinded him.

He heard pounding footsteps, followed by jeering laughter.

"Heathen, you can't escape!" It was Head Patroller Waters. He'd taken over his trade after killing Rickard's father. He clutched a hefty pipe and swung at Jonah.

Jonah raised his hands to block it.

That was the last thing he remembered before everything went black.

Chapter 39
EMOTIONAL HAZARD

Supreme General Aero Wright

Soldiers, arrest Major Rothman," Aero ordered.

When they seized her arms, she came out of her trance. "But it was my right to terminate his life," she said as Zakkay and Grimes restrained her. "Sir, you know it's true! The punishment for his treason is death. You were going to let him live."

Aero wanted to hate her. He wanted to feel justified in lashing out. But all he felt was a deep sadness. He met her gaze and held it for a long moment. "This makes us no better than him. Don't you understand that?"

Danika flinched like he slapped her. Her eyes darted to Vinick's body, splayed out on the floor with her Falchion jutting from his chest. "Sir . . . I'm sorry . . . I don't know what came over me," she stammered. "I must be an emotional hazard."

"I accept your apology," Aero replied. "But I still have to detain you."

"Of course, sir," she said softly. "I understand."

Aero ordered her incarcerated in the Disciplinary Barracks

along with Majors Doyle and Wright. His mother didn't even glance at him when his soldiers marched her off the bridge. After they'd vanished into the elevator, Wren met his eyes and offered him the barest slip of a smile.

"Well, that went well," she said in a sour voice.

Only the two of them lingered on the bridge. He'd sent the other commanders back down to round up their units and return them to their barracks. He had to put the whole ship on lockdown until he knew it was secure. He needed to broadcast a message to his soldiers, shore up his leadership, and contact Myra to let her know that their uprising had succeeded. But his mind swarmed with loose tangents and emotions.

"You were right. I never should have trusted Danika," Aero said, tugging his hand through his hair. It still needed a trim . . . badly. "Not after what Vinick put her through. He created a true emotional hazard."

"Danika did have a change of heart," Wren pointed out. She knelt down by Vinick, studying his face. It was contorted with pain. "I mean, she could have sunk her Falchion into your heart instead. At least she chose a better target this time."

Aero exhaled. "I guess that's progress." He crossed the bridge and gazed through the window at Earth, tilting slowly under the glare of the sun.

"I must confess," Wren said. "I'm not upset Vinick is dead."

Aero didn't want to agree that cold-blooded murder could somehow be right. But the reality was far hazier than his outsized ideals. People weren't machines. They were emotional and fallible. They made mistakes. They acted on impulses; sometimes good ones, sometimes evil ones. The truth—once he allowed himself to feel it—was that he was relieved that Vinick was dead.

"Me neither," Aero said. "He was dangerous."

Wren nodded. "And he would have continued to be dangerous even if we'd locked him up for the rest of his life or banished him to Earth."

Her words were true. Aero couldn't deny them.

"Sir, what are you going to do with Danika?" Wren asked.

"I don't know," he said with a weary exhale. Already the burden of command felt heavy on his shoulders. "We're at war, so for now, we'll keep her detained in the Disciplinary Barracks. Then I'll recommend a trial before the Majors. Maybe we can find a way to rehabilitate her. We should consult with the Medical Clinic."

"Good idea, sir. Maybe they can help her." Wren's tough exterior cracked slightly. Aero could tell that she felt bad for Danika. She knew that the girl had been abused and manipulated by Vinick.

A flash of light in the window caught Aero's attention and made him snap back to the threat barreling toward them. Quickly as he could, he brought Wren up to speed on everything they knew about the Fourth Continuum. She'd learned about the reappearance of the mysterious colony when Danika interrogated her, so she wasn't totally in the dark.

"Can you check on their location?" Aero asked, gesturing to the consoles.

The Second Continuum had powerful sensor arrays, and they were closer to the Fourth Continuum and had no atmospheric interference. Wren tapped a few buttons, pulling up their ship on the monitors. Drills jutted out of its hull like spikes, barely visible against the dark backdrop of space. The signal was strong; the ship didn't waver.

"Looks like Doyle was tracking their position," she reported, tapping at his old console. Her eyes skimmed over the screen. "Drakken isn't even bothering to cloak their signal anymore. It's almost like he wants us to know they're coming."

"That makes sense," Aero said. Through the pulsing of his Beacon, he could sense Drakken's menacing presence. "We already broke through their cloaking shield, so they lost the advantage of surprise. Now, they're hoping their speed will intimidate us."

"I concur," Wren said, hitting a few more buttons. The view of the colony shifted. "Drakken hopes we'll surrender without a fight and give him the Doom."

"Exactly," Aero agreed. "How far away are they?"

Wren tapped a few keys. "Based on Doyle's calculations, we still have about twenty-three days before they reach Earth's orbit. They're moving fast, but they'll have to decelerate as they get closer or they'll whip right past us."

"A little over three weeks," he said. "To train a whole army."

"And erect a shield," Wren added. "Don't forget that part. We have to find a way to counter that nuclear arsenal, or he'll just blast us to bits—"

An alarm sounded on the bridge. Wren hit more keys and frowned.

"Incoming signal, sir."

Aero raised his eyebrows. "Origin?"

"The First Continuum," Wren replied, tapping away. She looked up in confusion. "Someone named . . . Noah? He says he doesn't have a last name."

"Open communication lines," Aero said with a smile. "He's a friend."

"Captain Wright," a perfectly modulated voice said. "Or should I call you Supreme General Wright? I take it your mission was successful. I picked up the signal from the escape pod moments ago. They'll be landing outside our door any minute."

"Vinick is dead," Aero said. "The ship is mine."

"Very good, Supreme General." His voice swelled to indicate pride. "I'll commence a download from your Beacon and brief Professor Divinus. Myra is taking the elevator to the surface to greet the escape pod. Would you like to watch my feed?"

Aero knew that it wasn't strictly necessary. The escape pod would carry Kaleb and Tinker safely to Earth. That's what it was designed for. The only reason his pod crashed was because Vinick had shot it down. The impulse was sentimental and a waste of his precious time now that he had a whole ship to command.

"Noah, put it through," he said anyway. He wanted to see the look on Myra's face. Wren arched her eyebrow, but he ignored it.

He paced to the front of the bridge, where he was closer to the monitors. The screens came to life with grainy security footage of the courtyard framed by crumbling buildings. A speck of silver appeared in the sky. Parachutes drifted behind it. The escape pod drew closer and closer, finally landing with a gentle thud.

A few seconds later, the door sprung open. Tinker bounded out with a goofy grin stretching across his lips. Kaleb followed after him with a slight hitch in his gate. They made their way across the Yard, toward the ancient library. Snow still blanketed the ground, but it had melted in places. Their breath puffed out in smoky tendrils. The footage cut to another camera angle, showing the door to the First Continuum inside the library.

Myra burst from the elevator and rushed down the marble hallway. The footage kept cutting to different camera angles as they tracked her progress through the building and out into the blinding sunlight. When she saw Tinker climbing the steps, she broke into tears. She ran to him, sweeping him up in her arms. Aero felt his Beacon pulse with a flood of emotions. Tears welled in his eyes too.

In his head, he heard her voice. *Thank you, thank you, thank you, thank you . . .* It was less a message and more a sentiment, and it kept repeating.

"Tink, look how you've grown!" Myra said in the footage.

She set Tinker down with an exaggerated groan and then, almost shyly, approached Kaleb. The limp in his gate kept him from moving quickly. Aero saw the crumpled look on Myra's face when she glimpsed the extent of his disability, and even more so when she saw the raised bands of scar tissue encircling his neck.

"Hey, I'm not that fragile," Kaleb said with a wink. And then he hugged her fiercely, crushing her small body into his much larger frame. That was when Aero felt something else . . . and it wasn't entirely pleasant. He cleared his throat.

"End transmission," he ordered. "Thank you, Noah."

"Of course," Noah replied. "Ending transmission."

The monitors snapped off and went blank.

A long moment passed while Aero wrangled his emotions, stuffing them back down into his heart. He enjoyed being able to feel so many incredible things now, but he still wasn't used to the way that they could wound him like a dagger to the chest.

Wren stood up from the console. She gazed through the windows at Earth, tilting slowly under the sun's glare. "Earth looks different now, doesn't it?"

"It does," he agreed. "Only . . ."

"It doesn't feel like home yet," she finished for him. They were both experiencing the same thing. They felt torn between this ship—their first home, the place that had housed and nurtured them—and their future home on Earth.

"Sir, are you ready to address your soldiers?" Wren asked. "We shouldn't let too much time pass. Vacuums in leadership produce unrest. We should seize the moment and shore up your position, otherwise the soldiers will grow restless."

Aero turned to her and saluted.

"Yes, Major Jordan," he said. "Will you do the honors?"

She cocked her eyebrow. "Major, huh?"

That would have passed for insubordination under more formal circumstances, but it was still just the two of them alone on the bridge, and the familiarity that had been bred from everything they'd survived together ran deep.

"Right, I'm making changes around here. I've got some rather large vacancies to fill. If you don't approve of my choice, then I will take your wise counsel under consideration—"

She held up her hand to silence him.

"Promotion accepted, sir," she said with a salute.

She made her way over to Doyle's old seat and keyed in a few commands. "Supreme General Wright, the ship is yours. You may begin your broadcast."

Aero squared his shoulders, knowing that every movement, every word would be transmitted to the thousands of soldiers in their barracks. He had to brief them on Vinick. He had to update them on the Fourth Continuum. And most of all, he had to tell them to get ready because they were about to deploy to Earth and go to war.

Chapter 40
EVACUATION

Seeker

Ready?" Crawler asked, bounding up to Seeker. In his hand, he clutched a metal shard poked with holes, fashioned into a crude visor. "They're gathered in the city."

The throne room was empty, aside from ratter skeletons littering the floor. Seeker's eyes passed over the obsidian throne, the stone altar, the arched windows, the flying buttresses supporting the towering ceiling. She knew that this was a dead place. Still, leaving it wasn't easy. Though the power had failed, the colony had served its purpose. It harbored them for a millennium of exile, most of it in complete darkness.

Seeker turned away. "It's time to go," she agreed.

"Seeker . . . why so sad?" Crawler asked. His arm brushed against hers, sending a shiver rippling over her skin. Crawler was large for a Weakling. Many weeks of feasting on ratters, buggers, and tubers had filled out his frame. His russet coat looked glossy in the Beacon's pulsing light. He was the first to rally to her cause, and in the ensuing days, as they prepared to evacuate the Seventh Continuum, they'd grown even closer.

Seeker wasn't sure what to call it. She didn't think it was *love*, like she'd overheard Noah talking about—she wasn't about to do something illogical or crazy for him—but it was pleasant enough. She liked Crawler, she decided. Maybe that was it. Though the goose bumps pricking her skin might have told a different story.

"Home . . . leaving our home," Seeker growled back, leaning into his side and letting him comfort her. He stroked her arm in a gentle rhythm to soothe her.

"This isn't our true home—you taught me that."

"The Brightside?" Seeker said.

He nodded. "That's our home now."

Seeker took in the throne room one last time. Memories cascaded through her head, but they felt distant and hazy. Her life had changed so much since she'd left. Crawler was right. She knew it with every inch of her body. *It's time to leave.*

"Come on," she said. "Let's get out of here."

They galloped through the castle. Crawler led the way down the great hall and into the cobblestone streets of Agartha. For the last several days, they'd been making preparations for their journey to the Brightside. Once Rooter surrendered and the Weaklings united behind her, everything fell into place quickly.

Slayer rounded up the hundred or so Strong Ones who still survived, lurking in the tunnels. Seeker admitted them to the castle. She ordered the Weaklings to share their offerings with their exiled, starving brethren. She also had them take the Strong Ones along on their hunting trips, teaching them how to feed themselves. Despite Crawler's insistence that she take Rooter's place on the throne, Seeker eschewed it, preferring to sleep on the floor like the rest of her pack. She'd never enjoyed the trappings of comfort; being their leader didn't alter her habits.

They'd also been scouring the city for scraps of metal, shaping them into visors to protect their sensitive eyes from the burning orb in the sky. Seeker had told them all about the Brightside—both the wondrous, breathtaking parts and the fearsome ones. She explained about the nasty, burning, stinking light, though she knew that no words could do it justice. Soon they would all see it for themselves.

Seeker and Crawler whipped through the city streets. The castle loomed behind them, falling into darkness the farther away Seeker got. A few twists and turns later, they reached the central square, where a fountain burbled away. The Weaklings and Strong Ones stomped their feet when they saw her approaching.

"Seeker, the Strongest of the Strong Ones," they growled.

All of them clutched visors. Some had already slid them over their eyes. A few carried rucksacks stuffed with ratters. Some had slung tattered fabric across their shoulders for extra warmth. Many carried bone spears strapped to their backs with strips of leather. There were about eight hundred of them. That was all that was left.

Seeker raised her arms to signal for quiet.

"Weaklings and Strong Ones, we are now one pack," she declared. "We are the inhabitants of the Seventh Continuum— and the time has come for us to return home." She paused to let those words sink in. "Crawler has divided you into groups. We will have to take turns in the Moving Room that will carry us to the Brightside."

She gestured to Crawler.

"The first group," he said, "follow Seeker."

Crawler would stay behind to supervise the evacuation and leave with the last group. Seeker led her party to the Moving Room and opened the door. Some of them cowered away as the metal rippled and retracted into the wall.

"Don't be afraid," Seeker said, ushering them inside the elevator. "Hurry, friends! This way!"

Once they were all crowded inside, the door contracted behind them, sealing with a deep rumble that shook the floor. She directed them to secure their visors over their ears and hold on to the railing. Though Seeker had ridden it many times before, she still got that horrible tumbling feeling as the elevator accelerated, hurling them upward with tremendous speed. She felt her ears pop, more than once. Sounds of whimpering reached her ears, but she focused on holding on to the railing.

About twenty minutes later, the elevator shuddered to a stop. Everything went quiet, and then the door opened with another deep rumble. Blinding light spilled into the elevator. In the crush of eternal darkness, Seeker had lost track of time, but it looked like midday. A fresh wave of cries erupted from the group. Some of them pressed themselves against the back wall and scratched at it, seeking an escape route.

"It burns!" Slayer shrieked. "Nasty light . . . it burns!"

In her panic, Slayer had knocked her visor off. She clawed at her eyes, trying to make it stop. Seeker scrambled over, helping Slayer slide the visor back into place.

Seeker gestured for the group to follow her into the Brightside. But they stayed back, crowding into the shadows where the light couldn't reach them.

"Don't be afraid—the light can't hurt you," Seeker coaxed, letting it fall on her skin. They watched with rapt attention through their visors. She wriggled her fingers. They danced in the light, but no harm came to her.

"Follow me, hurry," she called, bolting from the elevator.

Clean, fresh air that smelled of dirt and snow hit her nostrils. She inhaled deeply, savoring the scent. She wouldn't miss the musty, recirculated air of the underground. Her feet tramped down into a few inches of snow. It felt cold but stimulating. She bounded to the precipice that overlooked the valley, where a rushing river of fresh snowmelt churned away. She heard footfalls pad up behind her.

Slayer halted by her side. "Seeker . . . what is this place?" Her voice shook with adrenaline. She craned her neck for a better view, her feet slipping on the icy snow.

"Slayer . . . careful," Seeker growled. "Watch the cliff."

Even with her close call, Slayer couldn't take her eyes off the view. She stayed there, by the edge, scanning the horizon. The visor worked to protect her sensitive eyes from the sun.

She didn't seem afraid anymore; she seemed euphoric. Seeker took comfort in that knowledge. Slayer would adapt, she could tell. They all would.

"This is the Brightside," Seeker said softly. "Our true home."

o   o   o

They set up camp in the shallow caves that pockmarked the mountain, while they waited for the other groups to arrive in the Moving Room, which they did about every thirty minutes, like clockwork. Crawler kept everything running on time. Seeker felt deep gratitude for his help. In a few short days, he had become invaluable to her.

She dispatched Slayer to recruit a few others to greet the newcomers to the Brightside and help orient them, making sure they kept their visors on and didn't go slipping off the mountainside or wandering too far away from the group.

That night, she dispatched five hunting parties, and they all returned with rucksacks full of ratters and buggers that they rooted out of the deep caves that dotted the mountainside. She taught them how to scoop up the fresh snow and put it in their mouths, letting it dissolve into water. "This is what happens when water gets too cold. This is called snow, and when clouds come like those, it falls from the sky," she explained, tossing a handful up to show them how it worked.

Some looked amazed, while the others looked distressed. But all of them craned their necks up to watch the dark clouds rolling in over the mountains, threatening to hurl precipitation at them. A few of the younger ones fresh out of their birthing season frolicked in the snow, hurling icy balls at each other and howling with delight.

At the end of their first day, Seeker sent a report to Myra, informing her that the evacuation had gone as planned and that they would start to make their way back to the First Continuum on foot. *We'll be waiting for you,* Myra communicated. *Hurry . . .*

That was followed by a quick flash of Drakken's ship. Then the signal terminated. The mountains made it hard to communicate, but the message was crystal clear:

The Fourth Continuum is coming for them.

When Seeker settled down to sleep—curled up next to Crawler, the warmth of his fur making her pleasantly drowsy—she felt more at peace than she had in many long weeks. The Fourth Continuum and their threats hovered still over everything they did, of course. But for this moment, cradled in the mountainside, while a light snow drifted down, pattering at the ground, she felt that this was right where she belonged—with her people and Crawler—free from the Darkness of the Below.

o   o   o

For the next few days, they journeyed through the mountains at a rapid clip, descending from the mountains to the gently sloping foothills. Her people were hearty and strong. They stopped only to slurp fresh water from the streams that ran through the mountains and camp during the peak daylight hours in caves, alternating turns hunting for food and sleeping. She kept a few guards posted while they camped, even though it seemed like an unnecessary precaution. This land was mostly bereft of life.

"Seeker," hissed one of the guards. "Seeker, wake up!"

She was coiled next to Crawler, but she roused to find Bruiser nudging her shoulder. "What is it?" she grumbled, wanting nothing more than to sleep for another few hours and rest her weary body.

"Something crashed from the sky," he hissed, sounding afraid. He prodded her shoulder again. "Slayer said to get you right away. You have to come quick."

Seeker grumbled. "Water falls from the sky sometimes. It's fine. No need to be alarmed. It's called rain, and it's normal—"

Bruiser shook his head. "Not water . . . something big with lights."

That got her attention. "Show me."

She left Crawler, who was still sleeping soundly, and picked her way over the slumbering bodies in the cave, following Bruiser into the twilight. Slayer galloped over. It was dark enough that she didn't need her visor. It was pushed over the crown of her head. After the incident in the elevator, she never went anywhere without it.

"Seeker, something came from the sky," she reported. "It was big and had flashing lights. It crashed down over there." She pointed to the next ridge.

"Slayer, you're sure?" Seeker asked.

But one glance at their faces told her they'd all seen the same thing. It wasn't weather related, she knew that much. The skies were clear, beginning to fill with twinkling stars. Slayer followed her gaze to the sky.

"What do you want to do?" she asked.

"Slayer, get your spears and rouse a few others," Seeker decided after a moment. "Let's track it down." Slayer and Bruiser nodded and vanished back into the cave. They reappeared with their regular hunting party, clutching bone spears and knives.

"Show me where it fell," Seeker said.

Slayer grunted her agreement and signaled to her hunting party. They led Seeker down the hillside and over to the next ridge. The sun still hadn't finished setting. Long shadows kissed the earth, lengthening ahead of them like a dark path. Slayer was sure-footed on the narrow, snow-ridden paths. She never strayed or stumbled.

They reached the next ridge, where they came upon a smoking crater in the earth. Strips of tattered silvery cloth led away from it. Seeker peered over the edge and recognized what it was right away—an escape pod. Footprints in the snow snaked away from the ruined ship. Two dark figures stirred in the shadows behind them.

Slayer and Bruiser pounced on the intruders, aiming their spears at their throats. The rest of the hunting party surrounded them with their weapons raised. The two men dropped their Falchions into the snow, jabbing their arms in the air.

"Starry hell, we surrender!" one of them cried. His eyes looked wild with fear. "Don't hurt us! We're lost and have no rations, please help us!"

Seeker eyed the golden blades gleaming in the last of the daylight. These were Aero's people, but she couldn't tell if they were his friends.

"What're your names?" she asked, pacing in front of them. She picked up one of the Falchions, feeling the light-weight weapon. It was still morphed into its default form. It surged with tingling power in her hands.

The men watched her warily. "I'm Major Kieran from the Second Continuum," the first one said. He was tall and thin with buzzed blond hair. His eyes flicked to his companion, who was bigger and had a darker complexion. "And that's Major Cole. A traitor took over our colony and murdered our people. Fearing for our lives, we fled. We set our escape pod to locate any life-forms, and it landed us here in these mountains."

"We didn't have time to pack rations," Major Cole added. His voice caught in his throat. "Please have mercy. We haven't eaten in days."

Seeker felt a grin snake across her lips. Major Kieran flinched back, probably mistaking it for a snarl. "A traitor took over your colony?" she said, emphasizing the words carefully so there was no misunderstanding. "That's why you escaped?"

The men exchanged a glance. "Yes . . . he's dangerous and unstable," Cole said. "He murdered our Forgers, took over the army, and was coming for us next. We had no choice but to flee from our home."

Seeker stalked around them. The sun finished setting and cast a veil of darkness over the landscape. But her eyes remained sharp even in the low light. She studied their faces carefully. "What was this traitor's name?"

"Aero Wright," Cole said. "He was banished, but he came back."

"That's him," Kieran confirmed. "He's an emotional hazard."

The carefully crafted lie slipped so easily from their lips. If she didn't know better, she might even have believed it. "Aero Wright is my friend," she replied, baring her teeth. "And you're the real traitors."

Their eyes lit up with fear, but Seeker plowed forward. "But we will grant you mercy . . . for now." She turned to Slayer and Bruiser. "Bind their hands with straps. We're taking them with us. Aero can decide what to do with them later."

o   o   o

When Seeker returned to their campsite, she sent a communication to Aero through her Beacon, letting him know that she'd apprehended Majors Kieran and Cole and would be bringing them to the First Continuum. Aero seemed amused to learn that they'd fled to Earth and searched for life-forms, hoping to locate a friendly colony, only to land right in the midst of Seeker's party from the Seventh Continuum.

They lied and said you were the traitor, Seeker communicated. That was met with a solid bout of laughter from Aero. She felt it through her Beacon.

Starry hell, they must have been surprised when you turned up, Aero replied. *I wish I could have been there to see the look on their faces.*

The communication ended.

Seeker and her people set out in the dark of the night. The prisoners had their hands bound behind them. They stumbled frequently in the dark, but Slayer and Bruiser kept them moving. At first, they balked at eating ratters and buggers, but hunger soon got the better of them and they choked them down. Seeker marveled at the differences between their colonies. She remembered the first time she came across Myra and her friends. They thought she was a monster. But she had thought the same thing about them before she bonded with the Beacon.

Over the next few days, the landscape grew flatter as they approached the coastline. Her Beacon pulsed and delivered directions from Jared, as he led them northward toward the First Continuum. They continued to travel at night, when it was most comfortable for her people, and sleep during the day in whatever shelter they could find, though sometimes they lay out in the open under the stars. Her people were adapting well to the Brightside, getting used to living without ceilings and walls.

Two days later, Jared's voice echoed through her head.

Seeker, I'm picking up a signal.

Seeker sat back on her haunches. They'd been traveling all night, and dawn was about to break. The horizon was already painted with searing pink light. Her visor was tucked in her rucksack, but she fished it out, preparing for daybreak.

Where's it coming from? Seeker thought, pushing her energy into the Beacon. It flashed brighter. A second later, she heard Jared's soothing voice in her head.

Somewhere . . . above us . . . up in the sky . . .

Seeker craned her neck up. She could just make out a fleet of silvery ships. With astonishing speed and grace, they grew larger and swooped down. They hovered overhead. Her people scattered like ratters and hid behind the rocks. Only Crawler stayed steadfastly by her side, though he cringed away from the sky.

Seeker wasn't afraid. She grinned up at them.

"Don't be afraid," she growled. "Old friends."

In a coordinated formation, the ships lowered vertically. Their engines kicked up grit and dust, hovering a few feet off the ground. A door cracked open in the side of the first ship. Wren stuck her head out. Her hair had been freshly buzzed and she sported a new deployment uniform, but she still wore the same feisty expression.

"Need a lift?" she yelled to be heard over the roar of the engines. She arched one golden eyebrow. "I'll bet your feet are getting pretty sore."

"What took you so long?" Seeker growled. She tried to sound stern, but her tone betrayed her affection for Wren. She was glad to see her friend.

"Hey, a little gratitude here?" Wren said in mock annoyance. "Starry hell, we had to overthrow a Supreme General, wrest back control of our army, and take over command of a whole colony. Think that's easy?"

"So did I," Seeker said. "And it didn't take me nearly that long."

They shared a laugh. "We've come to transport your people to the First Continuum," Wren said, gesturing to the ships. "Supreme General Wright's orders."

"Supreme General?" Seeker said.

"Yeah, and I'm Major Jordan. What about you?"

"Just Seeker," she replied and meant it. She didn't like fancy titles.

Wren spoke into her headpiece. All at once, the ships cracked open their bay doors, revealing large cargo spaces fitted with benches and restraints. With the help of Wren's soldiers, Seeker rounded up her people and loaded them into the transports. Once she was sure they were secure, she boarded Wren's ship, settling into a bench next to Crawler. She noticed that his hands were shaking as he buckled his harness.

In the cockpit, Wren hit a few buttons on the console and gripped the controls. She spoke into her headset. "Hold tight, we're about to lift off," she announced. "The weather looks clear. Should be a smooth ride to the First Continuum."

The sun lurched over the horizon as their fleet launched into the sky, sailing through the blue expanse and carrying them to the place where they would make their final stand. Seeker snaked her fingers through Crawler's hands, feeling the secure warmth of his grip. His shaking stilled as he squeezed her hand back. She wanted to savor these last few moments of peace before war broke over their world like a dark tempest. She remembered the last image that Myra transmitted to her of Drakken's ship.

He's coming for us, she thought. *And he's coming soon.*

PART V
UNITED WE STAND; DIVIDED WE FALL

War was always here. Before man was, war waited for him. The ultimate trade awaiting its ultimate practitioner.

—Cormac McCarthy, *Blood Meridian*

Chapter 41
A FISHING EXPEDITION

Myra Jackson

The saltwater lapped over her boots, staining them dark brown. Myra could smell the ocean on every breath; she could taste the brine on her tongue. The rocky shoreline stretched out in both directions, curving out of sight. A brisk wind whipped down from the grizzled sky, chilling her cheeks and drawing blood to their surface.

It's still winter, Elianna communicated. *Spring hasn't come yet.*

Spring, Myra thought, savoring the unfamiliar word like a piece of sweetfish on her tongue. Images rushed through her head—verdant, lush meadows bursting with wild flowers in every color imaginable; hummingbirds flitting between the cupped blossoms, lapping up the delicate nectar like it was candy; earthworms writhing in the fertile soil, still damp with morning dew. They were Elianna's memories.

Next to her, Tinker stooped down and stuck his hand in the ocean. "Holy Sea, it's cold," he said, jerking it out. Myra shot him a reproachful look.

"It's still winter. Be careful, or you'll make yourself sick."

"No, I won't," he said. "That's a myth."

"How do you know? Isn't that why they call it *catching a cold*?"

"Wren told me about it," he said excitedly. "When we were in the Second Continuum. Colds are actually caused by something called a virus."

"It's true," Kaleb called from the beach, where he was dragging a heavy crate across the sand. He looked healthier than he had in many weeks. "We had a lot of time to kill in that barracks. Talking helped keep us from going crazy."

Myra could scarcely believe they'd been back for a week already. She studied Kaleb. Something was different about him, though she couldn't put her finger on what exactly. He seemed *whole* again. Maybe that was it.

"A virus, huh?" Myra said. "Wren told you that?"

Tinker nodded. "She told me lots of stuff."

Myra still wasn't Wren's biggest fan, but she kept that to herself. She shifted her gaze to the crate. Kaleb dragged it over.

"Tink, want to help me get this open?" Myra asked.

Together, they pried the top off, revealing Myra's deep-sea probe. It looked like a miniature submersible. She'd spent the last few weeks building it. Only a few days ago, she'd finished her plans, welding the last joints together and programming in the coordinates Noah provided for the Thirteenth Continuum. But today was the real test. Would the vessel prove seaworthy? Or would it sink like a stone in the tempestuous sea?

Myra glanced up the beach, where Aero was waiting in the transport. He was talking heatedly into his headset, most likely to Wren about some issue that had cropped up with their new army. Between his duties commanding his soldiers and their plans for the Fourth Continuum, he always seemed distracted lately. She wondered if it would always be this way—if something would always drive them apart.

They lifted the probe from the foam casing and set it on the beach, where it sank into the sodden sand. The waves lapped at it. It looked wonky and small compared to the endless swathe of unquiet water.

"Think it'll work?" Kaleb asked, eyeing it. He ran his hands over the smooth exterior that Myra had welded together from scraps of metal.

She set her lips, studying her creation. "I don't know," she said bluntly. "The deep sea presents so many challenges. If the probe can withstand the pressure and get close enough to our colony, we might stand a chance."

"Papa will find the signal, won't he?" Tinker asked.

"Of course he will," she replied. "He's a brilliant Engineer. Since we can't build a real sub, this little probe is our best chance of getting a message to him."

What she didn't say was that it was a long shot. Their father would have to escape from the Pen somehow. And even then, he would have to be looking for the signal to find it. But she quelled her fears for her brother's sake.

"Play the message again," Tinker begged. "Please."

"But you've already watched it four times." Even so, she hit a button on the remote in her pocket. Her tinny, electronic voice echoed out of the probe.

Papa, it's Myra. We made it to the Surface, just like you hoped! I'm sending this probe back to let you know it's livable again. We made it to the First Continuum, though we lost Paige and Rickard along the way . . .

She let the message play a little longer, but one glance back at the transport told her that Aero was growing impatient. He was still talking into his headset and looked upset. Her Beacon flared, confirming that something bad had happened. He needed to get back to his troops right away. Myra turned her attention back to the beach.

"Tink, Kaleb, help me launch the probe," she said, swiping the hair out of her face. The wind was growing stronger, but it wouldn't affect the probe once it plunged underwater. Carefully, they lifted it, carrying it into the ocean. Cold water sloshed up to their knees. They set the probe into the waves. It bobbed gently, caught in the sway of the mighty sea. She pulled out the remote and keyed the button to power it on.

With a placid rumble, the probe whirred to life. The jets cut into the waves, idling and waiting for her next command. Kaleb grinned. "Nice work, Jackson."

"Ready?" Myra asked, feeling a rush of excitement.

"Wait, can I do it?" Tinker asked, his eyes darting to the remote. She handed it over. He bit down on his tongue in concentration while she showed him the correct sequence to depress. He aimed it at the probe. "Now?"

She nodded. "Go ahead, Tink. Send it to the Holy Sea."

He hit the buttons. The probe bobbed on the waves, but as soon as he finished keying in the signal, it leapt to life, spitting out water and spraying them. The currents were powerful, but the small probe sped away. She had based it on her father's blueprints, which she memorized before they escaped. They watched the probe power through the waves. When it got another twenty feet out, it dove beneath the surface and vanished from their view, bound for the Thirteenth Continuum.

Or what was left of it, she thought.

They were running out of oxygen. Even if her father received the message and the coordinates, it was unlikely that her people could escape from their dying colony. It would become their tomb before too long.

o   o   o

"Aero, is everything okay?" Myra asked as she climbed into the transport.

Tinker and Kaleb followed behind her. She slid into the copilot's chair, while they claimed seats in the first row of benches and fastened their harnesses. Aero sighed and yanked his headset off, massaging his ear where it had left an imprint. "More problems with the Seventh Continuum soldiers," he said wearily.

"Anything new?" she asked, buckling her harness.

He shook his head. "Wren is trying to train them, but they

hate taking orders. Their barracks are filthy. They won't wear their uniforms. They refuse rations and insist on hunting for ratters. That takes away from valuable training time."

"They do love their Falchions," Myra said. Aero had armed them with the extra blades forged by the Foundry. Seeker and her soldiers had taken to the modern weapons instantly. The bonding process went unexpectedly well.

Aero frowned. "But they refuse proper training."

"Well, your soldiers haven't exactly helped the situation," Myra pointed out. "That bullying incident last week really offended them."

She knew that Aero would rather forget about how a group of soldiers from the Second Continuum was caught bullying the Seventh soldiers for being "primitive humanoids." Discrimination was a real problem, one they hadn't solved yet.

He jammed buttons on the console. "I made an example out of them," he said a bit defensively. "My soldiers were punished for that infraction."

"Not harshly enough, in my opinion. A few extra shifts scrubbing latrines and some missed rations isn't exactly a hardship. They were caught abusing them."

"Only with words. They didn't lay hands on them."

"Words have power." She aimed her fiery gaze at him. "If Major Zakkay hadn't caught them, it might have turned out much worse. Your soldiers had unsheathed their Falchions and were preparing to morph them. I read the report."

"Look, I'll run my army," Aero shot back. He hit a button, making the engines roar. "And you can worry about the rest. Unless you'd like to be the Supreme General? Trust me, it's a lot of responsibility. I don't get much sleep these days."

The truth was visible in the dark circles that rimmed his eyes and in the hollowness of his cheeks. But Myra still felt a surge of irritation. "You think I don't know about responsibility? At least you were able to save your colony. My people are still suffocating under the sea, remember? I've got no way to rescue them . . ."

She trailed off when she felt a tug at her sleeve.

"Please," Tinker rasped. "Don't fight . . . it doesn't help anything."

They lapsed into tense silence. Aero slid his headset back over his head, effectively cutting off communication. She knew that Tinker was right. Fighting didn't get them anywhere. They needed to get along if they had any hope of surviving the coming war. But her emotions got the better of her. She spent the rest of the short flight back to the First Continuum in silence.

o　o　o

Their transport swooped over their encampment in the Harvard Yard. Flurries blustered around, but the view was clear. Myra leaned toward the cockpit window, taking in the aerial view of the army they'd cobbled together from their surviving colonies. Second Continuum soldiers milled about, passing in and out of the pop-up tents where they lived and slept. Some were lined up to receive rations, while others were grouped into formations and running combat drills. They moved with urgency and purpose.

She spotted the Seventh Continuum encampment on the other side of the courtyard, near the crumbling remains of the Science Center. Unlike the area that housed the Second Continuum, which was orderly and well kept, this section had tents arranged haphazardly. Rubbish and rat carcasses littered the snow. It also looked deserted. She didn't spot any of the Seventh soldiers. They preferred to sleep during the day. This was only one of the many reasons why integrating their colonies remained a challenge.

"Our ways . . . different," Seeker had explained in their first security meeting after returning to the First Continuum. "My people have never been outside our colony. We have to give them time to adapt." Myra knew that Seeker was right. But that was the one thing they didn't have—time.

She was jerked out of her thoughts as their transport touched down in the airfield and taxied up to the other ships.

According to Professor Divinus, this used to be a field where students played a sport called football. It involved throwing, carrying, or kicking a leather ball and players tackling each other. The game sounded silly and seemed to have no constructive purpose. Why people spent time, energy, and resources on it was beyond her understanding. The professor only shrugged when she voiced her confusion.

"It was a fun distraction, I suppose," he offered weakly. "A way to channel our primal aggressions."

"Hey, at least they weren't murdering people for sport like in the Roman Colosseum," Aero said with a grimace. "I got a taste of what that was like."

"People actually played this *football*?" Myra asked uncertainly.

"For about two hundred and fifty years," Divinus replied. "But eventually, the sport was banned due to traumatic brain injuries. The university maintained the field, but only because it was designated a National Historic Landmark. See those columns? It was actually built to resemble the Greek and Roman stadiums like the Colosseum."

Myra decided that an airfield seemed like a much better use of the space.

Aero powered off the transport and engaged the cooling systems, tugged off his headset, and clambered from his seat. "See you at the security meeting?"

He didn't wait for her response before he disembarked from the ship, bounding down the retractable stairs. A few of his soldiers fell in with him—Majors Zakkay, Tabor, Grimes, and Malik. They'd been waiting at the airfield. Myra couldn't hear what they said to Aero, but uneasiness wafted off them. They started back toward the encampment, talking heatedly. Aero was visibly upset by whatever they were telling him.

There was nothing Myra could do about it now. It was *his* army—or so he'd made abundantly clear. She tore her eyes away and helped Tinker out of his harness. They followed Kaleb from the transport, whose engines were still cooling. Maintenance soldiers swarmed the vessel and tended to it. She watched Aero's back as he marched off toward the encampment and wondered what new problem had cropped up this time.

Sorry . . . another incident with the Seventh soldiers, he communicated through the Beacons. But then his attention was pulled in another direction.

But not that sorry, she thought back.

She hoped Aero could feel her annoyance, but he probably wasn't paying attention. Only Tinker seemed to notice. He watched her warily as they picked their way over the crumbling bridge that spanned the rushing river. They passed under a rusty gate, heading for Widener Library. The old depository housed the First Continuum.

Her thoughts snapped back to the deep sea probe. Her hand crept into her pocket and felt for the remote. She wondered if her father would intercept her message or if trying to contact the Thirteenth Continuum was just an exercise in futility.

Elianna spoke up. *Myra, I know our people—they're resilient, scrappy, resourceful, and they will not go quietly. That probe gives us a chance to give them invaluable information. We must have faith that your father will receive it.*

You're right, Myra thought back.

She just wished she believed it.

Chapter 42
INSUBORDINATION

Supreme General Aero Wright

"Starry hell," Aero cursed when he saw the graffiti spray-painted on Sever Hall—bold, white, and jarring. Taking Myra to the beach that morning had been a mistake. His presence carried weight around here; when he was away, that absence was felt by the soldiers. That led to unrest—and in this case—outright mischief that threatened to undo their weeks of hard work. The unity of their army was already fraying.

"Sir, are you okay?" Major Tabor asked carefully. She exchanged a worried glance with Majors Malik, Zakkay, and Grimes.

"No, I'm not," Aero said in a harsher voice than he intended. He threw his arms up at the graffiti. "It's getting worse, isn't it? I left you in charge for *three* short hours, and I come back to this mess? Majors, how did you let this happen?"

Their eyes jerked to the jagged letters dripping down the bricks. The paint was still fresh, not even dry yet:

FILTHY, STINKING BEASTS!
BEWARE THE 7TH HUMANOIDS!

Tabor flushed. "Sir, I was dealing with that last ship-ment of rations from the mothership. They were improperly secured and leaked during transit—"

"No excuses, Major," Aero snapped. He hated the sharp-ness of his tone but couldn't help it. "At least you had the sense to block off the area. Get this cleaned up before anyone from the Seventh wakes up and sees it. We're just lucky they're nocturnal. The last thing we need is more fallout after that other incident."

"And the offender, sir?" Zakkay said tentatively, handing him a tablet with the soldier's file displayed. Aero skimmed it while Zakkay continued briefing him.

"He's being detained. We identified him from Noah's secu-rity feeds and pulled him out of his combat unit's barracks. It appears that he acted alone."

"Is this related to last week's incident?" Aero asked.

"Not directly," Malik said, but his voice caught.

"Indirectly then?" Aero said.

"Sir, we suspect it may have inspired him to act out," Grimes spoke up.

"Exactly," Malik added. "Insubordination spreads like a virus. Once it's loose, it can be difficult to contain. Last week's incident hit a nerve with our soldiers. They're disgruntled with all the changes. They're having a hard time adapting."

Aero felt a sharp pain in his temples. "Major, you mean we're going to have to deal with more of *this*?" he asked, though he already knew the answer. He couldn't take his eyes off the blasted graffiti. The Majors exchanged uneasy looks.

"There is one option," Tabor said. "That could work."

"Spit it out, Major," Aero said.

"Execute him," Tabor said. "We make an example out of this soldier. That level of deterrence might work. The lighter punishments we doled out last week didn't have any impact. If anything, they encouraged further infractions."

"For vandalism?" Aero said. "Don't you think that's a bit extreme?"

Tabor set her lips. "Not if it enforces order."

She didn't flinch when she said that. The delicate muscles of her face displayed no emotional cadence. Aero shifted his gaze to Malik, Grimes, and Zakkay, but they stood in solidarity with Tabor and also displayed no emotions. His temples throbbed even harder. He had to fight to keep from wincing at the pain. Clearly, the vandal had done something really stupid and harmful, but did he deserve to die for it?

"That's it," Aero ordered. "I've heard enough. Let's get this over with. Major Zakkay, bring the soldier to my tent. The rest of you, get this mess cleaned up."

The Majors saluted and rushed away, clearly relieved to be dismissed from his presence. He couldn't blame them. He made his way over to the latrine station and splashed cool water on his face. Droplets trickled down his cheeks but did little to ease his headache.

He straightened up and surveyed the encampment, which took up the entirety of the courtyard and spilled into the surrounding areas. It housed over four thousand soldiers, neatly divided into ranks and units, all at his command. When he was at the Agoge, he—like most of his classmates—often fantasized about what it would feel like to be the Supreme General. He never imagined that it would actually happen, even though his father commanded their ship. Biological relationships didn't influence their ranking in the army. But an unprecedented chain of events had carried him to this lofty position.

Yet, all he felt was a bone-deep weariness. He brushed his hand over his hair, clipped to the quick again, and headed back to his tent. He didn't want to see the encampment. Didn't want to think about the lives that he would soon be commanding into battle. Didn't want to imagine how many of them would perish on this field.

About ten minutes later, Zakkay arrived with the graffiti artist. He was a scrawny boy, clearly fresh out of the Agoge. He couldn't even grow stubble yet. Electronic restraints bound his wrists and ankles, though he still had his Falchion belted to his waist. He stumbled over the restraints, but Zakkay held the boy upright. *He is just a boy, isn't he?* Aero thought. He wondered if that was how Vinick had seen him.

Aero approached him. "State your name, soldier."

The boy tried to salute, but the chains jerked his wrist down. "Private Wilson Jamal Houston," the boy said. Even his voice sounded squeaky and immature.

"Do you know why you've been arrested?" Aero said, doing his best to project authority. Not many years separated them. The boy nodded as his cheeks flamed crimson. "I forbade this kind of discrimination against the Seventh soldiers—"

"But sir, they're primitives!" the boy cut him off.

Aero felt fury rising in his chest. He towered over the boy, reaching for his Falchion. "You will respect my command and your fellow soldiers—or I'll strip you of your Falchion and ship you back to the mothership. Is that understood?"

The boy struggled in Zakkay's grip. "No, sir! I won't fight next to those filthy beasts from the Seventh. You're arming them with our sacred weapons! The Falchions belong to *our* colony. Supreme General Vinick would never have allowed this!"

"Vinick was a traitor and a murderer," Aero said, failing to keep the anger from his voice. "Soldier, I'm declaring you an emotional hazard. I won't have you infecting our ranks with your insubordination. Major Zakkay, ship him back to the mothership on the next transport. Pending a medical evaluation, we'll decide on the proper punishment. But first, strip him of his Falchion. He is no longer a soldier in my army."

Even as he said that, Aero hated himself for having to do it. This was a boy. Deployed to a strange and barren planet. Preparing for war. What did he expect?

Obedience, came his father's voice through the Beacon. *You're commanding an army now. Without obedience, everything will devolve into chaos.*

I know, but we're punishing children, Aero thought back.

They're soldiers, his father communicated. *You can't change the rules for this boy because you feel sorry for him. He violated your orders. He must be punished.*

The Major led Houston away, pushing him out of the tent and into the encampment. Soon Aero heard the boy's screams reverberate into his tent. They escalated into animalistic shrieks. Zakkay must have taken his Falchion. Aero shuddered at the thought; his hand went straight to the hilt of his blade. He felt the fresh charge surge through it. He couldn't imagine the psychological pain of losing it. They'd throw the boy into the Disciplinary Barracks. Aero hadn't resorted to executing him, like Tabor had suggested. At least, not yet. But he couldn't avoid the decision forever.

Maybe he was too soft. Maybe Tabor was right. Maybe that's why all this insubordination was happening. His headache grew even worse. Aero flopped down on his cot, the thin mattress squeaking under his weight. Wren found him in the exact same position an hour later, doing the exact same thing—brooding.

"Sir, the security meeting," she said as she rushed into his tent. "Sorry, I overslept. Hurry, we're going to be late. You know that makes Noah testy."

The last thing that Aero wanted to do right now was talk more. But he couldn't skip it. This was yet another thing that he had to do. Before he was the Supreme General, he thought his life was regimented with an unrelenting schedule. But this was worse. Back then at least, there was downtime. Regular meals in the Mess Hall. Plus, a solid eight hours built into the schedule to sleep each night. Now, if he could get five uninterrupted minutes during the day or a few hours of sleep at night without some emergency cropping up, it felt like a luxury. His father spoke up.

Now you understand the burden of command. It's not for the faint of heart.

"You've got that right," Aero muttered, feeling every one of his seventeen years. His birthday had come and gone like any other day that warranted no celebration, just an adjustment of his age in his personal files.

"Sir, are you talking to me?" Wren said, arching her eyebrow.

"My father," Aero said, pulling himself up from his cot. He turned away, though he could feel her worried eyes still on him. He pushed the thick flap open. Bright sunlight spilled into the tent. "Did you hear about the graffiti?"

"Graffiti?" she said, squinting at the light. "That sounds bad."

"Well, it's certainly not good. Come on, let's go. I'll brief you on the way to the meeting." They marched toward the steps that led up to Widener Library, which kept watch over the courtyard like a grumpy caretaker.

o   o   o

Another damn meeting, Aero thought as the elevator descended to the First Continuum. He hated all this constant talking, analyzing, and agonizing over every little detail. He wished they could just implement their plan and carry on with it. Wren shifted stiffly next to him. She also seemed irritated.

"Tough day?" Aero asked.

"More like . . . a tough night," she said wearily. "I tried to run some Falchion drills—the operative word being *drills*. It ended up in a brawl, injuring several of the Seventh soldiers. Two broken bones. Stitches. I had to put the whole camp on lockdown so I could escort them to the Medical Clinic. I couldn't risk them venturing into the Second encampment alone. Clearly, I was right to worry, given your vandal."

"Right, it was a good idea to chaperone them," Aero said. "The integration isn't going as smoothly as we'd hoped. We'll have to keep taking extra precautions."

She nodded. "Anyway, I didn't get back to the Seventh camp until the sun came up. Got about three hours of shut-eye, but then I had to be up for this meeting."

Aero cocked his eyebrow. "Ah, meetings. Your favorite."

"Starry hell, you hate all this jabbering as much as I do."

"More, I'll wager," he said with a rueful grin. "I'm starting to appreciate what my father went through when he was the Supreme General. You think it's all about being the best soldier, but really it has nothing to do with that. Mostly, you spend a lot of time talking and putting out fires, and very little time actually fighting."

She studied his face. "Do you miss it?"

"Miss what?"

"Being a normal soldier, not having the burden of command."

Usually this would be considered insubordination, but their relationship extended beyond that of commander and soldier. Plus, he relished the chance to speak freely. "Well, I did command our unit," he pointed out. "But mostly, I had to follow orders from the Supreme General and the Majors. I didn't have to make every single decision. So yeah, I guess I miss that feeling of having somebody else in charge."

"You could always step down," she said. "I'm sure Major Tabor or Malik would be thrilled to step into your shoes."

Aero shook his head, though he wished it were that simple. "I'm the Carrier, and my father entrusted the Beacon to me. Besides, our army is hanging together by a thread. A change in leadership would spur more unrest, maybe even outright revolt."

"You're right. Forget I said anything."

A few moments of silence passed as they continued to descend.

"The vandal was only a boy," Aero said finally, letting the uncertainty filter into his voice. "I skimmed his file. Less than a month out of the Agoge. Scared and angry . . . and really confused."

"But still dangerous," Wren cut in. "His vandalism threatened the security and safety of the entire army. You have to punish him—and strongly."

"Tabor wanted to execute him."

Wren looked up sharply. "For vandalism?"

"Tabor thinks I need to send a message to the troops or we're going to face more incidents—that it's the only way to stop it from spreading like a virus."

Wren's eyes lingered on him. "So . . . what did you decide?"

"I put it off," he said. "I declared him an emotional hazard, stripped him of his Falchion, and shipped him back to the mothership. I couldn't do it . . ."

He trailed off. Wren reached over and laid her hand on his arm. The intimate gesture made his skin tingle. Their eyes locked. She squeezed gently. "You did what you thought was right," she said. "That's all you can do. That's all any commander can do. Tabor isn't in charge—you are. You have good instincts. You always have . . . sir," she added quickly. She pulled her hand away, crossing her arms over her chest.

They didn't speak again until the elevator spit them out. "Supreme General Wright, you're late," Noah said as soon as they stepped into the chamber and felt the cool rush of the underground air. "Major Jordan, so are you."

"Thanks. Tell us something we don't know," Aero grumbled, increasing his pace. They weaved past the cryocapsules. He glimpsed the embryos drifting in stasis.

"The Forger is running late too," Noah replied, missing the sarcasm. "He didn't respond to my summons, so I sounded an alarm in the Foundry. That got his attention."

"The Order's work is more important than another meeting," Aero said, picturing the new Foundry that had been set up in the unfinished chambers of the First Continuum. The sprawling, sparse rooms with their raw rock walls and exposed pipes suited the Foundry. With the surviving Forgers—about twelve of them—the young Forger had set up a makeshift workshop. They were laboring around the clock to fashion new weapons for the Seventh soldiers and charge the existing ones.

"Not according to the professor," Noah said. "He says the meetings are key to refining our battle strategy. Also, Ms. Jackson agrees with him."

"If we don't have enough weapons, how are we supposed to fight the Fourth Continuum?" Aero said, feeling his frustration at everything being directed at Noah. But he couldn't help it. "The Forger should have been excused from this meeting."

"I regret that it's not my decision," Noah replied. "You can take it up with the professor in the meeting. We have procedures in place for addressing such issues."

Aero bit his tongue. Noah was only a computer, after all. Arguing with him would prove futile. He and Wren proceeded to the control room. The Forger fell in with them. The faint odor of burning metal wafted off his robes. Soot blackened his fingers.

"Supreme General Wright," he said by way of a greeting.

"After you, brother," Aero said, gesturing for him to enter the control room, where they found Myra, Kaleb, and Professor Divinus already seated at the long table. Holographic images of the Fourth Continuum were projected overhead. Myra shot him an irritated look as he slid into the chair next to her. A few minutes later, Seeker and Crawler loped through the door. Aero hated meetings, but Seeker hated them a hundred times worse. Regardless, all the colonies had to be represented here.

"I'm calling this Assembly of the United Continuums to order," Professor Divinus said once they'd taken their seats. As Divinus droned on, Aero sank deeper into his chair, wishing that it was his cot and he could shut his eyes and drift away for a few moments. He could already tell this meeting was going to be a long one.

Chapter 43
THE ASSEMBLY

Myra Jackson

Professor, are there any updates on the Fourth Continuum?" Myra asked once they'd all taken their seats. She shot an annoyed look at Aero, who was sitting next to her. He was late. *Again*. They were all late. But for some reason, Aero's tardiness bothered her the most. But she didn't bring it up. They already had enough problems.

"They're two weeks away," Divinus reported. He flipped to a projection showing their trajectory through space. "They're having to decelerate as they approach, or they'd shoot right past us. That buys us a little time, but not much."

Myra looked up from her agenda, focusing on the projection. They were getting closer—she could feel it like a physical force. The ship no longer faded in and out. The signal was growing stronger as they closed the distance to Earth.

Aero turned to the Forger. "Brother, how are the defenses coming? Has your Order made any progress on the shield? Without it, Drakken can fire on us remotely with his arsenal. We need to force him to deploy his troops."

"My sworn brothers and sisters are working around the

clock," the Forger said. "That's why I was late to the meeting. But we've encountered a few delays."

"How serious?" Myra asked. "Two weeks isn't much time."

The Forger nodded to Professor Divinus, who pulled up a map of their encampment. "The First Continuum and the surrounding grounds are a larger surface area than we've ever had to protect before."

"Brother, can it be done?" Wren asked, her eyes glued to the map.

The Forger nodded. "I have confidence in my Order. But remember, the shield won't keep out Drakken's troops. They'll be able to pass through the barrier. The energy field only deflects their weapons."

"Of course, but forcing Drakken into a ground war evens the odds," Aero explained, while Noah projected a simulation that illustrated his plan. "We can meet them on the battlefield in one-on-one combat. At least that gives us a chance."

Myra frowned. "But we'll be outnumbered, right?"

Aero exchanged a look with Wren. "The Fourth Continuum is a much larger ship than our home colony. With their advanced technology, we believe they were able to sustain their population during the exile. Based on Noah's estimates, we'll be outnumbered about two to one."

"And the Seventh soldiers?" Myra asked, glancing at her agenda. She knew she was bringing up a sore point, but they couldn't ignore the myriad of problems facing them. "How are they adapting to the training regimen?"

"Training has proven challenging," Wren said. She was trying to sound diplomatic, but frustration edged into her voice. "We've armed over half of them with Falchions, but teaching them how to use them—well, that's been difficult, to say the least. They've had trouble adjusting to the surface environment and continue to keep a nocturnal schedule, which conflicts with the rest of our army. We're keeping them segregated in their own encampment. So far, integration has been impossible—"

"Because nasty soldiers bullying my people," Seeker growled, her hand darting to her Falchion, which remained sheathed in the scabbard belted to her waist. It stood out against her long, dark hair. Crawler reached for his Falchion too.

"Your soldiers calling us filthy names," Crawler added, glaring suspiciously at Wren. "And threatening us with their shiny blades. And they smell funny . . . too clean. We don't want to be around their stink. If they threaten us again, we fight back."

"Actually, it's because your soldiers won't follow my orders and keep trying to kill each other in training drills," Wren said. She turned to Aero. "Sir, they're not ready for Falchions. I warned you this would happen! They're delicate weapons—"

"My people can handle Falchions," Seeker growled. "You're the problem. Why do we need all this training? Running around and pretending to fight? Why waste precious energy on fake drills? It makes no sense. My people will be ready to fight when the time comes for real battle. Until then, we rest and save our energy."

Wren threw up her hands. "Did you hear that? How can I train them when their leaders tell them to disobey me? They can't even perform basic tasks like lining up in formation and marching in a straight line. Even children at the Agoge master that in the first week. They end up shoving each other and breaking into a brawl. It's complete chaos. Starry hell, I'm lucky if I don't get sucker punched trying to break it up."

Seeker and Crawler glared at Wren, but Myra interceded before they said something they regretted. "Seeker, the training drills are important so your people can learn to fight alongside the Second Continuum. Even if they seem pointless, can you convince them to listen to Wren?"

"If she can convince her soldiers to stop writing filthy messages on walls," Seeker growled. "We know about the graffiti. They tried to cover it up."

"Filthy soldiers," Crawler agreed. "Nasty soldiers."

Aero grimaced, holding his hand up for Wren to stay out of it. "That was the actions of one soldier acting alone. He is being punished harshly. I apologize for any offense it may have caused your people. My intention in cleaning it up was to prevent further damage to their morale."

"Too late," Seeker snarled. She leaned forward, the light catching her sharp jawline. She'd added a layer of lean muscle to her frame. "My people are threatening to defect—unless you turn the soldier over to us, so we can punish him our way."

"Oh yeah?" Wren asked, still stewing. "And what is that?"

"We let our people decide," Crawler said, narrowing his eyes. "Death by stoning, most likely. Since we don't have a chasm nearby to toss him into . . . and well . . . Seeker banned Feasts. Though maybe we should bring them back."

"Great, that's a relief," Wren said, rolling her eyes. "You won't eat the poor kid. No wonder our soldiers are calling you names. Maybe you deserve it—"

"Major Jordan, that's enough," Aero cut her off. "You're not helping. Don't make me reconsider your assignment to train the Seventh—or your promotion."

Silence descended over the table.

"Apologies, sir," Wren said, looking down. Her cheeks colored with shame. "I misspoke. I shouldn't let my emotions get the better of me like that."

"Hey, you don't have to be so hard on her," Kaleb said, glancing at Aero. "Look, she's under a lot of pressure. We all are. She's doing the best she can."

Myra was surprised that Kaleb came to Wren's defense. She felt a tickle of jealousy. *Since when did he care about this strange girl from the Second Continuum?*

"Kaleb, I respect your opinion at this Assembly," Aero said in a sharp tone. Sharper than necessary, now that Myra thought about it. "But Major Jordan serves under my command. How she conducts herself is my business. Is that understood?"

The two scowled at each other. "No wonder your soldiers are disgruntled and spray-painting the bloody walls," Kaleb muttered under his breath. That set off a fresh round of bickering, this time between Aero and Kaleb.

Myra felt her head start to throb as each member retreated

to their own factions and defended their alliances. This was the last thing they needed. She pounded on the table to get their attention, casting a withering gaze over the table.

"Hey, we're all on the same side here. The person sitting next to you isn't your enemy. Commander Drakken is the real enemy. Let's not forget that."

Aero looked sheepish. "You're right . . . sorry." He turned to Seeker. "I'll come to your camp and apologize personally for the incident this morning. But under no circumstances am I turning my soldier over. He serves in my army, and he's my responsibility. I will punish him in accordance with our customs and laws."

Myra held her breath. "Seeker, does that sound acceptable? Can you convince your people to stay and listen to Wren? We need their help if we're going to have any chance against Drakken."

Seeker and Crawler whispered to each other. Crawler sniffed and growled. More heated whispering ensued, and then Seeker turned back to the table.

"We accept your offer of an official apology," she said. "But if anything else happens, we want the soldier turned over to us for punishment. Is that clear?"

"Aero?" Myra asked. "Can you agree to that?"

"I don't like the terms," he muttered. "But fine."

The tense atmosphere in the meeting settled down a little . . . but not much. Myra glanced at her agenda. They had already veered wildly off course.

"Before we move on to the next order of business, have we finished our discussion of the shield?" she asked, trying to restore some semblance of order.

"I hate to bring it up," the Forger ventured. "But there's one other problem with the shield. It won't hold forever. My brothers and sisters believe the Fourth Continuum will figure out a way to break it, given their advanced technology."

"How long will we have?" Myra asked.

The Forger shrugged. "That depends on Drakken."

Myra felt her mind whirling with a thousand different

problems, each more daunting than the last. Her agenda seemed completely useless now. "So the shield and the ground war will do nothing more than buy us a little time?"

Aero grimaced. "Right, that appears to be the situation. The shield will deflect their long-range weapons. His troops will be able to march through the energy barrier. We can fight them off, but as soon as Drakken breaks the shield, he'll fire his warheads at us. There's always a chance that he won't break it . . ."

"A chance," Myra repeated. "But it's slim, isn't it?"

"Confirmed," Noah chimed in. "Ms. Jackson, I've run the calculations. The odds are not in our favor. Most likely outcome—Drakken will defeat us and gain access to the First Continuum. He can then hack my systems and obtain the secret of the Doom."

Noah's complex risk calculations materialized overhead. Myra didn't even try to follow them. What difference did it make? She knew they were accurate. With each flash of her Beacon, she could feel Drakken drawing closer to Earth.

"That means we've got only one option," she said softly, "if we're going to win this war."

"And what's that?" Kaleb asked, turning toward her.

Myra jabbed her finger at the projection. "We've got to find Drakken's weakness, something we can exploit and use against him. Something that he's not expecting."

"By the stars, she's right," Aero said. "Professor, did we learn anything from the Foundry's Archives? Maybe something we can use against Drakken?"

"Ah, yes," Divinus said. "Noah, can you pull them up?"

The air crackled with energy as the data materialized, written in ornate, sloping handwriting. Divinus manipulated the documents with a flick of his fingers.

"I did stumble across something curious," Divinus said. "It appears there was a relationship between Supreme General Bryant Stern and Shira Ramses. She was the Carrier for the Fourth Continuum at the time of their disappearance."

"A relationship?" Kaleb said. "You mean . . ."

"Yes, I surmise from his logbook entries that it may have been romantic in nature," Divinus confirmed. "We learned from our early studies on the Beacons that the devices can have an influence over the Carrier's emotional states, though it's difficult to quantify. Clearly, Stern harbored feelings for Ramses that exceeded the bounds of their official relationship, though I don't know if she reciprocated them. Before he could confess them to her, the Fourth Continuum vanished—and Ramses with them."

Myra couldn't help glancing at Aero. She wondered, were her feelings for him merely a by-product of the Beacons and their special connection? Or were they real? And more importantly, would she ever be able to unravel the two tangents?

"Professor, did Stern love her?" she asked as her eyes tracked over the logbook entries. Phrases like *ache of her loss* and *tugs at my heart* leapt out.

Divinus gave a sharp nod. "I believe so, but of course, some of that is speculation on my part. Stern communicated with Ramses regularly through the Beacons, so he knew the Fourth Continuum better than anyone. That's what makes his logbook entries concerning their disappearance even more troubling."

"Troubling . . . how?" Aero asked, exchanging a look with Wren.

"Remember Stern wasn't a scientist, so his understanding was limited," Divinus hedged. "But it appears that the Fourth Continuum was working on some kind of advanced networking experiment."

"Networking," Myra repeated. "Like computers?"

"This goes beyond computers," Divinus said. "We're talking about *human* networking. The idea came out of the Beacons and their ability to connect and preserve human consciousnesses. Technology tends to build on itself. One breakthrough leads to another and so on. But we know little beyond the vague descriptions in his logbooks."

Myra felt frustrated. "How does that help us?"

Divinus shrugged. "My dear, I'm not sure. But it's all we've got."

"What we need is a way to access the Fourth Continuum," Aero said. "Get into their computers, spy on them. Noah, can you break through their security protections?"

"Negative," Noah responded. "They're too strong. I've tried, but it's unlikely I can crack them. It's an intelligent program. That means every time I try to break into their network, it gets smarter and learns how to block me better."

They continued discussing Noah's failed efforts, but Myra was barely listening anymore. Her eyes fixed on her wrist, where the Beacon pulsed languidly. Suddenly, a crazy idea dawned on her—it was a long shot and highly dangerous.

"Wait, we should use the Beacons against Drakken," she said excitedly. "Like he used them to spy on us. We can hack into his mind and find his weakness."

She held up her wrist, but Kaleb looked upset.

"No way," he interjected. "In fact, I suggest we deactivate them now, since all the Carriers are back safely. The Beacons are dangerous and unpredictable."

"Myra, he's right," Aero agreed. "Drakken has already demonstrated his ability to manipulate us through the Beacons. Damn it, he almost killed you last time."

Her shoulder still ached where he'd stabbed her, but she ignored it. Her eyes flashed with defiance. "He tried—but he failed. I've kept him out since then."

Professor Divinus fixed her with a sympathetic smile. "My dear, you know how I feel. The Beacons were designed to preserve your history and lead you back to the First Continuum. To push them beyond their original intent could prove perilous and consequential in ways we haven't even considered. Human minds were never meant to be connected this way, especially not with Carriers in such close proximity."

"I disagree," Myra insisted. "Turning them off is a huge mistake."

"Myra, didn't you hear the professor?" Kaleb said. "You're not thinking clearly. You must listen to reason.

He's not even talking about Drakken. The Beacon could be damaging you. Is that what you want?"

He reached for her arm, but she yanked it away.

"No, you're the ones who aren't thinking clearly," she said in a louder voice than she intended. She felt protective of her Beacon. "If we deactivate them, then we destroy what small shreds of connectivity we have left. Just look at what's happening to our army—we're already dissolving into factions."

"Myra is right," Wren said. "Don't believe me? Come spend time in the Seventh encampment. I'm not the biggest fan of the Beacons either. I agree with Sebold. I don't trust them. But the last thing we need is something else driving a wedge between us."

"Better than getting killed in our sleep," muttered Seeker. Crawler thumped his foot on the floor. Myra had come to learn that meant he agreed with something.

"Exactly," Kaleb said. His eyes looked haunted. "I already lost Paige and Rickard and probably my family. I don't want to lose you too. It's not worth it."

Seeker nodded. "Drakken . . . dangerous and very strong. He could use the Beacons against us. They're a weapon in his hands."

Myra burst to her feet. "But that's it, don't you see? We can turn the tables on Drakken. I can use the Beacons to find his weakness. I'm getting better at controlling them. I've been practicing my mind exercises while you were gone. Drakken got me that one time, but I learned how to keep him out. It hasn't happened again."

"But what if you get tired?" Aero said. "Or sick? Or have a moment of weakness? That's all Drakken needs to destroy you. And it's not just you. As long as the Beacons are active, we're are all at risk."

"Aero is right," Divinus agreed. He flared with emerald light, seeming to age before their eyes. "My dear, it's not safe. We should put it to a vote of the Assembly."

"Why can't you see this is our chance?" Myra said. She anticipated the results of a vote. Ironically, Wren was the only one on her side. "Give me twenty-four hours to break into Drakken's mind. That's all I'm asking. If I fail, we can turn them off."

"If you're not dead," Kaleb grumbled, clearly unhappy.

The Assembly fell into uncomfortable silence.

Finally, Divinus called for a vote. "All in favor of giving Myra one last day before we deactivate the Beacons say *aye*."

"Aye," rang out around the room. There was only one abstention. It was Kaleb. He wouldn't meet her eyes. He didn't want to lose her—he would rather lose the war.

"It's settled," Divinus said. "Six in favor, one abstention. My dear, if you haven't succeeded in the next twenty-four hours, then Noah will deactivate the Beacons."

"Yes, Professor," said Noah. "Standing by."

The rest of the meeting passed quickly, as Myra sped through her agenda. She had only twenty-four hours and didn't want to squander them. Despite boasting about her abilities, she wasn't sure she could do it. She needed all the time she could get.

As soon as the Assembly adjourned, she rushed out. "Hey, Myra, wait up," Kaleb called after her, but she pretended not to hear. His limp held him back.

She felt bad for ignoring him, but time was of the essence. She could deal with his hurt feelings later. She rushed back to her chambers, which the service bots had tidied in her absence. The door contracted behind her, sealing her inside.

"Noah, lock my door," she said, snatching a tube of rations from the tray on her bed. She squirted the gluey paste into her mouth. She felt suddenly famished. Plus, she didn't want hunger to distract her. Noah's voice echoed through her room.

"The professor won't like it."

"Did he forbid it?" she asked between swallows. "Or give you a command?"

"No, he didn't. That was my opinion."

"Then you can't refuse."

"My apologies," Noah replied. "Locking door now."

She heard the satisfying beep as the door locked. Finally, she had peace and quiet—and a chance to put her skills to the test. She climbed onto the bed, feeling the soft mattress depress under her weight. She shut her eyes and stilled her thoughts. *Elianna, you have to guide me,* she thought. *Help me keep all the noise away.* She could feel the Beacon surge with power and Elianna's ethereal presence with her.

Her mind fell into absolute stillness. She could hear the hissing of the vents and taste the dust and antiseptic tinge of the air on her tongue. But that all dropped away as her consciousness hurtled from the underground chamber where her body remained, through the layers of rock, bursting through the surface and careening through the atmosphere and out into the vacuum of space. *I'm coming for you,* she thought.

This had to work—she needed to find Drakken's weakness.

Or they were all dead.

Chapter 44
ESPIONAGE

The Carriers

Myra catapulted through outer space—or rather, her consciousness. Her body remained behind, meditating on the bed in her underground chamber.

No, take me further, she thought. *Take me to his ship.*

She visualized the Fourth Continuum—sharp drills jutting out of the ebony hull—and locked onto Drakken's signal. She hurled through the vacuum of space, past the blaze of stars and their slowly tilting planet. Ahead, she spotted the ship. Silent and menacing. She pierced through the exterior hull and alighted inside a Docking Bay that housed their warships. She levitated and passed through the wall, floating down the corridor.

She entered a laboratory, her eyes falling on the crew in their red lab coats. They couldn't see her with their milky, dead eyes. One walked right through her projection, clutching a tablet.

So this is how Drakken does it, she realized. *How he spies on us.*

She passed through laboratory after laboratory, filled with more crew members dressed in lab coats. They were all wearing strange caps with wires plugged into the pale flesh of their skulls. Their movements looked robotic and mechanized. Their dead eyes still didn't see her. She floated deeper into the ship, searching for Drakken's signal.

Tell me your secrets. Reveal them to me.

Her Beacon flashed, guiding her through the labyrinthine corridors. She passed through a sealed door and into a familiar room. *I've seen this place*, she thought. *In Drakken's transmission.* Windows stretched to the ceiling, revealing the expanse of space. Drill points dipped into view. The room was empty—save for a chair.

She startled when she saw Drakken ensconced there. He looked even more fearsome up close. Thick scars snaked up his neck, marring his face in a crosshatched pattern. Wires and tubes plugged into his sallow, flabby flesh. His Beacon pulsed steadily on his wrist. He was sleeping—or doing whatever he did when his eyes were shut. Even in repose, she could feel menace wafting off him like heat.

Tell me your secrets. You can't hide from me.

Her lips moved but no sound emerged.

She caught a flash from her Beacon—

For a split second, she saw through Drakken's eyes. Only it was like seeing through a thousand eyes at once. The sensory overload felt oppressive. Her head exploded with white-hot splinters of pain as her neural synapses tried to absorb all of the viewpoints. She could see every room in the ship simultaneously. Every laboratory. Anywhere there was a crew member. And then she understood how it worked.

I found his weakness, she thought in triumph.

But then Drakken's eyes popped open. They focused as if through a haze. They locked onto her projection—he could see her. His face contorted with fury.

Get out, girl! he screamed. *You've violated my ship!*

The words hit her as if fired from a blaster. They slammed her against the floor. Her ghostly form became solid—it became vulnerable. Every part of her body screamed out in pain. She gasped for breath as Drakken rose from his commander's chair. Black smoke poured from his mouth, his ears, his fingertips. He morphed into the Dark Thing. The smoke sharpened into knifepoints. They stabbed at her all at once—

She felt searing pain. *Elianna, get me out of here!*

Myra was expelled from the ship with such force that it felt like it snapped every bone in her body. She plummeted to Earth in a blaze of sparks and smashed through the ground. But still she was connected to Drakken.

Get out, girl!

His voice shook the dreamscape, making it shatter into a million pieces. Myra struggled to breathe, but her lungs constricted and her heart stopped.

Chapter 45
ACHILLES' HEEL

Myra Jackson

Myra woke with a gasp. Adrenaline pumped through her veins like an electric current. Her chest ached like every rib was broken. Her vision looked blurry; she couldn't see clearly. A mask pressed over her mouth, cutting into her cheeks. She flailed and clawed at it, trying to rip it off, but something held her down. That made her panic more.

"Hold still, my dear," Professor Divinus Said. "You're going to hurt yourself." "Professor, her vitals are stable," Noah reported. "The odds of resuscitation were approximately one in five thousand twenty-one. I'm surprised it worked."

"Thank god," Divinus said. "I thought we'd lost her."

"So did I, Professor," Noah replied. "A few more seconds, and her odds of resuscitation would have decreased to worse than one in a million."

What were they talking about? Myra wondered hazily.

Her vision slowly cleared, the room coming into focus around her. The service bots hovered with their mechanical appendages. It took her a moment to understand what they were doing. They were performing CPR on her. One bot pushed down on her chest, while another pressed a mask to her lips that forced oxygen through them. Unable to help, Divinus was pacing behind them. He kept flickering with worry.

"What . . . happened?" Myra asked, still out of breath. The words came out muffled by the mask. She searched her memory, but came up blank. It was like it had been wiped clean. Divinus signaled to the service bots. They withdrew with worried beeps, but continued monitoring her vitals.

He regarded her seriously, tugging at his beard. "My dear, you died. Your heart stopped for several minutes."

"What . . . how?" she said, feeling pain in every part of her body.

"We're not sure," Divinus said. "Everything was stable. And then out of nowhere, you flatlined. Several bones in your body shattered. It was almost like you got hit by something. You're lucky Noah was monitoring your vitals. He unlocked your door and summoned the service bots to resuscitate you. Another few seconds, and it would have been too late."

"Professor, that is correct," Noah said. "I should point out that her injuries mimic those one would receive from falling from a great height, which is strange. I was monitoring her location the whole time. She never left her chambers."

Myra shuddered as a memory leaked through. *Drakken ejecting her from his ship . . . falling and falling through the sky . . . plummeting to Earth . . .*

"That's because I *did* fall," she said quietly. "You have to believe me. I got inside the Fourth Continuum. I broke into their ship, but then Drakken caught me spying on him. He morphed into the Dark Thing and tried to kill me. I had to get out of there . . . "

Divinus's eyes flicked to her Beacon. Deepened concern spread over his face. "That was only in your dream. Your body never left your chambers."

"But my mind did. Professor, you know it's possible—"

Kaleb appeared at her door. His eyes lit up with fear

when he saw her, surrounded by the service bots and their medical probes.

"Myra—what happened?" he said and rushed to her side. He glanced at the professor as understanding came over him. "Wait, she tried it, didn't she?" he said, gesturing angrily to the Beacon. "Drakken almost killed her again."

"Right, I'm afraid so," Divinus said, giving his beard an agitated tug. "Her heart stopped this time. Fortunately, the service bots were able to resuscitate her."

Kaleb glared at him. "By the Oracle, I knew this was a terrible idea. Those Beacons are dangerous. We should have deactivated them long ago."

"Drakken . . ." Myra said. "He caught me spying on him . . . but I got through his protections. Don't you see?"

She felt a jolt of excitement, though it could have been from the drugs the service bots had injected to jump-start her heart. She tried to sit up, making the bots beep in protest and force her back down. "Myra, he almost killed you," Kaleb said in disgust.

"Almost," Myra said. "But he didn't . . . and now I found it."

"Found what?" Divinus asked, raising his scraggly eyebrows. His visage flickered with interest, making him appear younger. "My dear, what did you learn?"

"Drakken's weakness . . ." she trailed off, searching her memory.

Disconnected images tumbled through her brain. *Crew members in red lab coats moving through their laboratories. Drakken resting on his commander's chair. Wires plugged into his brain. His eyes snapping open and locking onto her. Get out, girl! Dark tendrils stabbing at her.* She tried to remember more, but came up blank. It was like it had been erased from her brain. Weariness flooded through her.

"I knew it . . . his weakness. But I lost it. I can't seem to remember."

Kaleb wrenched his hand through his dark curls. "This is madness. I don't care if you figured out his weakness. You could have died in that dream." He turned his fiery gaze on

Divinus and jabbed his finger at him. "And you're encouraging her."

"I also had my reservations," Divinus agreed. "But if Myra has discovered his Achilles' heel, then that could save us. It may have been worth the risk."

"Achilles' heel?" Myra said with a frown. "What's that?"

"It's from an ancient myth," Divinus explained. "When Achilles was a child, his mother dipped him in magical waters to make him invincible. But she held him up by the heel, so that became his one vulnerable spot. His enemies used it against him, shooting him in the heel with a poisoned arrow. He died a few days later."

He looked at Myra expectantly. "My dear, did you find it?"

She hated disappointing Divinus, but her mind was blank. "I knew it . . . but I lost it," she said, punching her pillow in frustration. The service bots beeped their alarm.

"Professor, her vitals are dropping," Noah reported. The bots descended on her with an oxygen mask and needles. Myra tried to swat them away, but her hand felt like it weighed a thousand pounds and stayed rooted to the bed. Her vision blurred again.

"My dear, rest now," Divinus said worriedly. "You're gravely injured. We can try some memory retrieval exercises when you're better. In the meantime, Noah will check if your Beacon downloaded anything useful. The service bots will care for you."

"Fine, but no sedatives," Myra managed through her exhaustion. She shot the bots a warning look. "I want to stay sharp."

"But Drakken could kill you," Kaleb said, leaning over her bedside. He laid his hand on her shoulder. "Myra, don't act crazy. Please take the drugs."

"Drakken won't hurt me. He'll keep his distance."

"How can you be sure?" Kaleb asked.

She struggled up in bed, ignoring the service bots' panicked beeping. "Because I could feel it," she said in a firm voice. "He's afraid of me now."

o o o

For the next few days, Myra recuperated in her chambers in a haze of pain. Several of her ribs had been broken. Her body looked like an ugly patchwork of black and purple bruises. The service bots set her bones and bound her ribs with thick bandages. They gave her medicine to speed her healing. Still she refused the pain medication. She wanted to stay awake and sharp—she wanted to remember everything.

But the harder she tried to summon her memories, the more elusive they became. "*Bloody* dreams," she cursed. "*Bloody* Beacon. *Bloody* Drakken."

The only response she got was a slew of worried beeps from the service bots. One clamped an oxygen mask over her face, despite her adamant protests. Defeated, she gave into their frantic ministrations. She felt somebody climb into her bed and snuggle against her side. She knew it was Tinker. Careful not to disturb her IV line, she pulled him closer. "I love you," she whispered into the crown of his head.

"You're getting better fast," he rasped. "I can tell."

"But not fast enough," she muttered. "And I still can't remember."

"You will," he said. "I believe in you. You'll remember."

She wanted to believe him, but her mind remained frustratingly blank. She was starting to doubt herself. Had she really found Drakken's weakness? Or was it only a hallucination? Her broken bones said it was real, but her mind wasn't sure.

Kaleb came to visit her daily. Every time her wrist slid out from underneath the covers, he couldn't hide his disgust at the Beacon. His presence should have comforted her, she knew. But it only made her feel like she was suffocating. Whenever he visited, she found herself pretending to sleep, even when she was wide awake.

A few times, she caught him whispering to Wren in the corridor outside her chambers. The exchanges sounded heated, urgent for some reason. But she couldn't make out their muffled words, nor did she have the energy to try. They were probably worried, she decided. It seemed like everyone was worried about her lately.

Aero also came to visit, though less frequently, and whenever he did show up, he always seemed distracted. Through the Beacons, she could sense that he cared but also that he was preoccupied with his troops. Training the Seventh soldiers wasn't going well. Even more alarming, the Forgers still hadn't gotten the shield to work. In the first test, the shield held for only ten seconds before it gave way.

"My brothers and sisters will get it to work," Aero insisted. "We still have ten days left until Drakken is within firing range—it will hold."

"Ten days," Myra replied. "That's not much time."

"It'll work," he said tersely. He started backing away toward the door. "I'm so sorry, but I have to go. You'll let me know if you remember anything?"

Before Myra could reply, he had already disappeared through the door. His footsteps faded away. The service bots zipped in, feeding her nutrients and medicines through her IV line, changing her dressings, and generally fussing over her. Eventually, she lapsed into a dreamless sleep. Drakken didn't try to attack her again. His complete absence unnerved her. He was dangerous, but knowing what he was doing made her feel safer. Now that he was gone, she felt even more afraid.

What's he planning? she wondered with a stab of anxiety.

She tried to voice her concerns to Kaleb, but he didn't understand. "Wait, let me get this straight. Drakken isn't trying to kill you—and that worries you?" he said in an exasperated voice. "Myra, sometimes I don't get you. This is the best outcome we could possibly hope for. Maybe he'll turn his ship around and leave us alone."

Myra shook her head, though it made her ribs throb. "Not a chance. I saw inside his mind. He wants to control the First Continuum, and he wants the secret of the Doom. I could feel it when I broke into his ship. His thoughts are focused on it. It's become an obsession. He won't turn back. He's coming for us . . . and soon."

"Fine, whatever you say," Kaleb said with a weary sigh. "You realize, that might not have even been real? It could have been a hallucination, right?"

"It was real," she insisted, even as doubt gnawed at her heart.

"Okay," he said, knowing it was futile to argue. "But as soon as we convene the Assembly, I'm moving for a vote to deactivate the Beacons." He raised his hand before she could object. "Don't try to change my mind, Jackson. It won't work."

"Of course, you're right," she said demurely, even as her hand crept under the covers and stroked the warm metal affixed to her wrist. She didn't want her Beacon turned off. The very thought made her want to retch.

As the days passed—seven now, by her count—she grew more frustrated that she still couldn't remember his weakness. It teased at the edges of her consciousness, taunting her with its elusiveness. She also continued to be unnerved by Drakken's complete absence. She couldn't feel him through the Beacon at all.

"Holy Sea . . ." she cursed under her breath.

Trying harder won't make it come back to you, Elianna communicated in a gentle voice. *You have to relax and let go. Drakken has great control over his Beacon. He's using it to suppress your memory. But you're stronger than him. I can feel it.*

He made my heart stop, Myra thought. *How am I stronger?*

You survived, didn't you? Elianna communicated. *Any other Carrier would have died. You came out with a few broken ribs and some bruises. That's how I know.*

So I have to not try, and then I'll remember? Myra thought in annoyance. *Do you know how crazy that sounds? I'm just supposed to lie here and wait for it to come back?*

No, you're supposed to calm your mind, Elianna replied. But Myra wasn't listening anymore. She was too frustrated. Her mind buzzed with a litany of grievances and irritations. Though something from their conversation seeped into her brain. She stopped trying to remember. She stopped replaying the dream on a maddening loop. She let her mind drift away, unfettered, but now there was only blankness. That was almost worse.

The service bots whirred into her chambers. One gave her an injection. The sharp tip jabbed into her the inside of her elbow, pumping medicine into her bloodstream. She watched the needle protruding from her flesh—and that triggered a memory.

The images snapped into vivid focus:

Wires plugged into pale flesh . . . dead eyes . . . robotic movements . . .

She shot up in bed, causing the service bots to emit worried beeps. The needle twisted in her arm, making her wince. She tried to hold on to the images and tease out their deeper meaning. But as soon as she focused on them, they disappeared again, swallowed up by the murky waters of her subconscious mind. She could feel Elianna's disappointment. Myra flopped back on her pillow, giving up on trying to remember. She didn't need to hear Elianna's admonishment to know it wouldn't do any good.

Chapter 46
FIRING RANGE

Supreme General Aero Wright

Aero left Myra's chambers and headed for the Foundry, nestled in the back of the First Continuum. Abandoned mining equipment lined the corridor, frozen in the middle of burrowing into bedrock. As he rounded the bend, the Foundry's glow seeped into the corridor. The smell hit him next, familiar and deeply comforting—the smoky tang of fire, spicy aroma of herbal tea, and acrid scent of burning metal. The air grew warmer the closer he got. Droplets of sweat pooled on his forehead. He increased his pace.

A minute later, the corridor opened up into the large cavern that now housed the Foundry, though not in its former glory. They had stripped some of the machines out of the Second Continuum and transported them down here, but they hadn't brought everything for one simple reason—they didn't have enough Forgers to operate them all.

His eyes grazed over the red-cloaked figures rushing around with calm but deliberate energy. Only twelve Forgers had survived, including the young brother who'd accompanied them to Earth. Their faces looked youthful and unlined. Most were fresh out of the Agoge. Aero missed the old Forger fiercely.

As if hearing that thought, the young Forger looked up from his work. He switched off the machine, set his tools aside, and swished across the cavern. "Supreme General Wright, it can't be that bad," he said with the barest slip of a smile.

"Brother, it's that bad," Aero said. "And worse."

"Well, I'm pleased to report we've forged ten new Falchions," the Forger said. He gestured to the blades, levitating in the back of the Foundry. "We've almost finished arming the Seventh Continuum soldiers," he added with a bob of his head.

"Falchions are great, but what about the shield?" Aero said, hating the way his voice came out sounding so impatient. "Drakken will be within firing range in three days. And that's only Noah's best estimate. Their ship vanished off our sensor arrays late last night. They must have improved their cloaking shield. Noah can't hack it."

The Forger frowned. "That is concerning," he agreed, lowering the hood draped over the shaved dome of his head. "We already know he's coming, so why would Drakken put energy into cloaking their signal?"

Aero sighed. "I don't know, and that's what worries me."

"As for our shield, we haven't fixed the bug yet," the Forger went on. "We've been working on it, but I had to give my brothers and sisters a break to rest. The machines needed it too. We must be careful not to overwork them."

"Three days isn't much time," Aero said. He probed his Beacon, but he couldn't feel Drakken. He had vanished off their sensors—and also from their Beacons.

What was that bastard up to?

The Forger nodded. "Sir, I have full confidence in my Order. Fear not, we'll get the shield working. It will offer some protection, but remember—it won't hold forever."

"I know," Aero said, frustration creeping into his voice. "We're working on finding Drakken's weakness. Myra still hasn't remembered anything." He paused and lowered his voice. "Between us, I'm not sure what really happened in that dream. Maybe she did break into his mind—or maybe she imagined the whole thing."

The Forger laid his hand on Aero's shoulder. "Have faith in her, Supreme General. Our prophecies tell of the *Chosen Ones*. You cannot defeat Drakken alone. You need the other Carriers if you're going to survive this new Doom."

"I know," Aero said. "Only . . ."

"You're fragmenting," the Forger said with a knowing look. "I can sense it in the Assembly meetings. Seeker with her people, Myra with her dreams, you with your army. You must find a way to pull together and trust each other again."

"Easier said than done."

The Forger clapped Aero on the shoulder. "My friend, don't worry about the shield. My Order will uphold our part in this battle. We've been preparing for this for more than a thousand years—we're not about to fail you now."

"Thanks, brother," Aero said, bowing his head.

The Forger returned the gesture. "My apologies, but I must return to my work."

With another bow, this one deeper and more formal, he swept across the chamber and started manipulating one of the machines. Usually spending time in the Foundry helped Aero clear his head, but he left feeling more confused than before his visit.

His head told him that all this nonsense with the dreamscape and prophecies defied logic. A hostile colony was about to descend on them with the firepower of a hundred armies. His training told him that fighting back with Falchions and battle strategy was their only hope of winning. But was there another way?

Would Myra find it?

Did he really need her and Seeker?

The doubt lingered in his mind as he threaded his way through the chambers and boarded the elevator. "Noah, take me back to the Surface," he said.

o   o   o

Aero returned to his tent, feeling exhausted. The sun had set long ago. He slurped water from the pitcher by his cot and then climbed into it. He didn't have the energy to seek out his Majors and get an update; it would have to wait for morning.

He sank into his cot, pulling up the scratchy blanket. His dreams came fast and furious, turning into nightmares. His father came to him, but before he could open his mouth to speak, Drakken impaled him through the heart with a shadowy tendril. His father's face morphed into Myra. Blood spurted down her chest, staining her tunic.

Her lips moved:

Why don't you have faith in me?

Her voice penetrated his dream and bombarded his brain. He tossed and turned, sweating through his blanket. Suddenly, panicked screams broke through the thick membrane of sleep, jerking him awake. Aero bolted upright.

An alarm blared over their encampment.

He burst from his tent and sprinted into the courtyard. In the predawn light, a silent explosion blossomed and ignited the sky. Through his Beacon, he heard jeering laughter. He knew instantly that it came from Drakken. He had broken his silence.

"Starry hell, what did you do?" Aero hissed.

Chapter 47
DISSENSION IN THE RANKS

Seeker

T he shield failed—it was weak and feeble," Bruiser growled, gesturing angrily at the sky. Behind him, the setting sun cast long-fingered shadows over the derelict Science Center. "We should flee back to the Darkness of the Below before it's too late."

The Seventh soldiers emerged from their tents and gathered in the courtyard to listen. Their Falchions gave off soft chinks. Sharp whispers cut through the air.

"Drakken's coming for us . . . bringing the Doom . . ."

"He's the Strongest of the Strong Ones . . ."

"Safer in the Darkness of the Below . . ."

Drawn by their aggrieved voices, Seeker ducked out of her tent. Her eyes narrowed when she saw Bruiser speaking to the soldiers. Seeker scented the air and tracked Crawler down. She found him by the water station.

"Look, there's another gathering," she growled.

Crawler looked up, droplets dripping off the soft fuzz of his face. He swiped them away with the back of his hand. "Is it Bruiser again?"

Seeker grimaced. "Who else causes all the trouble?"

"Well, he has some competition." Crawler sat back on his haunches. His eyes glowed like saucers, refracting the camp's light. "Come on, let's put a stop to it."

But Seeker hesitated.

"Seeker, what's wrong?" he asked.

"What if Slayer's right about everything?" she whispered, glancing around to make sure they were alone. "We're exposed out here with nothing to protect us."

"The Forger promised they'd get the shield working."

Seeker dropped her tough façade. "But what if they don't? There's still time to leave. We have three days before Drakken's in range. You heard Noah in the meeting. The odds are not in our favor. I'm the reason they left the Darkness of the Below. I'm the reason they're putting their lives in danger for another colony who treats us like animals."

Doubt and fear filtered into her voice. *I'm a Weakling*, she cursed herself. *Always have been, always will be.* Crawler met her eyes and held her gaze.

"We were always meant to leave. That wasn't our home— it was our tomb. Now, come on. Bruiser is a filthy, nasty coward. We can't let him decide our fate."

"I know, you're right," Seeker said, leaning against his side. It was a strange sensation, trusting another person like this, though she still felt confused about the right path forward. She understood why Bruiser wanted to flee from their camp and seek refuge in the Darkness of the Below. Her gut was telling her the exact same thing.

Run!

It screamed at her.

Leave this cursed place, where the Light burns and the sky leaves all vulnerable to the wrath of the stars! There are no walls or ceilings to protect you!

But she stuffed the urge back down. She signaled to Crawler to follow her. They loped through the flimsy tents, that were nothing like the solid stone edifices of their home, and emerged in front of the Science Center. Night had fallen, but still they could see clearly in the dim light. Bruiser raised his arms, speaking to the anxious crowd.

"Why are we waiting around for Drakken to devour us?" he declared to raucous cheering and foot stomping. "We should leave tonight, while we still can."

The Seventh soldiers raised their Falchions. Most were still in their default forms; the soldiers weren't skilled at morphing them yet. Sparks popped and sizzled from the curved blades, lighting up the courtyard. Seeker tried to get their attention, but her voice got drowned out by the rowdy crowd. Crawler bounded to the front.

"Fellow Strong Ones, listen to Seeker," he growled, puffing out his chest in a show of strength. "She is our Carrier and the Strongest of the Strong Ones—"

"Not for long," Bruiser snarled, pacing around agitatedly. "If she keeps following these nasty, filthy Second Weaklings. They can't get their shield to work. They won't protect us from Drakken. He's the Strongest of the Strong Ones—"

"Treason," Crawler growled. "Drakken is our enemy."

"Are you challenging me?" Bruiser said, leaping in front of him. He pounded on his chest. "Crawler, I'll rip your puny Weakling body to shreds!"

That caused another eruption of jeering and foot stomping. Seeker watched helplessly, feeling like she was losing control over her people. She scrambled over to a plastic crate of untouched rations by the tents and clambered on top of it.

"My people," Seeker said, trying to project her voice and make it sound deeper. "Drakken is strong, but we're stronger. The Forgers promised to get the shield working. We still have three days before the Fourth Continuum gets into range."

"Three days," Bruiser snorted. "Too short."

"We should flee to the Darkness now," Slayer added. "While we still can."

"But don't you understand?" Seeker said, sweeping her gaze over their frightened faces. Hundreds of Seventh soldiers were gathered there. "Maybe we'll be safe in the Darkness of the Below for a short time, but Drakken will hunt us down like ratters and kill us. I've seen into his mind—he wants to destroy everything with the Doom."

Nervous whispers roiled through the crowd.

"We don't trust the stinkin' Second Continuum," Bruiser growled. "They call us *beasts* and *humanoids*. They think we're filthy animals. How do we know they won't hunt us down and slaughter us too? After we fight this war for them?"

The crowd roared with anger and thrust their Falchions in the air, emitting more sparks. Seeker was losing control over them. They weren't listening to her. Order and obedience didn't come naturally to her people.

But then a loud voice shot through the crowd.

"Because you have my word that won't happen," Wren said, looking like she'd just woken from sleep, though her voice sounded clear. "Where I come from, our word is our bond. You will have an equal place at the table in this new world order. I swear it on my Falchion." She lifted her blade into the air. "And on my life as a soldier."

"Why should we trust you?" Bruiser said. He stalked around her much smaller frame, but Wren didn't shirk back in fear. "Your people call us filthy names."

"The act of a few lone soldiers," Wren said, frustration seeping into her voice. "They're young and inexperienced. Like your people, they're terrified of Drakken and the Fourth Continuum. They acted inappropriately—and they're being punished harshly, I swear it. We armed you with our sacred weapons. Isn't that a show of trust?"

"Not all of us," came a shout from the back. The speaker held up her bone spear. "Where are our Falchions?"

"Patience," Wren said. "They'll be ready soon. The Order of the Foundry is working around the clock. It takes time to forge new blades. Their focus is on the shield now. Too many of them were slaughtered—"

Her voice was drowned out by disapproving shouts from the crowd. They were angry and scared. They didn't want to listen. Seeker caught Wren's eye and gestured for her to stand down. She waited for the crowd to calm; it took several minutes.

"Two more days," Seeker said once they quieted. "That's all we're asking. If the shield still isn't working by then, those who wish to leave may do so. You won't be hunted down and punished for deserting. You will be free to leave."

Wren looked like she wanted to object. Desertion was the worst offense a soldier could commit. Her shoulders sagged. "Fine," Wren agreed. "Two more days."

The Seventh soldiers still looked fearful, but the fight drained out of the crowd. Sensing he had lost them, Bruiser backed down. He bowed to Seeker, but his eyes still had a cunning glint in them. "As you wish, Strongest of the Strong Ones."

Seeker let out a shaky breath. She had feared that she lost them.

Wren pointed toward the training field. "Since you're staying, it's time for Falchion drills."

Rumbles of protest erupted from the crowd, but Wren quickly stepped in. "Two days, that's all you're giving me. Right now, you're one sorry-looking unit. Let's form up into ranks and see if we can't whip you into a decent bunch of soldiers yet."

After a few false starts and one minor brawl that Wren had to break up, they formed into orderly ranks. "Soldiers, draw your Falchions," she commanded. With a clanging of metal, they unsheathed their blades, though not perfectly in sync like the Second soldiers. "Shift them into your preferred weapon forms," she ordered.

The golden blades morphed into spears, swords, and battle-axes, though many soldiers failed and saw their weapons pop back into the default form. Luckily, no Falchions melted down, which was always a risk with untrained soldiers. Standing next to Wren, Seeker clutched a long, gleaming dagger in her hand. She had adjusted to wielding a Falchion easily, probably because of her connection to the Beacon.

"Forward march," Wren called out. Her voice echoed through the courtyard.

The units lurched ahead, again not entirely in sync, but at least they were listening to her orders and mostly following directions. Their footfalls pounded the ground. In the back of the unit, a scuffle broke out. "Stepped on my foot!"

"Quit shoving, you filthy beast!"

"Who you callin' a beast, Weakling!"

The two soldiers started wrestling. Others around them joined in. "Stop," Wren yelled, futilely. She clutched a talwer in her grip. "Soldiers, hold your positions."

But it didn't do any good.

The whole drill devolved into complete chaos. Those who weren't actively brawling formed a loose circle around the fighters and took wagers on the winner. Suddenly, an incendiary blast of light tore through the sky. The soldiers froze, even those in the middle of pummeling each other bloody. They jerked their frightened eyes up.

"It's Drakken," Bruiser screamed. "He's coming for us."

The crowd stampeded, trampling each other in a rush to seek cover. They weren't used to being exposed. The explosion expanded, lighting up the predawn sky, though no sound accompanied it. It was somewhere far away, but still visible to the naked eyed.

An alarm blared through the encampment.

Wren watched the explosion. Her hand shot to her Falchion. "Starry hell, what happened?" she choked out over the blaring alarm.

Seeker barely heard her. Her Beacon throbbed, delivering a message intended for the Carriers. When she heard it, fear shot through her body like an electric charge. She gripped her Falchion tighter, knowing it wouldn't protect them.

"The Second Continuum . . ." Seeker said, feeling sick to her stomach. Her eyes glazed over as she listened to her Beacon. "They're gone . . . all of them. I heard their screams. He wanted us to hear them. He wanted us to know what he did."

Fear cut across Wren's face. Her gaze fixed on the golden device clamped to Seeker's wrist. It pulsed wildly with emerald light. "Seeker, what do you mean?"

Chapter 48
THAT'S NO ASTEROID

Danika Rothman

Danika paced around the Disciplinary Barracks. She felt twitchy and anxious. She wasn't used to having no schedule to follow. *Nowhere to be, nothing to do.*

Her whole life had been regimented into strict allotments of time—Falchion drills, combat training, studying, eating, training, eating, sleeping, repeat. Why couldn't Aero have imprisoned her on Earth? At least then she'd be where all the action was. Most of the army had deployed, leaving only a bare-bones crew aboard their mothership.

A bare-bones crew, Danika thought. *And us prisoners.*

Her eyes flicked to the door; it was sealed and locked tight. Armed guards were posted outside. The barracks wasn't tiny. It was stuffed with bunks and meant to house a whole unit, but Danika shared it with only one other occupant. Her gaze shifted to the copper-haired woman lounging on the upper bunk, shoved up against the back wall.

Lydia Wright.

Her name shot through Danika's head. It felt strange that her bunkmate had no military title anymore. They'd all lost their rankings when Aero took over command of the ship. Danika might have saved herself from this fate. She might have kept her ranking, and if not that, at least a place in the army under the new Supreme General. She had just needed to play along, do her part and follow his orders, and not cause any trouble. But she hadn't been able to contain her emotions. She regretted skewering Vinick with her Falchion, even though the bastard deserved it. She was wrong to disobey Aero's orders. That's what had landed her here, in this hellacious purgatory.

"Starry hell, you're going to wear out the floor if you keep it up," Wright complained from her bunk. Their relationship wasn't exactly cordial at this point. Too much idle time. Too much had gone wrong for both of them. "Or drive us both crazy."

"No thanks to your son," Danika said. "He should get it over with and execute us already. Why make us wait here like this? Why not deploy us to Earth? They're badly outnumbered. They need every Falchion they can get."

"No doubt ours have already been repurposed," Lydia said with a shudder. Danika also felt a deep chill at the memory of her lost blade. It haunted her still. "They wouldn't waste fine weapons like that, especially since we slaughtered most of the Forgers."

"The Seventh Continuum," Danika said, continuing to pace. She couldn't stop it. It was the only thing she could do in the confined space. "They must be arming them."

She'd heard the rumors about the newest members of their army. Gossip always had a way of filtering through the ship. Even though most of their soldiers had deployed, transports still ran back and forth, delivering supplies and stoking the rumor mill.

"They're not soldiers," Lydia snorted, sitting up . Her eyes flashed with hatred. "They're foul beasts. They don't deserve to bond with our sacred weapons. One of our soldiers is locked up down the hall simply for calling them by their true names."

"Well, your son treats them with more respect than us," Danika pointed out. She knew that using that familial term went against their teachings and drove her cellmate crazy, but she didn't care. She had nothing left to lose at this point.

"That traitor is an emotional hazard," Lydia said in a sharp voice. "When he turned five, I left him at the Agoge with the Drillmasters—and the little deserter ran away. Ambushed me in the middle of a training session with my combat unit."

"He actually ran away?" Danika said, shocked. "From the Agoge?"

"Sure did," Lydia said with a sniff. "So I marched him right back to the Drillmasters. Made it clear that I never wanted to see his little face ever again. He put up a fight and cried like a baby, but he never ran away again."

Lydia kept ranting about her son and his traitorous ways, but Danika was barely listening anymore. Something had caught her eye outside the window. The circular portal was set into the thick wall. She covered the distance, pressing her face to the panel.

"By the stars, what's that?" she said softly.

A ray of light streaked toward their ship. Her first thought was that it was an asteroid or space debris. They were orbiting Earth. All kinds of space junk and derelict satellites still floated out here from Before Doom. But the trajectory looked too direct. Something seemed to be propelling it toward them with great speed.

She had one last thought before the alarm started blaring. *That's no asteroid.*

She opened her mouth to scream, but the sound never had a chance to form. The warhead tore through their hull—and then it detonated. Highly flammable oxygen ignited as it bubbled outward into the vacuum, along with other trapped gases. The explosion was soundless—at least to the human ear—but no less destructive. Shrapnel shot out into space at all angles and continued in straight lines with no gravity to direct it.

Danika didn't have time to make sense of her life as it flashed before her eyes. One second, she was standing in the Disciplinary Barracks aboard a massive space colony; the next, she was obliterated in a white-hot flash. Just like that, she was dead. Lydia was dead. The bare-bones crew left aboard the mothership was dead.

They were all dead.

Chapter 49
THE SHIELD

Myra Jackson

Alarms blared in the First Continuum, but Myra felt it through her Beacon first. Drakken's horrific laughter rang in her ears. She saw through his eyes for a split second as he gave the command to drop their cloaking shield and fire on the Second Continuum. It took only one warhead to tear the entire colony to shreds and kill every last soul aboard. Aero and Seeker saw it too. Drakken wanted them to see it.

Then he transmitted a message: *Carriers, behold the power of my arsenal. The Second Continuum is no more. Surrender now and deliver the secret of the Doom—or this shall be your fate. You have twenty-four hours.*

No . . . you're still three days away, Myra thought frantically.

You think your precious supercomputer doesn't make mistakes? Drakken replied with another bout of laughter. *His calculations are wrong. He doesn't understand the power of our nuclear thrusters. He based his estimate on the original blueprints, but we've modified the thrusters significantly over the last seven hundred years.*

Before Myra could reply, the communication terminated. Drakken had blocked them from his mind, shutting them out like turning off a screen.

It took a second for Myra's disorientation to fade and her vision to focus. She was still slumped on her bed, hooked up to the IV line. She ripped the cord out, drawing a splatter of blood across the crisp sheets. The service bots raced around in distress, but she ignored them and kicked off the blankets. She didn't care that her body still felt broken and ached fiercely with every step. She wasn't going to lie around in bed anymore.

The alarm continued blaring, accompanied by the flashing of strobe lights. "Emergency," Noah announced. "Carriers, report to the control room."

Myra limped to the door. "No, not the control room."

"But the professor said—"

"I don't care what the professor said," Myra said when she reached her door. She had to stop to catch her breath. Laying around in bed for days had sapped her strength. "Have the Assembly meet me in the Foundry."

"The Foundry?" Noah repeated.

"Yes, that's a direct command," Myra said. "Tell the others now."

She heard Noah's announcement go out as she staggered into the corridor. Kaleb rushed from his chambers. Tinker poked his head out of the next room.

"Myra, what's happening?" Kaleb asked, hurrying to her side.

"It's the Second Continuum . . ." her voice caught in her throat. Tears she didn't even know she'd been crying spilled down her cheeks. "Drakken . . ."

She didn't have to say anymore.

"He destroyed them, didn't he?" Kaleb said, his eyes tracking over her face. He saw the blood dripping down her arm. "Wait, did he hurt you again?"

"No, I'm fine," she said. "It's from the IV line. I ripped it out."

Before he could object, or tell her she was acting crazy again, she added, "Look, it doesn't matter if I'm hurt, or even if I die. Drakken is coming for us in twenty-four hours. Noah made a mistake."

"Twenty-four hours?" Kaleb said, shocked. "But the shield isn't working."

"That's why we're going to the Foundry." She grasped Tinker's arm, pulling him toward his chambers. "Tink, I need you to stay in your room and lock the door."

Tinker planted himself in the corridor. He got that obstinate look, like when he'd already made up his mind. "No, I'm coming with you," he rasped.

"It's too dangerous," Myra insisted. She kept him out of the Assembly meetings for the same reason. He was precocious, but he was only eight. His ninth birthday was still a few weeks away.

"I don't care," Tinker said. "I can help."

"How can you help us?" Kaleb asked. "It's safer if you stay in your chambers."

"While you've been in your Assembly meetings, I've been going to the Foundry every day," Tinker said with a sly smile. "I like their machines. They've been teaching me. They say I can become a Forger and join their Order. I think I'd like that."

Myra wanted to argue with him and insist that he stay in his room, where it was safer, but she knew better than to try and change his mind. Besides, maybe he was right and he could assist them. Right now, they needed all the help they could get.

o   o   o

They arrived at the Foundry a few minutes later. The scene resembled controlled chaos, with the Forgers rushing around while alarms blared. The young Forger's gaze fell on Myra and widened. He swept across the chamber, weaving through the machines.

"Brother, I'm sorry about your colony," she said, rushing up to him. "But we've got more urgent problems now. Noah's calculations were wrong—we've got only twenty-four hours before the Fourth Continuum is in range. We need to get that shield working."

"Drakken will bring about another Doom unless we stop him," the Forger said, shrugging off his hood. "Our prophecies foretold of his coming. I am only sorry they have proven correct. I hoped that humankind would learn another way."

Professor Divinus materialized in the Foundry in front of Myra. "My dear, I heard what happened. Noah picked up the transmission. Drakken dropped his cloaking shield."

Noah spoke up, sounding contrite. "I apologize for my mistake."

"It's not your fault, old friend," Divinus replied. "We were working with too little information. They kept their secrets hidden. That's why Drakken put the shield back up, so we wouldn't know he was targeting the Second Continuum—"

"That bastard waited until the mothership was in orbit over our encampment," Aero said as he stormed into the Foundry. Wren followed with Seeker loping behind them. "He wanted us to see it with our own eyes. What kind of monster does that? I'm waiting on casualty figures from the explosion. The warhead left none alive."

Seeker jerked his eyes to the Forger. "What about the shield?"

"We've fixed the bugs," he replied, "thanks to Tinker's help. He's been apprenticing under me for the last two weeks. He's very good with our machines."

Tinker smiled shyly from behind Myra. "Tinker's been helping you with the shield?" Aero said, sounding surprised. "But he's only a boy."

"So was I when my Order chose me from the Agoge," the Forger said. "Perhaps you remember when they came to escort me from our class? I thought I'd graduate and serve in a Medical or Engineering unit, but fate had a different path in store."

"I remember feeling relieved," Aero said. "Like I had been spared."

"Same here," Wren chimed in, her hand darting to her Falchion.

"Not an uncommon sentiment," the Forger said. "We are taught to worship soldiers and the heat of the battle, but my Order is what makes it all possible." He started across the chamber. "If you'll come with me, I need the Carriers' help."

"Our help?" Myra said. "With what?"

"The shield," the Forger replied, continuing over to one of the larger machines. "We need to harness the Beacons to power it. Actually, Tinker designed the program."

"You did?" Myra said, fluffing his hair.

"Yeah, I like the machines," he said. "I told you that."

The Forger gestured for them to join him by the machine. "This is how we generate the shield. The reason it keeps failing is because our power source isn't strong enough. We need to use the Beacons to boost the charge."

"Of course—like when the probe targeted our campsite in the desert," Aero said, thinking back. "I used my Beacon to boost the shield's power and protect us."

"Exactly," the Forger said with a bob of his head. "Only this is a much larger surface area, so I will need all three of you and your Beacons this time."

He had them assume lotus position. Then he and Tinker attached golden wires to their wrists, connecting their Beacons to the machine. Tinker approached the control panel and toggled a few levers. He bit his lower lip.

"Ready?" the Forger asked.

"Yup," Tinker replied, flipping a switch. "All systems are go."

Myra braced herself, but nothing happened. "Why isn't it working?" she asked, glancing warily at the wires snaking from her wrist.

Aero frowned. "Right, we have to channel our life force through the Beacons and into the machine to launch the shield. The Beacon is a conduit, and our life force has more power than any of these generators."

"Holy Sea, how do we do that?" Myra asked.

"That's what I wondered the first time," Aero replied.

Professor Divinus joined them in the circle. His projection rippled. "Remember the mind exercises? Clear your thoughts and feelings and let yourself drift off."

Myra did as instructed, finding her calm place quickly. The dreamscape unfolded around her. Soon, Aero and then Seeker materialized into it. She could still hear the professor's voice droning on.

"Now imagine you're holding up the shield . . ."

The dreamscape shifted to their encampment, where the alarm still blared. Panicked soldiers rushed around in the predawn light, trying to locate their units and lock down the courtyard. The Majors were shouting orders, while over in the Seventh camp, Crawler was forming his soldiers into units as best he could.

The Carriers moved through the courtyard like ghosts; the soldiers couldn't see them. Myra felt her Beacon throb faster, matching the racing of her heart.

Hold my hand, she thought to Aero and Seeker.

When their hands locked, power surged from their Beacons, engulfing their bodies in emerald fire. Myra focused on the shield. She imagined a dome enclosing the camp and the First Continuum, protecting them from Drakken's warheads.

"The Carriers are doing it . . ." she heard Divinus saying, though it sounded like it was coming from far away. "Tinker, now! Activate the shield."

Suddenly, a translucent dome materialized over the court-yard. But it flickered, threatening to disappear. *No!* Myra thought. *I'm supporting you!*

The fire from their Beacons built into a towering inferno and shot out toward the shield. The flames hit it—and this time it turned solid. The soldiers froze, tilting their heads to the sky. "The shield!" they cheered. "It's working! Look at the sky!"

But Myra could barely hear them.

She felt Aero and Seeker clasping her hands—and that was when a memory surfaced. She didn't know if it was triggered by the linking of their Beacons, if that was what finally broke Drakken's suppression spell, or if her mind had simply grown strong enough to crack through it. But she finally remembered the thing that had been eluding her. And this time, it didn't fade back into the depths of her subconscious mind. It stayed, like something powerful and true. Like the shield that now blazed over their heads.

Aero squeezed her hand, and so did Seeker. *We hear you*, they communicated. *We see your memories like they are our own.*

Peacefulness washed over Myra, but then it was gone. The dreamscape shattered around them. She felt a strange sucking sensation, and then they were back in the Foundry. Myra blinked, waiting for her vision to clear. Tinker unfastened the wires from her wrist. When he saw her eyes pop open, he grinned his lopsided smile.

"We did it," he said. "The shield is up and running."

Behind him, the strange machine whirred and flashed with emerald lights. He coiled the wires and checked the control panel, adjusting a few levers.

"Well, let's not get too excited yet," Wren said with a frown. "I hate to be a downer, but according to the Forger, the shield won't hold forever. It only buys us a little bit of time before Drakken breaks it. You saw what he did to the Second Continuum."

Myra felt a surge of hope. She met Wren's gaze.

"I remembered his weakness."

Chapter 50
THE SNAKE'S HEAD

Aero Wright

Caught in a swirl of black emotions, Aero claimed his usual seat at the long table next to Kaleb and Seeker. He couldn't stop picturing the explosion tearing through the predawn sky, painting it white hot and crimson. Professor Divinus materialized in the spot at the head, while Myra had eschewed her chair in favor of pacing around the room.

The Forger and Tinker stayed back in the Foundry to monitor the shield's strength and keep it running. Aero had dispatched Wren to the Surface to assume command of the army in his absence. "Sir, I want to be in that Assembly meeting," Wren had protested when he gave her the command. "You'll need my support in case Myra . . ."

"In case Myra what?" he demanded.

"In case she goes rogue again," Wren shot back. Her eyes flashed with defiance. "Sir, don't let your feelings for the girl blind you. She's emotional, unpredictable, and impulsive. That can cause serious damage. This isn't a simulation, sir. We're talking about fighting a real war here. And it's against an army that's larger and better equipped than ours.

Our Falchions are powerful, but they have limitations. They were designed that way on purpose. The Fourth Continuum imposed no such limitations on their arsenal—"

"Major Jordan, that was an order," Aero cut her off. He couldn't let his feelings get in the way of commanding his soldiers—and that included Wren. She needed to follow his orders and not question them. "You're the only one I trust up there."

Her eyes still looked defiant, but he saw sadness in them too. She snapped off a salute. "Yes, sir."

He watched her march toward the elevator. Why did he feel bad for issuing orders to his underlings? Surely, his father never felt so conflicted when commanding his soldiers. But then his Beacon flared and he heard his father's voice in his head.

Of course, I felt conflicted—and I didn't have to face such daunting challenges. Trust your judgment, my son. In these dire times, that's the best you can do

Myra's voice jerked Aero out of his thoughts. "Noah, can you download my memories from the Beacon and project them?" she said, still pacing excitedly.

"Already one step ahead of you, Ms. Jackson," Noah said. "Projecting your memories now."

The air above the table blazed with light and came alive with Myra's memories, projected in three-dimensional clarity. She materialized inside the Fourth Continuum and floated down the corridor. Aero watched with great interest. Two crew members dressed in red lab coats marched past, carrying vials filled with strange liquids. They couldn't see her.

"Here—see these devices on their heads?" Myra said, indicating the golden crowns encircling their temples. Wires extended from them, plugging into their scalps.

"They're peculiar," Aero said, leaning forward to study the projection closer. "I've never seen anything like those implants before."

"Nor have I," Divinus added with a frown. He stroked his beard, scrutinizing the strange devices. "It looks like they're connected directly to their neural synapses."

"Exactly," Myra said excitedly. "Remember Stern's logbook entries about the Fourth Continuum's experiments? I think they succeeded in building on the technology from the Beacons. They figured out a way to link their consciousnesses together."

"Like human networking?" Aero said with a frown.

Myra nodded, gesturing to her Beacon. "Look, we know it's possible to use this technology to connect our minds together. Only there appears to be one big difference between the Beacons and these implants."

"Dead eyes," Seeker growled, studying the crew members with their vapid gazes and jerky, robotic movements. "Drakken controls them through the implants."

"Right, that's what I think too," Myra said. "The Beacons connect us together, but each Carrier maintains free will. That's not the case with these devices. I saw into Drakken's mind. Harnessing the power of his Beacon, he sends the crew orders through their neural implants. They have no choice but to obey him—they're his slaves."

Aero took that all in. He studied the crew members' vacant expressions. "So Drakken controls them? How does that help us? That probably makes them better soldiers. They'll follow every order and fight to the death without complaint. Plus, if they're all linked together, that could increase Drakken's power. Like when you network computers. That makes them more powerful than a single machine."

"Supreme General Wright is correct," Noah said. "I'm technically made up of many computers networked together. That's what makes me a supercomputer."

Myra nodded. "That's true, it does increase their power. It's probably also why Drakken has such strong control over his Beacon. He's harnessing the collective consciousness of his crew. At first, I'm guessing the experiments were intended to amplify their minds in the pursuit of scientific knowledge. Cure all diseases. Heal the radiation-scarred Earth. Extend the reach of the mind beyond the body's fragile existence."

"But it all went horribly wrong," Divinus said, putting the pieces of their history together. "We know that Shira Ramses was the Carrier when the Fourth Continuum disappeared seven hundred years ago. We know about her from the Foundry's Archives. I'm guessing she was the first Carrier who gained the ability to control the ship like this."

Divinus's hands flicked through air, manipulating the projection and fast-forwarding Myra's memory. He paused it on one frame.

"Look at this laboratory." He focused in on the background, where the crew members were hovering over strange machines scattered throughout the sterile space. "They look like our cryocapsules, only they're not preserving animals."

"They're incubating babies," Myra said with a shocked expression. "They don't even birth children anymore. They make them in laboratories."

"Yes, I think so," Divinus said. "I'm guessing they have some horrific process for choosing their next Carrier. That must be how Drakken got these injuries."

He zoomed in on Drakken resting on his commander's chair. Scars crisscrossed every inch of flesh not covered by his crimson robes. Not even his face was spared.

"Again, how does any of this help us?" Aero asked with a frown. "Myra, you said you found Drakken's weakness? All this does is explain his strengths."

"But that's it, don't you see?" Myra said, pacing excitedly. "Human networking is what makes them so strong—but it's also their greatest weakness."

"My dear, please explain," Divinus said, flickering with confusion.

"Seeker said it first," Myra said, glancing at her. "They're Drakken's slaves. So if we take him out first, then we release the crew from his control. He's making them fight this war. They don't have a choice in the matter."

"Myra, you don't know that for sure," Kaleb said, gesturing to the images of the crew hovering over the table. "If we release them from their implants, they could turn out to be just as bad as Drakken. And we'd still be outnumbered and outgunned."

"No, they're like us," Myra insisted with a shake of her head. "I could sense it when I was on their ship. I can't explain how exactly, but I think the Beacon let me see into their minds through Drakken's connection. They're good people. They're just controlled by him. Remember how Padre Flavius made our people do terrible things? Aero, the same thing happened with Vinick in the Second Continuum."

"My home," Seeker added. "The Strong Ones . . . "

"Precisely," Myra said. "One bad leader can corrupt a whole colony. We know that from our history. So all we need to do is free them from Drakken."

Aero ticked through her plan, piecing it all together. His mind flashed back to his trial by combat with Danika. "So by your logic, we have to take out the snake's head," he said softly, growing more comfortable with this approach. "Just like the chimera."

"What is . . . chimera?" Seeker asked.

"It's an ancient, mythical beast with three heads—a snake, a goat, and a lion," Aero explained as Noah projected historical etchings displaying the ferocious creature. He pointed to the snarling heads. "Vinick programmed it into my trial, hoping the beast would kill us. Danika and I figured out that the snake's head controlled the other two heads. We just needed to take out the snake, and then the whole creature went down."

Myra nodded. "Then that's our plan—we take out Drakken and release his people from their mind-controlling implants. That's how we defeat them."

"Holy Sea, how do we do that?" Kaleb asked.

"Right, it won't be easy," Aero agreed. "Drakken will probably stay aboard the mothership and command his army remotely. That's what I would do. The Fourth Continuum is heavily fortified and defended. Maybe if we had the Second Continuum, we could break onto his ship and take him out. But without it, we don't stand a chance."

Noah flashed blueprints of the Fourth Continuum overhead, detailing their impressive defenses. "Also, the shield," Seeker added. "Won't hold long. Tinker said so."

"Exactly," Aero agreed. He thought through all the possibilities. "We would have to take a transport, somehow slip past the Fourth Continuum's defenses, break onboard their ship, get past his guards and locate Drakken. Oh yeah, and we'd have to do it really fast before he breaks our shield." It sounded impossible. "So basically, we're dead."

Silence descended over the table. Even Professor Divinus didn't try to lighten their spirits. "I sense your dejection," Noah said. "Professor, is there anything I can do?"

But nobody answered him.

Myra's memories continued to unfold overhead. She floated onto the bridge, where she found Drakken ensconced on his commander's chair. His eyes snapped open. *Get out, girl!* His Beacon flared as his voice tore through the dreamscape. His human form started to dissolve, morphing into the Dark Thing. His shadowy tendrils shot out. Before they could stab her, she plunged from the ship and back down to Earth.

"That's it," Myra said, her eyes locked onto her memory, which continued to play on a loop. She paced even faster, the wheels turning in her head. "By the Oracle, there's only one way we can get to him . . . it's a long short . . . and very risky . . . "

"Myra, what is it?" Aero asked, tracking her progress.

She skidded to a halt and bent over the table. "Listen, I don't know if this will work. It will take all of us working together. But first, we have to shield our minds from Drakken. He can't know our plan. We have to catch him by surprise."

Moments later, Aero felt hope flutter in his chest as he listened to Myra's plan. They'd first worked to shield their minds. When she finished, Divinus called for a vote.

"Aye," rang out around the table.

Only Aero remained silent.

"It must be unanimous," Divinus said. "For the plan involves all of you if it's going to work. Let me remind you,

Noah's new estimate has Drakken's troops deploying to Earth at approximately 0630 hours tomorrow. That gives us less than ten hours."

"Daybreak," Myra said. "He's coming at daybreak."

Aero narrowed his eyes. "Aye. Let's kill the bastard."

Chapter 51
ONE LAST NIGHT

Myra Jackson

One last night," Myra whispered to herself, burrowing under the thick comforter covering her bed. She shuddered despite the warmth it provided. She wished Tinker was with her—they'd always shared a room back home—but he was holed up in the Foundry, working with the Forgers to keep the shield running at full strength.

She knew that she should sleep in preparation for tomorrow. She was still recovering from Drakken's attack. They had a plan, but the odds of it succeeding were slim. And if it failed, then . . . well . . . she didn't want to think about it.

But the images forced their way into her brain anyway. She imagined the Harvard Yard strewn with the slaughtered bodies of her friends—Aero, Wren, Kaleb, Seeker. Their blood stained the earth crimson. Overhead, the shield fizzled and went dark as warheads sailed through the sky and slammed into their encampment, demolishing the First Continuum in one swift blast and heralding the coming of a second Doom.

She tossed and turned for what felt like hours. Finally, she shot up in bed, sweaty and shaking from her nightmare. The automatic lights were still dim—it was still night. She slipped from under the covers, slipped from her room, and padded down the corridor. It felt cold against her bare feet. She knew this was a bad idea and she should turn back, but her body continued as if on autopilot. She triggered the door next to her chambers.

"Well, come on," she said, poking her head into Kaleb's room. She could just make out his bed, shrouded by the gauzy curtains. "Don't make me ask twice."

A large form stirred in the semidarkness.

"Myra?" Kaleb said sleepily. "What are you doing here?"

But she had already started back down the corridor, suspecting that going to his room was a huge mistake. *Kaleb, faithful Kaleb.* He would follow her, she knew. She felt terrible for leading him on when her heart beat for someone else. Sure enough, his clomping footfalls echoed after her. She reached her room and climbed back into bed, slipping under the comforter. A second later, the door beeped shut. The drapes stirred and then settled. She felt Kaleb climb in next to her, sliding between the crisp sheets.

"No funny business," she chided. She tried to keep her voice stern, but it came out warm and affectionate. The armor shielding her heart was only a rickety façade.

"Of course, hands off," he said, holding them up. A sheepish smile broke over his face, lighting up his handsome features. "We could die tomorrow, you know?"

She grimaced. "Don't remind me."

He propped himself up on his elbows, fixing his eyes on her. She grew uncomfortable under the intensity of his gaze. "Sebold, what're you looking at?"

"Trying to memorize your face," he said with a shrug. "I want to make sure I remember it. Wren says your life doesn't really flash before your eyes when you die."

"Wait, you've been talking to Wren?"

Myra regretted asking the question as soon as it left her mouth. *Why should I care about who he's been talking to lately, when we could all die tomorrow?*

He fixed her with a teasing grin.

"Jackson, did I hit a nerve?" he asked, but then he turned more serious. "Look, I know you're not Wren's biggest fan. But we were locked up together with nothing to do but talk. She's a little prickly on the outside, but she's got a good heart."

"Guess I've only seen the prickly side," Myra grumbled.

"Well, she likes you. I know she does. She's just not good at expressing her emotions. They were taught to suppress them from a young age, so it's hard for her."

"Maybe," Myra allowed.

Impulsively, she snuggled into him, pulling his arms around her. He looked surprised, then pleased. He pulled her into his chest and buried his face in her hair. She felt him inhale. *Is he memorizing my scent too?*

"I thought you said no funny business," he teased.

"We could die tomorrow," she replied, and that was when she kissed him.

Kissing Kaleb felt like going home. Everything about him—the taste of his lips, the warmth of his mouth, the undulation of his tongue—seemed familiar. It soothed the homesickness that had taken up residence in her heart. She traced her lips over his scars, tasting this reminder of everything that they'd been through together.

She lost herself in the physical sensations, seeking to block out everything else—the conflict she felt about Aero, the throbbing of her Beacon, the Fourth Continuum barreling toward their door, her people running out of oxygen. She blocked it all out and kissed Kaleb harder, trying to fill herself up with his lips, his smell, his taste.

They pulled apart, breathless and both a little bit shocked by what had happened. Myra lapsed into a fitful sleep that felt like drowning. Her Beacon reached into her mind and carried her consciousness out across the night. Physically, she was still in her chambers, tucked under the thick comforter next to Kaleb; but she was also with the other Carriers at the same time—the fracturing of her existence.

o   o   o

Destroy. Destroy. Destroy.

Myra saw through Drakken's eyes. He sat in his commander's chair with his thoughts fixated on the upcoming war. His neural synapses fired off orders to his people as they prepared for battle, shedding their crimson lab coats and donning armor that glistened like obsidian in the harsh artificial light. They moved in perfect sync, thousands of them, arms and legs pumping. They slid their helmets down and picked up blasters. They clacked the safeties off. They marched into their warships in perfect formation.

Girl, your shield will fail—and we will be ready for it.

Drakken's laughter hit her like a punch.

Her shoulder ached where he had stabbed her. She pushed back against his signal, expelling herself from his ship. She plummeted back down to Earth.

o   o   o

Myra felt her arms and legs pounding the sodden earth. She galloped through the night, ducking around the rubble and chasing a ratter. The nocturnal world opened up to her with its unique smells and sounds and blue-black textures. The disorientation faded, and she understood—she was Seeker.

The night was moonless, yet she could see perfectly. The glow from the shield overhead bathed the crumbling buildings with emerald light. She dashed under an archway marked with a seal and a strange word: *Veritas.* Another figure pulled up next to her—it was Crawler. She recognized his scent. Soundlessly, they communicated, splitting up and tracking the ratter through the subterranean tunnels that wound under the buildings and through the musty earth. The creature was right ahead now.

She could smell it.

She unsheathed her Falchion, morphed it into a spear, and skewered her hapless prey. Sparks exploded from the golden weapon, fizzling out. The ratter twitched on the tip, dripping black blood on the concrete. After snagging a few more ratters, Seeker tracked Crawler down, and they devoured their fresh kill. The blood flecked their lips and hair. The meat tasted rare and delicious as it slurped down her throat.

Satiated, they snuck back into the Seventh encampment, where their soldiers were awake and active. Seeker led Crawler back to her tent, where they lay down together on a rough mat cast on the floor, eschewing the cot shoved against the canvas wall.

"Tomorrow, we will fight like Strong Ones," Crawler said, burying his head into her neck. He tried to pull her closer, but Seeker pushed him away.

"I feel like a Weakling," she said. Doubt surged through her. "Filthy Drakken. He is stronger than us. His soldiers will kill our people and feast on our bodies."

"The plan," Crawler growled. "It will work."

"But what if it doesn't?" Seeker said, untangling herself from his arms. Her hand darted to her Falchion. "I want to fight bravely and make our ancestors proud." Her hand dropped away. "But what if I really am a Weakling . . . like Rooter said?"

Crawler gripped her face roughly. "You already made them proud."

"No, I'm a coward," she confessed. She stalked around the tent in a loop. "I want to flee into the night and never return to this nasty, burning place."

"You led us out of the Darkness of the Below," Crawler said. "You found the Door in the Wall and hunted on the Brightside. You're the Carrier for the Seventh Continuum and the Weakling who became the Strongest of the Strong Ones. You inspired us to rise up. We're not starving anymore. Our bellies are full. We have Falchions. And tomorrow, we will defeat the Fourth Continuum—or die trying."

Seeker stopped pacing and curled up beside him. His warm breath kissed her neck, but still she felt afraid. "The shield won't hold for long," she whispered. "Tinker told me. Drakken will find a way to break it. He's already trying. The

Forgers are doing everything they can to reinforce it. But Drakken will fire on us as soon as it fails."

"Seeker, are you afraid to die?" Crawler asked.

She thought about it. Back in the Seventh Continuum, when she was a Weakling always hunting for her next meal, she woke up every day expecting it could be her last. Death seemed so certain back then, but now that had changed. She'd already outlived her own life expectations. She no longer woke up every night expecting to die. Crawler made her feel even more hopeful. She'd started to believe in the possibility of living—really living. But now death loomed large again. So . . . was she afraid to die?

Seeker felt her doubt draining away, replaced by deep conviction. She turned back to Crawler and growled. "No, I'm not—I'm only afraid to die a coward."

"No chance of that," Crawler purred.

He crushed Seeker to his chest, and that was when Myra felt her consciousness being propelled out of their tent, away from the Seventh encampment, and toward two figures sitting on Widener's steps, their silhouettes illuminated by the shield. She swooped down toward them and invaded the taller figure. She saw through his eyes and felt through his senses. This host didn't fight her; he welcomed her more than the others. He pulled her into him, inviting her deep into the recesses of his heart.

He loved her.

o   o   o

A familiar voice reached Myra as she listened through Aero's ears.

"Did you ever think we'd be standing here like this?" Wren asked.

Her eyes fixed on the tents that made up their encampment in the Harvard Yard. Aero followed her gaze. A strange calm seemed to have settled over the camp. The soldiers talked quietly with their comrades, loitering outside their tent flaps, or they got what little shut-eye they could, knowing that this could be their last night.

"You mean, did I ever think we'd be standing on the threshold of the First Continuum, commanding an army against an invading colony that wants to bring back the Doom?" he asked with a cock of his eyebrow.

"Yup, that about sums it up," she said with a chuckle.

"Not even close," he answered. "I mean, I expected to deploy to Earth. But I never thought the Fourth Continuum would reappear. We were taught they had perished on Uranus. And, well, I thought my father would . . ."

"You thought he would command our army," she finished his thought. "And that we would only be following his orders like good soldiers."

"Following orders, not giving them," he agreed.

"You were first in our class at the Agoge," she pointed out. "Is it really that unexpected? You're a strong soldier, skilled with your Falchion. But it's more than that. You have what it takes to lead. I know it hasn't been easy, but you're the—"

"If you say *Chosen One*, I'm leaving," he joked but then turned more serious. "What about you? Did you ever think you'd ever be standing here like this?"

"I used to dream about moments like this," Wren said. "The lull before the coming battle, when all your training and hard work are about to be tested, when the noise of regular life drains away and everything becomes really clear. I thought it would be exhilarating. But now that I'm here, all I feel is overwhelming dread."

"That's perfectly normal," he started, but she cut him off.

"Damn it, don't try to make me feel better." Her voice wavered and broke. She slumped her shoulders forward. "I'm a coward, plain and simple. This is the truest test of a soldier, and I'm frightened. What's wrong with me?"

Aero laid his hand on her shoulder. They sat together quietly for a long moment, letting the shield's glow wash over them. Finally, he broke the silence.

"Fear isn't the measure of our true worth," he said, repeating what his father had told him. "It isn't even the measure of our abilities as a soldier. Fear is simply a normal emotional reaction to danger—and we are in grave danger now. We only become cowards if we give in to the fear and let it dictate our actions."

"You're just saying that to make me feel better," Wren said, feisty as always.

"Maybe," Aero conceded. He studied her face. "Well, did it work?"

"Not really." She held up her hands. "I'm trembling like a Falchion that needs a fresh charge. But you're not afraid, are you? Your hands are rock solid."

She reached for them. Her palms felt clammy, though his remained dry and steady. He felt the urge to pull Wren toward him and offer her physical comfort, but he resisted it. It would only make everything more complicated. Worse yet, she would probably resent him for taking advantage of her momentary weakness.

Despite his mental protestations, he didn't pull his hand away, and she didn't either. "My hands may be steady," he confided. His eyes stayed fixed on her face. "But that doesn't mean I'm not afraid."

"So are you?" Wren probed. "Afraid?"

"Well, I still have a hard time identifying my emotional state. But my stomach feels twisted in knots, my heart is thumping wildly, and my mind keeps racing. So I'm guessing that means I'm feeling something like fear, but I refuse to give in to it."

"In that case, may we fight bravely at dawn. And if we should die tomorrow, then may we die clean deaths at the hands of a worthy opponent."

Aero grinned. "That's more like it, Major. I was starting to worry about you."

"Sir, I'm sorry to report that my moment of weakness has passed," she said, returning his smile. "Now, you may remove your hand from my lap."

He waited for several seconds longer than was necessary before he obeyed. But instead of separating himself from

Wren, he ran his fingers through her freshly buzzed hair and tilted her face toward him. She looked shocked, but then her expression softened. He held her gaze and did not look away.

"We make the rules now," he whispered. "We're the ones in charge of this world. You know the plan is a crazy long shot. We may never get another chance."

"But . . . what does this help?" Their faces were only millimeters apart. Her eyes roved over his face. "By the stars, this will only complicate everything. It's likely we'll die tomorrow . . . you're right. But what if we don't? What happens then?"

"Major, I don't care anymore," Aero said and kissed Wren. She tensed, clearly shocked by his impulsiveness, but then she kissed him back urgently. Her lips moved against his lips, fumbling and inexperienced, but they quickly warmed to his touch. She pulled him down onto the steps, and in that instant, he lost himself in her taste.

o   o   o

Myra came back to herself—her consciousness flung back into her physical body. She was back in her chambers with Kaleb curled up next to her, snoring softly. *One last night,* she thought again. She felt a twinge of jealousy, but it was unwarranted. Hadn't she done the exact same thing with Kaleb only a few short moments ago?

She settled into the pillowy softness of her bed and pressed herself to Kaleb, holding on to him for as long as she could. That was when she slept deeply and fully, entangled in his long limbs, until the automatic lights brightened, ratcheting up their intensity. Noah's voice echoed through the room.

"Myra Jackson, this is your wake-up call," he said. "The Fourth Continuum's estimated time of arrival is in one hour and thirty minutes. Please report to the control room. Professor Divinus is waiting for you."

Kaleb stirred next to her. He was suddenly wide awake. "I'm sorry . . ." he started as everything came flooding back. She silenced him with a quick peck.

"Don't be sorry." She sprang from bed, tugging on her

tunic. "Please, let's not spoil it by talking about it either." She started toward the door but turned back.

"Don't worry, I'll check on Tinker," he said, recognizing the look on her face. "I'm planning to go the Foundry anyway. I've got a feeling the Forgers could use all the help they can get."

Myra hadn't seen Tinker since last night, when she had stopped by the Foundry on her way back to her chambers. "Please, tell Tinker . . . I love him."

"Of course," Kaleb said, sliding from bed. She could see the scars on his chest in their full and terrible glory. He grabbed his tunic. "Even though he already knows."

"And Kaleb . . ." she started.

"I already know too," he said as Noah's voice blared out again.

"Myra Jackson, you're late. Report to the control room."

Hating that she had to leave, Myra dashed into the corridor, tugging on her canvas shoes. Was this the last time she'd ever see him? She prayed it wasn't, but the odds weren't in their favor. Suddenly, she caught a flash from her Beacon.

Destroy. Destroy. Destroy.

That was accompanied by horrible laughter that rattled her skull, making her double over. She grabbed her temples as pain surged through them, struggling to understand the message. Drakken was coming . . . no . . . that was wrong . . .

Drakken is already here.

Breaking into a sprint, Myra tore through the corridor and burst into the control room, where she found Divinus already seated at the table. Several images floated over his head. One showed the Fourth Continuum's ship, hovering in orbit. Black flecks broke away from the mothership and shot down toward Earth, trailing twin tails of fire and gas.

"My dear, they're deploying," Divinus said. "Phase one of our plan is engaged. Their long-range weapons are locked on us, but they're refraining from firing—"

Suddenly, an explosion hit the shield and lit up the sky.

Myra saw it on the surveillance feeds. The control room shook, throwing her to the ground.

Red lights flashed and alarms blared.

"What was that?" she yelled, scrambling back to her feet. "Professor, I thought you said they were *refraining* from firing?"

On the screen, the shield was smoking but still protecting the encampment.

"They're testing the shield," Divinus said. His projection hadn't moved from his position at the head of the table. His fingers flitted through the air, flipping through the feeds. "Thankfully, it appears to be holding."

"But for how long?" Myra asked. Her eyes were fixed on feeds.

"The Foundry reports shield integrity at ninety percent," Noah announced as another blast rained down on the dome. "They're trying to reinforce it—"

His words cut off as another explosion tore into the shield, more powerful than the last one. The control room shook violently, but this time Myra was ready and braced herself. Once it passed, she pushed her energy into the Beacon, sending a message to Aero and Seeker. *Please hurry,* she communicated. *We don't have much time.*

Chapter 52
WELCOMING SHOT

Supreme General Aero Wright

Aero braced himself for the incoming explosion, managing to keep his footing. Not all his soldiers were so lucky. As the blast rained down on the shield, across the Harvard Yard, hundreds of their soldiers staggered and went down to their knees. The ground buckled under their feet. That was followed by the shrill blaring of alarms.

"Starry hell, what was that?" Wren yelled, glancing at the shield. Seeker and Crawler appeared next to them, gripping their Falchions. They also craned their necks up.

"Welcoming shot," Aero muttered. His Beacon throbbed as he caught a flash from Myra. "They felt it down there too. Drakken's testing the shield."

The blast radiated into the shield, fanning out. The shield warped and started smoking, but miraculously it held. *Otherwise, we'd all be burnt to a crisp*, Aero thought.

Aero gazed out over the Harvard Yard, where hundreds of units stood in formation. Their Falchions glinted, reflecting the light, a mixture of the shield's steady glow and the dawn sunlight spilling over the horizon.

"Incoming," Major Zakkay yelled. He had scopes raised to his eyes, trained on the shield. "Get ready for it. Five seconds . . . four . . . three . . . two . . . one!"

The next blast rained down in a fiery explosion.

The ground shook and threw them around. Aero felt Wren stumble into him. Many soldiers staggered around, looking frightened and straying from their positions. Aero was suddenly aware of how inexperienced they were. Training at the Agoge and fighting simulator drills wasn't the same as real combat.

"Hold your formation," he ordered, trying to head off the panic.

His officers—including Wren, Zakkay, Seeker, and Crawler—repeated the order to their troops. More enemy fire blasted into the shield. The welcoming barrage tapered off. The shield was smoking but still intact. *Shield integrity at sixty percent*, Myra communicated. Silence fell over the courtyard. Aero knew what was coming next.

From the highest step on Widener Library, he raised his voice. "Soldiers, unsheathe your Falchions," he commanded. "Prepare to engage the enemy."

Aero watched as the first wave of the Fourth Continuum's transports descended like a swarm of insects from Before Doom. The spiky black ships landed swiftly, plunging vertically and settling on the ground outside the shield. Their bay doors yawned open. Soldiers marched out, forming up into ranks. They clutched blasters and wore glossy black armor that was molded to their bodies. Helmets with faceplates protected their heads. They marched in perfect formation like automatons.

All at once, they marched forward in unison. Aero watched in awe. His soldiers were skilled and trained, but even they couldn't march like that. Myra was right—they were networked together, and Drakken was controlling them.

The first units reached the shield, pausing outside the translucent barrier. One unit marched forward, passing through the energy field unharmed. Like the Forger warned, the shield could deflect their weapons, but it couldn't keep their soldiers out. The next wave of transports clouded the sky, casting the courtyard into shadow.

His Beacon pulsed—and Aero caught a message from Myra: *Hurry, they're coming . . .*

"Soldiers, morph your Falchions," Aero commanded. His eyes swept over the courtyard, inspecting his units. The Second soldiers and the Seventh soldiers stood shoulder to shoulder, their divisions forgotten in the face of battle. "Shields first, like we practiced. Don't go on the offensive until you're close enough to inflict damage."

On his command, thousands of Falchions rippled and shifted into long shields, emitting golden sparks. "Hold your positions," Aero called, sensing nervousness in the ranks. Even Wren seemed tense next to him. "Wait for them to get closer."

The Fourth soldiers spilled into the Harvard Yard and unleashed an onslaught of shots that slammed into the Falchions. Most of the shots were deflected by the shields, but some of Aero's soldiers went down. But still Aero waited, keeping his soldiers back. Finally, when the Fourth soldiers got close enough, he issued his next order:

"Soldiers, attack!"

Aero watched as his army surged forward, engaging the enemy troops in a ground war. The courtyard erupted with blaster fire and golden sparks. Aero turned to Wren and caught her eye. Though it went against his every instinct, he forced himself to comply with their plan and issue the most important command of his life.

"Major Jordan, it's your army now," he ordered.

"Yes, sir," she said with a salute. "Good luck down there."

Together with Majors Zakkay, Malik, and Tabor, Wren plunged into the battle, wielding her Falchion in the form of a talwer. The Seventh soldiers, despite their freshly bonded Falchions and erratic training, fell on the Fourth Continuum soldiers with speed and ferocity. Crawler tore after them, snarling commands while he ran.

But Seeker didn't follow him. She sprinted over to Aero—and together they retreated from the battlefield, abandoning their soldiers to their fates.

"Feels filthy and wrong . . ." Seeker growled as they ascended the steps and vanished into the crumbling Widener Library. The roof had been torn off and the columns toppled, but some of the walls still stood. The sounds of combat—screams, explosions, clanging, howls of pain—chased them down the dim corridor.

"I know," Aero said, feeling sickened. "But it's the only way."

They dashed into the elevator, which was waiting for them. "Noah, take us down to the First Continuum," Aero yelled as soon as they crossed the threshold.

The door contracted, cutting off the sounds of battle. Aero felt his heart plunge along with his body as the elevator lurched downward. Abandoning his post and deserting his army when they needed him most felt tantamount to treason. One glance at Seeker told him that she was experiencing the same confusing mix of emotions.

Remember the plan, Myra communicated. *Don't lose faith now.*

When the elevator spit them out, they rushed through the chambers to the control room, where they found Myra and Divinus waiting for them at the table. Above their heads, in three-dimensional clarity, Noah projected security feeds of the battle raging on the surface. One feed cut to a close-up of one of his soldiers right as he took a blaster shot to the head. He convulsed and went down. Aero felt a surge of guilt again. He didn't even know the soldier's name. The courtyard was littered with dead bodies, mostly his soldiers.

"Starry hell, it's a bloodbath up there," Aero said. "They're slaughtering us."

"I know," Myra replied. Her voice sounded strained. Her eyes flicked over the feeds, taking in the bloodshed. "That's why we've go to hurry."

On another feed, Fourth Continuum soldiers were setting up machines at various points along the shield's dome.

"What are they doing?" Seeker growled.

Divinus followed her gaze. His visage quivered with worry, appearing to age two decades. "They're trying to break the shield," he said.

"Professor, you are correct," Noah reported. "Shield integrity is down to fifty percent. The Foundry is doing everything they can to reinforce it. Best estimate is . . . fifteen minutes to collapse."

That snapped them into action.

"Carriers, we haven't a moment to lose," Divinus said.

Though it went against his every instinct, Aero tore his gaze away from the feeds and slid into a chair. Seeker claimed the seat to his right. He could feel that she was struggling too. Only Myra seemed to have achieved some mastery over her feelings.

"Remember, we have to do this together," Myra said, meeting their eyes. "Forget the feeds . . . forget your soldiers. You have to focus, or we're all doomed."

It was harder than he expected, but Aero pushed thoughts of Wren, his Majors, and his army from his mind. The battle was only a distraction to keep Drakken's attention divided, so that he would be vulnerable to another sort of attack—one that wouldn't come in the form of a blaster or a Falchion.

"Carriers, shut your eyes," Divinus said. "This is where the real battle will be fought. Not with weapons, but with your minds. Are you ready for this?"

Aero searched his heart, feeling the reassuring presence of his father. *It feels wrong to leave your troops, but you are acting in their best interest.*

The tide of conflicting emotions died down. Aero felt his mind grow very still—and that's when he knew he was ready. Myra reached out and clasped his hand, and Seeker did the same. Their Beacons started to throb in sync as their minds melded together, until Aero wasn't sure where he ended and Myra and Seeker began.

"Drakken is powerful and strong, so you must stay connected," Divinus continued. "That's your only chance of defeating him. Close your eyes, and still your minds. Feel the Beacons pulse through you and connect you together . . ." Divinus kept talking, but his voice sounded distant.

"Shield integrity at forty percent," Noah reported, but Aero could barely hear him, nor could he hear the clanging and raging of the battle anymore.

United we are strongest, Myra communicated. *Stay united.*

That was the last thing Aero heard before the world of the First Continuum—the control room and its flickering feeds and whirring computers—faded away and he was somewhere else altogether. The dreamscape unfolded around him in perfect clarity—a world of their own making, cobbled together from their memories, wishes, and experiences. It was partly the venue from his Krypteia, with howling wind and carbon dioxide snow, but it was situated on the rocky beach where Myra's submersible washed up. Ratters skittered down the beach, vanishing into the caves drilled into the earth.

Aero focused on cloaking his presence in shadows; Seeker did the same thing. They hid in the blurry fringes of the world. Further away, Myra lay down on the rocky beach, letting the snow pile up around her. She was unarmed and defenseless. The ocean churned and frothed with whitecaps, beating against the shore.

Drakken, come and get me, Myra thought. Her Beacon flared—and he answered her call. Laughter tore through the dreamscape, accompanied by a menacing voice.

You're dead, Carrier.

Chapter 53
THE DREAMSCAPE

The Carriers

The Dark Thing materialized on the beach, answering Myra's siren call. Snow swirled around his shadowy form. The wind howled even harder. Storm clouds cloaked the sky, amassing and darkening. Drakken locked onto the girl, letting out another horrible peal of laughter. Myra tried to scramble away from, him, but she had nowhere to hide.

She was completely exposed on the rocky shore.

You can't escape, girl, Drakken taunted.

She froze, watching as he flowed over the beach like an unnatural fog. His amorphous form dwarfed her small frame, and then suddenly it began to shift and contract. The shadows took on solid form, revealing a man clad in obsidian armor. A black helmet with a faceplate covered his head. Spikes shot out of his arms, back, torso, and legs like daggers. His Beacon throbbed strong and bright. But he was no normal man—he was a monster, many times larger than Kaleb and Aero put together.

Drakken towered over her with his spikes aimed at her frail body. *Carrier, the last time you spied on me, I almost destroy you. This time, I won't fail.*

Please, don't hurt me. I'm alone and unarmed.

Drakken stabbed at Myra with his spikes. They shot out from his body like blades, aiming for her heart—

Leave her alone, you monster!

Aero's voice cut through the dreamscape.

Uncloaking themselves from the shadows where they'd been hiding, Aero and Seeker charged at Drakken with their Falchions drawn. Aero clutched a broadsword, while Seeker wielded a long dagger. Drakken roared with fury at their ploy. He tried to expel himself from of the dreamscape—but they'd been expecting that.

Drakken, you're not going anywhere, Aero said.

He pushed his energy into his Beacon. The device flared, igniting with emerald light. *Chains*, he thought. Fiery chains materialized, sprouting from his palms. They weren't really chains at all, only extensions of his willpower.

Seeker did the same as blazing chains spurting from her palms. They latched the shackles around Drakken's wrists, binding him to the dreamscape. He shrieked and writhed, trying to break the unnatural bonds, but they held fast. They concentrated hard on keeping him locked there. Their Beacons pulsed in sync, strong and united.

Myra stood up from the beach.

She no longer looked weak or afraid. Her Beacon throbbed brighter and stronger, enveloping her body with green fire. It burned down her arm, sprouting into a fiery sword. Drakken roared and wrenched against the chains. His Beacon pulsed weakly. The three Carriers—Myra, Seeker, and Aero—advanced on him.

Commander, you're the one who's dead, Myra thought.

They raised their weapons to strike him down.

Drakken fought back against their hold on him. His Beacon throbbed brighter. First one set of fiery chains snapped off one arm, and then the other. Freed from the bindings, Drakken lunged toward Seeker and slammed a tendril into her jaw. With a cry of pain, she flew through the air, landing on the beach with a dull thud. Knocked from her grip, her Falchion sailed into the ocean and sunk beneath the churning waves.

She didn't get up.

Aero screamed and stabbed at Drakken with his broadsword, but he pivoted away and deflected the blow with his tendrils. The Falchion skittered from Aero's hand, landing out of reach.

Now you will die, Drakken thought.

He grew taller, his dark form expanding impossibly large, and loomed over Aero. His spikes targeted onto the boy. Drakken stabbed at Aero, impaling him in the chest. Aero gasped in shock, clutching at his chest, and crumpled into the beach.

Aero! Myra screamed and ran to him.

But Drakken flowed in front of her and blocked her path. Myra raised the fiery sword clutched in her hand. Drakken reared back and let out another laugh.

Two can play at that game, girl.

A blazing sword sprouted from Drakken's palm. He gripped the hilt with both hands and swung at her. Their blades clanged together, releasing sparks that melted the snow. Myra felt the blow rocket up her shoulder, aggravating her old wound.

She broke the connection as pain shot through her arm. She could barely hold the sword up. The pulsing of her Beacon slowed, weakening. She glanced at Aero, who was bleeding profusely, and farther up the beach, at Seeker who lay lifeless in the snow. Overwhelmed by fear, Myra started to lose her concentration. Her sword flickered, threatening to vanish. It existed only as long as her mind could hold on to it.

You're weak and afraid, Drakken roared. He raised his sword to stab her. She cringed away, expecting to be struck dead when—

Leave her alone, Weakling!

Seeker leapt at Drakken with her claws extended. She latched onto his back, avoiding the spikes. Drakken staggered in surprise and turned on Seeker, leaving Myra alone. She scrambled away, gasping for breath. Seeker had just saved her life. Seeker slashed at Drakken, her claws tearing into his armor, but it was too strong. Her claws skittered off, causing no real damage. Drakken towered over her.

Carrier, you can't hurt me, Drakken sneered. *I'm too powerful.*

He reached out and seized Seeker by the neck, choking off her airway. Seeker gasped and struggled, unable to break his hold. He tightened his grip. Then with one sickening jolt, Drakken wrenched her neck and snapped it. Seeker dangled lifelessly from his grip like a ratter. Her Beacon pulsed one last time and then fell dark.

Noooooo! Myra screamed, but she was too late.

Drakken cast Seeker aside with a flick of his wrist. Her body landed on the beach with her neck twisted at an unnatural angle. Myra scrambled over to her, but Seeker dematerialized from the dreamscape before Myra could reach her.

Drakken unleashed more laughter. *Did you really think your ruse would work, Carrier? It's only a matter of minutes before we break your shield.*

He rose up over her, expanding in size. With each Carrier he vanquished, he seemed to grow stronger. Myra could feel it through her Beacon. Helplessly, she glanced at Aero, who lay bleeding on the beach. The pulsing of his Beacon had slowed dangerously. That made fear shoot through her like an electric shock. Her flaming sword wavered and started to fade from existence. Panic gripped her heart and squeezed it.

Our army is losing . . . the shield is almost broken . . . Seeker is probably dead . . . and maybe Aero . . . everyone I love will soon be dead too ...

Panicked thoughts whipped through her head. She felt dizzy and faint, sinking to her knees. Her Beacon grew weaker, and her sword even fainter. She knew that she should try to pull herself out of the dreamscape while she still could, but then everything they'd fought for would be lost. Another Doom would be unleashed upon the world.

That left her with only one choice.

Drakken's voice cut through the dreamscape.

Shield integrity is ten percent. As soon as we break it, I will unleash our warheads on your army and seize control of the First Continuum. The Doom will be mine.

He raised his fiery sword to impale her.

But Myra stood her ground, pushing all of her energy into her Beacon. It pulsed faster and brighter, sparking with emerald fire. This was her last chance. *Help me, Elianna*, she thought. *Please . . . help me . . . give me the strength to defeat him.*

It won't work, Carrier, Drakken snarled. *You're all alone.*

He stabbed at Myra, but she heard Elianna's voice.

He's only a man. You can kill him. You're more powerful. You have to visualize him that way. Force him back into his human form. Then you can defeat him.

Myra concentrated, focusing her attention on her Beacon. She locked onto Drakken. He roared, trying to resist, but she stripped the armor away from his form, revealing a pale, scrawny, scarred man. He shivered on the beach, weak and afraid.

Elianna's voice screamed:

Now, Myra! Do it now!

Myra felt her power increasing. The fiery sword blazed from her hand, strong and true. She aimed it at Drakken, thrusting the sword with the force of her mind. Her blade pierced him in the heart. Fire shot out of her Beacon and down the sword, igniting him in an inferno. He shrieked and writhed as the fire consumed him—and then he vanished from the dreamscape.

Only a smoldering black stain remained on the beach.

The sword retreated from her grip, dissolving as the flames tamped down, sucked back into her Beacon. *It's over, Myra*, Elianna thought. *Drakken is dead.*

Myra probed her Beacon and knew that she was right— Drakken was no more. The dreamscape began to crumble around her. Pieces fell from the sky, shattering like glass on the beach. The pull of a great void encompassed her being.

Then everything went dark.

Chapter 54
AFTERMATH

Myra Jackson

Myra regained consciousness in the control room, where chaos had erupted. Aero lay slumped in his chair. His eyes were shut tight. Blood seeped from many wounds—but his chest rose and fell in steady rhythm. He was alive. The service bots swarmed around his body, trying to staunch the blood flow. *Seeker*, Myra thought urgently.

She wasn't in her chair.

"Where's Seeker?" Myra cried, leaping to her feet.

Dizziness swept through her, but she forced herself to focus. She scanned the control room. Her gaze landed on a body twisted on the floor. The neck was bent at a tortured angle. The Beacon latched to Seeker's wrist didn't throb with light, not even faintly. The service bots were attempting to revive her. One injected her arm with medicine, while another pressed an oxygen mask over her face.

But she remained still and lifeless.

"Noah, it's been too long," Divinus said, materializing over Seeker with a grave look on his face. His features looked skeletal. "Call the service bots off."

"Yes, Professor," Noah said. "Time of death: 0721 hours."

Though it had felt like an eternity, almost no time had passed while they were in the dreamscape. Emitting a slew of beeps, the service bots retracted their appendages. Myra laid her hand on Seeker's arm, stroking her hair. Her flesh still felt warm.

"No, she can't be dead," Myra said frantically, wishing it was only a harmless dream. "She saved me from Drakken . . . she's the only reason I'm still alive."

"My dear, I'm sorry," Divinus said, flickering with regret. "We tried to revive her, but the damage was too severe. It appears that Drakken broke her neck. As we feared, what happens in the dreamscape has ramifications in the real world."

"No, bring her back. I know you can . . ." she trailed off. She knew the professor was right. The damage had been done. She'd witnessed it with her own eyes.

Seeker is really and truly gone.

Sensing her distress, the service bots beeped worriedly but stayed back. Myra felt deep sorrow sweep through her, drawing tears to her eyes that spilled down her cheeks. Her dizziness worsened, but she didn't care. It wouldn't kill her. Through her blurry vision, she caught a glimpse of the security feeds projected overhead.

The Fourth Continuum soldiers had surrendered. They staggered around the courtyard, looking bewildered and disoriented. The ground was littered with dead bodies, many of them from the Second and Seventh Continuums. She could tell by their silvery uniforms and the Falchions still clutched in their lifeless hands.

"Major, round up the Fourth Continuum soldiers," Wren ordered on another feed. "Confiscate their blasters, and throw them in the makeshift holding cells."

"Yes, Major," Zakkay responded with a salute. He gestured to Majors Grimes and Tabor, who got to work executing their new orders.

Myra felt a rush of relief. Wren had survived the battle, though not unscathed. A nasty wound that needed stitches marked her temples. Overhead, the shield still glowed, but weakly. Her eyes flicked to the readout:

Shield Integrity: 5%

Myra had defeated Drakken just in time. *The war is over—it's really over*, she thought in a daze. Her crazy plan had worked. But instead of exhilaration, all she felt was a great well of sadness that flooded her chest and threatened to drown her.

She reached out and closed Seeker's eyes. "I'm sorry, friend . . ." she whispered. "You saved my life. You saved all of our lives. You're a hero . . ."

Myra choked up as tears flowed down her cheeks. A shadow fell over her—it was Aero. He was still bleeding. The service bots tried to tend to his wound, but he shooed them away. "Leave me be," he told them with a grimace. "I'll live."

They scurried around in protest but stayed a few feet away.

Aero knelt beside Myra, his gaze falling on Seeker. "She was truly the Strongest of the Strong Ones," he said, though he didn't sound sad. "She fought bravely and died a clean death at the hands of a worthy opponent. May we all aspire to such an end."

Myra tried to derive comfort from his words. Their colonies had such different ways of dealing with death, she marveled. She felt gratitude for her friend's sacrifice, but also sadness that Seeker was no longer with them. She leaned into Aero's side and allowed grief to overtake her. She sobbed and sobbed, and Aero held her while she cried.

A few minutes later, a small cloaked figure darkened the doorway. It was Tinker. His head was shaved clean now. He wore the long crimson robes of the Forgers. His eyes shifted to Seeker and sadness flashed over them. Kaleb followed after him, rushing into the control room. He looked equally heart-broken when he saw Seeker.

"She's dead, isn't she?" Tinker said softly. He swished over to his sister, wrapping his arms around her. "I heard Noah's announcement. What happened?"

"She protected me from Drakken," Myra said, trying to keep her voice steady but failing. "He was going to kill me. She sacrificed herself for me . . . for all of us."

"She was very brave," he agreed, reaching out and stroking her forehead. He spoke in his usual blunt, monotone manner. But that didn't mean he didn't care. "Braver than all of us put together. She was my friend. I'll miss her."

"I know you were close to her," Myra said. "I'm so sorry, Tinker."

"That's not my name anymore," he said. "It was never my name."

"Jonah?" she said, reciting his true moniker. It felt strange on her tongue. He was named after their father, but her brother had always gone by his nickname.

"Brother—that's what he goes by now," Kaleb said, kneeling next to Seeker. He swirled his hand over his chest. "He's been chosen to join the Order of the Foundry and become a Forger."

Tinker nodded solemnly. "We leave our individual names behind once we take up the robes. Our only purpose is serving and protecting our sacred science. They haven't conducted the official induction ceremony yet, but I've been granted temporary status after proving my devotion by keeping the shield running."

"You're sure about this?" Myra said, feeling surprised. "It's been a stressful time. You shouldn't make hasty decisions. This is a lifelong commitment."

But one look at his face told her that he had already made up his mind. Her brother didn't do things lightly. She'd always expected that he would shed his nickname and replace it with something else when he grew up. But to replace it with no name . . . that would take some getting used to.

"I'm sure," Tinker said and left it at that.

Myra felt her surprise fade into understanding. Of course he would join the Forgers. All they did was *tinker* with their ancient machines. It was perfect for her brother. He had found his true calling, though it felt a little like she was losing him.

"You'll always be *brother* to me," she said and mussed his hair.

o   o   o

Seeker's funeral was arranged as their first order of business, after they rounded up the survivors from the Fourth Continuum and cleaned up the courtyard. The bodies of the Second Continuum soldiers who had died in the battle would be disposed of without ceremony, as was their custom; Aero and Wren insisted on it. It was decided that the deceased from the Seventh Continuum would be buried along with Seeker.

They all contributed to planning her funeral. The Seventh Continuum had their own burial rituals, but Seeker was also a Carrier, and that meant that she had a little bit of all their colonies in her now. She sacrificed herself to save them, so they owed her a great debt of gratitude.

Crawler led the funeral procession through the Harvard Yard and toward the crumbling remains of Memorial Church. Professor Divinus had suggested the location would best serve their needs. The edifice was originally erected to honor the men and women of Harvard University who died in World War I, so it seemed especially appropriate. The Assembly approved the idea unanimously.

The Seventh Continuum soldiers—those who had survived the battle—carried Seeker's body on their shoulders. Myra walked beside Aero, their Beacons flashing in sync. It was strange that they were the only two Carriers left alive. Seeker's Beacon was still latched around her wrist, but it had fallen dark. Myra hadn't been able to bring herself to remove it, and neither had anyone else.

Wren and Kaleb trailed behind them along with the Majors, while Tinker marched in his hooded cloak along with the other Forgers. His official induction ceremony was scheduled for tomorrow in the Foundry, but it was a secret ritual open only to the members of the Order, so Myra wasn't allowed to attend.

Not Tinker, she reminded herself. *That's not his name anymore.*

It still felt strange that he was joining this peculiar order of scientists from another colony. Strange, but also just right. Tinker had never fit in back home. He'd found his place in this new world order. That was worth everything. Myra glanced back at Kaleb. She still felt torn between two worlds—the old one under the sea, and her new home here at the First Continuum. Her feelings remained unresolved. That last night before the battle that she spent with Kaleb had only further confused the matter.

Why can't anything ever be easy?

Aero caught her eye, as their Beacons flashed in tandem. He'd read her thoughts and knew about her feelings for Kaleb. Her cheeks started to burn, and a shiver jolted up her spine. They hadn't talked about what had happened that fateful night. And she wasn't the only one who felt torn. Aero had spent the night with Wren. Myra quickly averted her gaze and tried to block Aero from her mind. It didn't work, not really.

Her Beacon flared again, brighter this time.

We're connected now, Aero communicated. *We always will be.*

They reached Memorial Church and passed through the arched doorway. The roof had been torn off the building, but the walls still stood, though they'd been licked by flames. Crawler led the way, carrying Seeker's body with his people. She was wrapped in crimson cloth donated by the Forgers. They laid her to rest in a pit they'd dug out that morning. Crawler lingered over her body. Tears welled in his eyes. He stroked the soft fur of her arm. *He loved her*, Myra understood with sudden clarity.

Then something miraculous happened.

The Beacon bonded to Seeker's wrist ignited with emerald light that illuminated the dilapidated church. The metal shifted liquidly, unlatching itself from her wrist. It had chosen Crawler to be the next Carrier for their colony.

Mesmerized by the ethereal glow, he scooped up the Beacon. He cradled the golden cuff tenderly in his palm. "The Gold Circle . . ." he whispered.

His people bowed down before him. "The Gold Circle protects us. We worship the Light in the Darkness. May the Light never go out, so long as we shall live . . ."

Myra raised her voice to join their chorus, which filled the church. In one smooth motion, Crawler latched the Beacon around his wrist. It flared with blinding light and sealed itself around his flesh. He blinked hard and stumbled, but Slayer caught him and propped him up. Myra reached out to him through her Beacon. She found his consciousness and connected with it. It felt like talking to an old friend.

Crawler, you're a Carrier now, she communicated. *You'll feel some disorientation from the bonding process, but it will pass as you grow accustomed to carrying the Beacon. Make sure to get some rest tonight.*

Welcome to our ranks, Aero added.

Crawler's eyes widened when he heard their voices in his head. "How is this possible?" he growled in amazement. And then his eyes widened even more. "Seeker . . . she's in here . . . in the Beacon. I can feel her . . . she's not really dead."

Myra knew it was true. Once you were a Carrier, you never really died. The Beacon preserved you—or rather, it preserved your memories, your essence, your thoughts, your feelings. What really made up a human consciousness?

Myra wasn't sure. Was Elianna Wade really *Elianna Wade*? Or merely an approximation of Elianna Wade preserved and projected by the Beacon? There was no way to know for sure. But did it matter really? The Beacon had found a new Carrier, and Seeker had found a new life beyond the limitations of her physical existence.

She wasn't really gone after all.

The funeral ended with them tossing a rock into the grave and saying this prayer: "We are born of the Darkness of the Below, and to the Darkness of the Below shall we return. The Gold Circle protects you. May the Light never go out."

As Myra cast her stone on Seeker's body—a hunk of obsidian birthed by the Doom's fires—she felt a wrenching in her heart. Seeker was covered by a layer of rocks, but her naked wrist peeked through the shrouding.

"May the Light never go out," Myra whispered to Seeker.

Aero waited for her by the door. They exited the church together to return to the First Continuum. The war was over, but the real work was only just beginning. They crossed the Harvard Yard and proceeded into Widener. The elevator descended with ear-popping speed and spit them out miles beneath the surface. The whole way down, she could feel Aero probing her thoughts, but she forced him out of her mind.

"So . . . have you?" he asked, resorting to talking out loud. Her control over the Beacon had grown. Defeating Drakken had the effect of making her stronger.

She avoided his eye contact. "Have I . . . *what*?"

"Made a decision yet?"

She caught a flash from his mind of her entwined in Kaleb's arms. So he did know—he had seen everything from that night. She pushed him out of her head with so much force that he staggered backward. A hurt expression crossed his face.

"I don't know," she said, digging her shoe in the floor. "What about you?"

"Right, I don't regret what happened with Wren," he said quickly. He seemed to be searching for the words, and they seemed to fail him for a long moment. "I think I had to know what was behind that door . . . before I could close it forever."

"So does that mean you're closing it?"

Her face felt hot and her palms sweaty. She wasn't sure if she had the right to ask him that, given her own confusion. He met her gaze and held it. The elevator continued to descend. Myra felt light-headed suddenly.

"This is my answer," he said, and then he kissed her.

There was no hesitation in his lips. She melted into the kiss, letting herself be swept away. Their Beacons throbbed together as their thoughts intertwined, melding them in this embrace. They stayed locked together until the door contracted.

"You're late, Ms. Jackson," Noah said right away.

Embarrassed, she pulled away from Aero and tried to keep her voice even. "Right . . . something happened at the funeral," she said quickly. "Crawler bonded with Seeker's Beacon. It chose him to be the next Carrier. He's resting now, but he will be joining us soon to go over the repopulation plans. Please inform Professor Divinus."

"Of course, Ms. Jackson," Noah said. "I look forward to receiving the new Carrier. The professor is waiting for you in the control room."

They proceeded through the chambers, weaving their way through the cryocapsules still locked in frozen slumber, and entered the control room, where Divinus was sitting at the long table. "It's time to initiate the revival process," he said, gesturing to the screens ticking through with detailed instructions. He flashed, aging backward to his teen visage. "Noah has already compiled the plans. Are you ready?"

Myra sat down at head of the table. "Yes, Professor. Let's get started."

o   o   o

That night, Myra didn't return to her chambers. Something was on her mind—something she couldn't ignore or avoid any longer. It wasn't fair. She went in search of Kaleb and found him in his chambers. She knew what she had to do, but that didn't make it any easier. She opened her mouth to get it over with, but he held up his hand.

"Wait, let me talk first," he said before she could speak. He looked nervous. "Look, you know I've been avoiding you since the other night. I guess it took me a while to realize how I really felt about everything. I've been meaning to talk to you for some time now. Well . . . it sort of just happened. I still love you, of course."

Myra felt confused, but then understanding washed over her. "It's Wren, isn't it?"

He looked surprised. "How did you know?"

"I've seen the way you look at her," she said, thinking

back to after Drakken stabbed her in the dream. She'd been in a haze of pain, but she remembered them whispering in the corridor. "Ever since you got back from the Second Continuum."

He exhaled slowly. "When we were locked up together, we grew close. I mean, nothing happened," he added quickly. "We wanted to talk to you first."

"Do you love her?" Myra asked. She studied his face.

"I think so," he replied. "I told her about the other night. And she doesn't mind. I gather that something happened between her and Aero too. She's still learning a lot about her emotions. I guess that night helped her to see things more clearly."

"Does she love you?" Myra asked.

"Well, that's kind of a new concept for her. But yes, I think she does."

"Right, that whole *no emotions* thing," she said with a knowing look. "I can't believe they actually thought that would work. I mean, I guess it helped their colony survive the exile. But it seems crazy to suppress how you feel, doesn't it?"

"Yeah, it doesn't really work," he said with a grin. "I can't imagine trying not to feel any emotions. It's been interesting learning about the other colonies and their cultures. Plus, she can kick my arse. That's kind of . . . hot."

"For sure," Myra said with a grin.

He blushed fiercely and shot her a nervous look. "So, you're not upset?"

She took his hand and squeezed it gently. "Not even close. I'm really happy for you . . . for both of you."

"Because you have Aero?"

Now it was her turn to blush. "Because I have Aero," she agreed.

Myra returned to her chambers alone. She was surprised to find that her heart didn't ache like before. It didn't wrench in half like when he broke up with her after the Trial, when all her friends abandoned her. Actually, she realized, her heart felt whole for the first time in many long years. This just felt *right* somehow.

She was happy for Kaleb, but she was also happy for herself. The guilt that she'd been carrying around since she first bonded with the Beacon and discovered her connection to Aero evaporated. Kaleb didn't need her anymore. He had found his better half. And the truth was—the truth that they'd been fighting against ever since they first started courting— they were never right for each other. As friends, they were a perfect match. As lovers, it never would have worked, not over the long term.

And especially not with the Beacon melded to her wrist.

She caught a glimpse of Aero outside, tinkering with a transport engine. He had learned a lot from her. Wren approached him, looking stricken, and mumbled a few words about Kaleb. *So they planned this*, Myra thought and smiled. She was smiling because she could sense Aero's reaction to the news through their connection. He was happy too. And more than that—in his steady way—he affirmed his feelings for her.

Myra, I love you, he communicated. *I've always loved you.*

Chapter 55
WORLD WITHOUT END

The Order of the Foundry

One Month Later

The Forger formerly known as Tinker swished down the corridor. His small hand slipped inside his robes. The long sleeves dripped over his wrists. They needed to be hemmed, but somehow that always fell to the bottom of a long list of priorities. He pulled the device from his robes to confirm his suspicions. It was still blinking. Satisfied, he slipped it back into his robes and continued through the chambers.

Her door was unlocked, but he knocked anyway. Back home in the Thirteenth Continuum, he had shared a tiny bedroom with Myra in their cramped compartment, but that felt like a lifetime ago. Since he joined the Order of the Foundry, he was supposed to cut ties with his family, but she violated that regularly by doing things—

"Tinker," she exclaimed, triggering the door. "I haven't seen you in ages." She was still wearing her official uniform with the Ouroboros seal emblazoned on the crimson tunic, tailored to her small figure. Above the seal, five words were printed:

PRESIDENT OF THE UNITED CONTINUUMS

"That's *not* my name anymore," the Forger said, feeling a swell of annoyance. It was amplified when she reached out and rubbed his shaved scalp.

She was freshly showered. He'd caught her on her way out to another Assembly meeting. He wasn't the only one who had been busy lately. When she wasn't trapped in the control room in endless meetings or supervising their terraforming and repopulation projects, she was usually with Aero—or fast asleep.

"If you insist, brother," she said with a roll of her eyes. "But I still miss your hair. Even Aero's got more than you," she added, slipping into her canvas shoes.

"My sworn brothers and sisters live to serve our sacred science," the Forger said with a deep bow. "Shaving our heads is more efficient and ensures that we don't succumb to vanity. Maybe you should try it." Before he could stop himself, a smile crept onto his face. He still harbored affection for his sister, even if it was frowned upon.

Myra patted her wild curls. They jutted out at all angles, refusing to be tamed. "No, thanks," she said, scrunching up her face. But then sadness flashed over it. "I guess it's one of the only things that still reminds me of her . . ."

Tinker didn't reply, but his thoughts leapt to their mother. He had no memories of her. She died giving birth to him—or so he'd thought until he learned the truth. Padre Flavius had her killed for asking questions about the Beacon. That made him remember the purpose of his errand. *Why does Myra always distract me like this?*

Without further delay, he produced the device from his robes. Her eyes fell on it and widened. "By the Oracle, is that what I think it is?"

"It's the remote for the unmanned probe you built," he confirmed, holding it up. It flashed with green light, but not in a regular pattern like she had programmed it. "It started doing that about an hour ago. I rigged Noah to alert me if it went off."

Myra studied the device. "The flashing looks strange . . . some shorter and some longer flashes." She looked up with a puzzled expression. "What could it mean? Is it some kind of malfunction? Could the battery be on the fritz?"

Tinker shook his head, which gleamed under the automatic lights. "I thought so at first too. But I checked the batteries and had my brothers and sisters consult on the device. It's functioning perfectly. My Order believes it's picking up an external signal. And whoever sent the signal, programmed it to flash in this pattern on purpose."

"External signal?" she said, her eyes studying the irregular flashing pattern. They snapped to his face. "But who sent it? Holy Sea, spit it out already."

"We believe it's a code," he said, pointing to the device. "I couldn't decipher the mathematical pattern. But my brothers and sisters recognized it right away. Apparently, it's an ancient signal language from Before Doom. It's called Morse code."

Myra looked up excitedly. "Well, what does it say?"

"It's not communicating words."

Myra frowned. "What then?"

"These flashes—they're numbers."

She glanced at the device in confusion. "Numbers? What could they mean?"

"Well, I can't be sure, but I believe they're coordinates."

He fished a portable tablet from his robes. "I fed the coordinates into Noah, and he spit out a location. It's for a beach not too far from here. A place that used to be called . . ." He consulted a map, zooming in on the sharp outcropping. "Cape Cod."

Myra breathed out sharply. "Papa."

o   o   o

Aero piloted the transport with Wren. The Forger formerly known as Tinker watched the landscape blur below them. He pressed his face to the window, straining for a better view. He still loved flying, though he didn't get out of the Foundry much anymore. Myra and Kaleb sat on the bench next to him.

They weren't talking, but the significance of this trip buzzed like static in the recirculated air of the cabin. Except for the Order, Professor Divinus, and Noah, they kept their mission secret . . . just in case.

The Forger felt confident in his Order's assessment of the signal. He also agreed with his sister—this code had their father's fingerprints all over it. In her message carried by the probe, Myra warned him about the Fourth Continuum, so he would know that a signal sent in code would be safer. But what if they were wrong about the message? What if the remote really was on the fritz? Or what if the signal was from someone else?

There were so many Continuums still unaccounted for—seven, to be exact. A mixture of underground and underwater colonies. All these doubts and questions whirred through his head. He tried to use his Order's mind exercises to quiet his thoughts, but he was still learning.

A few minutes later, Aero piloted the transport through the cloudless sky and landed effortlessly on the rocky beach. He powered down the engines. "Welcome to Cape Cod," he announced through his headset. Wren hit a few buttons. The bay door yawned open. A crisp sea breeze wafted into the cabin. Tinker tasted salt on his tongue. They clambered out into the bright sunlight, emerging on the shore, except for Aero. He stayed behind in the cockpit, finishing his landing check.

The Forger saw the silhouette of a broad-shouldered man limping up the beach in raggedy, hempen clothes. He was short but sturdy, with long hair and a trim beard. The man broke into a grin and held up his arms. More figures trailed behind the man. Farther down the beach, he saw the abandoned remains of a submersible. The Forger had to squint against the sun to see the man's face—and then it hit him.

"Rickard!" Myra yelled and ran to the man.

Chapter 56
EXODUS FROM THE DEEP

Myra Jackson

Is it really you?" Myra said as she ran up to Rickard.

"The one and only," he said, breaking into his trademark grin. He pulled her into a firm hug, nearly rebreaking her ribs. But she didn't care. She hugged him back fiercely. She noticed scars etched into his face that didn't used to be there.

"But ... how is this possible?" Myra said, feeling equal parts joy and confusion. Her brain struggled to make sense of it all.

"I told you I was like a bad case of the Pox, didn't I?" he said, finally releasing her. She winced, rubbing her side. "You can't get rid of me that easy."

"I hardly think the Patrollers bludgeoning you to death counts as easy," Kaleb said, reaching them and tackling Rickard with a hug. The two friends beamed at each other. "By the Oracle, how did you survive? We watched them kill you."

"Aye, the 'Trollers bludgeoned me. You got that part right. But not to death, though close enough." His face darkened as he swirled his hand over his heart. "My father didn't fare as well, I'm sorry to report. He passed from his injuries."

Myra and Kaleb returned the gesture. "The Holy Sea have mercy on his soul," they said. Before they could dwell on it, another familiar voice reached their ears.

"Myra . . . Tinker . . ."

It was their father.

He rushed up and swept them into hugs. Behind her father, through the tears welling in her eyes, Myra spotted Maude walking with Stella and Ginger Bishop, who had sprouted several inches. Maude looked different too. Her hair was swept back into a neat bun. She wore a simple blue uniform with a symbol stitched into the lapel.

"We also thought Rickard was dead," Jonah explained. "I guess Padre Flavius kept him locked up in his private chambers. Somehow, he managed to escape."

Rickard shuddered. "By the Oracle, good riddance to that Red Cloak."

"I'm guessing he didn't make the trip?" Kaleb said with a knowing look.

Jonah shook his head. "Padre Flavius put himself out to sea. He claimed our exodus from the deep would bring another Doom and that we would all perish. He locked himself in a portal with the Oracle. It was all very dramatic and pompous, though most of the colony cheered when the Holy Sea claimed him. A majority of the Red Cloaks and the Patrollers stayed behind, where they'll suffocate to death."

"Poor superstitious bastards," Rickard added. "We gave them the choice to come with us, but they decided to stay down there. Though it serves them right after all the damage they inflicted on our people."

Several more submersibles bubbled up from the depths. They were cobbled together from spare parts, welded into place using her father's design. Myra could recognize his handiwork anywhere. She watched them speed toward the beach.

"Wait, you built a whole fleet?" she said, scanning the

ocean and counting them. More kept rising up. "How many people made the journey?"

"My family?" Kaleb cut in. "Did they make it?"

Jonah nodded, patting his shoulder. "Your parents, brother, and little sister made it. They should be in the next wave. Chancellor Sebold defected from the Synod and joined our little uprising even before we issued the colony-wide evacuation order."

"Uprising?" Kaleb said in surprise. "Against the Synod?"

"You mean *my* uprising?" Maude said with a toothless grin. She passed Myra a satchel that she pulled from her pocket. "I'm the Chief, after all."

"Your uprising?" Myra said, peeling open the satchel, revealing a cluster of sweetfish. She popped one in her mouth, where it melted on her tongue in a tart, sugary rush. It made her eyes water with pleasure. "Maude, what do you mean?"

"After you escaped, the Hockers rose up against the Synod and took over the Engineering Room," Maude explained. "We'd been planning the revolt for some time, but your little escapade into the Holy Sea was the catalyst we'd been waiting for. We broke your father out of the Pen to help us defeat the Synod. That was when he informed us about the Animus Machine. That whole . . . it's breaking down and I can't fix it, you're all going to suffocate to death, Hocker, Factum, and Plenus alike."

Jonah snorted. "I think I said it more eloquently than that."

"Right, it was a very rousing speech," Maude grinned. "Anyway, he told us we were wasting our time fighting the Synod and that what we really needed to do was build more submersibles—and fast. So we hatched Operation Surface and seized control of the Spare Parts Room and the Docks. But then Padre Flavius and the 'Trollers raided our headquarters in the Engineering Room."

"Yeah, that wasn't pretty," Jonah said, gesturing to his head. "I took a nasty blow to the temples. Luckily, Rickard saved my life and pulled me into the pipes. The rebels escaped using your secret ways, and we barricaded ourselves in the Docks."

"My secret ways?" Myra said, surprised. She was the only one who ever used the pipes and ducts to get around the colony. She couldn't imagine others doing it.

"Yup," Stella answered. "Remember how you taught us?"

"When you broke us out of the Pen?" Ginger added. Or at least, Myra thought that was the order in which they spoke. It was still impossible to tell the twins apart, with their matching shocks of red hair and freckled faces.

"Your secret ways saved us more times than I can count," Jonah agreed, fixing Myra with a proud smile. "Once we reached the Docks, we barricaded ourselves inside. But we still had no idea where to go once we left the colony. I knew if you were alive, you would try to get us a message. So I used the old computer system to scan for signals. Most people forget that it's right there with terminals hardwired into the colony."

"The central computer," the Forger said. "Of course, that's genius. There are terminals all over the colony. You could access it from anywhere, though almost nobody used it anymore. They'd forgotten about it, like you said."

"Well, I learned about it from you," Jonah replied. "You always loved those terminals. I had to pry you away to keep you from being late to the Academy."

"So you got our signal?" Myra said. "You found our probe?"

"Yup, one fine morning, your little sub popped up on our radar," Maude said. "And thank the Oracle it showed up when it did. We were getting ready to swim blindly into the ocean. The oxygen levels were dropping to unsustainable levels."

"Exactly," Jonah agreed. "So I rigged up a reply message using an old code I found in the computer and issued an evacuation order to the entire colony. It went out over the system, broadcast to every sector."

"How'd you defeat the Synod?" Kaleb asked. "And the 'Trollers?"

"In the end, we didn't need to defeat them," Maude said. "They lost all their support. Unrest had spread through the colony. When the oxygen levels dropped even more and the evacuation order went out, most Factum came over to our side. They realized we were right about everything, including the Synod and their lies."

"Papa, I knew you'd get my message," Myra said, hugging him again. It felt amazing to have him right here with her. She could scarcely believe it.

"Aye," Jonah confirmed. "And I knew you'd crack my code."

"Actually, he did that part," Myra said, gesturing to her brother.

"Tinker, of course," Jonah said. "Why am I not surprised?"

"With the help of my Order," the Forger replied. He looked down and a little color crept into his cheeks. "Also, that's not my name anymore," he said softly.

"Oh right, Tinker goes by Brother now," Myra said. "He's been inducted into the Order of the Foundry. It's this ancient group of scientists from the Second Continuum. That's one of the outer space colonies."

Jonah cocked his eyebrow. "So that explains the fancy robes?"

"And the shaved head," Myra added. "It's all a little . . . strange."

The Forger scowled. "Fine, you made your point."

They all laughed, but then Myra turned more serious. "Papa, so much has happened since we left home. I don't even know where to start."

"Plenty of time for that later. I'm just happy you're both alive," Jonah said, clasping her hand. His gaze drifted up to the sky. "So this is the Surface? By the Oracle, it's even more beautiful than I imagined. Is that . . . the sun?"

"The *sun* and the *sky* and the *clouds*," Myra said, looping her arm through his elbow and leading him toward their transport. Tinker walked with them, his robes quietly swishing around his ankles. "Oh, wait until you hear about *weather*."

"Weather?" Jonah said, frowning. "What's that?"

Myra launched into an explanation, while Wren sent out

a message calling for additional transports, as more submersibles burst through the ocean and sped toward the shore. Dressed in their crude hempen clothes, the colonists from the Thirteenth Continuum staggered onto the beach and stared at the sky with wild-eyed wonder.

"Mom . . . Dad . . . Jack . . . Ella!"

Kaleb spotted his family and ran to them. Now that his father wasn't sitting on the Synod, he looked different—friendly almost. Wren approached them hesitantly, but Kaleb pulled her over and introduced her with obvious pride.

"This is Wren," he said. "She's from an outer space colony."

He pointed up to the heavens, though his family regarded him with baffled expressions. They couldn't fathom that somebody could live in the sky.

Myra listened to her father's enthusiastic chatter as he peppered her with more questions about the Surface. She could scarcely believe that their little family was reunited. So many times over the course of their strenuous journey, she had doubted that this moment would ever come to pass, and yet here they were.

As they fell back into their familiar patterns—her father and her animatedly exchanging ideas, her brother's attentive silence—it felt like almost no time had passed. But of course, it had. They weren't the same people anymore. That much was evident from the scars cut into their flesh, lines drawn on their foreheads, and other less visible traumas that they each carried—and the Beacon steadily pulsing against her wrist.

But they had survived. That was enough for now.

Epilogue:
THE UNION OF SEA AND STARS

Myra Jackson

Myra looked up from her tablet. Her eyes blurred as they attempted to focus on the control room. "The president doesn't get days off. I told you that."

"Sure, you do. We make the rules, remember? That was one of your big selling points, if I recall." He nuzzled her neck playfully, but she pushed him away and scrolled through her incredibly long to-do list.

"Supreme General, that is not entirely correct," Noah chimed in. His disembodied voice echoed through the room. "President Jackson can propose new rules, but the Assembly must ratify them. This isn't a dictatorship."

"Right, I don't care," Aero said, pulling her up from the table. "I'm declaring this a holiday. I already told the Assembly members. I gave them the day off too."

"Wait, I object," Myra said, clutching her tablet to her chest. "What about our meeting? And what's a holiday?"

"Before Doom, holidays were special days that commemorated an event of historical significance or honored an important person," Noah said. "People often took the day off work and government offices and courts closed for the day."

"Exactly—they took a day off," Aero said. "It's a new concept for me too. But I want to embrace better ways of doing things."

"And what could we possibly have to celebrate?" She gestured to her tablet, which displayed the status of their farming and repopulation projects. "We've only just begun all of this. We haven't even launched the main cryocapsule phase yet."

"Presidents' Day?" Noah suggested. "That was one of my favorites."

"I was thinking our anniversary," Aero said, snatching her tablet away and holding it out of reach. He keyed in a few commands. "I had Noah check the archives and the data from our Beacons. It's been one year since we first . . ."

"First *what*?" she demanded, making him blush. She grabbed her tablet back triumphantly, only to see that he'd locked the screen and changed the passcode.

"First dreamed about each other," he finished. "Or whatever you call it."

She smiled in spite of herself. "A good dream, wasn't it?"

"Certainly got my attention. Now come on, I've reserved a transport. It's not easy to get one these days, with so much going on. But I pulled a few strings."

Myra gave up on her tablet and the mountains of work clamoring for her attention and followed Aero from the control room. They stopped by the Foundry on the way out, where they found her brother and father working on a strange machine. Her father had a toolbox out and splayed open. He grasped a wrench and bent over the control panel, but her brother grabbed his arm.

"If you tighten that, the whole thing is going to blow."

"Brother, watch and learn," her father said and did it anyway. He tightened the connection. They waited—and the controls blazed to life. "Told yah," he declared triumphantly, shutting the panel. "I've been doing this a long time, remember?"

"Papa, maybe you should join the Order," Myra said.

Her father looked up. "Nah, I'm not much for robes. The Red Cloaks left a bad taste in my mouth. Plus, I want to hang on to what I've got," he said, patting his thinning hair. He'd aged in some ways, but his eyes still shone with youthful energy.

"Robes and hair? That's what you care about?" Myra joked. "What about preserving their sacred science? And maintaining their ancient machines?"

"You're assuming they'd take me," her father shot back.

"We'd be honored to have you join our Order," said the Forger formerly known as Xander. He strode across the Foundry to greet them. "Your father is a natural with our machines, but I shouldn't be surprised. I see where you get it from now."

Myra studied the machine they were working on. "What's this one for?" she asked. "It looks different from the other machines." Indeed, it had a larger display and control panel marked with thirteen flashing green lights.

"As you know, your father and brother are spearheading the reconnaissance mission to contact the Continuums that remain unaccounted for," the Forger formerly known as Xander explained. "Your brother designed this machine to contact them and search for signals from their Beacons. Our hope is that some of them survived."

Jonah nodded. "I've got my Engineering team building unmanned probes to deploy to the deep-sea colonies," he said gesturing across the Foundry.

Myra spotted a girl about her age with long, dark hair and a studious expression ordering around the much-older Master Engineers and a few younger Forgers. The Foundry and the Engineering Room had melded together seamlessly, maybe because of their shared love of science and anything with mechanical parts.

"Who's that over there?" Myra asked.

"Charlotte's in charge of the probe project," her father said. "She's my pledge from the last graduating class from the Academy, before the uprising."

"And the underground colonies?" Aero asked. They already knew the fate of the space colonies. The Third Continuum, also known as the Mars colony, failed hundreds of years ago due to an air leak. The Second Continuum's mothership was destroyed, but after defeating Drakken, they'd taken command of the Fourth Continuum's vessel.

"Crawler and his Seventh soldiers are going to head up that mission," her brother said. "They're most adapted to the underground environment. If we fail to pick up signals, the Seventh soldiers will fly them to the colonies and deploy them."

"We call it Operation Survivor," her father added with a sweep of his arms. "What do you think, Madame President? We were waiting to brief the Assembly on our efforts until we got this little machine up and running." He patted it affectionately.

"Head Engineer Jackson, I think you've made excellent progress," Myra said in her official voice. The clanging sounds and smoky, metallic smells of the Foundry made her heart happy. She yearned to work on the machines alongside her family.

She reached for a wrench, but Aero shot her a look.

"Holiday, remember?" he said in a lighthearted voice.

Her father set his wrench aside and stood up, rubbing his hands on his coveralls and smearing them with grease. "Wait, aren't you supposed to be in one of your Assembly meetings? What are you doing slumming it in the Foundry?"

Myra rolled her eyes. "Aero forced me to take a day off."

"Good job, son," her father said. "Where we come from, Factum rarely got time off. But all of us need a break sometimes, or we'll wear down like old cogs."

"Thank you, sir," Aero replied formally. "It was the same back in my home. But I'm hoping we can make some changes around here."

"Please, call me Jonah," her father replied, clapping him on the shoulder.

Aero looked even more uncomfortable. Myra had to stifle

a grin. She grabbed his hand, pulling him away. "We're off on a mysterious adventure," she declared.

"Have fun," her father said, while her brother waved. Jonah's eyes crinkled up as he watched them exit the Foundry and disappear into the corridor. Myra wondered if he was thinking about her mother, Tessa, and when they first started courting.

o   o   o

The elevator sprang open to clanging and banging noises and dust swirling in the sunlight shining down through the missing roof. Myra and Aero stepped into the corridor, their eyes falling on the scaffolding erected against the walls. Workers clutched tools and worked on rebuilding the library. Myra waved to a few familiar Factum, and then she and Aero descended Widener's steps. The fallen columns had been carted away, the rocks piled up by the Science Center for use in their many rebuilding projects.

"Never ceases to amaze me," Myra said, taking stock of the Harvard Yard. She'd been holed up in the First Continuum for too many days, she realized as she squinted in the midday sunlight, wishing she had Seeker's old visor to protect her eyes.

"You and me both," Aero said, grasping her hand.

The courtyard had been transformed by a massive farming project, turning it from a scorched wasteland into a lush, verdant paradise with neat rows of crops stretching their delicate tendrils toward the sun. The rows teemed with workers from all the colonies—the Second, Fourth, Seventh, and Thirteenth Continuums. It hadn't been easy, but thanks to the Medical units from Aero's home and the doctors from the Thirteenth, they were able to rehabilitate most of the Fourth Continuum soldiers.

A jovial voice cut through the Yard.

"If it isn't President Jackson," Maude called, hoisting her hand to her brow. Her skin glowed, partially from her daily nips of firewater, but also from working all day in the sun. She moved down a row, tying up the cornstalks, while Greeley followed her with a crate filled with rich, loamy soil. Something wriggled in the dirt—earthworms. They'd been freshly hatched from the cryocapsules. Greeley laid the glistening creatures by the plant's roots, letting them burrow into the damp earth where they belonged.

"Don't be shy, stranger," Maude added. "Give an old lady a hug."

Myra crossed the Yard, inhaling the earthy scents of growing things. The sun beat down, warming her shoulders through her tunic. She wrapped Maude up in a tight hug. "Holy Sea, I've missed you. This whole President thing keeps me busy."

"Tell me about it," Maude said with a grin. "I don't miss being Chief. I'm enjoying my retirement. Now I see why Farming was such a popular trade."

"You'll always be Chief to me," Greeley interjected, setting his crate down and draping his arm around Maude's shoulders, making her giggle like a schoolgirl.

"Oh, stop it, Greeley," Maude said, swatting his arm away playfully. "You always were a sentimental fool, weren't you?"

"Guess you bring it out in me," Greeley shot back.

He wiped his hand across his brow, leaving a trail of dirt. The Bishop twins ran up, clutching woven baskets filled with fresh tomatoes, peppers, and cabbages. They waved shyly at Myra, still regarding her as a hero for escaping from the Synod.

"Stop by and visit our dwelling one of these days," Maude said, gesturing to Sever Hall, which they'd rebuilt into permanent residences for the settlers.

"Only if you have buttercake," Myra said with a grin. "And sweetfish."

"And ginger beer," Aero added. He'd fallen in love with Maude's brew from the very first taste. "Maybe with a shot of firewater," he added.

"I'll have plenty of everything if you promise to darken my doorway," Maude said. The Bishop twins nodded eagerly at the idea of a sugar-laden party. Before Myra could say anything else, Maude shooed her away.

"Off with you, Madame President. I know Aero's got a plan." She passed him something that Myra couldn't see, making her feel even more in the dark.

"Am I the only one he didn't tell?" she said, trying to sound annoyed.

But a smile broke over her face and ruined the charade. Using her Beacon, she tried to pry into his mind and figure out his plan, but Aero kicked her out with a teasing admonishment before dragging her toward the airfield. When they arrived at the transport, her produced a shred of cloth, which he fashioned into a blindfold.

"Close your eyes," he said.

o   o   o

Aero landed their transport, setting it down softly but firmly. "Welcome, Madame President," he said, hitting the button to open the bay doors. They'd taken one of the smaller transports. The cabin felt cozy. Warm air gusted in through the door.

"Cape Cod?" she guessed, unbuckling her harness and inhaling the unique fragrance of the ocean—brine, iodine, dampness, sulfur. She was still blindfolded, but she could hear the unmistakable music of waves crashing against the shore.

He pulled off her blindfold. Her eyes fell on the rocky beach. "Well, you've been complaining about how you miss the sea lately," he said, following her gaze. "So I thought I'd bring you out here. Plus, we rarely get any time alone together."

She planted a kiss on his lips. "Thank you," she said, kissing him more deeply. "I have missed it, more than you could ever know."

They climbed from the transport. Her feet sank into the sun-warmed sand. She peeled off her shoes and then raced up the beach, kicking up grit as she went. Laughter spun from her lips, tinkling in the salty air. Aero's boots, with their stubborn clasps, took longer to remove. "Starry hell," he cursed, ripping the second one off.

He caught up and tackled her. They landed in a tangle of limbs on the soft sand. She let out another peal of laughter, gleeful and happy. They lay there on the beach, twisted in each other's arms, while waves sloshed over their bare feet. It felt amazing to be out here, just the two of them, without ceilings or walls pressing down on their heads, or rules restricting their words, thoughts, feelings, and actions. It felt free.

They watched as the sun plunged toward the ocean, putting on a kaleidoscopic light show. "Sunsets," she marveled. "They never get old, do they?"

"Especially not at the beach," he agreed, planting another kiss on her lips.

They watched until the sun vanished, swallowed up by the sea. The air stayed warm on these summer nights. The weather hadn't started to turn cold yet. Still, she snuggled into the warmth of his chest. The sky turned blue-black and filled with stars.

"We're missing dinner," she said as the moon appeared overhead, showering the beach with pale light. "But I don't want to head back yet. Though I should warn you—my father might send out a search party if we don't turn up soon."

"I considered bringing rations." She made a face at the mention of the bland, gluey paste. "Right, that's what I thought. So I snagged some sweetfish from Maude. It's her last batch. Also, I have a feeling your father isn't coming after us just yet."

They shared the candy, passing the satchel back and forth, though Myra ate more than her fair share. She couldn't help it. Sweetfish were her absolute favorite. There was a time when she thought she might never get to taste them again. Her gaze skipped across the ocean, following the trail of moonlight to where the saltwater tipped the sky, the union of sea and stars. She tried to imagine what it would look like when they released fish and marine animals and set birds free into the skies.

"Aeternus eternus," she whispered, brushing her lips

against his Beacon. The ancient words felt like a prayer—to everything that was and everything that would be.

"The end is the beginning," he whispered back, tracing his fingertips over the snake that marked her Beacon. It flared in response, sending shivers up her arm.

The moon set, and still they lingered on the beach. The sun rose at dawn and kissed the sky, and still they lingered. It rose higher and higher, painting cornflower blue hues over the ceiling of the world. Only then did they stand, their joints stiff, their skin dusted with sand, and their hearts glad. Their transport loomed in the distance, waiting to carry them back to the First Continuum and all their unfinished work.

Myra's mind swirled with the hundreds—maybe thousands— of tasks left to do to carry out the professor's plans. She was in charge of this crazy operation now. This Continuum Project. So much depended on her decision-making. Could they revive all the cryocapsules? It was going well so far, but they'd touched only the first few chambers of insects and similar creatures. Could they live peaceably upon this fair Surface, planting and tending to it until it was as rich and green as it was in Elianna's memories?

Her Beacon flared, sending images of Tulsa at the peak of summer cascading through her mind—the skies crammed with insects, the fields thick with crops, the skies alight with a million stars. She could smell the humidity in the air, taste the life on her tongue. *It once was,* Elianna communicated. *And so it shall be again.*

Myra blinked as the memory cleared from her vision like the lifting of a veil. She worked hard to quiet the clamoring of her doubts and worries, like the professor had taught her. Instead, she concentrated on this moment on this beach with this soldier. The waves beat against the shore, rhythmic and old as time. She felt Aero's strong arms envelop her, pulling her close. She tasted salt and sweetfish on his lips.

It was then that Myra realized something important.
We're finally home.

THE END

ACKNOWLEDGMENTS

THIS BOOK WOULDN'T EXIST without the help of so many incredible individuals. Their belief, wisdom, inspiration, and guidance shepherded me through writing my first ever trilogy and launching it into the world. These words can never adequately express my deepest gratitude, but here it goes. To my phenomenal book agent Deborah Schneider at Gelfman Schneider/ICM. Also, to my film agent Josie Freedman at ICM and my UK and foreign rights agents at Curtis Brown. As always, I know I'm in great hands with all of you on my team.

To Turner Publishing—look at what we did! Three freaking books! Thanks to my editors, Stephanie Beard and Jon O'Neal, and my publisher, Todd Bottorff, and everyone at Turner Publishing for taking this risk and championing my books. I'm forever grateful.

And to the Lemon Tree House Residency for Writers, where I began typing the first pages of this manuscript in the bucolic rolling hills of Tuscany. The landscape and history of Italy inspired many important aspects of this story (the

Roman Colosseum!). I'd also like to thank all the amazing indie bookstores that have supported me and this series, especially Mysterious Galaxy, Book Soup, Skylight Books, and Powell's.

To my parents—Jeri and Jonathan Rogers. I composed and revised big chunks of this book at their mountain haven nestled in the Blue Ridge Mountains. Thanks for inspiring, supporting, and harboring me while I tried to untangle the intricate plotting and finish this trilogy with a bang. I think I succeeded, no? And of course, my unending gratitude and love to my husband, Will, and my fluffy companion, Commander Ryker. You'll always be my Number Ones.

Finally, to my dear readers—thank you, thank you, thank you. For taking this journey with Myra and Aero and all their pals. For carrying this story from my fingertips into the real world. For showing up at my book events, posting reviews, and sending me messages on the dark days when I needed to read them the most. This book marks the end of one part of the story, but the Continuum Universe will live on. It's not over; it's never over. The end is the beginning.

AUTHOR Q&A
with Kester Nucum of LILbooklovers

What inspired you to write The Continuum Trilogy?

Originally, I came up with the idea during the BP oil spill in the Gulf of Mexico. I was sitting at home and watching the TV news coverage of the oil spreading over the top of the ocean and suffocating birds and fish. As I stared at the dark sludge, feeling horrified, I started to wonder what would happen if we couldn't live on the surface anymore. I couldn't shake the idea. I kept asking myself more and more what if questions. In this way, the idea for the Continuum Universe started to form in my mind. At first, I thought of having underwater colonies, but quickly realized that we would build Continuums in multiple environments to maximize our chances for long-term survival—underwater, underground, and in outer space. In this way, the idea kept growing bigger and bigger, until I knew the story needed to expand into three books.

Your books take place throughout many of the Continuums, and each one had a different history and culture to it. How did you build each Continuum so uniquely?

Exactly, the original concept involved putting different societies into extreme isolation and exploring how they evolved differently. I had the idea for the underwater Thirteenth Continuum first (due to inspiration from the BP oil spill). I've always been fascinated by the deep-sea environment and how we know more about the surface of Mars than our own ocean trenches. Often when I'm worldbuilding, I rely on historical allegory to guide me. In this case, I based the history of that colony on the Dark Ages. I was interested in exploring how we went from a pinnacle of civilization with the Roman Empire and fell into a dark age, losing knowledge and technology. I also wanted to show how a democratic society modeled on the United States of America could devolve into a totalitarian state ruled by an oligarchy named the Synod. That's why I included the constitutional amendments in the beginning of the first book.

For the Second Continuum—the lone surviving space colony, or so we think—I wanted to make them a military colony ruled by discipline and order, very different from the religious, superstitious Thirteenth Continuum. So, I turned to ancient Sparta for guidance on how to build that colony's world. I realized along the way that while they had advanced technology and remembered their history, they still suffered in a different way. Their overreliance on logic and systemic organization led them to suppress their emotions and revile romantic love.

With each colony, each new environment, came a chance for me to build a different society. The underground Seventh Continuum devolved significantly, living in complete darkness with no technology. In their desperation to survive, they even turned to cannibalism. Influences included Lord of the Flies and also Gollum from the Lord of the Rings (who is also a devolved hobbit). This aspect of the trilogy that involves the different colonies really makes it stand out.

Why did you decide to include flashbacks, excerpts, records, and quotes throughout the books? What impact do you think it made to the overall storyline?

Great question! When I originally conceived of the

Continuum books, I needed a way to lead the survivors back to the Surface. Thus, the Beacons were born. I didn't want to rely on a map or something that felt old-fashioned. I had the idea for a device that was given to each colony—and worn by a young Carrier—that would bond with them and preserve their memories and history, as well as serve as a homing beacon to lead them back to the First Continuum and the trove of life and information preserved there. This gave me a way for Myra to learn the history of her colony through the first Carrier Elianna Wade, who we first meet in the prologue. By making the memories interactive, I think it gives the reader the experience of learning the history of the Doom along with Myra. Those chapters are some of my favorite parts of the first book.

The quotes—from many of my favorite works of literature—and the historical records and documents cut to the core of the book's main theme. What do we choose to preserve? What do we save from the Doom? What matters most to humanity? What happens if we lose our history, art, and culture? These inclusions stand as a warning—here is what we stand to lose if the Doom happens. Here is how we could devolve from a democracy to a totalitarian religious state.

Practically, they also speak to Noah's role in the Continuum Project. He's a supercomputer, and his name stands for the National Operation to Archive Humanity. It's also clearly a biblical reference to Noah's Arc. The historical records come from Noah, who is tasked with preserving our history for the future recolonization of the planet. The famous saying goes, "Those who cannot remember history are doomed to repeat it." (Santayana, but often repeated).

Your books switch between different POVs of many of the main characters, including Myra, Aero, Seeker, Jonah, and others. Who was the easiest to write? Who was the hardest? Which character was your favorite?

When I started working on this story, I knew it had to be told in rotating POVs to properly explore the full expanse of the huge universe. The main POVs in the first book belong to

Myra and Aero, but we also hear from Sari Wade, Professor Divinus, the Synod, and briefly Seeker in the epilogue. As the books continue, the POVs expand to include more characters. The most challenging to write was Seeker, who really comes to life in Return of the Continuums. Because she's so devolved, I had to work extra hard to make her relatable. Also, she undergoes a major transformation. I knew the book would either live or die with her voice. I'm pleased that she came out so strong, in my humble opinion.

I love all the characters in different ways. Surprisingly, writing antagonists like the Synod and Commander Drakken was really fun. I also loved writing Jonah, Myra's father. I'm glad I was able to continue following his journey through all three books. Some of the characters who I absolutely adore, but that don't get their own POVs (yet) include Tinker, Maude, and Wren.

When writing your series, did you shock yourself? Were there some scenes and possible character deaths that surprised you?

Yes, many surprises came in writing the books. One of the first big ones came at the end of the second book when Myra and Aero finally connect in person and reach the First Continuum. I realized pretty quickly that Noah would deactivate the Beacons after they had served their purpose. And then it dawned on me that it wouldn't be the sparks flying romance I had first imagined. Without the Beacons to connect them, Myra and Aero were really just strangers. Furthermore, they came from such drastically different colonies that they had little in common. So that was a fun surprise to explore to what extent the Beacons shaped their feelings and connection, and to what extent they really did love each other.

Another surprise came in the third book when I realized that Vinick was going to slaughter the Forgers. It was a really difficult scene to write, since I love the old Forgers so much. Later in the book, when I was writing the confrontation on the bridge with Vinick, I realized that Danika was going to kill him, something I also hadn't expected. Another tough one was destroying the

Second Continuum, courtesy of Commander Drakken. It helps to raise the stakes in the book. I realized at a certain point that it had to happen, but that didn't make it easy to write.

As I was reading your books, I felt like I was watching a movie! Did your background in movies affect how you wrote The Continuum Trilogy?

Yes, for sure. I care a lot about the structure of my books, which is something I learned working on screenplays in Hollywood. I also tend to write very visually, especially since I build such expansive worlds. I have to be able to envisage a scene in order to write it. It has to feel real to me—like a fully imagined world. I think that's part of why Hollywood has always been so interested in adapting my books for the big screen. The exciting news is that we've just attached a director, and we're moving forward with making them into films. It's a long road to actually make the movie, but this is a huge step forward. So keep your fingers crossed!

Many of the main characters progress and change throughout the trilogy as they learn new things about the world and people around them. How would you want your book to change and impact your readers?

Like most dystopian authors, I hope my books serve as a warning of what could happen if we continue down certain dark paths. As much as I love the fictional world of my books, we don't really want to be living in isolated Continuums because we destroyed Earth, right? I also hope that my books inspire empathy for other people who come from different backgrounds. At heart, we are all part of humankind. I hope we can remember that.

Out of all the quotes you used before each part, which one was your favorite and why?

Wow, that's a hard one! I chose so many from my favorite writers and placed them throughout all three books. I love the epigraph at the beginning of this book. One is from Einstein, and the other is from J.K. Rowling. I still get chills when I read them again.

How does it feel finishing writing The Continuum Trilogy?

Both exhilarating, but also sad at the same time. I love writing the end, but then I always go through a mourning process where I miss my worlds and characters. Through the process of working on the books, a process that consumes years of my life, they become like my friends. Myra and Aero have been with me for years. So, it's a bittersweet experience. But I also feel really proud of this trilogy and how it came together. I think this third book is my favorite. It was also the hardest to write. I was juggling so many POVs and having to pay off so much.

In your opinion, what makes a YA dystopian novel stick out from other books in that genre? What would you say makes The Continuum Trilogy stand out from other dystopian books?

I would say that my books are actually post-Dystopian. They show how we emerge from the dystopia and rebuild our world. I always say that tonally, they're more like Star Wars than some other dystopian works. They have hope at their core always. My characters always have hope, even as the obstacles pile up. They never stop believing they can survive and make the world a better place. My books also read more like science "faction," incorporating real science. Also, it's not a game—the stakes are real. I find a lot of recent books involve elaborate constructs.

What can we expect from you in the future? Will we see more of the Carriers and the Continuums?

Yes, I sure hope so! I'd love to write a prequel series about Professor Divinus and the Carriers at some point. I think it would be fun to explore the rich backstory more. I'd also like to write some subseries set in other colonies, like the Third Continuum (the Mars colony). It's worth noting that I did leave the door open at the end of The United Continuums to explore what happened to other colonies. But in the meantime, I'm already working on a new book idea. It's in the same genre—YA science fiction—and involves a lot of outer space elements. I'm excited to start writing it later this year. I'm also focused on packaging the Continuum Trilogy for film.

AUTHOR'S NOTE

AND SO WE COME to the end. This book—indeed the entire trilogy—was conceived in a world that felt markedly different from the one into which it's now being born. You know what I'm talking about, don't you? To quote Neil Gaiman from his essay introducing *Fahrenheit 451* which also appears in *The View from the Cheap Seats:* "This is a book of warning."

Science fiction, especially dystopian fiction, isn't meant to be predictive. It's meant to warn. Don't go here. Don't do this. Pay attention now. Or else. I warned you, didn't I?

Dystopian authors take scenarios that exist now and project them into the distant future. If you continue along this path, we say with our keystrokes, here's where you could end up. The surface of the Earth will be reduced to a smoldering, radioactive wasteland, all organic life utterly destroyed. You'll be trapped in far-flung colonies scattered across the universe, isolated from fresh air and sunlight. You'll be lost to the depths of the sea, the cold expanses of space, or the dark recesses of the underground, condemned to a millennium of exile.

That's if you're lucky.

That's if you've been *chosen.*

When I was considering what caused the Doom, I had options. Oh, so many delightful and colorful options—climate change, natural disasters, alien invasion, etc. I thought long and hard about different scenarios. But here's the thing. The core of this trilogy, the deep theme of the books, concerns humanity's predilection for self-destruction, so I knew it had to be something that humankind did to ourselves.

The idea first came to me during the BP oil spill in the Gulf of Mexico, when black sludge was spreading over the surface of the ocean. I was watching the news and thought—what if we couldn't live on the surface anymore? We caused that oil spill. We did it because we invented machines and electric grids and cars that rely on oil to power them, but in our greed, in our rush for creation, in our need for unbridled progress, we unleashed great destruction on the ocean, the very thing that gave us life in the first place. That's why I knew that both protagonists and villains in these books had to be human. The cause of the Doom also had to be manmade. In the first book, President Wade writes in his journal entries:

> *Every day I see what mankind is capable of: our resilience, our innovative spirit, our capacity for adaptation under exigent circumstances. Our citizens work tirelessly to produce the food, water, and power that keep us alive. But every day, I am also reminded of the Doom that we unleashed upon the world. The two sides of our psyche: creation and destruction. Which will win out? I can only hope the former . . .*

In casting my gaze around at different options, I landed on a threat that only intensifies with each passing day (a threat that I hoped was behind us)—nuclear proliferation. Today, on April 5, 2017, as I type these words, I woke up to news that North Korea tested another ballistic missile. That test succeeded. Their weapon can reach Japan. Meanwhile, our President has vowed to massively increase our military spending and nuclear capabilities. Does this start to sound eerily familiar? As a writer, it is possible to scare yourself sometimes. To say—hey wake up—I didn't mean for my books to be prophetic. I made them up, damn it. They can't actually come true.

Fortunately—and this is where I find solace—my stories don't just present the myriad problems. They show us how we can come out of the dystopia and survive the Doom. Myra and Aero and their crew have something big in common—hope. They discover that their colonies are doomed, yet they fight to return to the Surface and rebuild human civilization from the ashes of the long-dead world.

Preserve.

Hope.

Resist.

Change.

Professor Divinus and his sworn brothers and sisters saw the Doom coming and put into effect a contingency plan. In the First Continuum, they saved seedlings and embryos using advanced technology. In programming their supercomputer Noah—which stands for The National Operation to Archive Humanity—they also preserved art, literature, culture, history, music, film, etc. What is humanity worth without culture? Without knowing our roots?

In this new dark age, always remember the importance of culture. Remember that you can resist what is happening, like Myra and Aero and their friends. You have a choice; you have a voice. You are stronger than all this. I hope this book carried you away to distant worlds and helped you escape, but that it also brought you back to our reality with hope rooted firmly in your heart. Always know that we are stronger together; we are stronger when we are united.

This is a book of warning, like Neil Gaiman wrote—but it's also a book of hope. I hope that our greater selves will prevail in the end. That our proclivity for creation will save us. That it will win out over our tendency toward self-destruction. The two halves of humanity's dueling psyche.

Remember, the end is the beginning. World without end.

Aeternus eternus.

Jennifer Brody
April 4, 2017
Los Angeles, California

JENNIFER BRODY lives and writes in Los Angeles. After graduating from Harvard University, she began her career in feature film development. Highlights include working at New Line Cinema on many projects, including *The Lord of the Rings* trilogy, *The Golden Compass*, and *Love In The Time of Cholera*. She's a member of the Science Fiction and Fantasy Writers of America. She also founded and runs BookPod, a social media platform for authors.

You can find her online at:

@JenniferBrody

www.jenniferbrody.com

www.facebook.com/jenniferbrodywriter